PRINCES AND PAWNS

ALL THE QUEEN'S KNAVES BOOK FOUR

KATE SPARKES

SPARROWCAT PRESS

For every square peg who tried to reshape yourself to fit a round hole.

PART I

CHAPTER ONE

The music at the Ambling Goat was as terrible as it was loud, reliably increasing in volume and dissonance as each evening wore on. The food was no better, consisting mainly of a stew that had, according to local legend, been simmering over the fire for at least a hundred years, with vegetables, meat, and generous servings of water thrown in as needed. But the Ambling Goat remained a thriving landmark in Cottsbridge for one important reason.

It existed.

Aside from the Ambling Goat, which offered eating, drinking, and dancing, as well as a few rooms beneath its thatched roof for the rare travellers who ventured so far north, Cottsbridge didn't have much going for it. It had farms and a sawmill, a blacksmith, and a tannery. It had sheep for wool and cows for milk. Its citizens had learned long ago that they needed to be self-sufficient if they wanted to survive, and that was enough.

There was no library, no theatre. Survival didn't require such frivolities.

The boredom would have been enough to drive Sorra mad if she couldn't drink and dance every once in a while, and the Ambling Goat offered a chance to do both when she could scrape together enough money to pay her way—or better yet, find someone willing to cover the expense for her.

It had been months since anyone new had come to town, but

tonight a fresh crop of soldiers had stopped on their way to the Gate, the only pass through the mountains to the north. They were an unimpressive crew, as every group of them had been in the past—some fresh out of training and in need of experience, some a little too experienced in all the wrong ways but not quite terrible enough to be discharged from the king's army.

Sorra sat on the open plank stairs in the corner and sipped her gin, observing the visitors over the edge of her glass as she considered which of them might be worth knowing better.

None of the younger soldiers would do. The poor pups had spent the evening pathetically enraptured by local girls who blushed prettily and sipped their drinks, batting their eyelashes and offering the promise of a kiss by night's end if their suitors were lucky. It was the same every time soldiers passed through—the same gestures, the same dances, the same expressions on young men's faces as drink helped them imagine themselves heroes in search of ladies fair.

Those poor, bumbling fellows were enough to make Sorra lose faith in humanity—or at least lose interest. But there were a handful of others, a little older, a little more rugged, playing cards at one of the long, wooden tables that surrounded the dance floor. They wore the same dusty grey uniforms as the younger ones, but on the more experienced soldiers they fit like second skins instead of costumes.

The dealer was grizzled and rough, stoop-shouldered but broad and strong. To his left sat his apparent opposite, lean and quick, with sharp features and beady eyes. He sneered aggressively at anyone who looked his way and slapped cards down as though he might intimidate them into obedience.

Sorra dismissed them, too.

But to the dealer's right sat a soldier Sorra guessed to be in his mid-twenties, with the toughened look of someone who'd lived more life than his years should have allowed. Red-haired, bearded, and handsome enough to draw her attention even with the three long scars that crossed his right cheek.

Good enough for tonight, anyway.

One couldn't afford to be too picky in Cottsbridge if she didn't want to spend the night alone.

The redhead considered what his opponents had already laid down, then produced a high card from his sleeve before laying out his hand and collecting every bit of cash from the table. No one but Sorra seemed to notice his trick, and the others groaned over their defeat.

That was fine. Sorra didn't mind a cheat as long as he was a competent one.

She stood and brushed the dirt from her skirt. The dress wasn't especially fine and the hem was worn with age, but it fit her nicely, flaring out when she danced and hugging her torso in exactly the right way for a night like this. She considered the card players again and released her hair from the coiled braid she'd worn at the back of her head, letting dark waves fall over her shoulders to frame the dress's low neckline.

The air on the dance floor was heavy with the musk of workers who had spent the day in sun-baked fields and the equally unpleasant scent of the floral perfume someone had doused herself in. Sorra held her breath as she wound through the crowd, careful not to spill her drink on anyone's shoes.

Someone grabbed her arm. She turned, then shook herself free, trying not to let her distaste show. "Gavin."

"Evening, Sorra." He was already drunk, his words slurred, but he looked as fine as ever. Her first infatuation. Her first for many things, in fact. "You want to get out of here?"

Sorra raised her chin so it felt like she was looking down at him, though he was slightly taller than her. "Why? Have those mean old soldier boys stolen everyone else's attention?"

Gavin grinned and stared down the front of her dress. "They can have it. No one interesting here 'cept you. We were good, right? Let's give it another go. I don't care what anyone says about you. I can handle it. Nobody needs to know."

Sorra pressed her lips together and resisted the urge to slosh her drink in his face.

Perhaps he hoped she didn't remember how he'd handled things five years ago. He'd told her then, too, that her problems meant nothing to him, that he'd take her away from Cottsbridge when she was old enough to marry him. He'd also insisted that their relationship remain secret for her own good and had sulked every time she questioned his true intentions, telling her all would be well if she could just trust him and keep her mouth shut until he worked things out.

And then he'd married Luella Boyle, and the trouble Sorra had caused at the wedding became a fresh stain on her reputation—one she didn't regret at all.

Or maybe he had forgotten, at least temporarily. The romance that had hardened her had been nothing more than a passing fling for him, an exciting risk taken with a girl who didn't know to be cautious with a man seven years older. Sober, he knew enough to avoid her and the potential trouble she'd bring. Drunk, the ugly truth of him floated closer to the surface.

Selfish desire. Disloyalty. Desperation.

Sorra had made more mistakes in two decades than most people made in a lifetime, but she prided herself on never making the same one twice.

No more secrets. No more "for your own good."

And definitely no more Gavin.

She leaned closer to be sure he'd hear her over a shrieking fiddle solo. "Go home to your wife and your squalling baby. I wouldn't have you if every other man in Andonia was rotting in his grave."

Sorra patted him on the arm and flashed a bright smile, her spirits buoyed as she left Gavin stung by the knowledge that he'd been rejected by the only unmarried woman in Cottsbridge no one else wanted.

A young soldier, his sand-coloured hair sweaty from dancing, had seated himself at the card table, straddling the wooden bench as he caught his breath and sucked back a pint of ale.

Sorra took the empty seat next to the red-haired soldier, her back to the table. She nodded at the cash piled next to him. "Looks like tonight's your lucky night, stranger."

He turned to her with an easy smile and looked her over with a subtle glance. His gaze lingered on the pale wine-stain birthmark that painted her left cheekbone and temple, then shifted to meet her eyes.

"Suppose it might be," he said.

"Care to share your good fortune?" Sorra swallowed the remains of her drink and set the empty glass on the table.

"I'd love to." He motioned to Abraham, who stood behind the bar looking disapprovingly over his patrons as though they weren't the only reason he could afford to keep body and spirit together. The old innkeeper muttered something to himself as he pulled a bottle from under the counter and made his way toward them.

"Evening, Abe," Sorra said as he poured her a fresh drink.

He looked her over with baleful hound-dog eyes. Up close, the patchy grey stubble on his chin and the nests of hair spilling from his ears threatened to become a distraction.

"Sorra. I hope we won't have any trouble tonight."

"When have I ever caused you trouble?"

The innkeeper sighed. "Never. Makes me think it's only that my turn hasn't come yet."

Sorra looked away.

This was the other half of the problem with living in a small, isolated town—not much happened, but when things did, they became everyone's business. Abraham had surely heard about the sheep she'd accidentally let out of the Ekersens' field when she worked for them, leading to catastrophic loss when wolves attacked the herd. She'd been blamed for the cows at the Goldbrook family's dairy farm drying up when she worked there, too, and the inexplicable invasion of frogs that had choked the waters of their pond after she'd talked the good farmers into giving her a second chance.

Abraham hadn't yet made the mistake of hiring or befriending her, and he'd been spared any tragedy beyond plagues of customers. He had good reason to be wary, but she hated him a little for putting a damper on the scrap of cheer she'd mustered to see her through the evening.

The innkeeper took her new friend's money, sighed again, and wandered back to the bar to take up his post.

"I should have another," the young soldier said as Sorra turned to face the table. He raised his hand to draw Abraham's attention again, but the dealer pulled his arm back down.

"We're leaving in the morning." The dealer's voice matched his face, rough and worn. "I won't have you slowing us every time you need to heave into the bushes."

The lean soldier, who up close reminded Sorra of a weasel nosing his way into a henhouse, scowled. "Let him have his fun. He'll need something pleasant to remember when he's collecting nightmare tinder a few days from now."

The blond boy blinked slowly. "Nightmares?"

"Sure. Did we forget to tell you what roams beyond the Gate?"

Sorra tried not to look too interested. If there were secrets being shared, she didn't want to be the reason the conversation stopped.

"Reinbard." The dealer's voice carried a warning note. "Leave the boy alone."

The blond laughed. "Don't worry, sir. I can handle his tall tales."

The weasel-faced soldier, Reinbard, smiled grimly. "We'll see how brave you are when you meet a goblin. They're not like you think from the stories. Tall as a man. Long claws. Sharp teeth. So strong and quick they'll tear your throat out before you can draw your pathetic little sword." He gestured toward the redheaded soldier. "Ask Stuart. He might not have remembered how he got those scars if you'd asked him a few towns ago, but it's all coming back as we get closer." His smile faded. "Guess we wouldn't have agreed to come back if we'd remembered."

Sorra didn't turn to stare at Stuart's scars, and he didn't speak up to confirm or deny their origin.

The blond soldier, who looked even younger now that his confidence had escaped him, looked uncertainly at the dealer. "Sir?"

The dealer nodded toward the dance floor. "Go on. Have fun. I'll tell you when it's time to think about anything else."

The hairs on the back of Sorra's neck prickled. She swallowed her drink in a few gulps, letting its sharpness steal her attention away from the hollow resignation in the older man's eyes.

People rarely spoke of the Gate or why the pass needed to be defended, and when Sorra turned her normally active imagination to the idea of what might lie beyond it she couldn't come up with a single idea. No one else seemed to have any, either, and even the map on the schoolhouse wall ended at the northern mountains.

Some said it was worse in the south, that folks who lived farther away couldn't even consider the concept of "beyond the mountains" without their thoughts clouding over. They said magic caused the forgetting, but Sorra had never heard who had made it so, or why.

Or heard anything about goblins, for that matter. Reinbard seemed willing to let the matter drop, but he glared at the table as he tapped his bitten-down fingernails against its scarred surface.

The young soldier stood and straightened his jacket. "Guess I'll try to wear my feet out dancing before I wear them out marching."

"Good lad." The dealer collected the cards and shuffled them with slow, clumsy movements that made Sorra want to snatch them from his hands to show him how to do it with a bit of flair.

Stuart reached for Sorra's empty glass and held it in the air. Abraham glanced toward them, then looked away without acknowledging the request. Sorra told herself it wasn't personal. When that idea didn't stick, she told herself she didn't care.

The music died down, offering a temporary reprieve as the musicians made their way to the bar for refreshments. A few determined couples kept dancing to the hum of conversation that remained.

"Is everyone in this town as charming as the old barman?" Stuart asked, setting the glass on the table.

Sorra wrinkled her nose. "Most of them, unfortunately."

"Not what I heard," the dealer said, not looking up from his studious manipulation of the cards. "We don't hear much about this town when we're down south, but there was a rumour about a family of sisters here who have special gifts. Magic of some kind. Beauty, charm, incredible talents." He grinned at Sorra, revealing tobacco-brown teeth. "Don't suppose you're one of 'em?"

Sorra's stomach knotted. "Hardly. I'd love to hear the story, though, if you're in the mood to tell it."

Love wasn't quite the word. She'd heard the story more often than she'd heard any lullaby or fable when she was growing up, and her life would have been greatly improved if she'd never had to hear it again. But the fact that it had spread to the south interested her. It had always seemed that Cottsbridge and its inhabitants must disappear from the soldiers' memories as surely as knowledge of the Gate did when they went home, either by the same magic or because it was just so forgettable.

If people were talking about her sisters, Sorra wanted to know.

The person sitting at the next table moved, drawing Sorra's attention. She hadn't noticed this stranger among the crowd, though the dark crimson cloak and the hood that shadowed their face would have made them stand out on a less busy night. The only clues to the person's identity were the hands, delicate but strong, their dark skin crossed by paler scars.

It seemed to Sorra that this person had leaned closer to listen, but she couldn't be sure.

"Four sisters," the dealer said. "Apparently they were blessed by a faerie creature at birth. Or a witch, maybe. One sister with great beauty, one could spin wheat into gold, one with great charm, and one..." He paused, frowning. "Music, I think it was."

Sorra passed her empty glass from one hand to the other, sliding it across the uneven tabletop as she considered her response. "A lovely story. I'd say girls as extraordinary as those ones would have long since moved on to a larger city and better opportunities, though."

"I suppose." The dealer set the cards into a messy pile and rested his meaty hands over them. "There was something else to it. Another gift. A compass that'd point to... I dunno. Fate or something."

"Or something," Sorra echoed, and decided not to offer anything more. If he wanted to, the old man could get the rest of the story from almost anyone in town.

Gods know they never let me forget it.

Reinbard gave his head a shake, seeming to free himself from whatever thoughts had held him captive. "Greatness. Not where we're going." He glanced at Stuart's winnings. "It's been a good night for you, though. Bit too good for my liking."

Stuart flashed him a charming smile. "Just a temporary bit of luck. I'm sure the cards will go your way next time if you're more careful about how much you drink."

Reinbard narrowed his beady eyes, completely uncharmed. His hands balled into fists. "If I didn't know better, I'd say luck had nothing to do with—"

The musicians cut him off, breaking into what sounded like four different tunes simultaneously.

"Dance with me," Sorra said, more an order than a question, and pulled Stuart to his feet. He pocketed his winnings, shrugged at his companions, and let Sorra drag him to the dance floor. The table and Reinbard were quickly out of eye- and earshot.

"I appreciate the graceful exit," Stuart said as they wound their way between dancers. "Reinbard isn't usually a bad sort, but when he's in a dark mood he'd pick a fight with a hatrack if he thought it looked at him the wrong way. I should warn you that I'm not much of a dancer, though."

Sorra smiled back at him as she led him past the musicians. "Let's pretend we danced, then, and skip straight to the part where we rest." She pushed the door open and stepped out into the cool and blissfully fresh air outside.

Let him think she was saving him from a fight and not running from the talk of blessed babies and grand destinies that had haunted her for twenty years.

Four blessed daughters.

It seemed no one had mentioned the fifth.

The music was more pleasant when muted by the inn's thick log walls. Sorra stepped into the yard and glanced at the stars. Most were hard to see through the light from the inn's windows, but the brightest of them were always there, refusing to be outshone.

She turned to Stuart. "Was teasing the boy with talk of goblins just part of Reinbard's dark mood?"

"No, that was true. All of us who have been to the Gate before have been on edge as our memories have returned, but not all of us are mean enough to take it out on the new recruits." He drew in a long breath and frowned as he looked toward the miserly lights of Cottsbridge at the bottom of the hill, then lifted his gaze to the dark mountains beyond. "The forgetting is a mercy, I suppose. You don't even realize there was anything to forget. Even now I'm only half sure of anything I saw up there, but the closer we get, the more sure I am that there are dangers none of us knew to speak of a few days ago."

"Could you run?"

"If I wanted to live as a fugitive, sure. But it wouldn't be a long life. Crimes against the king's army are taken seriously, desertion included." He smiled at Sorra, warm but a little uncertain. "Besides that, I wouldn't run even if I could. My job isn't easy, but it's important. We guard the pass to keep our people safe, and it's been centuries since a goblin set foot on Andonian soil."

"You're heroes." Sorra's throat tightened. The scars on Stuart's cheek spoke of the danger the soldiers would soon face, but they were going out into the world, changing it for the better. Even knowing how they must all dread it, she couldn't help feeling a little jealous.

"I wouldn't say that," Stuart said. "We've all got dust on our shoes and secrets in our pasts."

Sorra nodded. "Let's forget the past, then. And the future. Thinking about either feels like a waste of a perfectly good present."

"Exactly what I was thinking." Stuart looked down at her. "You're sure you're not the beautiful sister from that story?"

Sorra snorted out a breath. "If you want to flirt, you might aim for at least a whiff of sincerity."

"I am entirely sincere." Stuart brushed Sorra's hair back from her face, exposing her birthmark. "You have a unique sort of beauty."

Sorra shivered. It was rare that anyone but her sisters touched her, and with them it was usually to fix her hair or wipe dirt from her face. Her aunt Corinne hadn't laid a hand on Sorra since her birth, touching her only through a willow switch or a wooden spoon when correction was required.

This was different. Not real—his lie slipped as smoothly from his lips as the winning card had from his sleeve, and she knew it for what it was. But it was something. It was a sensation, a soft touch and a warm hand, something she could have for a little while before she had to return to the daily work of being the family's failure.

As long as she didn't let herself believe it, a pretty lie wouldn't do any harm.

"You like unique, then?"

He arched one eyebrow. "I do. Unique and troublesome in particular."

"Then this really is your lucky night." Sorra considered the hard line of his nose, the gentle curve of his lips, and the dark eyes that were focused entirely on her. She rested a hand on his chest and drew her fingers over the smooth curve of muscle beneath his uniform. He smelled like he'd bathed after arriving at the inn.

Worth a go, anyway, she decided, and allowed her body to respond as he leaned in to brush his lips over hers. Cautiously at first, she noted, then more firmly when he found her not only accepting but welcoming.

Dishonest but not presumptuous. Gentle but strong.

A girl could do worse.

Sorra pulled back. "Do you have your own room, or are you bedding down in the stable?"

"A room upstairs, but not alone. Reinbard's going to be sulking at the table for a while, though, and the door has a lock."

"Good enough." Sorra took his hand again and led him around back to an outdoor staircase where they'd draw less attention than if they went inside. One more bruise to her reputation wouldn't make much difference, but there was still a small, beaten-down part of her that insisted such things mattered even when she ordered that part to stop being such a ninny.

For a while it would be her and another person behind a closed door. No sisters, no stories, no magic. Just her own body and his, and the raw, pure honesty that came where words ended.

It wasn't much, but she'd take it.

CHAPTER TWO

Sorra wakened to the first hint of sunlight reaching its fingers through the room's only window, illuminating specks of dust floating in the air. She slipped out of bed, careful not to wake Stuart or jostle her aching skull, and reached for her clothes.

She hadn't meant to sleep. She'd only allowed herself to drift in its shallows, certain that the soldier who was supposed to be sharing the bed would soon be banging on the locked door and rudely ejecting her. All she remembered was a vague sense that Stuart had been snoring as she fell asleep. Now, all was quiet. No snoring, no crickets outside, no music or laughter or shouting from downstairs.

She looked back at the bed. Stuart had stolen the heavy wool blanket and pulled it up over his shoulders. All that showed on the pillow above it was his red hair.

"Goodbye, then," Sorra whispered, not wanting to wake him. Better to disappear before things could get awkward, or before he could—every god forbid—try to convince her last night had meant anything more than a bit of fun.

Not a *lot* of fun, but she had no regrets. Best to leave it that way.

She unlocked the door and crept barefoot into the hall, her shoes in one hand, headed toward the door to the outside staircase.

"Sorra?"

She froze, one hand reaching for the doorknob. "Abraham.

Good morning." She turned to find him watching her as he had the night before.

He raised one unkempt eyebrow. "Sleep well?"

No point denying where she'd been. Sorra stood straighter. "No. I suspect you have fleas in your mattresses."

"No one's complained."

"I'm complaining."

Abraham sighed. "Go on, before anyone else sees you. I won't tell your aunt you were here."

Sorra smiled. She hadn't expected to. "Then I won't tell anyone about the fleas."

"Very generous." Abraham's jaw muscles tightened. "You could do better, you know. Whatever people say about you, it doesn't matter. You have a choice."

Sorra's smile vanished as her heart turned to lead. She wanted to tell him that he knew nothing, that he had no right, that she had tried her best to make a place for herself in Cottsbridge, to exist without bringing trouble to every person whose life she touched. No one, save for perhaps her sisters, knew how hard she'd tried.

She could try to explain it to him, hoping for a shoulder to cry on, a sympathetic ear, or a mind that could comprehend how she'd been cursed by her own birth. But what then? She had no friends because misfortune followed her like a personal storm cloud, and no one liked getting wet in its showers. She had no job because new wagon wheels broke and canned foods went bad and chickens stopped laying when anyone hired her. She had no parents because—

Sorra answered him before her thoughts could pull her under.

"I'll take that under consideration, thank you." She pushed the door open, slipped her shoes on, and hurried down the stairs.

It was easy for Abraham to say she should do better, but he'd never offered her a chance to prove it, and he never would. Employing her might lead to the Ambling Goat burning to the ground. Sorra couldn't blame him for not risking action, but she wished he'd kept his cheap words to himself.

The air was already warming, the flies buzzing over droppings left by horses on their way to the stable. Sorra considered peering in to see them and to hear the snores of the low-ranking men who'd had to sleep in the loft, but she decided against it. They were unfamiliar horses and unfamiliar men, but there wasn't enough novelty left in either of those beasts to make it worth risking her aunt's wrath if Sorra didn't make it home before anyone realized she was missing.

Sorra hurried on, braiding her hair as she walked.

Cottsbridge spread out below her at the bottom of a gentle slope, every wooden house and struggling garden the same as it had ever been, the shallow river beyond unchanged and unchanging.

The main streets met at a crossroads at the centre of town, dividing it neatly into quarters. The King's Road stretched from the Gate in the north to more desirable locales far from the mountains in the south. The Cottsbridge Road ran only as far as it needed to, from the fields in the west to the sawmill on the eastern side of town. Other routes, which lay scribbled between tightly packed homes and businesses, couldn't be described as anything grander than lanes. The offshoot leading to the town hall had at one time aspired toward street-hood, but plans to pave it with cobblestones had been denounced as a waste of money. The lane had remained the serviceable pair of wheel-ruts it had always been, and most folks in town seemed greatly pleased by the lack of progress.

Sorra kicked a stone down the road. All was quiet, save for the occasional croaking of frogs in the pond as she passed the cattle field, then the bark of a dog somewhere in the distance. As she drew closer to town, though, voices joined in. Not many at this early hour, but workers were already heading out to the fields, and the baker would be preparing bread by now.

As long as Corinne's still snoring...

The buildings at the southern end of Cottsbridge stood with their backs to the outside world, windows staring warily down at the road. Sorra had barely stepped into their shadows when Davina appeared, seemingly from nowhere, to walk beside her.

"Out for an early walk, love?"

Sorra cast a sideways glance at her sister. "Of course."

The dealer at last night's card game had gotten scraps of the story right. Davina was one of the four blessed sisters, and her artistic eye had revealed itself when it became apparent that she wasn't playing with her food but painting with it. Once she had access to proper materials and lessons, she filled the house with drawings and sculptures that reinterpreted the stories her sisters read to her at bedtime. Ingrid's blessing of beauty had been recognized by then, as had Aurelia's ear for music and Grace's unique connection to the natural world.

Even now, when she'd probably rushed from their shared bed to the streets in search of her wayward sister, Davina's gift showed itself in the impeccable tailoring of the dress she'd made herself, the casual perfection with which she'd gathered her dark hair behind her neck, and the way her shining eyes drank in the world, gathering inspiration the way a crow might gather glittering trinkets to decorate its nest.

The legend of the blessing wasn't entirely untrue, but the old soldier had assumed too much.

Sorra's four elder sisters each had a gift, but simple versions of the story made it sound like each of them was only that one thing. Even at her most petty and envious, Sorra had always considered this a disservice and would have bloodied the nose of anyone who reduced her siblings to flat pictures from a storybook.

Davina wasn't only a skilled and imaginative artist. She was fearless, too, and kinder to Sorra than most folks. Ingrid looked like a woman sculpted by a master artist, but she also had a mind for numbers and had worked as a bookkeeper until her destiny led her away. Aurelia was a dreamer as much as she was a composer and had occasionally become lost in the woods when she'd followed her daydreams too far from the real world. And Grace's intuitive understanding of plants and animals offered her deep insights into humans, as well, which provided fodder for the scathing sense of humour she only revealed to her siblings.

The sisters all resembled their mother with their black hair, pale skin, and dark eyes, and the first four seemed to have been built from the same stock of flawless materials. Ingrid had been dreamed by the gods, but Aurelia, Grace, and Davina were each composed into their own kind of loveliness that hinted at the gifts each held within.

Sorra had always felt that she herself had been assembled by an untalented apprentice from leftover, broken shards, leaving her recognizable as a Dawson sister but somehow entirely separate from the others. Nose a little larger than was fashionable, hair that defied proper management, lips that refused to look anything but mocking when she smiled… almost correct, but never quite there.

None of her sisters carried the rose stain that cradled Sorra's left eye and, according to some, marked her as unblessed. They never said the same about any other child born with marked skin, but the people of Cottsbridge embraced any evidence they could conjure against Sorra.

"Someone from the south was asking about you last night," Sorra said.

Davina's steps didn't slow. "Me, or all of us?"

"All of you. Said he'd heard stories."

Davina seemed about to reply, then frowned and touched a finger to her lips as she turned slowly toward footsteps approaching from behind. Sorra hadn't heard them over the gravel crunching beneath her own shoes.

She expected Stuart, or the dealer from last night, or perhaps the cloaked figure who might have been listening to their conversation. Instead, she found a young woman wearing a forest-green skirt and matching waistcoat over a clean, white blouse with puffed sleeves. A top hat, too small to be of any practical use, perched atop her thick hair, which was pulled back behind her neck. Sorra tried not to stare, knowing how off-putting such a thing was, but noted that one of the stranger's eyes was dark brown and the other a subtle green-gold.

Odd, but appealing. Sorra wondered whether it made this young woman an oddity among her own people, or whether such things might be fashionable elsewhere.

The stranger smiled pleasantly and folded her bare hands in front of her.

No scars, and skin a lighter brown than that of the cloaked figure from last night. That made two visitors who weren't soldiers.

"Sorra Dawson, I presume?" she said. "And this must be one of your fabled sisters."

Sorra frowned at her. "You must be thinking of someone else."

She took Davina by the arm, fighting the urge to break into a run. Aurelia had sought her destiny and had followed it all the way to Embercliffe to share her talents in its concert halls. Ingrid had been stolen by the outside world not long after, and then Grace. The thought of someone enticing Davina away and leaving Sorra alone with their aunt was more than she could bear.

She silently cursed whoever had been spreading tales about them.

"I don't mean you any harm," the stranger said, her voice gentle and calming.

Sorra wasn't in a mood to be calmed. She turned her back and tried to drag Davina away.

But Davina resisted, planting herself like an oak and smiling at the newcomer. "Forgive my sister," she said, and shook her arm free of Sorra's grip. "We don't get many visitors here, and she doesn't trust the ones she can't... dance with."

The young woman's smile widened. "Fair enough. I'm not much of a dancer, myself, but I may have a business proposition for you. A lucrative one. Is there somewhere more private we can speak?"

Sorra searched the shadows and the rooftops for the cloaked figure from the inn, but there was no sign of them.

"Here's fine," she said, and gestured toward the water pump in Mrs. Blotchkin's yard. The old widow wouldn't hear their conversation any more than she'd heard the wayward dog that had broken down her door and helped itself to the contents of her pantry when Sorra had been employed as her caretaker.

It had been just as well, really. Sorra had helped with the canning, and although she'd followed every instruction, the dog had died of a creeping paralysis after helping itself to a jar of string beans.

"Very well." The stranger held the gate open and motioned the sisters through as though she owned the place. "It's not only soldiers who pay attention to stories. There's a young lord in Bruxbridge who heard about your family and asked me to make contact."

"And who are you to him?" Davina asked, polite but cautious.

The stranger folded her hands behind her back and looked up at the house's crooked roofline. "A humble shopkeeper, but I take an interest in the rare and unusual when it's profitable to do so. I'm here about the arrow."

Sorra and Davina exchanged a glance. "Not sure what you're talking about," Sorra said.

The stranger focused on Davina. "He's willing to pay well. That is, if the stories are true and you do, in fact, have an enchanted arrow in your possession that flies toward the bow-bearer's greatest potential destiny."

Sorra tried not to scowl. There was no reason for this stranger's knowledge of the arrow to feel like a threat, but it did.

Davina pursed her lips. "A thing like that would be valuable, indeed."

"Enough to pay your way out of here," the stranger agreed. "All of you."

Sorra's chest tightened painfully. She rarely allowed herself to think of leaving, no matter how desperately she wished for it.

"It's gone," she said, her voice cracking. "Our aunt sold it."

She left the rest unsaid—how Grace had brought the arrow home after she used it on her eighteenth birthday, how Corinne had tried to use it for herself, how it had struck the earth on her own property instead of leading her to greatness, or how the weeks when Corinne left to pawn the 'useless thing' in a distant town had been the happiest of Sorra's life in spite of the sadness she felt for Davina's lost opportunity.

Family business wasn't for outsiders.

"That's a shame." A breeze blew through the yard, turning the long grass into a pond of rippling green waves and carrying a hint of lilac from bushes to the southwest. The stranger looked from Sorra to Davina, then produced a business card from her waistcoat pocket and held it out between two fingers. Its corners had been clipped, giving it an eight-sided shape. "Should the arrow happen by some miracle to turn up in the next few days, I'm staying at the inn. If it should appear after that, you can write me at the store. This lord isn't a patient man, though. I suspect the value of his offer will drop as time passes, and he may lose interest entirely."

Sorra's cheeks burned, but she held her tongue. It was needlessly cruel for this woman to taunt them with the idea of riches and then accuse them of lying on top of it. She snatched the card before Davina could take it.

"Delian Carraway?"

"That's me."

"What's in a curiosity shop?"

"What isn't?" Delian bowed slightly and left the yard. "Thank you for your time. I hope I'll see you soon."

Sorra kicked the water pump, releasing her frustration and sending a bolt of pain up her leg. "Come on. Let's get home before today gets any worse."

"Don't say that, love." Davina didn't have to say the rest—that if it could get worse it would, especially where Sorra was concerned.

Four blessings had been bestowed on their parents on their wedding day, one for each of four future children. Who had blessed them and why was now a matter of debate, but the number was fact. Four blessed children, and one enchanted arrow that would guide them to their greatest destinies once they'd each reached adulthood.

But there had also been a warning about greed and overreaching. About a fifth child who would walk in shadow where her siblings danced in the sun, whose fortunes would mirror theirs as she followed a path that would bring dishonour to her family and destruction to everyone around her.

A child who was never meant to be born at all.

Davina was quiet as they followed the dusty road toward the little house that sheltered at the edge of the woods to the north, scorning the company of other buildings. Sorra had lived under Corinne's roof her whole life, but she'd never been sure it felt like home. Stepping through the kitchen door felt more like returning to a cage.

It wasn't all bad, though. Sleeping in the kitchen meant a chance to sneak food after she'd been sent to bed without supper, and with three sisters gone there was more room to stretch out in bed at night while Corinne snored away in her room under the steeply pitched roof.

Sorra changed into her plainest brown dress, then lay on the mattress in the corner while Davina put the kettle on.

The staircase in the living room creaked. Moments later Corinne appeared at the kitchen doorway, blowing in with all the warmth of a winter storm.

"Lazy," she muttered, and kicked the mattress.

"I've been up," Sorra said, motioning to her dress. *Longer than you have,* she thought, but didn't say. "Just resting my eyes."

Corinne sighed, long and trembling. She was a tall woman, broad and strong through the shoulders, with a face as sharp as her tongue. As she told it, she'd been a great beauty before she'd taken in her poor sister's orphaned children and been drained of her looks, her wealth, and any remaining hope of finding a husband.

She'd named her youngest niece Sorra only after the mayor said she couldn't register the child as Sorrow, and their relationship hadn't improved much in the years since.

Corinne sniffed disapprovingly and scooped a serving of oat porridge into a wooden bowl. "I don't suppose you've found a way to bring some coin home?" she asked, turning to Sorra with the pained expression of a suffering martyr.

"No." Sorra sat up and looked down at her hands, fearing punishment for what her eyes might reveal if she looked at her aunt.

"Of course not. But please, eat some of the porridge I've paid for." Corinne sighed again, and Sorra resisted the urge to ask whether she should perhaps see a doctor about the condition. "This is what I get for sheltering you and preserving the rest of Andonia from your curse. If I weren't so damnably charitable, you'd have been in a southern orphanage before your first birthday."

Sorra closed her eyes and prayed to Linnea for strength. It was blasphemous to pray to a long-dead queen instead of the gods of her parents, but she liked those old stories and could at least be certain that Linnea had once existed. She never could be sure whether the gods had done the same and figured the odds of receiving an answer were about the same either way.

"I'll take tea out front when it's ready," Corinne told Davina, and glided through the open door into the living room, then out to the porch.

Davina waited until the front door closed behind her, then sat on the bed next to Sorra.

"Don't mind her. I'm fairly sure the stories she spins about her selfless suffering are the greatest pleasure in her life."

"That would explain her frequent indulgence." Sorra rested her face in her hands. "I wish she *had* sent me away before I'd known to miss any of you. Or that—" She paused. "No. I don't wish we still had the arrow, because then you'd have used it and left me, too. I just wish we had the money we'd have gotten from selling it."

"About that..."

Sorra turned to her sister, her stomach twisting. "What?"

The front door creaked. "Davina!" Corinne called. "My tea?"

"Be there in a moment!"

The door closed again, harder than seemed necessary.

Davina offered Sorra a tight smile, then got up to pour water into the teapot and a chipped porcelain teacup. A jar hidden on a high shelf held the herb mixture that would prevent long-lasting consequences after Sorra's night out, and Davina added three pinches to the cup.

That, at least, wasn't a mistake Sorra had needed to make before her sisters had taught her to avoid it. Whatever chaos she might bring to the world, a child wouldn't be part of it.

When Davina spoke again, her voice was quiet. "I still have the arrow."

Sorra stood, her heart beating harder. "You what?"

Davina grinned. "The arrow Grace brought back was a fake. I made it myself after we—Grace and myself—realized Aunt Corinne thought it might only have one use left. You remember how desperate she was then."

"I do." It had been a few years ago. Corinne had watched her first two nieces leave without much fuss, complaining only when they didn't bring their grand destinies home with them to add to the household's wealth or reputation. Ingrid's happy marriage and Aurelia's fame had convinced her of the arrow's powers, and it hadn't surprised Sorra when Corinne had decided to use Davina's birthright for herself. "So all her despair when the arrow showed her nothing greater than the life she had…"

"Was the result of my little trick, yes." Davina's amusement faded as she looked toward the front door. "I should probably feel worse about that than I do."

"It served her right."

"Maybe. Anyway, Grace gave me the real one after Corinne had taken the fake, and it's been hidden away ever since."

Sorra gaped at her. The arrow that had led three of her sisters to their greatest destinies was lost. She'd never had reason to believe otherwise. But if Corinne hadn't sold it…

She paced the kitchen, thoughts whirling until they struck a wall. "Dav?"

"Hmm?"

"Why didn't you use it?"

Davina smiled, but to Sorra it looked thin and forced. "Give me a moment. Wouldn't want to keep the mistress of the house waiting." She poured two cups of tea and carried one out to Corinne.

Sorra tried to imagine how a person could choose a lumpy mattress in a dingy kitchen over a grand destiny that might involve fortune, fame, adventure, or love. It was as unfathomable as whatever lay beyond the northern mountains.

"You could use the arrow now, before we sell it," Sorra said when Davina returned.

"Could, yes. But should is another question." Davina slid Sorra's cup of medicinal herbs toward her. "I've seen where the arrow leads, and how happy our sisters are. But the words always troubled me. *Greatest destiny* implies more than one, doesn't it? A range. Not destiny as fate, but as the potential ending of a story."

"A happy ending," Sorra said. She'd loved fantastical adventure stories when she was a child, before Corinne sold the books the sisters had inherited from their parents. Her sisters did seem like heroines from the simplest tales. Ingrid had met her true love when her arrow hit the side of his carriage, and even if he wasn't the prince he'd have been in a storybook, he was strong and kind and wealthy. To Sorra's mind that was better than any prince. The royal family hadn't paid attention to Cottsbridge for generations, and its citizens were glad to return the favour.

Aurelia composing and performing and teaching music wasn't a bedtime story ending, but it was perfect for her, and Grace's letters came bursting with her joy as they told of the challenges and successes she found as she travelled Andonia studying flora and fauna, advising on agricultural issues, and publishing academic papers on topics Sorra barely understood.

Davina's destiny would surely be just as great—painting the ceiling of the King's throne room, a private studio and wealthy patrons, travel and acclaim and whatever else she desired.

"A happy ending. Exactly." Davina shrugged. "I know it seems silly not to leap at mine, and I did consider it when my time came. I touched the arrow, I felt its magic… but I decided I didn't want my life to be set in stone. I'd rather see what comes if I keep rolling the dice at every step. And then there were the other questions. Would my greatest destiny be different now from what it would have been if I'd shot it when I was meant to? Would Grace's have been different if she'd stood facing south instead of east? If the range of potential destinies is changed—"

"Enough, I understand." Sorra's head ached, as much from the conversation as from the previous night's indulgences. She sipped her medicinal brew and winced at its familiar bitterness. "And we'd always assumed the arrow wasn't meant for me, so you kept it hidden. But if we sold it now, it could change everything for both of us."

"Or we could find out whether the arrow works for anyone beyond the so-called blessed four and then sell it."

Sorra drained her cup, though the drink burned her throat on the way down. "Are you joking? It'd probably send me stumbling into a bottomless pit if it did anything at all."

Davina shrugged. "As you wish. But if you'd quit feeling sorry for yourself and think logically, you'd see that you above all others need something to point you toward your true potential, which I doubt is at the bottom of any sort of pit."

"I'm not supposed to leave Cottsbridge. It's not safe for anyone."

"But if there were a safe way out, the arrow will show it. If you—"

The clanging of the town's bell cut Davina off, hard and frantic enough that it reached them through the open kitchen windows. Sorra had only heard it a few times when the townsfolk needed to be alerted to some immediate danger. Without a word, she and Davina hurried out the kitchen door and climbed the shed to reach the back slope of the roof—the best place to spy on whatever was happening without Corinne spotting them.

Shouting soon followed the bells, and after a few minutes someone thought to holler toward the lonely house at the edge of the woods.

"Murder!" A man's voice, though Sorra couldn't tell who it was. "Body found at the inn, one of the soldiers killed in his bed!" He ran closer, apparently having spotted Corinne.

Sorra crouched behind the roofline, frozen in place.

The door was still locked.

But the window was open.

"What's this about?" Davina whispered.

Donnell, the tanner's son, hurried closer, bursting with the news and seeming more excited than troubled by it. "Soldier," he said again. "Supposed to be another fellow sleeping there with him, see, but that one was downstairs all night on account of the dead one having... y'know. Company. I suppose they'll be looking for his, er..."

"Company, yes," Corinne said. "How terrible."

Sorra slid down from the roof into the backyard, and Davina followed.

"I didn't kill anyone." The flatness in her own voice frightened Sorra as much as anything else.

"I know," Davina said. "But you were at the inn all night?"

"I was."

"And he was alive when you left?"

Sorra's mouth went dry. "I assumed he was. I slept more deeply than I expected. I thought he was doing the same. I didn't wake him."

She tried to force some movement or a gentle snore into the

memory and failed. Maybe someone had killed him after she left the room.

Maybe she'd been sleeping with a corpse.

Either way, Stuart was dead. She didn't need to hear his name or see a body to confirm it. She hadn't meant to hurt him, but then, she never meant to hurt anyone. If he'd taken a different woman to bed, he might be alive now.

Davina took her hand. "You were seen leaving this morning?"

"I was."

Sorra considered her choices. The idea that anything like a great destiny might be in the cards for her seemed preposterous. If she had a destiny, her family's blessing made it clear that it was anything but good and was best contained to one isolated village.

Then again, the alternative suddenly appeared to involve hanging. No one would speak up to defend her, knowing the soldier had died because of her even if it wasn't by her hand. It would be a chance for them to rid themselves of their bad luck without inflicting it on the rest of Andonia.

This wasn't just murder. It was the killing of one of the king's soldiers. If the locals didn't execute her first, she'd find herself on her way to Embercliffe to have her neck stretched. Or maybe to face a worse punishment, if such a thing were possible.

Surely that couldn't be her greatest destiny. And even if the arrow failed to reveal anything better, retrieving and selling it would put enough cash in her pocket for an attempt at escape, risks be damned.

"Dav?" she whispered. "I think it might be time to find that arrow."

Davina pulled her toward the woods, and they ran.

CHAPTER THREE

"Where in the world did you hide it?" Sorra ducked as the branch Davina had pushed aside swung back and nearly slapped her in the face.

"Somewhere Aunt Corinne would never know to look even if she figured out what I'd done."

Davina marched deeper into the forest, pausing occasionally to check a faint marking on a tree or judge the angle of her turn at a distinctive rock formation. Sorra had spent plenty of time in the woods over the years, either because she'd been banished from the house as punishment or because she'd needed to escape from people for a while. Still, she had to pay careful attention to note the invisible trail as it twisted between the trees.

They'd almost reached the river when Davina stopped at the base of a massive oak. It had fallen some time ago but still lived, even with most of its roots torn from the earth, its branches resting on the support of neighbouring trees. The disturbed ground beneath it blossomed with tiny wildflowers and blueberry bushes that had sprouted where sunlight reached the soil. Davina crawled beneath the roots and emerged with a long package wrapped in oiled leather.

Sorra sat on a rock as Davina unwrapped it and inspected the unremarkable wooden bow their sisters had used to shoot the arrow. As she strung it, Sorra looked over the three golden arrows that glinted in the sun, each with a smooth, narrow head of some darker material.

"You made spares?"

Davina wrinkled her nose. "Earlier, flawed attempts. See if you can choose the real one."

They all looked perfect to Sorra. She'd never touched the arrow, knowing it wasn't meant for her, but she'd been invited to watch when her sisters used it to seek their destinies. All three arrows were gold, all three had perfect white fletching, but the one on the left stood out. There was something more liquid about the way its metallic shaft reflected the light that filtered through the leaves above.

"That one," she said, pointing. "The others are good, though. I'm not surprised you managed to fool Corinne."

"And whatever poor soul she sold it to." Davina reached back into the space beneath the tree for a sturdy canvas knapsack and a leather belt with a sheathed hunting knife attached to it.

"You've been prepared for this," Sorra observed.

"Of course. There was always a possibility we'd need to escape, with or without the arrow's guidance. Do you remember how it works?"

"I think so. Our sisters each had to go alone after their first try. It only works once per person." She folded her hands behind her and took a step back. "You should do it, Dav. Find your destiny and come back for me. I'll wait here, and we'll go together. If I try it, I'll probably lose the arrow or run into some other trouble, assuming it goes anywhere at all."

She wasn't sure which outcome she was more afraid of—another failure to feel ashamed of, or confirmation that her blessing was a curse she'd never be free of no matter how hard she tried.

That's the happy ending I want, she thought. *The one without a shadow blessing.*

Davina shook her head. "I told you, I don't want to. Either you try it for yourself or I sell it." She picked the arrow up, turned it under a beam of sunlight, then held it out to Sorra. "Mother's diary never said it would only work for us, only that it was an ancient object and a precious gift. There's no reason it shouldn't work for you. If it does, we'll know which way to go to get away from here. I can't imagine your greatest destiny is being hanged for a crime you didn't commit."

Sorra unclenched her fists but didn't reach for the arrow.

"Come on," Davina said. "Any direction is better than none at this point. If you don't like where it leads, you'll bring it back and we'll figure things out on our own once we've sold it. At least you won't have to wonder what might have happened."

"Fine. But don't blame me when—" Sorra's tongue fell silent as Davina placed the arrow in her hand. It felt heavy, as much from its significance as from whatever material it was made from.

Davina smiled with more confidence than she could possibly be feeling. "It'll work for you. I know it will."

Sorra took the bow and nocked the arrow. She hadn't practiced much over the years, but it wouldn't matter. If the arrow intended to deliver her destiny, it would. It had flown halfway to Graftenburg when Grace had loosed it, but had left a trail to follow, invisible to everyone but her.

Each had followed her own path and had returned the arrow safely for its next use.

Sorra's arms trembled, and she lowered the bow. "Promise you'll get yourself out of here if I don't make it back."

"Of course, love." Davina leaned against the oak's trunk, arms crossed, looking pleased. "I've been considering how I might make my mark if we found a safe way to join Aurelia in the capital. Don't worry about me. I have a little cash saved, and I can earn more."

"Don't tell Corinne. Some shared expense will pop up if she knows you have money."

"Gods, no. Now stop stalling and let it fly."

Sorra huffed out a breath, raised the bow again, and closed her eyes.

Something in her mind said to turn to her left. She did, stopping when the urge to move ceased, leaving her filled with perfect peace and certainty she'd never felt before.

"You feel something?" Davina asked. She spoke quietly, as though trying not to disturb any magic that might be at work.

"I think so."

The arrow has never failed, Sorra reminded herself. *And Davina's right. Anything is better than here.*

She stood straight and pulled back on the string as she'd been taught, then opened her eyes. She stood facing a sunny clearing. The direction felt right in some way she couldn't define.

Please don't fail. I need a way out. Away from this place, away from my blessing.

As her fingers twitched to release the arrow, something bumped her from behind. She stumbled. The arrow went wild, shooting high into the trees to the right of where she'd aimed, leaving a trail of golden light behind it.

Sorra righted herself and spun on Davina. "You pushed me!"

But Davina was still leaning against the fallen oak. Her eyes widened. "Nothing pushed you. Nothing I could see, anyway."

Sorra blinked back tears. "I had it right. I felt it. Now it's wrong. What do I do?"

Davina stepped closer. "Do you see anything?"

Sorra looked up. "A ribbon of light."

"Then I guess you follow it." Davina didn't sound nearly as certain as she had before. "The magic worked for you. At least see where it went."

"I don't want to go alone." It felt silly to be afraid of a walk in the woods. Childish, even. But after so many years of seeing how things tended to go wrong for her, Sorra doubted her sister would judge her too harshly for her nerves.

"You have to. The trail will disappear if you don't." Davina fastened the belt and hunting knife around Sorra's waist. "Trust the enchantment for now and see where it leads. I'll be waiting."

"Right." Sorra straightened her shoulders and studied the arrow's trail as she would size up an enemy before a fight. She'd fought more than her share, though she wasn't usually quite this sober when she did.

She made sure the knife was fastened tightly to her waist, then jogged into the woods after the arrow before she could change her mind.

~

The arrow's shining trail seemed to go on forever, soaking her skirt as she crossed the broad, shallow river and sending her deep into woods on the other side that Sorra had never explored. She chased it through thickets of brambles and across a stream with muddy banks that pulled at her shoes, then screamed in frustration when the trail passed over a deep ravine that was too wide to jump across. She stomped up and down its near side but found no better place to cross, so had no choice but to climb to the bottom and scrape her hands on the rocks and roots she used to claw her way back up the other side.

The thought of giving up crossed her mind, but she dismissed it. The chase had become a matter of pride. No matter how hard the arrow wanted to make things, Sorra would not let a scrap of metal defeat her. The blessing might have thrown her off course, but if something better might wait beyond these obstacles, she would find it.

"Misbegotten spawn of a…" she muttered as she reached the top of the ravine, speaking between ragged breaths, finding herself at a loss as to how to properly insult an arrow. "Damned faerie," she said instead. "Witch. Bright One. Whatever you were. Blessing folks with one hand and cursing them with the other."

But she said it quietly. One never knew who might be listening.

Her stomach growled, and Sorra looked up to find that the sun had crossed more of the sky than she'd expected. The day was more than half gone, with no sign that she was catching up with the arrow. Its trail was just above her head now, but she didn't dare try to touch it in case doing so disturbed the magic.

"Stupid lords with their stupid money, too. Bet the arrow won't make him dirty his fancy shoes in a mud pit. Ought to sell him one of Davina's fakes just to teach him a lesson."

But she trudged on through the forest. A stone turned beneath her left foot, sending bright pain shooting up her leg as she gasped and fell.

Sorra lay on her back, staring up at the shimmering light shining through the leaves above her.

Failure, whispered a small voice in the back of her mind. *Go back and be hanged. The world will be better off.*

It was a voice she'd heard many times before, usually keeping her awake at night when she'd run out of ways to distract herself from it.

"I hate you," she whispered, not knowing whether she meant the voice, the arrow, the lord, the bearer of bad blessings, or herself for her pathetic need to prove she could do something right when everything in her life thus far had proved exactly the opposite.

But the arrow had worked, or at least tried to. Davina had said to trust it, so she would. At least for a few more steps.

"Get up," she ordered herself in such a stern tone that she didn't dare disobey. The twisted ankle wasn't as bad as she'd feared, but her progress slowed as she took care not to aggravate the pain.

"Linnea have mercy," she prayed, embracing her habitual blasphemy more vocally than she dared at home. "Let this actually lead to my destiny, and let it be good if it can't be great. Let the damned arrow not be lodged high in a tree or lost in a marsh, or—"

She pushed through a copse of aspens and froze as she took in the sight of a massive brown bear staring over its shoulder at her, the golden arrow lodged firmly in its backside.

CHAPTER FOUR

Sorra stepped back into the bushes, but it was too late. The bear ambled closer, snorting, as she searched for any chance of escape that didn't require outrunning the massive beast.

The nearest tree offering potential salvation was a willow with sturdy branches beneath its trailing canopy. Sorra ran toward it, sending sharp pangs up her ankle, and threw herself onto the lowest branch, scrambling higher until she felt safely out of reach. Her breath came in quick gasps, too shallow to offer what her body needed, and she clung to the tree until a wave of cloudy white dizziness passed.

The bear nosed the dangling greenery aside and stepped into the dome formed by the willow's hanging leaves. Filtered sunlight picked out the longer hairs of its coat, highlighting the ruddy brown fur with an aura of gold as the bear stood on its hind legs, pawing at the air, watching Sorra. Its breath came in audible grunts. Not growls, but just as frightening.

She couldn't look away from its claws. She'd seen the damage left by bears when they tore apart rotting logs as they searched for a snack. It was all too easy to imagine what this great beast's weapons would do to her tender human flesh.

"Go on," she called. "Shoo."

The bear's lips flared, showing yellowish teeth as its jaws opened. Then it rested on all four paws, grunted, and reached along its side with one forepaw. The limb wasn't nearly long enough to reach the arrow, and the bear growled with what Sorra would have called frustration if she hadn't known better.

It sat on its massive behind and looked up at her as if to say *Well? What are we to do now?*

"I think this is what we call an impasse," Sorra said. The bear cocked its head to one side. "I need that arrow, and you need it out before you get a nasty infection, but I won't risk my life to get it."

The bear lay on the ground, chin in the dirt between its forepaws like an oversized dog.

And I'm not leaving until you try, its voice rumbled in her imagination.

As a child Sorra had often pretended to have conversations with cows, barn cats, and anything else that didn't mind her company. She'd lost the habit as she grew up and began to see the world more clearly for what it was—not a thing she could improve with her fancies, but a hard place that she could only survive if she, too, became hard. Still, here she was, falling back into comforting habits that would do her no more good now than they had then.

Animals in storybooks might talk, might offer rewards for people who helped them. A real bear would more likely tear her throat out in one swipe.

Her ankle throbbed, and she pulled her stocking down to examine it. The flesh had swollen, but the pain was only a little worse after her climb.

"You're my destiny, I suppose," she said, and laughed so hard it frightened her. The bear looked up. "The enchanted arrow worked just fine for three of my sisters. Took them to their beautiful happy endings like the family blessing meant it to, but I knew something would go wrong for me. I didn't really expect it to lead to true love or fame like it did for them, but a way out of Cottsbridge would have been nice." She paused to collect her thoughts, then glanced down at the bear. "I'm sorry your rump got in the way."

The arrow shone in the sun, taunting her.

It was always going to be this way, she thought, knowing she'd probably cry if she said it out loud. The magic had worked. The arrow had been going somewhere, and in quite a determined fashion, until her blessing got in the way.

Sorra didn't let herself wonder what she might have found if not for the interruption, or if she hadn't stumbled and thrown it off course. Maybe there would have been something good at the true end of its trail, but she'd never know.

"Or it's some kind of joke," she said. The bear blinked slowly at her. "Maybe this is it—my great destiny is a twisted ankle and an angry bear, and there's nothing better for me after all. All I wanted was a chance to be free."

Sorra rested her back against the tree's trunk and took the knife from her belt to cut a long strip of cotton from the underskirt she wore beneath her dress. It was awkward work, but the blade was sharp, and she soon had enough to bind up her ankle. It still ached when she was done, but the pressure helped.

As she was tying off the cotton, the knife slipped from her hand and landed point-first in the ground. Sorra's throat tightened painfully as the bear leaned forward to sniff it, then settled back again to watch the strange creature in the tree above it.

It was a damnable choice to have to make. Either she could sit in the tree until the bear left her to wander home empty-handed or risk helping the poor beast, ending up with either an arrow to sell or a brutal death.

"Trust the enchantment," she said, mocking Davina's tone. "Didn't trust it for herself, though, did she?" She looked down at the bear. "I could help you. I might have to cut the arrow free, though. I don't think you'd like it."

The bear laid its head down again and sighed.

Sorra had made many foolish decisions in her life. She'd believed insincere promises, spent her scant coin on a false miracle or two, been kind to those who wished to harm her and unforgivably rude to those who didn't, and taken pity on a strange frog she found children tormenting on the road, not knowing that releasing it into the pond would lead to an infestation of nightmarish proportions.

But this, she decided, was unquestionably the most foolish.

She climbed down from her perch, watching for any sudden

movements from the bear. When she felt sure it wasn't going to attack, she plucked her knife out of the dirt, then cleaned it as well as she could on her skirt.

The bear still didn't move.

"Be a good bear and we'll both be on our way soon." She tilted her head to one side, eyes narrowed. "I don't suppose you're going to offer to grant me a wish for helping you?"

The bear's nostrils flared.

"Right," Sorra said. "Well, it'll be a funny story to tell your cubs one day."

The bear rolled onto its side so the arrow pointed toward the branches above them.

Sorra frowned. "Do you understand what I'm saying?"

It didn't answer. It wasn't behaving like a wild bear, though. Perhaps it had been tame, once, and had escaped from captivity as Sorra had so often dreamed for herself. She wished Grace could be there. She'd have known how to read the creature's movements, how to keep it calm.

The bear was a larger animal than it had seemed at a distance, and more fearsome. Sorra's heart thudded in a wild, panicked rhythm as she approached and laid a hand on its leg, barely resting any weight against the coarse fur. The bear snorted gently.

The arrow had gone through fur, skin, and a thin layer of fat and buried itself in the muscle beneath. Sorra tugged at the arrow, hoping its narrow head would pull free easily, and the bear snarled. She jumped back, knife held out, but the bear only lifted its head and looked at her, then at the arrow, as if telling her to get on with it.

Sorra approached just as cautiously as she had the first time and parted the thick fur around the arrow's shaft. It smelled more pleasant than she'd expected, like the bear had recently been napping in a meadow. "I won't hurt you more than I have to, I promise."

She pressed down on the skin next to the arrow, and the bear didn't react.

So docile.

A bear like that might let a person get close enough to cut its throat, and a person who managed that would have a much easier time retrieving her arrow. Safer, too, when things were so likely to go wrong.

But it's not the poor creature's fault this happened, she thought. *No more than it was Stuart's fault he met me. No more than it's my fault I was born.*

The world was hard, cold, and cruel, and Sorra had felt herself becoming its creature more and more with each passing year. But suddenly, if only for a moment, such a transformation didn't seem inevitable.

I may not have a grand destiny, but I do have a choice.

The blade slipped as easily into the bear's flesh as it had through the fabric of her skirt, widening the opening around the arrowhead and sending a thin stream of blood flowing over the dense fur. The bear snorted and dug its claws into the ground as Sorra worked the arrow free, careful not to twist it and catch on the torn flesh more than she had to. It was frightening and gruesome work, but it was soon done.

She backed away with the arrow in one hand and the knife in the other as the bear stood, its sides heaving, its teeth bared as it stepped toward her.

Sorra turned and ran, but her ankle gave out before she'd taken three steps. She fell, sprawling across the roots of the willow, bruising her knees and the heels of her hands as she landed and curled on her side, waiting for claws to meet her skin, praying the end would be swift as the bear's shadow fell over her and the fabric of her dress pulled tight across her hip.

A huff of warm, wet breath stirred the lock of hair that lay across her cheek, and she realized she wasn't dead. Still, she couldn't open her eyes or move until the bear stepped away, leaving her lying in the murky warmth of sunlight trapped beneath willow leaves. She blinked slowly and sat up.

The bear stood nearby, its head held high, sniffing the air.

Sorra touched her cheek and shivered as she remembered its warm breath. Those teeth had been so close to her throat, those claws had stood on her skirt, but she was alive.

"Good," she said, as much to the bear as to herself. "At least that's not what the arrow was leading me to."

She opened her hand, but the arrow didn't resume its interrupted flight. And when she stepped out of the willow's shelter and back to the place where she'd found the bear, its golden trail had vanished.

Whether it had meant to take her farther or not, this was where the path to her destiny ended. She'd tried not to hope it would lead her to a way out of her backward birth blessing, but it hurt to have the door slammed in her face.

That was the problem with hope. It insisted on sticking its nose in where it wasn't wanted and leaving a person worse off than she'd have been if it had never come at all.

Sorra turned to the bear, which had followed her. "I don't suppose you know how to get back to Cottsbridge?"

The bear blinked at her.

"The King's Road? Any road, really." She looked down at the arrow. "I don't want to go back to my horrid aunt's house or that wretched town, but my sister is waiting. I don't know what happens after that, but it's a start."

The bear swung its head from side to side, testing the air again, and plodded into the woods, crashing through a stand of young birch trees.

Probably off to find some nice berries, Sorra thought, wishing she could forget her troubles so easily. Still, it had chosen a direction that wasn't far off from where she thought the road might be, given that she hadn't crossed it on her journey. She walked after the bear, reasoning that at least it was clearing a way forward.

Even if the arrow's path had been a cruel joke, any direction was better than none.

She quickly lost the bear's trail, but reached a broad road that stretched north and south.

After a backward glance to make sure some glorious destiny wasn't about to materialize, Sorra turned south, heading toward Cottsbridge for what she hoped would be the last time.

CHAPTER FIVE

The last traces of sunset glinted off the river as Sorra approached the bridge, pausing at the edge of the woods to make sure no one was watching for her. There was no movement on the road or at the rocky shoreline, and no lantern light approached as darkness fell.

If they thought she'd run away, they rightly believed she'd be a fool to head north. There was nothing there but the Gate and a village or two that the soldiers would search as they continued on their journey.

Something rustled in the trees behind her. She turned, half-expecting to see the bear, but it was only a fat rabbit that disappeared back into the darkness when it caught sight of her.

Sorra waited for dusk to settle over the river, then cursed the full moon and the clear sky as she hurried across the bridge. Davina waited in the woods not far ahead, waving for Sorra to join her. They stepped deeper into the tree cover before either spoke.

"What happened to you?" Davina asked.

"I shot a bear."

Davina gaped at her. "You what?"

"It let me remove the arrow, but it seems my greatest destiny was for me to injure my ankle and end up back where I started."

"You… what?" Davina squeezed her eyes closed and took a long breath.

"It didn't work for me, Dav." Sorra swallowed back the pain that would do her no good if it came out in her voice. "Or rather, it did, but my destiny is a dead end."

"That remains to be seen." A distant look came into Davina's eyes, and Sorra suspected she'd be overthinking all of this long after Sorra hoped to have moved on. "In any case, we have pressing matters to deal with."

"The sheriff?"

Davina cast a glance in the direction of the house. "He hasn't dropped by yet, though he must have witnesses to your presence at the inn by now. Aunt Corinne's already been in to collect gossip, but she won't tell me anything."

"What's next, then?" Sorra asked. "Have you spoken to that woman who approached us this morning?"

"No. I didn't want to make promises until I had something to offer."

Sorra looked down at the arrow, which felt like nothing special now that it had served its purpose for her. No urging, no direction, no sign that it was anything but a ridiculously fancy bit of metal and scraps of feather.

Its magic was hidden, waiting for its next use. No different now from Davina's beautiful fakes, and no one who hadn't felt its magic would know to expect anything more.

"We could sell her one of the arrows you made," she said. "Then we'll still have this if you want to use it after all, or to sell another time."

Davina frowned. "That's dishonest."

"Who and what is honest these days?" Sorra weighed the arrow in her hand, liking her idea more as she thought it through. "Corinne got away with it, didn't she? No one will know the difference until we're gone and it's too late for any of them to find us, and I'd say a rich man can spare the money. Besides, that shopkeeper will be trying to cheat us, too, so she can keep more of that lord's money for herself."

"It's a bad idea, love," Davina said, softly but firmly.

Sorra smiled as though it didn't matter. "You're right, I guess." She'd made her decision. Davina might be too honest to do what was best for them both, but someone had to. "You go find that shopkeeper and tell her I'll meet her under the bridge later tonight. I'll take care of the negotiations. We'll pack once Corinne is asleep, and we'll be on the road before sunrise."

Davina shivered. "I don't want you meeting with that woman alone."

"You don't trust me?" It wasn't difficult for Sorra to sound hurt. "I can't go into town, and I can't go home until you've sent Corinne off to bed with the pleasant thought that I've run away for good. I can take care of this part, though. Please let me do something useful."

"I—" Davina paused, obviously struggling between wisdom and affection. "You'll be careful?"

"I will."

"You won't provoke her or overstep?"

"I won't. I also won't take less than the arrow is worth, but there has to be common ground somewhere. She's a businesswoman, and we're giving her what she wants. How much trouble can she cause?"

"All right." Davina looked at the arrow one last time. "Aunt Corinne thinks I'm at the inn now, gathering news. I'll deliver the message to our buyer."

"Good." Sorra's stomach rolled.

Davina walked away, then glanced back. "Be careful. Don't do anything I wouldn't."

Sorra flashed her another bright smile, and Davina went on her way.

When she was sure her sister was gone, Sorra paused to tighten the fabric binding her ankle and walked deeper into the woods. Everything looked different in the dark, but she soon found the first landmark that would lead her to the cache of fake arrows.

Maybe Davina was right about it being a bad idea, but the odds of a stranger giving them anything like what the real arrow was worth were too slim. They'd need plenty of money just to get to another city, never mind to start a new life. Cash would be the only security they'd have, and if there was even a chance that they could hold on to the arrow to sell again later, she saw no choice but to take it.

Davina would thank her eventually, and what she didn't know wouldn't hurt her.

That shopkeeper won't suspect anything, she told herself. *If Davina's imitation was good enough to fool Corinne, it'll be good enough to fool her.*

CHAPTER SIX

When Sorra was six years old, Ingrid had read her a story about trolls living under the river bridge, ugly creatures that would snatch bad children who tried to cross and eat them for supper. It hadn't taken Sorra long to decide to walk to the bridge alone so she could see the trolls, and to be disappointed to find nothing beneath it but the remains of an old campfire and a rotting blanket.

Years later she'd realized the story wasn't really about trolls at all, but about less obvious threats that waited for children who wandered too far from safety—threats like humans who might at first seem kind and trustworthy.

The story was about a true thing, but the trolls were a fiction created to make subtle dangers real to those who had the most to fear.

Still, as Sorra cautiously descended the river's bank weighed down by the firewood that now filled the knapsack from beneath the oak, she found herself watching not for bandits or wayward soldiers, but for trolls with stony skin and bone-crushing jaws.

The firepit was still there, though Sorra couldn't say who used it or when. Tonight, it was hers, and she set out the dry branches, leaving the enchanted arrow hidden in the knapsack and setting the best of Davina's replicas on top of it so she wouldn't confuse the two. She made a nest of kindling collected from the bullrushes at the river's edge, lit the fire, and settled in to wait.

And wait.

When she couldn't sit anymore, she paced, judging the ache in her ankle to be a fair price to pay for the easing of her boredom. When that wasn't enough, she threw rocks into the water and observed which shapes made the most satisfying sounds as the river swallowed them.

Finally, long past midnight, footsteps crunched on the road above her. Three people slid down the bank. Sorra faced them, wishing she'd brought a weapon larger than the hunting knife she still wore on her belt.

"I didn't realize it would be a party," she said. "I'd have brought refreshments."

As they stepped into the firelight, Sorra recognized Delian, the shopkeeper she and Davina had spoken to that morning, now dressed in a perfectly tailored calf-length jacket of dark wool that she wore buttoned to her throat, black boots, and riding gloves. The one next to her wore a red, hooded cloak—the same person who had listened to her conversation at the inn, though at that time Sorra hadn't seen the darker stains at the cloak's hem.

The third hovered at the edge of the firelight. Her face, too, was shadowed by the hood of the violet cloak she wore over a long, black skirt.

"We appreciate your hospitality nonetheless," Delian said, nodding at the fire, "though we won't be staying long. Things have gotten a bit sticky in your little town since we last spoke. Seems best to leave before anyone's suspicions turn from the victim's mysterious paramour to the strangers lodging in the next room."

Sorra looked to the red-cloaked person. "Did you kill him?"

"I did not." A feminine voice, but rough and husky. She lowered her hood, revealing a deep scar that cut down the left side of her face, lovely as a cracked porcelain doll but with the sharp eyes of a predator. "My guess would be one of the soldiers he cheated last night."

"Did you tell the sheriff?" Sorra asked. "A witness who could suggest another suspect might—"

"No." Delian smiled apologetically. "We don't involve ourselves in other people's business. It doesn't tend to end well."

Especially when it's mine, Sorra thought.

"You have it?" Delian asked.

Sorra retrieved the false arrow. In the light of the fire, it appeared a perfect match to the one she had chased through the forest earlier. "We'll need to discuss the specifics of payment. This is a valuable item. It led three of my sisters to great success and happiness. One can only imagine what it would do for a lord who already has power and wealth behind him."

The shopkeeper raised one eyebrow. "Indeed. All he lacks is direction. So, subject to verification—"

Sorra's stomach dropped. "Verification?"

"Of course. Gale?"

The third stranger stepped closer and plucked the arrow from Sorra's hands before she could object. Beneath her hood, Sorra caught sight of rosy cheeks, pursed lips, and dark eyebrows furrowed in disapproval. "Fake. There's nothing there."

The girl—Gale—tossed the golden arrow out over the river, where it disappeared without a splash. Sorra noted that she was missing the first finger on her right hand.

Delian sighed. "We could have sold that." She turned to Sorra, every trace of good humour erased from her expression. Behind her, the woman in red pushed her cloak back over her shoulders. Her scarred hands hovered near the twin knives strapped to her belt, but she didn't draw them. She didn't need to. The quiet confidence of her movements left Sorra certain the young woman could kill a person before her victim realized it was happening.

Stupid, stupid, stupid.

"I—I didn't—" Sorra stammered.

"Didn't know we'd have a witch with us?" Delian smiled, cold and grim.

Sorra's skin crawled as she looked into the young woman's strange eyes and wondered who, exactly, she was dealing with. The others were more frightening on the surface. One a battle-scarred warrior, the other a witch—a criminal who used magic illegally and was probably quite dangerous if she were at all competent. But they both seemed to be taking orders from Delian, if that was even her name, which probably made her more of a threat than either of them.

And certainly no simple shopkeeper.

"No." Sorra stood straighter. Running wasn't an option, so talking it would have to be. "That is, I must have gotten it mixed up with—"

"This?"

Sorra jumped at the sound of a deep voice behind her. She hadn't seen a fourth member of the party, but now a young man in a charcoal-grey suit stood next to her knapsack with the true arrow in his hand. He passed it to the witch, who nodded.

"I can't confirm the exact nature of the enchantment without testing," she said, "or verify that it will work for our buyer. It feels..." Her voice trailed off, but no one else spoke. "It's what he asked for."

"Good enough." The fellow who'd taken the arrow tossed a heavy cloth bag at Sorra.

She snatched it out of the air and opened the strings to verify that its weight came from real coins. Even without counting she could tell it was a fair price—more gold than she'd seen in her lifetime.

Banknotes would have been easier to carry, but she wasn't going to complain.

"Will that do?" he asked.

"I suppose," Sorra said, then glanced at the red-cloaked woman's knives again. "That is, it's plenty, thank you." She looked over the four travellers, remembering the shop's name and the city written on their leader's business card. "Your lord must be either desperate or foolish."

The witch narrowed her eyes. "What makes you say that?"

Sorra collected her empty bag and slung the straps over her shoulders, then pocketed her payment. The weight of the coins pulled at her dress, and they jingled faintly when she moved. "He gave you this much to pay me for something he couldn't be sure existed, and presumably enough to cover travel expenses for four and make it worth your time to come all the way here from

Queen's Run. So he's desperate, or so rich he doesn't know the value of a coin."

"Or both," Delian said. "The high-born can be absolute idiots about so many things." She shot a sly smile at the man, who now crouched by the fire, warming his hands. He had a roguishly handsome face of the sort Sorra never found among the locals or the soldiers who passed through.

He glared half-heartedly back at his companion.

"We should move on," the one in red said.

"Of course." But the shopkeeper stepped closer to Sorra, guarded by the watchful gazes of her friends. "May I offer a piece of advice?"

"Why?" Sorra's voice came out as a whisper as she imagined an attack, her body left beneath the bridge, her coin stolen back as the strangers left with the arrow.

"Because I'm feeling generous." The light from the fire danced in Delian's mismatched eyes. "I'm willing to forgive you for trying to trick us, but only because I'd have done the same if I didn't know better. Others won't be so generous. If you want to play dangerous games, make sure you understand the rules." She smiled. "And never underestimate your opponent."

"Thank you," Sorra said, unsure of how else to respond. All she wanted was for these people to vanish so she could get to work forgetting them.

The one in red walked with an uneven gait as they followed the riverbank upstream, strong but unnaturally deliberate, as though her steps caused her pain. The witch walked close beside her, whispering something, and the other two followed.

Delian had confessed to being a trickster, and the witch hadn't hidden what she was. The man might be a burglar or a pickpocket. The other woman could be a mercenary of some sort, paid to protect the others, her scars proof of past fights fought and survived.

Criminals. Maybe as bad as what Sorra's blessing promised she would become, maybe not. But they had a purpose. They were doing things. They seemed to fit together in a way that Sorra had never fit in anywhere, and as they disappeared into the night, she let herself hope she might find her own place in the world once she'd left Cottsbridge behind.

Or my imagination's running away with me again, she thought, and rubbed her eyes. After two nights with little sleep, there was no telling where her fancies might take her.

But that dangerous feeling of hope had returned. Perhaps the arrow itself was her destiny—not for where it had led her, but for the bag of coins that would buy her way out of Cottsbridge. Corrine had always insisted that the best Sorra could do was to make herself inconsequential to limit the scope of her villainous destiny, that seeking more or better could only lead to disaster.

And maybe she was right. But if a better life were possible despite her unfortunate birth, Sorra was sure she wouldn't find it waiting by the river.

She gave the buyers a head start, made sure the fire was out so she wouldn't add the bridge to her list of accidental arson charges, and walked toward home, one hand clutching the bag of coins in her pocket to assure herself the witch hadn't enchanted them to disappear.

The lights were off in the house as Sorra approached hours after midnight, ready to fill the empty knapsack with her few belongings before she fled forever. The pack of scoundrels under the bridge were right—it was past time to get out of town. Sorra listened at the open front window for several minutes, then lifted the knob, easing the weight on the door's hinges so they wouldn't squeak and give her away.

Clear, cold moonlight outlined the familiar shapes of the sitting room—the threadbare sofa, the rocking chair, the stone fireplace, and the clutter of Corinne's collection of brass, glass, and porcelain objects she called "finer things."

Davina sat up from where she'd been lying on the sofa. "How did it go?" She spoke in a barely audible whisper.

"Fine." Sorra decided she wouldn't tell Davina about the fake arrow. It didn't matter now, anyway. She pressed the bag of coins into Davina's hand. "We got what we need."

The stairs creaked, and the sisters exchanged a panicked look.

"Go," Davina said. But before Sorra could take a step, the oil lamp on the mantel flared to life, blinding in its sudden brightness.

Corinne, wearing her lace-trimmed nightgown and a smile fit for a dog that had just downed a stolen roast, put out the match with a flick of her wrist and set it next to the lamp.

"What's the rush?" she asked. When neither Davina nor Sorra answered, she stepped closer, her eyes sweeping over them and landing on the cloth bag in Davina's hand.

Corinne moved past them and locked the front door. "I think we should all sit down and have a little chat, don't you?"

CHAPTER SEVEN

Corinne stood with her back to the door, arms crossed, daring either of her nieces to speak.

Sorra glanced at the closed door to the kitchen. Beyond it, the back door offered a chance of escape.

"I wouldn't," Corinne said. "You won't get far before I summon the sheriff."

Sorra's hands tightened into fists, but Davina motioned for her to be still.

After a lifetime of being ordered to control even the slightest hint of her temper, of being warned that it was a sign of her true nature surfacing, Sorra had learned to keep it on a tight leash. Still, the pressure kept building, the urge to leap at Corinne and silence her becoming so strong that holding still made Sorra physically ill.

But for Davina's sake, she stood with her fists pressed tight against her thighs, trembling with anger. Davina's way was quieter, always observing and waiting and carefully judging before acting. Not one scrap of Sorra's soul wanted anything to do with that sort of plan, but neither of them could afford to let an impulsive action further upset things.

"If turning her in is your intention," Davina said, "I don't suppose we have much to discuss."

Corinne sat primly in her favourite rocking chair, legs crossed at the ankles. "We'll see."

Neither Davina nor Sorra moved, either to flee or to make themselves comfortable.

"I didn't kill that soldier," Sorra said.

"I believe you." Corinne's voice became lower and softer. "That is, I believe you didn't slit his throat. But you and I both know you're responsible even if you're not directly at fault. If that poor man's life hadn't brushed up against yours, he'd be alive now."

Sorra didn't object. She couldn't. Not when she'd had the same thought herself, and not when everyone in Cottsbridge would think the same.

Corinne nodded as though Sorra had answered. "It's the same for all of us, isn't it? You never mean harm, but it comes. To me. To your poor parents. To your sisters."

"Leave us out of this." Davina stepped closer to Corinne. "Sorra hasn't harmed us."

Corinne smiled at Davina with sympathy that pained Sorra more than cruelty or her usual indifference could have. "The others are flourishing now, aren't they? All because the arrow led them far from here. Far from her. It couldn't have done otherwise, could it? The same would have been true for you if you'd taken me up on my offer to use the arrow before I sold it. You knew your greatest destiny had to be to abandon her, so instead you suffer with the rest of—"

Davina's expression hardened. "Shut up."

Sorra's heart sank, heavy as stone. "Is that true, Dav?"

"No." Davina spoke to Sorra but didn't look away from Corinne. "I mean, yes, she offered. Yes, I was afraid the arrow would lead me away from you as it did the others, and I chose to stay. But what I said before was true—I had other reasons." She turned to Sorra, her eyes shining. "You have not harmed me, and I've never feared your bad luck. Whatever challenges we face after we leave this place will make life more interesting." Her trembling voice dropped to a whisper. "Whatever comes, we'll both be better off than we are now."

"Better off," Sorra said, her voice thick and rough, "but it won't be your best life."

"It can't be," Corinne said. "Not with you in it. What's true for

Davina is just as true for me and for the rest of Cottsbridge. You've proved over and over the truth of the birth blessing—*Destined to walk a path which is a dark reflection of her sisters', bringing turmoil and trouble to every life she touches.* I've known for two decades that it was my unfortunate duty to keep that darkness contained to the best of my ability, and our community has shared that burden for the sake of Andonia. When I shot the arrow and it landed here, I knew I wouldn't be free as long as you lived."

Sorra laughed. "That wasn't the real arrow." She barely managed to keep herself from adding *you pathetic cow.* "The real one is gone now, and good riddance. You will be rid of me, and free to make the life you've always wanted, or to find a new excuse for not having it."

Corinne's lips tightened as she pushed herself up from the chair. "Real arrow or not, its message was true. I am trapped here as long as you live. I can't allow you to leave. The more lives you touch, the more your curse will spread and harm Andonia. You've seen the extent of your sisters' greatness. Who's to say what destruction you might cause if you're set free to mirror their destinies? What sort of villain or monster you might become?"

"She won't let that happen," Davina whispered.

A gentle breeze blew through the open window, carrying in the cool, damp-smelling night air. Something creaked on the porch—Corinne's second-favourite rocking chair, perhaps, though Sorra found it hard to convince her racing heart that it wasn't the sheriff paying a premature visit.

Corinne reached out to touch Sorra's cheek, the first affectionate gesture she'd ever offered. Sorra flinched away.

"This is for the best," Corinne said, letting her hand fall to her side as she moved toward the door. "I'm going to tell the sheriff I overheard you confessing to murder. It's the greatest mercy I can offer. No one, least of all you, should have to live under the weight of your destiny."

"You can't do this." Sorra wasn't sure whether the tears she blinked back were welling up from anger or despair, but she knew they wouldn't buy her any sympathy. "I don't want to die. Please, just let me go. You never have to see me again."

Something hit the door hard. Not a knock, but a thud, followed by a harsh scraping against the wooden panels.

Corinne picked up a silver candlestick from the table next to the door and backed away. "Who's there?"

Another thud, hard enough to crack the door up the middle, was the only answer.

Sorra froze. The back door still offered a chance at escape, but she couldn't be sure the sheriff or the soldiers weren't out there, waiting for her to run.

The door crashed inward, and the hulking form of a huge, brown bear stumbled into the room, looking lost and confused as it took in its surroundings and the humans staring at it.

Corinne shrieked and threw the candlestick at the beast. It bounced off the massive skull with a loud crack.

The bear roared and raised one forepaw to rub at the injury, then glared at Corinne. "That hurt!"

It spoke in a deep, rumbling voice, thick and a little slow.

Sorra stood rooted to the floor, any thought of flight gone as she struggled to understand. It was the bear she'd met earlier, no question. But that bear didn't belong in Corinne's house.

That bear didn't talk.

No one answered, and the bear cleared its throat. "I beg your pardon," it said, setting its paw back on the floor. "I wouldn't have barged in so rudely if it hadn't sounded like someone was in trouble." It turned to Sorra, looking sharper and more intelligent than it had earlier. "I have a proposition for you."

CHAPTER EIGHT

Davina stepped between Sorra and the bear. "Who are you?"

The bear grunted and pawed at the floor. "Someone's destiny. Or so I've been told."

A strange voice. Masculine to Sorra's ear, though perhaps any bear would sound that way if they made a habit of conversation.

Corinne sank into her rocking chair and gripped its arms tight, her gaze darting between the bear and the opening where the front door should have been.

The bear turned his head from one side to the other, taking in the cluttered room, then looked to Sorra. He was out of place in the cabin, too large and too wild, but seemed more at ease than Sorra felt.

"I've come to make you an offer," he said, "and with a sincere apology for my rude silence earlier today. I hadn't spoken in so long that I wasn't sure I knew how, and it took some time for me to understand the meaning of what had happened. To decide I could trust you enough to make my proposal."

"Perfectly understandable," Sorra whispered, automatically offering the polite sort of response that had been drilled into her since childhood. Her voice had fled, and she wished her body could do the same. There was no immediate threat, but her heart wouldn't stop pounding and her mind seemed to be entirely stuck on the idea of *talking bear*, which left no room for planning or reasoning or arguing against the cold dread that pooled in her stomach.

The bear took a step to one side, creating a clear path between Sorra and himself. His shoulder pushed against the threadbare armchair that faced Corinne's rocker, filling the silence with the uneven scrape of its legs against the floor.

"An offer," the bear repeated. "I am in need of a companion to come and live with me—to keep me company, to tend to my home. It seems fate has named you, and that it has timed our meeting most fortuitously." He glanced at Corinne, let out a faint growl, and looked to Sorra again. "You said you were hoping for a way to escape this place, and I heard enough through the window to understand why. If you will agree to stay with me for a year, to leave your home and share mine, to respect me and not harm me, I will in return keep you safe from this woman and anyone else who would harm you."

Sorra licked her lips to wet them, but her tongue was just as dry. "Including yourself?"

The bear's lips pulled back in what was either a smile or a grimace. "Including me, and for as long as you abide by our agreement. I have no wish to harm you. Your surroundings will be humble, but I can offer food, shelter, and conversation. If you agree to leave your home, your family, and the ills of human society behind, I will help you escape your current troubles."

Corinne stood. "You can't take her. I haven't suffered under the weight of this family's destinies for all these years to let her get away now."

The bear growled and clawed at the floor, carving ruts into the wood. "Her destiny is no longer your burden to carry. The arrow brought her to me."

Corinne glared at Davina. "You gave her the arrow?"

Davina didn't answer. She might not have heard, focused as she was on the bear.

"You don't understand," Corinne said. The bear flashed its teeth at her, and she bobbed a quick, clumsy curtsey. "Kind sir," she added. "The situation is complicated."

"And it's out of your hands," the bear said. "Your part in her story is finished. Set aside your own plans for how it will end. This is not for you to decide."

Corinne crossed her arms and went to the window, turning to face the breeze that brushed her hair back from her face. "Give me a moment to think."

The floorboards creaked as the bear stepped closer to Sorra. "Promise to stay with me for one year, to be my companion, to do me no harm, and to respect the rules I set, and I will carry you away from this place."

Davina took Sorra's hand, her fingers like ice against Sorra's flushed skin. "Where would you take her?"

"A safe place, but secret. It would not be safe otherwise."

"And who are you? You didn't say."

The bear sighed. "I did not. I cannot. I am what I am, and I meant what I said. Unanswered questions will do no harm as long as they're left in peace. I will care for your sister for as long as she keeps her end of our agreement, should she choose to make one at all."

"And when the year is over?"

"She will be alive and well, and she will be free to stay or leave as she chooses."

Sorra squeezed her eyes closed, though it seemed dangerous to do it in the presence of such a fearsome beast. She couldn't think when she was looking into his eyes.

One year.

The offer was beyond strange. It was nonsensical. She had no choice but to accept the fact that a talking bear existed but struggled to understand why such a creature would want a human companion. For conversation, perhaps—other woodland creatures likely didn't offer much in that regard. And maybe approaching most humans was too dangerous, prone as they were to doing things like locking extraordinary creatures up or making them perform for money.

He was asking her to promise not to do that, to leave society behind for a time so he could have a companion on his own terms. They'd met by accident, she'd somehow impressed him, and that was that.

It was a wildly impossible idea, but was it any stranger than an arrow leading to her greatest destiny or the undeniable fact of the creature it had led her to?

I do have a destiny. A strange one, but maybe there's still a chance for it to be a good one.

Sorra opened her eyes. The bear was watching her, and Davina was watching the bear, her brow furrowed with whatever thoughts were churning behind it.

And Corinne was gone.

Sorra brushed past the bear to stand in the doorway. Corinne hadn't made it far but was walking toward Cottsbridge at a fast clip, her white nightgown blowing in the breeze.

Sorra considered running after her, tackling her to the ground, forcing her back to the house. But her cries would draw attention, and the attack itself would be reason for the sheriff to haul her in even before Corinne got her accusations out.

Instead, she turned to the bear, her mind a little clearer after a few breaths of night air and her nerves oddly calmed by the knowledge that what was in motion could no longer be undone.

The only question was which direction everything would go.

"I give it ten minutes before she's back with the sheriff and a bunch of soldiers," she said. "Can the three of us leave now and discuss our agreement in a safer place?"

The bear turned to face her, knocking over a spindle-legged end table and sending a dusty vase of glass flowers crashing to the floor. "No. I leave now, with or without you. If you wish to come, it will be we two alone, with our agreement in place." He lowered his head. "Please. If I am your destiny, you are mine. Let us see what comes of it."

Sorra clenched her jaw.

If I don't like what comes, at least I'll be alive to figure a way out of it.

"I agree," she said. "If you promise to get me away from here, provide for me, and keep me safe, I'll stay with you for a year."

Davina paled. "Sir... bear, if you'll keep watch here for a few minutes while we pack her things we'll all be safer."

The bear nodded and went to the doorway, filling its width with his broad body as he sat on his rump to wait.

The kitchen felt strange when Sorra entered. It was the same one she'd left that morning, the same one she'd gone to bed in almost every night of her life, and one she might suddenly never see again. Davina closed the door to the living room and lit the lamp on the worktable, her trembling hands casting strange shadows on the walls.

Sorra shrugged the empty knapsack off her shoulders. She'd forgotten it was there but was glad to have it.

Hurry, the voice in her mind whispered, uncharacteristically helpful even if the urging was unnecessary.

She stuffed a spare dress into her bag, along with undergarments, socks, and a second sweater after she'd pulled her favourite on over her dress. She might not need it on such a warm night, but winter would come eventually…

There was no way to pack a single bag for a year-long journey in just a few minutes. She turned to Davina for help and found her sister wringing her hands in the sort of unhinged agitation that was usually more Sorra's business.

"Dav?"

Davina gave her head a quick shake, then rolled a thick wool blanket that she tied to the bottom of the knapsack. "Sorry. Thinking. Over-thinking."

"You are good at that."

"I wish you hadn't agreed so quickly."

Sorra paused, the stockings she'd been meaning to mend since the spring half-balled in one hand. "I don't have much choice, do I? He's my way out. I'll never get away on my own, not with soldiers after me."

"I know." Davina's wavering smile, clearly forced, felt like a knife to Sorra's gut. "And you can't go back on an agreement with a magical creature. Once the deal is done, the consequences can be grim. You didn't ask what they'd be, and now it's too late."

Hurry, the voice whispered again. Sorra stuffed the stockings into her pack but couldn't think of what should come next. "He is magical, isn't he?"

"The talking bear? I think the odds are that he is, yes." Davina collected a book of matches, a little cooking pot, and a tin cup as she spoke. "It's not the kind of thing they teach us about in school, but you know the old stories as well as I do—the Bright Ones who lived here before humans, goblins and sprites and whatever else, tempting offers and doom for those who broke their promises." She shoved the items into the knapsack, squashing the clothing beneath to make room.

Sorra's legs weakened, and she sat on the edge of the bed. "He said he meant me no harm."

"And that he'd keep you safe from himself and others as long as you obeyed him, which is why I'm not urging you to flee while he's distracted." Davina spoke quietly, her words tight with urgency. "The arrow led you to him, but I don't understand what any of this means."

The world sharpened around Sorra, then swam like it did when she felt a fever coming. "You said to trust the arrow."

"I did. And I do. But things are complicated for you thanks to the blessing. I was only thinking of the arrow and your happy ending, but how else do the old stories end? The girl who agreed to serve a king in exchange for a beautiful voice only to be transformed into a bird and kept in a cage to sing sorrowful songs for his pleasure. Or the foolish boy who agreed to..." Davina paused, frowning. "I can't even remember, but he was changed into a donkey and got worked to death. Or the princess who fell in love and married a handsome man who turned out to be a goblin."

Sorra took a deep breath before she answered. She understood Davina's concerns but wished she'd kept them to herself if it really was too late to change her decision. "Those are just stories, Dav. Warnings about not trusting people."

"So we thought." Davina crouched and took both Sorra's hands in hers. "Now I'm wondering whether the stories were truer than we realized when we were so cleverly picking them apart. You can't afford to trust him too easily. This offer of escape might be destiny's way of keeping you alive, but you have to make sure there's not a darker side to it. He said you'd be free to leave alive at the end of the year if you choose, but I worry he's going to try to win you over so he can get more from you later."

Sorra wanted to argue, to remind Davina of how they'd made

fun of the stupid decisions people made in those silly stories, to say she knew better.

But Davina was right. She had trusted too easily before. Bad enough when the punishment for it was a stained reputation and a broken heart. Far worse now, when it might be the loss of her freedom or her life.

Davina stood. "You can't run from him unless he sets you free, and you can't afford to antagonize him—you've agreed to be a good companion, and if you break your promise, he might kill you. But you can guard yourself for a year." She reached for the jar of contraceptive herbs and handed it to Sorra. "You're bound to him by a promise. Best to be sure you're never bound to him or anyone else by a child."

Sorra laughed, more from surprise than any sort of amusement. "Dav, if a bear tries to get me in a situation where I need these, I'll have bigger problems to worry about."

"And if he's not a bear?" Davina took the jar back and tucked it deep in Sorra's knapsack. "I want this to be your happy ending, love. I do. I want it to be your greatest destiny."

"But things don't work that way for me. I know." Sorra forced herself to her feet. "I'll be careful. But this is where the arrow led me, which means it's better than hanging or whatever would have happened if we'd escaped on our own. I'll be free of Corinne, and now you're free, too."

She said it for her own sake as much as Davina's. Somewhere in the back of her mind the old chorus of *stupid, impulsive, never looks before she leaps, trouble at every step* had started its familiar refrain that flowed from her brain to her guts, twisting them into knots.

"It'll be fine," she said, closing the knapsack and hauling its straps onto her shoulders. "I'm going to get away, and I have a place to stay until everyone forgets they're looking for me. All I've agreed to is a year, and I won't be tricked into more. I'll find you and we'll be together again."

Davina wiped her eyes on her sleeve. "I'm probably scaring you for nothing. It's just—"

The bear nosed his way into the kitchen. "Lights on the road," he said. "More than a handful. I'm leaving."

Death or destiny.

The noose or the unknown.

Either way, the bear seemed like the right choice.

He has to be good. It has to be my turn for fair winds and sunny skies.

"I'm coming." Sorra let the bear out into the yard, then pulled Davina into a tight hug as he disappeared into the night. "I'll see you again before you even miss me."

Davina held her tight. "If he won't tell you who or what he really is, promise me you'll do everything you can to find out for yourself." Her words came out in a quiet rush. "If you learn that he's good, you'll know for sure that you've found your happy ending. If he's not, you'll at least know whether it's worth the risk to break your promise and run. Pay attention to the empty spaces—what he doesn't say, what he doesn't do. That's where he can't help telling the truth."

Sorra shivered. "I promise."

It was good advice. Davina's always was when Sorra chose to listen.

The bear waited in the yard, crouched with his belly pressed to the ground.

"Best you ride," he said. "I can run faster than you."

Sorra only hesitated for a moment, the absurdity of charging into the woods on a bear's back far outweighed by the knowledge of what happened to those convicted of crimes against the king's army.

She climbed on, hauling herself up by handfuls of the bear's fur, her legs spread across his broad back in a most unladylike fashion behind the great hump of his shoulders.

Davina watched, framed by the light in the kitchen doorway.

Before Sorra could wave goodbye, the bear stood, leaving her no choice but to hold tight with both hands, and bolted for the woods.

CHAPTER NINE

As the bear carried her away from home, it seemed to Sorra that she was living out two stories. The events and settings of each were identical—the bright stars against a blanket of dark velvet overhead, the warmth of the bear beneath her and the icy chill of the river as he splashed across it, soaking her skirt.

But the stories would lead to different endings, which changed everything about them in the present.

In one, the arrow had led to her greatest destiny. Her happy ending wasn't shaping up to look like her sisters', with love or fame or fortune, but why should it? Her life before hadn't been like theirs, either, and the utter absurdity of her knight in shining armour being a shaggy-pelted talking bear wasn't necessarily a bad outcome. If the arrow had led Grace to a creature like this, no one would have doubted his good intentions or the blinding shine of whatever future lay ahead.

Sorra wanted to live in that story, where every step away from Cottsbridge was a step away from the shadow of her blessing, a bit of magic out of a bedtime tale. It was easy enough to be carried along with it at first—or at least, once she was sure no one was coming after them on horseback. If she let herself think of it as her first grand adventure, everything from the snap of fallen branches beneath the bear's paws to the distant howl of a wolf could only add to the thrill of her dramatic escape. Her rescue, in fact, by a creature who had saved her because he thought her worthy of protection from an unjust world.

She wanted to believe she deserved such a happy ending after her miserable life in Cottsbridge.

But Sorra wasn't accustomed to imagining the best, and doubts would have clouded her mind even without Davina's warnings. The other version of her story, darker but just as believable, was one where her blessing had thwarted the arrow's attempt to lead her to a great destiny. She'd accepted the bear's offer believing that only magic could have placed a talking bear and a potential rescuer in the arrow's path but hadn't questioned *which* magic. He might be a witch. Or a creature descended from the Bright Ones who had once ruled this land, most of whom were said to care nothing for humans except as pets or servants... or worse. He'd saved her life, and in exchange she'd given him control over it.

One story promised the ending she wanted. The other reflected the reality she'd lived every day of her life, where pretty promises hid dark intentions.

Sorra forced herself to breathe.

I'm alive, and that's enough for now.

But the tension between wishes and fears, between *could be* and *maybe not*, felt like it might tear her in half. She supposed she might survive either story, in one as a rescued damsel with an unlikely new friend or in the other as the girl who defeated the monster.

But only if she knew which was true.

She clung to the fur on the bear's shoulders and huddled close as he ran on. They were well away from the cabin, the town, and anything familiar before he slowed to a walk. Sorra held tight with her legs to keep her balance as she wrung the water from her dress. Her heavy knapsack shifted uncomfortably with every step.

"Thank you for getting me away from there," she said.

Best to get on friendly terms with him either way, and it didn't seem he was going to start a conversation.

The bear snorted. "I wasn't anticipating such an exciting departure, or for you to come with me at all. I'd meant to enter in a more civilized fashion, but I caught the end of your conversation through the window—her threat, your pleading. I didn't understand until then how dire the situation was."

Sorra relaxed slightly. He still seemed nice enough, even now that they were alone. "And I wasn't anticipating any sort of rescue. Certainly not to have a bear save me, or to be my destiny. If that's what you really are."

"We can only hope so."

The bear didn't take the opening to continue the conversation. Sorra let him walk in silence until the questions itched her mind badly enough that she had to scratch at them again.

"Where are we going?"

"Far enough that they won't be able to follow."

Not what I asked, Sorra thought. An answer, but not one that offered anything useful.

That doesn't mean he's bad, she told herself, though her stomach squirmed. *Only that he's not skilled at understanding the implications of a question. He's actually doing quite well for a bear.*

She smoothed a clump of fur she'd been gripping in one fist. "What's your name?"

The bear's right ear twitched. "What makes you think I have one?"

Sorra shrugged, though he couldn't see it. "You should, anyway. If I'm to spend a year with you, I can't just call you 'bear.'"

The forest became denser as they walked, the space under its canopy darker between thick oak trunks and patches of spindly pines. A stand of birches came into view ahead, stark and pale in what little moonlight reached them. In Sorra's mind, they became slender ladies waving to urge her on in her adventure and, at the same time, a menacing crew of skeletal wraiths waiting to give chase.

In this case she had the luxury of believing neither. They were trees, nothing more, and letting her hopes or fears colour reality would only complicate her search for the truth.

Find out what he is and forget the rest, she told herself.

If he is what he says, learn to accept that goodness is possible.

If he's not, at least you'll know.

"Shall I give you a name?" she asked.

"If you'd like. Whatever pleases you."

Sorra settled deeper into the steady sway of the bear's steps. "I can't name you after anyone I know. Maybe not a human name at all."

"Probably best that way," the bear said.

"Destiny would be far too silly as a name."

"Indeed," he rumbled. Sorra thought he sounded amused but couldn't be sure.

"Arrow? That's how we met."

He snorted. "A fine name for a horse."

Sorra decided not to point out that he was the closest thing she had to a noble steed. She also decided not to ask how a bear knew what sorts of names people gave their pets and beasts of burden.

"Forest, then? Or Blade, for the knife I used to cut the arrow free." Silly names. She wasn't in a silly mood, and the attempt at humour felt brittle. "Or Bow, for the one I shot the arrow with."

The bear's steps slowed, then resumed their former pace. "Be serious."

"Maybe I am." Sorra paused, considering the idea. "Not like bow and arrow, though. Beau, the name."

The bear tensed beneath her. "I thought you didn't want to choose a human name."

"But I don't know any human who uses it. There was a dog in Cottsbridge called Beaumont when I was a child, and they called him Beau. A great shaggy thing with fur a bit like yours. His name would work for you. And maybe a person's name is best if I'm to think of you as a friend."

He sighed. "Very well."

He didn't seem thrilled but didn't offer any further objections. Or any other conversation, though Sorra waited again.

"Thank you," she said, some time later.

"For what?"

"For letting me do that. Giving you a name makes you feel more... I don't know."

She did know, though. A name made him feel more known, or perhaps knowable, even if she'd named him herself. Not a something, but a someone, and that felt far better. But saying so out loud would feel like admitting a weakness that required accommodation.

Beau carried tirelessly on. The forest was quiet save for the occasional movement of animals as he passed their hiding places. The great bear didn't seem troubled by any of them, and Sorra found herself relaxing further. She had to shake herself awake several times so she could pay attention to her surroundings, though there weren't many landmarks in the dark woods she might use to find her way home.

The forest thinned, and the sound of running water ahead reminded Sorra of how little she'd had to eat or drink recently. Her bladder awakened, too, and began whining about how long it had been since she'd tended to its needs.

Without her asking, Beau crouched at the edge of the stream. Sorra slid to the ground and winced. Her legs had stiffened after hours of riding, and she had to stretch them out carefully before she could take a step.

"Would it be all right if I went over there to relieve myself?" she asked, gesturing toward a fallen tree a short distance downstream.

Beau lifted his nose and sniffed. "There's no danger. I'll wait."

Sorra squatted in the shadows, knowing it was probably silly to consider modesty in front of an animal that left its droppings all over the woods, then wiped herself with a handful of leaves after checking them carefully to be sure they wouldn't leave her with a painful rash in an undesirable location.

A person only had to make that mistake once in her lifetime.

Beau was sitting by the stream when she returned, and he watched as she cleaned her hands and scooped clear, cold water into her mouth.

"I could walk for a while, if it's easier." She stood and dried her hands on her sweater. "I don't mind."

That wasn't quite the truth. Her ankle was still sore, and exhaustion was catching up with her. It would be rude not to offer, though, and there was no point making a bad impression.

"I don't mind carrying you," he said. "It will be faster, and we still have a long way to go."

Sorra watched the movements of his mouth, wondering how it

all worked. Animal voice, human words. There was something strange about how he said them, slow and cautious, like he practiced each sentence in his head before he spoke, but it felt so natural that she was tempted to pinch herself in case it was all a vivid dream.

"Thank you," she said, realizing she'd become distracted and forgotten to answer.

He crouched, and she climbed onto his back, finding it easier this time to keep her balance when he started walking.

Beau didn't speak, and Sorra lost track of the time and distance that passed in silence.

"Your home is a long way from Cottsbridge," she said at last, fearing she'd fall asleep and topple off his back if she didn't have conversation to keep her awake, hoping she might lead him into revealing a hint of what lay beneath his scowling brow and thick coat.

And hoping, too, that he'd decide it was safe to explain things now that they were alone.

"It is," he said. "You must be exhausted. Do you need to stop for a longer rest?"

"No," Sorra said through a yawn. "I'm used to late nights and lost sleep, and they've never been brought on by anything as exciting as this."

"Oh? And what sort of work did you do that kept you awake so late?"

Sorra smiled. It was the kind of question a person would ask of a new friend, not someone he meant to harm. "I did a lot of jobs, though none of them at night." She counted them off on her fingers. "Minded a few children over the years. Milked cows. Worked the fields. Did a bit of work for the blacksmith. Assisted an older woman in town, reading to her and such. Helped customers at the general store for a week or two. Rebuilt a few stone walls, fixed fences, bit of trapping. Tended pigs and sheep. Lots of things."

Beau glanced over his shoulder. "You can't have worked at any of them for very long, then."

Sorra had heard implied disapproval too many times in her life to miss it now, even in a bear's voice.

She forced a cheerful grin. "Haven't found what fits me yet, I guess."

Letting him think of her as flighty felt better than saying she'd been sacked every time. Safer. The narrowing of his eyes said it would be all too easy to ruin this fresh start simply by revealing the truth about herself.

"I see," he said, and looked away.

Sorra's cheeks warmed. "Does this disappoint you?"

Beau's answer came slowly and after a long silence. "It surprises me. When we met, you spoke as if—that is, you seemed like a certain sort of person. Seeking your destiny, a blessing on your family and taking your turn. I'd given up on finding the companion I sought, but then you were so brave, so kind, so in need of help that you might be open to the idea of..." He trailed off. "Forget I said anything. I don't doubt you are who you said you are. Breadth of experience can only be a benefit in a companion, and I look forward to hearing more of what you've learned and how you've grown through your life's winding path."

The pit in Sorra's stomach turned into a nest of vipers that writhed and snapped at her insides. It was the longest string of words Beau had offered since they'd left Cottsbridge, but all they'd revealed was that the arrow might have played a cruel joke even if he wasn't a monster.

"You saved me because you think I'm good? And heroic?"

"Of course." Beau's voice warmed. "I required a companion who would be kind, gentle, understanding, wise, and trusting. I risked coming to you because you showed yourself to be all those things, and brave as well to have faced a wild bear instead of fleeing and leaving him to suffer. I didn't feel the magic of your arrow, but it seemed that you had to be my destiny, and I yours."

And there it is.

It was almost a relief to know something had gone wrong. Catastrophe was familiar territory, and knowing it had arrived was easier than waiting for the blade to fall or pretending to believe all was well.

And maybe if I play this right, she thought, *I can escape before the blessing makes things worse for either of us.*

Sorra slid to the ground without asking him to stop, stumbling and catching herself before she could fall. She backed away, putting space between them, though she knew it would do her no good if he decided to break his promise not to harm her.

"I'm not what you want," she said. "If you wanted someone like that, you should have taken Davina."

Beau's ear twitched. "But the arrow brought you to me. Not her."

Sorra drew a long, trembling breath and let go of the pride that had kept her from wanting him to think badly of her. "Please listen," she said, holding out her hands in a placating gesture she hoped he'd understand. "What I said when we met was true. My parents received a blessing that gave them lovely and talented children. Four of them. And that enchanted arrow led three of my sisters to their greatest destinies."

"You did say that," Beau rumbled.

"Well, I'm their fifth child. The opposite of the others, actually. The dark side of their blessing, meant to bring as much bad to the world as they're meant to bring good." Sorra swallowed back the thickness that filled her throat. "I'm not wise or clever—I wasn't allowed to finish my schooling because Corinne decided ignorance would make it easier to keep my wings clipped. For the good of the rest of Andonia, you see. And I'm not brave and kind. I only faced you down so I could sell the arrow to make my escape. Because no, I didn't kill anyone. But I did spend the night with the soldier who died, and you might as well know I'd have swung even without Corinne's false testimony. Everyone in town would be happier with me dead. I'm trouble. Every job I lost was because I brought disaster on those who gave me a chance to be good and useful."

Beau's nostrils flared. "You lied to me."

In spite of her fear, Sorra's temper sparked, hot and bright. "I did not! I didn't know you understood a word I was saying, so I couldn't know it mattered whether I kept the worst parts to myself. If you took what I said and made assumptions about who I was and how I was somehow your greatest destiny, that's your fault."

Beau opened his mouth again as if to speak, then closed it and gave his head a hard shake. "Then what of the arrow? You implied that its magic worked for you until its path ended with me."

Sorra took another step back. "I don't know. Maybe you were the only way I could escape hanging, and this is the end of it. Or maybe I'm supposed to pretend to be what you want, but I…" Her shoulders slumped. "I can't. I'm not perfect, but I am trying to be honest. I didn't lie."

"I suppose not." Beau sighed. "I should have known it wouldn't be so simple."

"Nothing ever is for me. Or for those who let me into their lives, unfortunately." Tears pricked at her eyes, and she wiped them away on her sleeve. *This is good,* she thought. *Better to know.*

There's a lesson to be learned here, whispered the shadowy, slithering voice in her mind. *It wouldn't hurt so much if you hadn't let yourself imagine that someone wanted you.*

Beau stood as still as the ground beneath him, his eyes closed. Whatever he was thinking or feeling, it didn't seem like he was preparing to attack.

There was still a version of destiny that didn't end with his claws at her throat if she chose her words carefully.

"We could end our agreement, if you'd like," she said. "You've had a stroke of misfortune in becoming my destiny, but that can end here. I'm willing to release you from your promise of a safe home if you'll release me from the year I promised you. And if you'll let me go without hurting me, of course. No hard feelings needed over a misunderstanding. And I promise I'll never tell anyone about you."

Sorra's heart raced. *Let me take back my mistake,* she thought, not addressing anyone in particular. *Just this once.*

And it was clearly a mistake. Maybe spending a year as someone's greatest disappointment was better than hanging, but not by much.

Beau let out a rough breath. "No."

"No?"

He hung his head, defeated. "This may not be what either of us hoped, but I made a promise that I intend to keep. If I leave you here, you'll die before you find a way out of the woods. If I take you back, you'll be executed for a crime you didn't commit. There's no safe place for you among humans when your supposed crime is fresh in their minds, and I won't have your blood on my—my paws."

Sorra pretended not to notice his hesitation over the familiar phrase and hoped he'd think she shivered from the cold and not apprehension.

Beau crouched, inviting her onto his back. "I don't fear any shadow that might hang over you as much as I fear many other things, and I don't suppose you'll be able to cause much trouble where we're going. You will come with me as we agreed, and you will be safe. Nothing has changed."

But his tone said that everything had changed, and that he regretted his part in their bargain as much as she did hers. More, perhaps. Whether his plans for her had been delightful or horrible, she sensed that she'd somehow ruined them by not being the docile, sweet companion he desired.

But he was right. She wouldn't make it far in the human world as a murderer on the run. A quiet place to hide until autumn's rains washed the ink off her wanted posters might be a decent destiny, if not exactly a great one.

It only promised my *greatest*, she reminded herself as she climbed up again, trying not to pull too hard on his fur. Maybe there hadn't been many options for the arrow to choose from.

She tried not to think about the range of bleak destinies that might technically be considered greater than hanging.

"Beau?"

He took a long breath before he answered. "Yes?"

"Who are you, really? And why do you want me?"

"I believe I made it clear that I wouldn't answer that sort of question." There was an edge to his voice that hadn't been there before. Restrained, but not kind or happy.

"You did," Sorra said. Then to herself, she added, *but you didn't make me promise not to ask.*

He didn't say anything more, and she decided not to irritate him further. She rested her chest against his back and laid her head on her arms, her fingers twisted tight in his fur.

The bright, happy ending version of her story had popped like a bubble, but Sorra didn't feel any closer to the truth than she had before.

I'll find it, though, she promised herself, and yawned. *If the blessing wants to hurt me, so be it. But it had better be ready for me to fight back.*

CHAPTER TEN

When Sorra opened her eyes, the sky had lightened.

She sat up straight, sending a bolt of pain up her back, which had stiffened as she dozed.

"Where are we?" she asked, rubbing her hands against her arms. The air was warming already, but the chill of the night had seeped into her bones.

"The southern reaches of the northern mountains," Beau said. "Nearly to my home. To yours, for now. Just a little farther to climb."

Sorra didn't ask more. If this were truly a happily ever after, she might have imagined his home as a grand manor house with invisible servants and more food than she could eat in a lifetime, isolated but magical and perfect. But with the blessing's foul winds blowing, anything could happen, and imagining the best would only make reality more painful. The only reasonable thing to do seemed to be to imagine the worst, so Sorra proceeded accordingly.

Beau had offered shelter, but what qualified as such for a bear might not meet her idea of acceptable accommodations.

A cave, maybe. She'd need to act unbothered even if it were full of bats and bugs, so he might like her better and be open to the idea of improving things in the future.

There was so much she now realized she should have brought with her. An axe. More blankets. More clothing. More food. But regret wouldn't fix anything. And for the moment, neither would worry.

Beau walked on, carrying her through a forest of widely spaced spruce trees with skeletal trunks stretching toward a patchy canopy of green needles. Birds flitted between the branches, twittering and squabbling, and a rabbit darted from its path to hide in a clump of bushes. Sorra closed her eyes and focused on the sun against her face, the sweet-sharp bite of the woods in her nose, and the clean air in her lungs.

Over a lifetime of making herself small, of doing less so she wouldn't risk disaster by trying for more, she'd learned that small pleasures still existed, and that they were the fingerholds that might keep her from slipping into despair.

This wasn't a destiny like those offered to her sisters, or whatever the arrow would have had in store for Davina. It wasn't love, and likely not even the sort of companionship she might have hoped for when she'd agreed to Beau's plan. It wouldn't be a castle or servants or the approval and acclaim she tried not to let herself dream of. In the end, it might be a disaster.

But in this moment nothing was hurting her. She wasn't hurting anyone. And her companion wasn't sighing about how grateful she should be that he hadn't cast her out yet, which was an improvement over Corinne's morning greetings.

Small pleasures. Best to enjoy them while they lasted.

"Here we are," Beau said.

Sorra tried to prepare herself to hide her horror at her new living conditions, already practicing how she'd compliment what she could before mentioning amenities her fragile human form might require if he wanted her to survive through the winter.

At least let there be no bugs or bats, she thought. *Please.*

When she opened her eyes, there was no cave, and no sign of a terrible prison like Davina might have feared. Instead, Beau had stopped in front of a log cabin with a pair of small sheds built behind it, lit by buttery sunbeams that cut through the trees. The cabin was old and spotted with moss, and in place of windows it had small, glassless openings cut into the walls. It was smaller than Corinne's home but well kept, moss notwithstanding, and the porch at the front door showed signs of recent repairs. The roof was done with wood shingles, lighter in places where they had been replaced in large patches.

Set against her expectations, it almost looked like a palace, or at least like a place where a person could survive and be safe for a year.

It seemed Beau understood humans better than she'd feared.

"This is your home?" she asked.

Beau crouched to allow her an easier route down, then pawed at the ground and stretched his back. "The woods are my home. This will be yours. I hope it will serve."

Sorra stood with her arms crossed, surveying the area around the cabin. There was no road. No neighbours. It would quickly become a lonesome place, but for the moment the quiet and the lack of human company seemed entirely desirable given what she'd left behind.

"May I go in?"

"Of course." Beau followed her onto the porch, which creaked under his weight.

Sorra paused with her hand on the latch. A rusty hasp stood open on the outside of the door, with an equally rusty padlock dangling open from it.

"Sorra?"

"Sorry."

He stood beside her and followed her gaze to the lock before she could look away. "Ah. I'd forgotten that was there. It won't do you much good to lock it when you go for a walk, unless you find a key. Not many thieves in these woods, though." He glanced at her. "That wasn't your concern, was it?"

"No. I mean, I only—"

He frowned. "You're not a prisoner here. Take the lock down if you want. Throw it away. I have no need of it."

Sorra felt herself blushing, though she knew there was no need to feel ashamed of a little caution. She opened the door, then stepped aside and motioned for him to enter first. When he'd squeezed through the doorway, she took the lock and slipped it into her pocket. She couldn't see how a bear would make use of it but felt better having it in her own hands.

She stopped just beyond the threshold to look over the single room inside the cabin. It was tidy. Plain enough that Corinne would have turned up her nose at it, but Sorra was glad to see an iron stove with cut wood stacked beside it, rickety wooden chairs at a roughly carved dining table, and a large bed in the corner dressed with a faded brown quilt.

Cobwebs had gathered on the firewood and in the corners, but those would be easy enough to banish.

There was only a little room for storage—a few shelves on the kitchen wall, a boxy pantry with a curtain for a door in the corner, a single cupboard beside a rusty sink, and a pine chest set at the end of the bed. But there were a few dishes on the shelves, a kettle on the stove, and half-melted candles in tarnished silver candlesticks.

To compensate for the lack of proper windows, someone had nailed sheets of thin white cotton over the openings in the wall, allowing air and light in without offering insects the same privilege.

The only decorations were a dusty brass clock on the mantel of a fieldstone fireplace and a rectangular rug in the centre of the room. Its faded pattern of red and green flowers had been worn nearly to threads and was covered in a fine layer of brown fur.

Sorra turned to Beau, who stood in the kitchen. "Do you sleep in here?"

"I've waited out a few storms. It's yours now, though. Toss the rug out if you don't care for it."

"No, not at all. I only wondered." She paused, searching for words that would erase the previous night's conversation and coming up with nothing.

"There's an outhouse next to the shed out back," Beau said, sounding a little uncertain, or perhaps uncomfortable. "And a river a short distance away where you can draw water. I believe there's a large metal tub stored under the porch if bathing in the wild doesn't appeal to you. Not much to eat here at the moment, I'm afraid, but the meadow we passed not far back has berries if you'd like to pick some for your breakfast."

He spoke cordially, evenly, without a trace of the disappointment or anger he'd revealed back in the woods. Sorra didn't trust it. He could express emotion, and the lack of it made her wonder what he was hiding.

She'd always preferred honest conflict to false civility but decided to follow his lead.

"Thank you." She removed her knapsack and sat on the bed. The mattress sank under her weight, but whatever it was stuffed with was at least soft, and it didn't smell of mildew. "I might rest, first."

"Of course. Perhaps I should see what I can find for you to eat. Give you time to settle in and sleep."

"That would be nice. Thank you. Again."

"Very well."

Beau left without another word, and when Sorra made her way to the door to look out after him, he was gone.

"Very well," she repeated, making her voice as low and rumbly as she could manage. His presence had been awkward, but his absence was just as bad, leaving her feeling more alone than she liked in this strange new place.

She closed the door and walked around the perimeter of the room, tracing her fingers over the warped scrap of oak countertop, the table and the backs of the chairs, and the mantel. The big clock's hands weren't moving from their position at five past eight, but the key at the back of its casing tightened when she turned it. There wouldn't be much need for a clock if she had no appointments to keep, but the idea of marking time was comforting when everything else felt uncertain.

Though her eyelids were heavy, Sorra decided to finish her exploration before she let herself rest. If Beau wasn't going to tell her anything about himself, maybe the cabin would offer more.

A closer examination of the kitchen didn't reveal anything interesting. Bowls on the shelf, pots and pans in the cupboard, and nothing but spiderwebs, mouse droppings, and a few jars of vegetable preserves in the pantry, plus a tin canister of salt.

On her way to the chest at the end of the bed, Sorra paused to pull the rug up, hoping for a trapdoor that would lead to the cellar, but found nothing except pine boards.

She set it back in place and opened the chest. It held extra blankets, a clean feather pillow, and a few items of men's clothing—worn trousers, a shirt, and a damaged wool sweater.

She frowned and touched the sweater's tattered hem, remembering how Beau's claws had damaged Corinne's floor.

A bear had no need of clothes. Or a cabin. Or a bed.

This place had belonged to someone once, so what had become of them? It wasn't hard to imagine a person torn to pieces by a bear who wanted a secluded home for the companion he desired. Or worse—perhaps she wasn't his first companion, and the one before her had displeased the bear and suffered the consequences of breaking their agreement.

It would explain the lock on the door. She took it from her pocket and buried it beneath the clothing in the chest.

There were simpler explanations for the convenient home he'd provided—an abandoned cabin he'd stumbled across, a legitimate purchase somehow.

The hairs on Sorra's arms stood on end. It felt as though someone were watching her from the kitchen, but when she spun to look, she was alone.

Don't be stupid, she told herself, but the advice felt supremely unhelpful when she couldn't decide whether it was more foolish to jump at every shadow or to cling to every scrap of hope.

Neither, she decided. *Don't assume anything for now. Just keep your eyes open, stay focused for once in your life, and see what comes of it.*

It sounded like something Davina would suggest, which made it a comforting idea. Not having her sisters around to keep her on the right path felt strange and frightening, but maybe that was the answer—do as they would advise. Or better, try harder than she ever had before to do as they would do.

She thought it over as she removed a few items from her backpack, setting the pot, cup, and jar of herbs in the pantry and piling most of her clothes on the chest at the end of the bed, leaving only the essentials packed in case she needed to grab her bag and run.

He wanted someone like Davina and got me instead.

If I can be like her, he might like me.

And if he likes me, he might trust me... and let me see who he really is.

He seemed to be forcing politeness to win her over, and two could certainly play at that game.

Sorra curled up on the bed, her lightened pack hugged to her chest, her back to the wall.

I'm not like my sisters, she thought. *But if they're what he wanted, I can pretend. Just for a while.*

CHAPTER ELEVEN

Sorra sat up and rested her head in her trembling hands, willing the anxious shriek of her thoughts to fade. She didn't remember dreaming, though the orange light from outside told her she'd slept the day away, and nothing had frightened her awake.

But her fear didn't need a fresh catalyst. Waking in a stranger's bed with no idea what would become of her might be enough to give anyone a jolt.

Sorra hurried to the door and hauled it open, just to be sure she could.

Not a prisoner.

She breathed in and waited for her heart to slow.

The air was cooling already. Back in Cottsbridge it would be another warm summer night, but things were different here in the mountains.

She closed the door and went to the chest at the end of the bed, kneeling as she opened it. The rusted lock sat where she'd left it, undisturbed.

Nothing felt safe, but the sight of it offered a sense of control that calmed her.

So get on with it, then.

There was already wood in the stove and plenty of kindling. Sorra stuck one of the long matches packed into a box at its side and soon the warm smell of burning wood filled the cabin. The logs stacked next to the stove wouldn't last long, but perhaps there was an axe in the shed.

She glanced at the clock. It told her nothing useful about the true time, but the hands had moved, and that pleased her. If she set it to noon when the sun was overhead, it might be close enough for her needs.

The cabin warmed quickly once she had the fire crackling. Sorra pulled back the curtain that shielded the little pantry, halfway hoping that some magic had stocked its shelves while she slept, but she found only the same paltry offering of dusty old jars that had sat there earlier. She was considering whether it would be better to go hungry or risk dying with a stomach full of rotten preserves when a scratch at the door made her jump.

Calm down, she ordered herself as she crossed the room to open it.

Beau stood on the porch, a large fish cradled gently in his mouth.

"Is that for me?"

Beau blinked at her. "Ihsfurngl."

Sorra took the fish. It wasn't twitching, but it was still wet and slippery, its eyes bright and its flesh firm. Her stomach groaned.

Beau licked his lips. "It's for you. I'd have come earlier but didn't want to wake you if you were resting."

Sorra set the fish on the counter, then remembered her new commitment to proper manners. "Come in, please. You said there's a stream for water?"

"Straight out back. I believe there's a bucket on the porch." He paused. "I could accompany you if you'd like."

"No, I'll find it. Make yourself comfortable."

Sorra wasn't sure why she refused his company except that she felt too much like herself after her nap, unfinished and sharp around the edges. A short walk would clear her mind and give her time to put on her best face.

To become like her sisters, to whatever extent that might be possible.

He nodded but followed her onto the porch.

"Shout if you have trouble," he said.

"I will."

Sorra took the bucket, then set it down outside the well-ventilated little outhouse while she relieved herself. With that done, she followed the sound of burbling water into the woods, keeping her eyes and ears sharply focused even when no prowling mountain cats or wolves showed themselves.

Be brave, she reminded herself. *He wants brave. Kind. Polite.*

She collected a bucket of water and hurried back to the cabin.

Beau settled on the rug at the centre of the room while Sorra set the iron pan on the stove, then cleaned the fish.

She was lighting the dusty old candles when Beau broke the conversational silence she hadn't noticed, focused as she was on the delightful prospect of food.

"Set the parts you don't want on the porch," he said, nodding at the pile of bones and guts she'd left on the counter.

"I was—" Sorra began, then caught herself. Lovely Aurelia would never snap *I was going to do it in a minute*, whether it was true or not. Grace might have gotten away with it, choosing the perfect gentle tone and adding a hint of a *you silly thing* laugh, but Sorra knew well enough how it would come out of her own mouth, saucy and a little surly.

She nodded, gave him a thin smile, and did as he asked, sliding the slimy entrails into a large bowl and setting it outside. Then she set water to boil in the kettle so she could finish the cleaning later and placed the fish in the pan, hoping it wouldn't stick too badly without oil or butter.

It only took a few minutes to cook, but the absence of conversation pressed down heavily on Sorra now that she'd noticed it. Beau sighed and rested his head on his paws.

Talk, dummy. He wants a companion, not a silent domestic performer. Win him over. Figure him out.

She cleared her throat and tried to sound sincere and humble. "I think I owe you an apology."

She didn't really think any such thing but was accustomed to taking the blame for misunderstandings back home, and the habit seemed likely to serve just as well here.

He looked up. "Oh?"

"Back in the woods last night, when I snapped at you."

"Ah."

Sorra turned the fish, leaving only a bit of skin sticking to the pan. "I was rude." *And so were you,* she thought, but kept that part to herself. "Blame my exhaustion, blame the years I've spent being unfavourably compared to my sisters and the feeling that you were doing the same, blame my empty stomach, whichever you like. I may not be quite what you were expecting, but I'm not all bad. Not even mostly bad, I hope."

She removed the pan from the heat. The fish smelled good enough to clear the bitter taste of her forced apology from her tongue, but she made herself wait for it to cool.

"Apology accepted," Beau said. "I fear I made a poor impression as well, in spite of my efforts to do the opposite. I assumed too much, and I was angry because..." He sighed. "I wasn't angry with you. Not really."

It wasn't quite an apology, but it was something. Whatever his intentions, he seemed willing to attempt a fresh start.

"Good."

She couldn't wait any longer, and dug into the fish, not caring that she burned her fingertips and tongue as she scooped the flaky flesh from the pan into her mouth. It was gone far too quickly, and she realized only after she was finished that she'd forgotten to season the meal.

Salt would be good for cleaning up, though. She busied herself at the sink with the hot water, an old rag, and a bit of salt from the pantry to scour the countertop as she tried to think of something clever to say.

"Did you build this place with your bear hands, then?"

She glanced over her shoulder. Beau narrowed his already tiny eyes.

Sorra held up her wet hands. "I mean... Bare hands? Bear?"

He looked up at the rafters. "I didn't build it. I've only done repairs."

Silence followed, heavier than before, as Sorra tried to decide whether he'd actually said *rebears* or whether she'd only misheard it in his strange voice. Either way, she supposed it might be some attempt at a joke.

She cleaned the pan next, scrubbing it out and setting it on the counter to air dry, savouring the knowledge that Corinne wasn't going to pop in to nag her about drying it properly and putting it away. She sat at the table, pleased with the fullness of her stomach and the warmth of the stove.

"That could rust if you don't dry it," Beau said, in the same tone he'd used when he'd questioned her spotty employment history.

Sorra tensed but tried not to let her irritation show. Her sisters would know to smile and do as he asked, and perhaps they'd thank him for the advice. She doubted she could do the latter without sarcasm creeping into her voice, so she stood and dried the pan on her skirt, then set it in its place on the shelf.

Your sisters wouldn't have been so lazy in the first place, whispered the dark voice. Sorra ignored it.

She turned to Beau, forcing a bland smile. "Better?"

He shrugged, an oddly human gesture that Sorra filed away in her mind. "Makes no difference to me. I prefer my fish raw."

"Then why mention it?"

"A pan is a useful tool for you. It would be a shame to see it ruined."

Sorra gritted her teeth. He wasn't wrong, and that somehow made his vaguely condescending advice harder to take.

She waited for him to say anything else, but he seemed content to let the maddening silence drag out. "I'm very grateful for the meal," she said. "Was there something else you wanted?"

Impolite, whispered the dark voice.

Beau's eyes widened. "I thought you might be accustomed to company at home. If you don't wish to have any..." He stood.

"No. Stay. Please." Sorra dragged her chair to the edge of the rug and sat. Sending him away wouldn't get her any closer to answers. "I'm being rude again. The last few days have been overwhelming and exhausting, but that's no reason to take it out on the bear who got me away from that mess."

She thought back, counting through the calendar, and realized it might be more than that. If her body's cycles were working as they should, she was due for a few days of fouler-than-usual moods.

And won't that be fun, she thought as she contemplated whether moss would be absorbent enough if she stuffed her undergarments with it and whether the smell of blood might change a friendly bear into a wilder sort of animal. She and Davina had packed some useful things, but they hadn't thought to prepare for that little inevitability.

The fire crackled in the stove. The sun had set, and an owl hooted somewhere near the cabin. Sorra glanced around the room, searching for a way to ask Beau about himself that would sound more like conversation than prying. There was nothing, but nothingness in itself had potential.

Not *great* potential, but she'd work with it.

"It seems quiet here," she said. "What do you do for fun when you're not wandering close to human settlements in search of company?"

"Bears don't need to have fun."

"You're not exactly a normal bear, though, are you?"

"What gave that away?"

Again Sorra couldn't tell whether he was joking, so she didn't answer.

Beau let out a snuffling breath. "I suppose I like to look at the stars on clear nights. Catching fish is amusing in its way."

Sorra pulled her feet up onto the chair and rested her chin on her knees, trying not to look like she was filing every dull scrap of information away for later examination.

Beau seemed ready to let the conversation die again, but he sat up straighter as though an idea had struck him. "You asked because you're bored. What do you do for fun, then?" He seemed pleased with himself for remembering to ask.

He was trying as hard as she was, in his clumsy way.

"The stars are certainly nice," she said, though she'd rarely stopped to admire them on her way home from late nights at the Ambling Goat. "Dancing, though I'm clumsy. Music, but only listening—I'm not much of a singer. I don't suppose you have any wine or anything hidden away around here? That helps boredom quite a lot."

It seemed impossible that a bear should manage the clear disapproval Beau displayed on his face, but there it was. Sorra hated how it made her stomach sink.

"No," he said. "I don't suppose avoiding reality would serve me well."

He frowned, and Sorra narrowed her eyes to look closer. She was sure his face was more expressive than a bear's should have been.

"Life is what it is," he said. "Better to face it head-on."

"I don't know about that," Sorra said, unable to resist the urge to test the waters. She smiled like she was teasing. "A break from it every once in a while isn't the worst thing."

"I wouldn't know." He scratched his chest with a forepaw. "Anything else you enjoy?"

Sorra thought it over. "I used to like reading, but I haven't seen any good books in a long time. Usually have to make things up to amuse myself."

The habit of daydreaming had persisted longer than her imagined conversations with animals, and her wandering mind had led to disastrous lapses in concentration on more than one occasion. It was hard not to drift away when she found it so easy to visit a better reality.

He'd think her silly and flighty if she said so, though.

"Would it amuse you to tell me a story?" he asked.

Sorra's cheeks warmed. It had been a decade since anyone had asked that, and longer since she'd said yes. "No. Thank you."

His lips pulled back, baring his teeth in an uncomfortable attempt at a smile. "I suppose we'd best see what we can do to make your time here pleasant, then." He turned, considering the cabin as though he'd never really looked at it before. "Not much like your last home, is it?"

"It's certainly emptier. Corinne's treasures were always a little stifling, though. I appreciate the lack of lace doilies here."

"What would make it more comfortable for you?"

Sorra pulled her sleeves down over her hands. There was so

much she wanted and needed, and so little a bear could provide. She weighed her thoughts carefully, not wanting to offend by asking for the impossible.

"Food. More clothing. Soap would be nice, for myself and for cleaning up." She considered her body's upcoming trials again. "Fabric, a needle, thread, towels. Things I should have thought to pack for a long stay. I understand if you can't get them, but—"

"I'll see what I can do."

"Really?"

He smiled again, a little more naturally. "No promises, but I'll try. Anything else that would make you happy?"

Sorra spoke without thinking. "Answers, more than anything. About you, about this cabin, about whoever lived in it before and what happened to them."

Beau's nostrils flared.

"You asked what would make me more comfortable," she said, knowing that more words wouldn't help but unable to stop herself. "I'm trying to be honest."

Beau stood. There was nothing especially threatening about his posture, but the fur on his shoulders had lifted like a cornered dog's.

Sorra stood, too, knocking the chair over as she backed away.

"I told you not to expect answers," he rumbled. "I have given you a home, which I swear to you was empty when I found it. I have given you food, and I will prove my good intentions by providing for your other needs."

"And I'm more grateful for that than I can say." Sorra's voice trembled.

"Then why must you pry? You seem to think badly of me when I've only done good for you. Is it not enough that your arrow has revealed me as your destiny? That I saved your life?"

Sorra's mouth went dry. "It's not that I'm ungrateful. I want to believe you're good. But I can't trust you if I can't know you, and your past, your intentions, and your true nature are as much a part of you as your words and actions." She risked a step closer, her hands held open. "Perhaps you don't know what it's like for humans, how we hurt and betray each other, how sweet promises and good manners can be used to lower a person's defences, opening them to a knife in the back. If you grew up as a bear—"

He growled. "I won't discuss that."

"I'm not asking you to tell me about your childhood, I'm asking you to understand me!" Sorra raked her fingers through her hair and paced away, risking an attack from behind for the sake of releasing a bit of the frustration that coursed through her. "I've learned not to assume anything about anyone, to watch for signs of danger where others wouldn't. My life is like… it's like crossing a bridge in the dark, knowing there are missing planks you need to watch out for, knowing the boards that look solid could actually be rotten. I want this to be my greatest destiny, but my blessing taints everything. I don't need your darkest and most shameful secrets. I only need something solid under my feet before you ask me to walk with you."

She turned and found him watching her, his expression unreadable.

"I see," he said.

"Do you?" She sat on the edge of the bed. There was so much more she wanted to say, but anything she might add would likely make things worse. She didn't think she'd said anything terrible, but he sounded displeased. "I'm sorry. My tongue always gets away from me. I'll try to… I won't pry anymore."

He pawed at the carpet. "I should leave. You must be tired."

"I slept all day. We can talk more."

"No."

She followed him to the door.

"Don't be angry, Beau."

The fur on his shoulders twitched. "I'm not. We'll speak tomorrow."

Sorra opened the door. Much as she hated for him to leave on a sour note, it was better than being trapped with an irritated bear. He brushed past her and hurried into the dark forest without another word.

Sorra closed the door and sank to the floor.

"Good job, Sorra. Very nicely done." She pressed the heels of her hands to her eyes.

Acting like her sisters hadn't done much except preserve the awkward politeness Beau had decided to offer. Letting herself show through had been worse, and asking questions had given her nothing except more certainty that he was hiding something important.

But if a lifetime of failure had taught her anything, it was to learn from her mistakes. To try harder, and to change course if that didn't work. Then to change again until she'd exhausted her options.

Questions wouldn't work, so there had to be another way.

If only she knew what it was.

CHAPTER TWELVE

Sorra knew she was dreaming—a strange one about a talking bear and a house in the woods, and one that seemed reluctant to release her from its grip so she could face the day properly.

But as she fought her way free, the world refused to settle into its expected reality around her. The mattress felt wrong, the blanket didn't smell of the kitchen, the light wasn't right.

Doze, then, she told herself. *It's safe here. Everything else can wait.*

If only.

She forced her eyes open and sat up, feeling strangely empty as the truth of her situation hit her square in the chest. It hadn't been a dream. A talking bear had carried her away from home on his back. She did live alone in a cabin.

And, most real of all, she did need to use the outhouse, then figure out how she was going to survive on trout and berries for the next year if it turned out Beau wasn't quite the provider he'd implied.

She pulled her grey sweater on over the undergarments she'd slept in and stepped outside. The sun was fully up, the birds chattering in the trees, the air warm. A perfect summer day, but Sorra was in no mood to enjoy it. When she returned to the cabin, she dove back under the covers, wishing she'd been wakened earlier by Davina preparing breakfast, even if that meant dealing with Corinne.

At least there were eggs at home. And tea.

But soon Beau scratched at the door. Sorra pulled the blankets higher, hoping she could pretend to be asleep until he gave up and left.

The latch clicked, and Sora peered out from under the covers as Beau's snout appeared in the opening. "Are you awake?"

He can open the door. Fantastic. He'd told her he used the cabin to get out of the rain, but she hadn't considered the idea that this strange creature would be able to enter her new home whenever he wished.

Be good. Be polite.

"Just now," she said. "Come in." She sat up and brushed her fingers through her tangled hair.

Beau entered, leaving the door open behind him. "You're still in bed."

"I am."

"Are you getting up?"

Sorra's shoulders tensed. "I'm considering it."

"You should. There's work to be done." He turned and left, not closing the door behind him.

Sorra forced herself out of bed.

The nerve, she thought as she shed the sweater and slipped into her brown dress, trying to ignore how unpleasant it smelled after the previous few days' adventures. *Judging me for catching up on sleep when he probably dozes all winter, when I have nothing to get out of bed for anyway.*

Or so she'd thought. Their agreement had done a poor job of identifying what she'd be expected to do during her time with him, and 'work' could mean anything as long as it didn't step outside his idea of doing her no harm.

At least that might offer a hint about his true intentions, though.

She squared her shoulders and stepped onto the porch.

Beau stood in the sun near the bottom of the steps, his forepaws hidden behind several large, woven baskets packed to the brim with a variety of goods.

Sorra hurried down the steps to dig through them, her bad mood vanishing like morning mist in sunlight.

Everything she'd asked for the previous night was there, and more.

Three new dresses in shades of grey, a few lengths of soft unbleached cotton, and a sewing kit she could use to make alterations. A pair of boots—not particularly fine leather, but sturdy, and they fit well enough when she slipped them onto her bare feet. A straw hat to keep the sun off her face. Glass jars filled with peaches, beets, cucumber pickles, and plums. A box of tea. A deck of cards. Two round loaves of bread and a pot of butter. A bow with arrows. A dozen eggs.

Beau paced anxiously nearby, watching as Sorra pulled three books from the bottom of the final basket. The first was an illustrated volume on edible plants. The next was a thick tome called *Travels Within* that looked to be a fictional story but closer examination revealed to be the sort made up of boring contemplations, complaints, and long, winding sentences that tried to make a cloudy sky seem meaningful.

The kind of book teachers expected students to appreciate even though the pages didn't have a scrap of real excitement in them, and likely the kind of book Beau's ideal companion would have devoured.

Sorra forced a smile and set the book aside, then reached for the third.

Her smile warmed.

Beau stepped closer, frowning at the book as Sorra paged through the thick volume of bedtime stories. It was old and musty-smelling, with no pictures like in the books she'd learned to read as a child, but she spotted a few titles she knew—*The Goose and the Bullfrog, The Gryphon's Bride, Answel and the Lion*. Not particular favourites, but there was comfort in their familiarity.

"That's a mistake," Beau said as she paused on the first page of an unfamiliar story entitled *Green Grass*. "I didn't intend to bring you something meant for children."

"It's fine."

"I'll get you something more useful."

Sorra shrugged as though it didn't matter. She wanted the book but had no desire to ruin a pleasant morning with an argument over the usefulness of fanciful stories, or for him to think less of her for enjoying them.

"You don't need to trouble yourself with replacing it," she said. "I'll need kindling for the stove. This will do in a pinch. Or I could leave it in the outhouse for when I need pages for—"

"I understand." Beau looked away.

She tossed the book aside, and he relaxed. "Did I forget anything?" he asked, gesturing at the gifts with his nose.

Sorra looked over the goods spread across the ground and the dresses laid out over the baskets. There was no wine, but when she broke open one of the loaves of bread, the smell was more than intoxicating enough to satisfy her for the moment.

"I was shamefully unprepared yesterday," he added. "I hope this will make you more comfortable."

He seemed agitated.

No, she realized. *Anxious. He cares about my answer.* There was something endearing about his uncertainty, and she liked it better than the stiff courtesy he'd offered the night before.

"It's wonderful," she said. "Thank you."

He lowered his head, obviously relieved. "I told you I intended to provide what you need. I hope this puts your mind at ease."

Sorra lifted the bread and inhaled again but stopped short of taking a bite.

"I've been told it's dangerous to eat food of magical provenance." She hoped he'd reveal something about where it had come from—a nearby village, perhaps. That would be useful information, even if it wasn't about him directly.

"I wouldn't worry," he said. "You've already made a deal with me. I doubt a little bread would pull you in any deeper if I had nefarious plans." He paused, and Sorra had the strange idea that he was teasing her. "It's your choice, though. You can eat this food or find your own in the woods."

He waited, probably knowing as well as she did which option she'd choose.

Sorra took a bite of the bread, savouring the heavy, nutty grains and the hint of honey. It didn't seem cursed, but even if it were she thought she'd find it hard to regret partaking.

"I nearly forgot," Beau said. "Look in the dress pockets."

Sorra set the bread aside, her heart fluttering as she searched. It felt like a game, like what a birthday would be if it were celebrated rather than lamented—food, gifts, excitement. For a moment she forgot to be suspicious, and she allowed herself to expect something good.

Her fingers closed around a hard object, and she pulled it free. A silver cuff bracelet shone in the sun, and Sorra slipped it over her left hand, admiring its intricate braided design.

"It's lovely," she whispered, her throat tight for once with delight instead of fear or shame. "I've never had anything so pretty."

"I'm glad you like it," Beau said. "You should have lovely things, and a better life than what you've known."

Sorra closed her eyes, clinging to joy that might slip like sand between her fingers.

"I can get other things if you want them," Beau said. "Other foods, though perhaps nothing too extravagant. Different entertainments, perhaps?"

Sorra looked over the bounty laid out before her. It was all good. And it was all from him. He would bring more, but the idea of relying solely on his generosity made her uneasy. Everything he offered was a debt she owed him, and anything she relied on him for was something he could take away.

Even if he was as good as gold and as pure as sunlight, that wasn't a position she could afford to put herself in.

"What about things like gardening tools and seeds?" she asked. "Supplies to do my own baking?"

Beau tilted his head in a way that reminded Sorra of a confused dog. "You don't have to do those things. Maybe in your old life, but not now. I'll make sure you have all the cakes and vegetables you want."

"I believe you," Sorra said, choosing her words carefully so as not to reveal too much. "And I do trust you to provide all of that. In fact, cake sounds lovely. But you asked what would make me comfortable, and I..." She laughed helplessly. "It's a long story. Let's just say that I'm most comfortable if I don't have to depend on other people, even if they want me to. Besides, now is as good a time as any to cook and tend and repair and learn. I can't really hurt anyone but myself with my mistakes, so no one will stop me from trying again. Maybe I'll finally find something I'm good at."

She meant it to sound like a joke, the kind of gentle self-deprecation people always found charming in her talented sisters, but it felt too real when she said it.

Beau was silent for a few seconds, watching her. Then he nodded. "The soil here is poor, but maybe a garden is just what this place needs."

A question formed at the tip of Sorra's tongue, but she held it back.

It would be natural to ask where he'd gotten everything. He might even be expecting it—he seemed to be bracing himself and kept glancing into the woods as though planning another escape, anxious even now that he knew his efforts had been worthwhile.

A shadow passed over Sorra's mind, dulling the morning's pleasantness.

It all looked so lovely on the surface. A misunderstanding overcome. A new friend providing for her needs.

But she'd learned through hard experience to pay attention to what could lie beneath pretty words and unearned generosity. *I hope this will make you more comfortable* could easily mean *I hope this lets you stop asking questions.*

It wasn't certain, but in the cold light of her blessing, it was terribly clear. He had given her so much of what she'd asked, almost enough to distract her from the fact that he hadn't offered the one thing she'd said she needed most. He clearly wanted to win her over, and instead of earning her trust with answers, he'd decided to buy it with the kind of trinkets, attention, and affirmations she'd craved all her life.

Sorra hadn't known she could hate her blessing more than she always had, but in that moment she wanted to scream at it to let her have one happy moment that wasn't tainted by it.

The question of what he might be hiding remained, but it wouldn't do to follow her impulses and ask. Her impatience the night before had only led to Beau closing himself off more, and to his current readiness to flee from her curiosity. Patience had never come easily to her, but perhaps that was another skill she might learn here, and one that would be more useful than baking or pricking her fingers on sewing needles.

Davina had told her to find answers in what he did or didn't do, in his absences and what he didn't say, and Sorra's heart fluttered as she realized Beau had already shown her more than he'd likely meant to.

He has a way of getting things—a village or a human contact or pure magic.

He still wants to win me over even though I'm not what he wanted. Whatever his reason for needing a companion, he can't give up on those plans.

It wasn't much, but it was more than she'd learned by questioning or pleading for answers. He might reveal more as time passed. As long as he kept his end of the agreement, she could afford to be patient, maybe even enjoy the goodness this destiny offered while she tried not to stumble over whatever the blessing might throw into her path.

No more questions. Only observation and putting him at ease.

Just until I know for sure.

Sorra smiled. "I'm sorry about last night. It's not easy for me to adjust to things changing so quickly. I've landed on my feet for once. It's strange."

"But good?"

"I think so." She brushed the breadcrumbs from her dress. "So tell me, what work am I to do?"

"Oh, terribly difficult things." Beau's lips pulled back in a smile that seemed far more natural than the previous night's attempt, if no more human. She wondered if he'd been practicing. "You're going to need to carry all this inside and find places for it, see whether the dresses need altering to suit you, and decide whether there's anything else you need to be happy here." He stepped closer and nudged the wooden hunting bow with his nose. "I thought this might be useful if you got tired of trout."

"Ah. Well, I'm very grateful," she said, "but I'm afraid I'm not a very good shot."

Beau cast a glance over his shoulder toward his rump. "I did wonder about that."

Sorra smiled again, more easily than she'd expected. Perhaps acting good and cheerful wouldn't be so hard, after all.

"Thank you," she said. "Again. How will I ever repay you for any of this?"

"Hmm." Beau scratched at the ground. "I'll just help you with this, then?"

Not an answer, Sorra noted. *Not even a scrap of a hint of a peek beneath his surface.*

But that might come.

She piled the items back into the baskets, and Beau picked one up and carried it into the cabin. The basket's handles were perfectly shaped to fit his mouth.

That felt like it might hint at something. Sorra added it to the pile of information she wasn't quite sure what to do with.

She picked up the book of bedtime stories and paged through it again.

This, too, was something. He didn't like the book. Maybe it was just a strange bit of snobbishness that made no sense in a bear, or maybe it was something else. There was magic in those stories, and maybe more truth than he wanted her to see.

But it was more than that. Sorra thought back over what he hadn't said, and more importantly what *she* hadn't.

I didn't tell him the name of the book.

She wasn't sure whether the fact that he could read—and upside down, at that—should come as a surprise given how he spoke and thought and acted.

But it means he learned it somewhere.

He has a past. An education. A teacher.

The barest bones of answers, though he hadn't offered them.

She smiled to herself, stuffed the book deep into another basket, and followed him inside.

CHAPTER THIRTEEN

The first twinge of pain blossomed in Sorra's lower belly as she was washing her old dress two days after Beau had delivered her new ones. She left the washing to soak in the yard, went inside to avail herself of the cloths she'd sewn the day before, and returned to work hoping the event—which was always a relief as much as a painful burden—might prove to be no more than an inconvenience this time.

Not long after supper that night, she lay in bed, curled up on her side, arms wrapped protectively around her torso. She'd made willow bark tea that had gone cold before she could finish it and had set a bowl next to the bed in case she couldn't keep the medicine down. All she could do now was try not to focus on what felt like a family of rats trying to claw their way out of her body.

The sky outside was darkening when Beau scratched at the door.

"Come in," Sorra called, though his company was near the bottom of the list of things that would improve the situation. He'd visited earlier, and the stilted formality of his attempts to be friendly had made his departure a relief.

He'd entered and pushed the door closed behind him before Sorra remembered her fear about wild animals and the scent of human blood.

"I know it's early to be in bed," she said. "I'm not being lazy."

Beau approached cautiously. "Are you injured?"

"No."

"Ill?"

"Not exactly. It's nothing that won't right itself in a few days. The ruby river floweth. The monthly curse of Nanjalan has returned. My time of woe is upon me. Take your pick."

"What—" he said, and stopped himself. "I see. Is there anything I can do to help?"

Sorra watched him carefully, analyzing the tone of his rumbling voice. He hadn't turned into a slavering predator. He also didn't seem confused as an animal might be, or embarrassed like most of the human men she knew.

Pain gripped Sorra's lower belly, squeezing hard, then released her to wait for the next round.

"I don't think so. But thank you for asking."

"Hmm." He sat next to the bed. "What would you usually do when this happens?"

"I've already had willow tea," she said. "It doesn't help much, but it's better than nothing."

"Anything else? I was planning to have more supplies for you in the morning. Perhaps I could—"

"I don't think so. The worst will be over by then, anyway. I hope." A hard knot formed in Sorra's throat. "My sisters and I had a flat stone we kept in the corner of the kitchen, as big as a dinner plate. If one of us felt particularly awful, the others would take the stone to the oven to warm it, then wrap it in blankets." She rolled onto her back and pressed her hands over the bright spring of pain that welled up from deep within her body. If Davina had been with her, she'd have set the stone there.

"And this eased your pain?"

"It did. The warmth, the pressure. I think being taken care of helped as much as anything." She forced a smile and tried not to miss her sisters. "It's only been me and Davina for a few years now, but that was enough."

Beau glanced at the kitchen. "The fire in the stove has gone out."

"And I have no rocks. It's all right. I've survived worse."

"No doubt. But if you wished, perhaps..." Beau stood with his forepaws on the edge of the bed, then slowly settled onto his forelegs, claws turned inward, and gently laid his chin where Sorra's hands had indicated. "Would this be at all the same?"

Sorra meant to tell him he didn't need to put himself out for her sake, to say again that she could handle it on her own. Then he stretched his neck forward and rested the full weight of his head on her. It wasn't like the stone, or like being fussed over by her sisters with the knowledge that she'd be doing the same for them soon enough. It was good, though, warm and heavy and comforting if she didn't think about the strangeness of being cared for by a wild animal.

"That is helpful," she said. "Thank you."

She knew she should still be afraid of him, in the long term if not in the moment, but there was something about his approach—uncertain, hesitant, curious—that made her think this wasn't a shallow ploy to win her over. That maybe he did want to be her friend, even if neither of them was what the other had been searching for in the forest that day.

A fly settled on his head, and Sorra brushed it away. The fur was shorter and softer than on his body, and she let her hand rest there. He didn't object.

"You must miss your sisters," he said, his voice rumbling pleasantly through her aching muscles.

Warm tears trailed over Sorra's temples. "I do. And sometimes I don't. Or both at the same time. It's complicated."

Beau looked sideways at her without moving his head. "Go on, if you'd like."

It would be better if she didn't say more. He seemed to have forgotten the unlikable bits of herself she'd revealed to him that first night. To offer more of her past would only give him more to judge or to hate, more reason to leave her or drive her away. She'd made that mistake with humans too many times.

But he'd asked for a story once and she'd denied him. Talking would take her mind off the pain. And if she lowered her defences, maybe he would, too.

"I've always had a complicated relationship with... well, everyone," she said. "My family is special. I told you about the blessing my parents received."

"Four sisters with wonderful gifts and destinies, a fifth fated to the opposite if she were born at all?"

"Essentially, yes."

"Who blessed them?"

"By the time I was old enough to ask, no one could say for sure," she said. "Our parents didn't talk about it with my sisters when they were little, and Mother's diary didn't go back that far." The final volume of hurried entries was all Sorra had ever known of her mother outside of her sisters' recollections, and it had never been enough. "She wrote about her fears regarding her fifth pregnancy, which had come as a surprise. She'd seen proof of the blessing already in my sisters, so she had no reason to doubt what would come. She said the fear was enough to make her wish my father hadn't earned the blessing at all. Besides a little about her hopes for where the enchanted arrow would lead her daughters, there were no more details."

"Interesting."

She had to force the next words out. The first evidence against her was common knowledge in Cottsbridge, and she'd never needed to explain it to anyone before. "During her pregnancy my father was offered a position on a trading vessel. He didn't want to leave her alone with so many children, so he left them with her sister Corinne."

Beau grunted.

"The vessel was lost at sea in a terrible storm soon after I was born. Word didn't come until a week later."

"And your mother?"

"Died of a fever not long after my birth."

Beau drew in a long breath and released it slowly. "And you believe your infant cries stopped your mother's heart? That they called the storm that took your father?" He spoke gently, but Sorra suspected he was less willing to believe it than the people of Cottsbridge had been.

"I don't think their deaths were a coincidence. No one does." She brushed her tears away with the back of her hand. "Corinne knew what I was, and she never let me forget it. Once I was born, there was nothing to be done but raise me, and the people of Cottsbridge... they tried. They taught me to turn away from anything they saw as a sign of badness coming out in me—anger, cruelty, greed. More than the other children, I mean. If a classmate hit me, it was written off as childish behaviour. If I hit back, it was a sign of terrible things to come. As I grew older, I tried to contain it all. I was as kind as I could be, I punished myself for carelessness and meanness so others wouldn't have to, I tried to be good like my sisters. But it usually went wrong, and even when it went right, folks were waiting for the shadow side of my goodness to show itself. Eventually their mission became not one of reformation, but containment. I couldn't be good, so I was supposed to focus on trying not to be bad, which eventually meant trying not to be anything at all." She wasn't sure why she needed Beau to understand how hard she'd tried, but she did. "They'll be better off now, without my chaos. Without having to act as the buffer between my terrible blessing and the rest of the world. Maybe that's what the arrow intended, really. Not my greatest destiny, but everyone else's."

The thought saddened her. Not success or love or joy as her happy ending, but an avoidance of harm to others. It was what she'd always been told she was supposed to want.

Beau adjusted the weight of his head to turn slightly toward her. "And your family?"

"You saw and heard what you needed to of my aunt, I think," Sorra said, and he nodded slightly. "My sisters were kind to me, even when the warning about my birth proved itself over and over. They grew and blossomed despite the shit they'd been planted in. I was the weed who should never have taken root anywhere near them. Three of them have moved on. Davina will, too, once she lets go of the idea of saving me from myself. So yes, I miss them. I miss their laughter and their wit. I miss their company."

"But?"

"But I don't miss their brightness, or how it made me look so dull. I don't miss comparing myself to them and coming up short in every imaginable way. I don't miss the guilt I felt every time some minor tragedy in their lives could be traced back to me. I love them desperately. And I think a small, horrid part of me also hates them for having so much to look forward to when I can't help feeling that this is an ending for me."

"That would make you a footnote in their grand stories, then?"

"I suppose. But it's best for everyone."

Beau looked as though he wanted to say something, but decided against it. Sorra knew all about holding her tongue, though it often ran wild in spite of her efforts.

"What?"

"I think," he said, speaking slowly and carefully, "that perhaps that's not true. Nothing is done until it's done, and you're still breathing. You said your townsfolk are better off without you, but from where I sit, it looks as though you're the one who's better off without them."

Sorra's chest squeezed tight. "It's kind of you to say so, but you don't know what they've been through because of me. I was nearly a woman before I understood that in most towns, in most children's lives, every day isn't filled with tension and mayhem. Much of that was unintentional, but not all of it. Sometimes I did things out of spite or jealousy or greed."

"As all children do," Beau said, his voice gentle. "And I don't doubt the blessing is real—you certainly have enough reason to believe it is. But even so, I wonder if they were wrong to restrain you." He thought for a moment. "I can see how you might be a challenge to the sort of people who believe children should be seen and not heard, or to those who want everyone to fit into their world like cogs in a machine. But I also wonder what might have happened if you'd been allowed freedom."

Sorra laughed. No one had ever spoken so kindly before when they'd called her a challenge, and it was obvious he still didn't understand.

But she didn't correct him. He wasn't telling her anything about himself, yet he was. Whatever sort of mind lurked beneath his ursine exterior, it was intelligent. Perceptive. Judgemental and a bit snobbish and not entirely unlike those people he'd just spoken of, but perhaps also willing to question his own assumptions.

It was something to add to the scant list of evidence she'd collected thus far.

"Laugh if you wish," he said, not sounding at all bothered. "You know better than I do."

"No, go on," Sorra said. Whatever he thought would surely be wrong, but it would tell her more about him.

Or it would at least be amusing to hear an idea that wasn't the same stale conclusions folks had reached before she could walk.

"Your sisters all developed the natural gifts the blessing offered them?"

"Of course. They had whatever the town could provide—education, access to gardens or musical instruments or whatever they needed to encourage their blessings. Why wouldn't they accept that?"

"Indeed." Beau yawned, and Sorra smiled. If he was getting comfortable it meant she wasn't imposing on him as she'd feared, and it was making his company quite pleasant. "My humble observation is that they still had a choice. You say one is a musician—could she have chosen to let her talent lie dormant? And if she had, if she'd for some reason decided to become a baker or a merchant, would the arrow have given her a different destiny?"

Sorra felt as though she'd been kicked in the stomach—not from the cramps, but from his words and the weight of a lifetime of hearing *if you just tried harder*. She held her breath until the feeling passed.

"Are you saying that I could just choose to not be... me? Because I've tried to choose that every day. If you knew how everyone had tried to keep me from growing into the blessing—"

His eyes widened. "No. The opposite, in fact. They tried to shape you into someone you're not instead of helping you find the best version of yourself. An oak sapling can't grow tall and strong if it's pruned to the shape of a rose bush and punished for not flowering."

Sorra's throat tightened. "Not an oak, though. More like a tree that's proved itself to bear poison fruit."

"And what tree could bear good fruit when it's forced to grow from poisoned soil?" Beau closed his eyes. Moonlight from the window near the bed traced his features and turned the tips of the long hairs on his shoulders to silver. "You've been dealt a bad hand, and magic is a tricky thing. Maybe I'm wrong, or only desperate to believe destiny is never set in stone. I—" His lips twitched, baring his teeth. "I apologize. It's not my place to speculate on what I don't understand."

"It's fine," Sorra said softly. "Say as much as you like. There's no harm in words."

He was right. He didn't understand. But the fact that he was trying pleased her in a way that felt strange and good.

Beau rumbled in his throat, sending soothing vibrations through Sorra's muscles. "If only that were true."

Sorra spread her fingers wide and stroked his head, smoothing the short fur back from his brow. His head grew heavier as he relaxed, and Sorra drifted with him.

Time passed, marked by the clock on the mantel. Sorra had learned that it needed to be wound every day and had remembered to do it before she'd started the washing. She supposed she'd forget such a minor chore soon enough, but at least the consequences of that mistake were small. Another noon would come, another chance to start again.

"Some people's fates are sealed from the moment they're born," Beau mumbled, his voice so faint that Sorra suspected he wasn't quite awake. "Maybe yours doesn't have to be."

Sorra bit back a question about what he expected of his own fate. It was becoming easier to keep them to herself, and for the first time she wondered what it would be like to let go of her suspicions entirely. He seemed so sincere tonight, so genuinely kind in spite of his awkwardness. So much like what she'd always imagined a true friend might be.

She'd once dreamed of adventure, even of being the kind of hero the blessing said she could never be, but life at this quiet cabin would be just as good if she could be sure Beau was what he seemed. If she could know he was really good—a unique creature born in the magic of these mountains, maybe, alone and needing a friend as badly as she did—all would be well for the first time in her life.

She continued to smooth the fur on Beau's broad head. She'd need to get up to attend to her body's needs soon enough, but for the moment she was closer to peace and contentment than she'd thought possible an hour before.

"Unfair," Beau mumbled. "Doesn't deserve more pain than she's... already..." He growled. "I can't hurt her. Please."

Sorra froze, not daring to breathe, but he didn't say more.

"Beau?"

He snorted and lifted his head, eyes wide. "What did I say?"

"Nothing."

"Was I sleeping?"

Sorra drew her legs to her chest and sat up, pulling the blanket higher. "I don't know."

He looked to the mantel—to the clock. Before Sorra could ask what was wrong he bolted for the door.

"Wait," Sorra called. "You don't have to—"

But he swatted and clawed at the latch, opening the door before Sorra could get up to let him out, and fled without another word.

Sorra gritted her teeth and pushed herself off the bed, glancing at the clock as she passed. Something about ten o'clock had sent Beau into a panic.

He was gone before she reached the door. She closed it, then picked her sweater up off the floor and pulled it on. Her whole body was shaking, and she wasn't sure whether it was from the loss of his warmth or from the words he'd spoken when sleep had softened the walls he'd built around his secrets.

Something about it being unfair that she should experience more pain, and not wanting to hurt her. Sorra didn't know whether she was the 'she' he meant. If she was, it raised the question of whether 'pain' meant her current isolation or something he wouldn't dare speak of when he had full control of himself.

The bedtime stories of her childhood haunted Sorra's mind as she made her way to the outhouse and back, whispering to her the unhappy endings of those who trusted the wrong magical creatures and found pain where they'd been promised safety or joy.

She'd thought them foolish once, but all it had taken was a scrap of kindness to lower her own defenses.

The mattress had gone cold when she eased herself back into bed and pulled the blankets tight around her shoulders. Her lower belly ached again, and a shameful part of her wished Beau hadn't slipped up at all. His strange words, spoken like a warning he hadn't meant to offer, had shattered the sense of peace and rightness she'd let herself slip into, and she wanted it back.

She wanted it to be real. The comfort. The conversation. The kindness.

But assuming anything could only lead to disaster. Her blessing would make sure of it, and if she let it win this time, she'd have no one but herself to blame. He'd uttered a warning. Only a fool would choose to ignore it, no matter how tempting the lie might be.

The shopkeeper she'd sold the arrow to spoke in her mind. *If you want to play dangerous games, make sure you understand the rules.*

"And never underestimate your opponent," Sorra whispered.

She didn't know what kind of game she'd stepped into, or whether Beau was an opponent at all—and she couldn't know, because he refused to tell her. But he'd revealed something tonight. More would surely come.

Beau's secrets could be more dangerous than his claws or his teeth, and she knew well enough that kindness could be a weapon.

But if she was careful and clever, maybe this time she'd walk away unharmed.

CHAPTER FOURTEEN

The scent of strawberries and pastry filled the cabin as Sorra finished drying her supper dishes. On the surface it had been a fine day. The sun had shone, the berries had been plentiful when she walked to the meadow to collect them, and now there would be a sweet dessert to share when Beau came for his evening visit.

If she thought of it that way, and if she thought of nothing else, Sorra couldn't find anything to complain about.

But it had been two weeks since the night when Beau had come so close to revealing himself to her before bolting from the cabin. He'd said nothing of it the next day—no apology, no explanation, no embarrassed acknowledgement of a strange moment. His courteous but distant demeanour had invited no questions or complaints, and she hadn't risked asking.

As the days passed, her new situation had settled into dull, peaceful routine. Polite inquiries as to each other's health and quality of sleep each morning, comments on the weather and acknowledgements of how it would soon change, but no deeper conversation about her past or her family, and certainly nothing about his. He provided everything she asked for, but he didn't make himself a part of the life she was struggling to construct in the lonely home he'd offered her.

The sense that she was living two stories at once had only deepened. In one, things were as they seemed, and the destiny offered by the arrow had saved her from the blessing, if only by removing her from any situation where she might harm another person. In the other, the blessing was still winning, and the placidity of this new life was lulling her into a sense of complacency that would be shattered when Beau revealed his secrets too late for her to escape their consequences.

The arrow or the blessing. The great destiny or the terrible fate.

The tension between them itched beneath her skin even as she smiled and cooked and pretended nothing was wrong, always aware of how important it was to keep up her end of the agreement.

Sorra wiped the last of the flour from the counter and swept the floor, barely aware of her own actions, her attention buried under thoughts she'd had a thousand times already.

Waiting and observing had seemed like a fine plan, but it had produced virtually nothing. She'd started to note Beau's behaviour in the evening and concluded that he consistently refused to stay past ten o'clock. She kept the clock wound and was sure she'd caught him glancing at it a few times. Even when he didn't, he became uneasy and restless an hour or so after the sun set. She'd asked him to stay, pleading sleeplessness and a need for company in the darkest hours of the night, but it did no good.

It wasn't much, and it told her nothing. There were no other patterns to his appearances and disappearances, or to which days he might ask whether she needed anything from him.

His gifts had continued. He'd brought warmer blankets, an oil lamp, a pen topped with a peacock feather, and a bottle of blue ink that was useless to her when she was forbidden to make contact with the world of humans, but she'd smiled and thanked him none-theless.

He offered each gift with humility, and he always seemed pleased by her gratitude.

He was pleasant. And generous. And she still felt she didn't know him at all.

She paced the cabin, her steps driven by the agony of not know-ing, which had to be worse than the pain of certainty, even if the truth might be terrible.

At least I'd know, and not have to feel like a fool for doing nothing.

The urge to rock the boat and force the truth to show itself grew stronger every day, but she didn't dare.

Not when it was still safer to float on calm waters.

Thinking the same thoughts over and over wasn't accomplishing anything except perhaps slowly wearing a track into the wood floor.

A distraction, then.

Sorra checked outside, but there was no sign of Beau. He'd visited earlier, and after an hour of stilted small talk she'd sent him to the meadow, claiming she'd heard wolves. He'd been happy to investigate, and she wondered whether he was as relieved to be free of her companionship as she was of his.

For now, she was alone.

She dug the depleted book of children's stories out of the wood box beside the stove. She'd been using the pages as kindling so Beau wouldn't think she'd lied about why she wanted to keep it, but she read them first. The simple stories hadn't offered any insights into her situation, and it seemed his wariness about the book might be another shadow with nothing of substance behind it.

Reading them was amusing, though, especially when she remembered Ingrid doing different voices when she read, and they provided an escape when her mind wouldn't be silent. Sorra sat at the table and opened the book to the first intact page, listening for the creak of the porch step that would alert her to Beau's arrival.

Winnifred and the Dragon

Not one she was familiar with. Sorra rested her chin on one hand and bent over the book.

Sharpen your ears, children, and hear the tale of Princess Winnifred, who was kind and beautiful and won the hearts of all she met.

Sorra rolled her eyes. These stories were always about sweet and beautiful girls, as though they were the only kind worthy of adventures and happy endings. An inexplicable number were princesses on top of that, which only made them less interesting. But she read on, knowing there was no sense wasting a few minutes' entertainment before the pages went in the fire.

The lovely princess was walking in the forest one day when a roar shattered its peace. Winnifred gathered her skirts and ran toward it, for it had sounded like a roar of pain.

"Stupid," Sorra muttered, and turned the page.

The story went on as they usually did, with the lovely princess remaining foolish but falling in love with a misunderstood dragon. Sorra sank into it as she had into her daydreams as a child, leaving her troubles behind in a cabin and a world that faded to shadows at the edge of her mind.

Princess Winnifred had taken on an admirable but foolhardy journey to the dragon's mountain when Sorra caught the scent of smoke—not a vividly imagined detail but irritating her nose. She looked up, blinking against smoke that stung her eyes, then leapt to her feet and reached for the dish towel to protect her hand as she pulled a charred pie from the oven. Its heat worked quickly through the fabric, and Sorra tossed it onto the table before it could burn her fingers.

The storybook fell to the floor in a flutter of pages. Sorra cursed and kicked it to the corner, then turned her attention back to the crisis at hand.

Worthless, the voice in her mind whispered. *Can't do any simple thing right, can you?*

Sorra opened the door to let the smoke out, then turned and glared at the pie, fists clenched at her sides, trying and failing to calm her breathing. Her eyes watered, and she told herself it was only from the smoke.

For two weeks she'd struggled with her new problem, never noticing how the old feelings of home had faded until they came crashing back.

Inadequate. Foolish. Stupid. Gullible.

"Everything all right?"

Sorra flinched at Beau's voice but forced herself to turn to him. He stood in the doorway, sniffing the air.

"I burned the pie."

"Hmm." Beau made his way around the table, then narrowed his eyes as he looked at her. "Is that all? You seem distraught."

Sorra took a deep breath of the smoky air.

"It's not just a pie." She wiped her eyes on the dishcloth. "It's a dozen pies and a burnt-down forge and a plague of frogs. It's you standing there trying to look like you're not thinking I'm stupid for letting it happen, but in my mind I have a dozen voices asking why I can't just try harder and do better."

"I don't think you're stupid," Beau said. "I don't suppose I should ask what happened?"

Sorra tried to smile. "Not if you want to make me feel better. The only worse thing would be to offer me a bit of condescending advice on how to not let it happen again."

Beau blinked slowly at her. "I certainly wasn't considering that."

"Good."

He sniffed at the pie. "It's not completely ruined."

"You think?" Sorra sighed. "I've never liked the taste of charcoal. You can have it once it cools."

"I will. Thank you."

There it was again. Polite. Accommodating. Damnably likeable now that he seemed to have decided to accept his contractually obligated companion for what she was, but still a blank wall when it came to showing her anything meaningful about himself that might prove it wasn't all an act.

He didn't seem like he was leading her to the kind of disaster Davina had warned of. But then, Sorra's most spectacular mishaps never did offer warning signs as she raced toward them. Her first supposed love, Gavin, had seemed like the answer to her prayers, and she'd taken him at his word when he'd said all would be pawell if she stopped doubting him.

And she'd only risked her heart that time.

The pie was still hot when Beau carefully took the plate in his teeth and moved it to the floor, then worked his way down to the sweet filling with his nose and his long, pink tongue. The combination of animal enthusiasm for inedible food and the care with which he avoided making a mess on the floor was unnerving.

What are you? Sorra thought for perhaps the hundredth time since they'd met. *Do monsters like burnt pie? Witches? Or just bears enchanted to think and speak as humans do?*

Do you know where my destiny is leading, and is that the pain you think I don't deserve? Or are you another victim of my blessing?

There were so many things he could be. Waiting hadn't gotten her any closer to answers, and something needed to change before her uncertainty ripped her apart from within.

But questions would only cost her what little progress she'd made.

He won't tell me anything. He won't show me anything.

...at least, not when he knows I'm watching.

There was only one time when she was sure he did things he wanted kept secret. She glanced at the clock. In an hour or so, he'd say he needed to leave. She might keep him a little longer if she played her cards right, and that would be better. If she asked for supplies, he'd have a destination to focus on, and perhaps be less alert to her if she followed him.

And then I'll see where he goes, or who he meets with in the middle of the night. Or at least where he's getting all these gifts.

The idea was thrilling and terrifying.

If he's bad, I can figure out how to escape a terrible destiny. If he turns out to be trustworthy, he never has to know what I saw, and I can find a way to be happy here.

She twisted the silver bracelet he'd given her around her wrist.

It could work, if I'm careful.

Of course, if he catches me...

It was a risk, to be sure, but it seemed one worth taking. In two weeks, waiting had done nothing but drive her halfway mad. And no wonder—what was inaction if not a repetition of past mistakes? It was time to get ahead of the blessing for once.

The idea calmed her, settling her mind with a sense of certainty even as she considered the dangers of getting caught.

Beau finished licking the pan and looked up at Sorra as though he'd forgotten she was there. "Thank you."

"Of course. I'm glad someone could enjoy it." She glanced at the pantry and the curtain that covered its well-stocked shelves, letting her fingers twist nervously on her lap. "I'd like to try again tomorrow. It smelled so good before it started burning, and there are plenty more berries in the meadow. But I'm out of flour and lard. I know it's my own fault, please don't feel like you have to—"

"I'm sure we can get you more by tomorrow."

"Thank you. I might be able to collect enough berries for two pies. I'll leave it up to you whether you want yours burnt."

Beau dipped his head in a bow. "I should leave you to your evening."

"No, please. Stay for a while." Sorra smiled, ignoring the anxious writhing in her gut. "It gets lonely when you're not here."

Beau nodded. "A little longer wouldn't hurt, I suppose."

Guilt knotted Sorra's insides. He'd tried to be kind and given her so much—everything except for the one thing she needed if she was to find peace here.

That, she would need to take for herself.

CHAPTER FIFTEEN

"Y ou're sure you have to go?"

Beau rose from his place on the rug and stretched. "I've taken up enough of your evening."

Sorra waited until his back was turned before she glanced at the clock. She'd talked him into learning a game using the deck of cards he'd brought her. It hadn't been a particularly good game, as he couldn't hold his own cards and needed her to lay them down on his turns, but it had kept him later than he'd stayed in weeks.

She wanted to remind him of his promise to bring her baking ingredients for tomorrow but held her tongue. She'd never pressed him about her needs before, and acting like she'd perish without fresh lard might raise suspicions.

Beau opened the door himself. "Goodnight, Sorra. I hope you have a pleasant sleep."

"Thank you," she said, trying to look tired. "I'll see you in the morning."

Beau picked up one of the baskets from the porch and slowly descended the steps.

Sorra closed the door behind him, slipped into her boots, and tucked a candle and matches in her pocket. She lifted the fabric at the corner of the kitchen window and peered out into the yard.

She'd expected to see Beau walking into the woods and hoped only to note what direction he'd gone. Instead she found him sitting on the ground with the basket next to him, his nose pointed toward the stars.

At least he didn't lie about what he does for fun, she thought. It was sort of adorable, and that made her feel worse about what she was about to do.

A few minutes later he stood, picked up the basket in his mouth, and headed west into the nighttime shadows of the woods.

Sorra doused the lamp, not wishing to see the cabin burn down in her absence, and stepped outside. The thick layer of pine needles on the forest floor muffled her steps as she followed Beau into the shadows, and she hardly breathed in case he might hear it. She spotted him between the sparse trees near the cabin and hung back so he wouldn't see her if he turned.

He didn't, though. He moved at a steady walk. There was no path, but he seemed to know exactly where he was going.

The night was clear, and the milky moon illuminated the forest with its cold light. More shadows would have been better, but Sorra decided she wouldn't complain. The answers were close. She felt it as much as she hoped it.

She'd see where he found the gifts he brought her, or spy on his meeting, or see what he didn't want her to see.

And if a small, foolish part of her was frightened enough to think that blissful ignorance would be better than learning an unpleasant truth, that was only more reason to keep going.

A twig snapped beneath her foot. Sorra darted behind a thick tree, pressing her back to it, praying Beau hadn't heard.

"Sorra?"

She winced but didn't answer. If he had to ask, he hadn't seen her. She held her breath and waited.

When she peered out from behind the tree, he was gone.

Sorra continued in the direction he'd been headed, watching and listening for any sign of him, examining the forest floor where the moon broke through trees that grew thicker as she left the cabin far behind. The needles and leaf litter on the forest floor were disturbed in long patches, but following the rough path was slow business.

Getting lost in the woods would be bad. Following the wrong

large animal could be worse, and if she let the blessing have its way, she'd end up doing one or the other.

She ran through a silent string of every foul word she knew as she picked her way forward.

The trail, such as it was, ended at a vertical rock face protruding from the side of the mountain. Even in the shadows, Sorra could pick out the darker opening that split the stone into the mouth of a cave.

A patch of brown fur clung to the rough stone at one side.

Sorra sat and watched, shivering with the chill in the air and the knowledge that not every creature roaming the woods at night would be as friendly as Beau. Her legs cramped from sitting, and she stood to stretch. Still there was no bear, and no light or voices from the cave.

There was no telling how long she'd been walking or waiting. Probably not as long as it felt, but long enough that Beau's reasons for leaving each night might have already been revealed, and she'd missed it while she was lurking outside like a cowardly lump.

Sorra steeled herself and poked her head into the cave. It smelled of guano and damp rock, and a faint dripping sound echoed from its walls. The air inside was black as burnt piecrust, and nothing moved in the shadows even when she picked up a stone off the ground and tossed it inside.

She pulled the candle and matches from her pocket. As the match flared to life, a dozen bats took flight in the shadows over-head. Sorra ducked, heart slamming, as they flew over her and left the cave.

But that was all. Nothing, bear or witch or otherwise, came to investigate.

She'd lost Beau, but if he'd gone into the cave as part of his journey, it seemed worth knowing what was inside.

The candle did little to cut through the blackness, but it allowed her to make her way forward, avoiding the worst of the mess on the floor.

Her pulse echoed through her body.

At first the cave seemed like any other, cold and messy and damp but entirely unremarkable. Sorra followed the soft plink of water until her candle's light reflected off the surface of a deep, dirty puddle.

The flame flickered in a faint gust of air. Sorra turned toward it, cupping her hand to protect her only source of light, and discovered a short upward slope that led to another opening in the cave's wall. Sorra turned sideways to pass through and stepped back out into the forest, scanning the ground for signs that Beau had passed by this way when he'd left the cave.

The bare stone offered nothing. She'd emerged near a river, though—the one the stream near the cabin fed into, and perhaps the one where Beau went to catch fish. She looked back to make sure the cave's entrance would be visible when she returned, then walked toward the water.

The trees here were smaller, as though the forest had been cut away and had grown back over time. At the edge of the river there were no trees at all, and when Sorra looked down, she found not the forest floor, but an uneven patchwork of flat stones forming the remains of a long-neglected road.

Sorra crouched to touch them.

A road meant people, or at least it had at some time in the past. It seemed clear that no one used it anymore, but it might still lead somewhere—to the King's Road, or even to a village. If it was the latter, that might be where Beau was getting all her lovely gifts. The idea of a bear, especially one as wary of humans as he claimed to be, doing a bit of midnight shopping was absurd, but she couldn't dismiss it outright.

His shopping habits didn't worry her, but his reasons for keeping them secret did.

She took a step down the road, then stopped herself. He had a good head start now, and she couldn't be sure he'd even come this way.

And he'd said as part of their bargain that she was to leave her family and human contact behind.

She stood for several minutes, shivering, weighing the risk of breaking their agreement against what she might learn if she followed the road.

I'm not in danger now. If I get back to the cabin safely, I can try again another night.

Or maybe things will get better and I won't need to.

Maybe he'll change his mind and explain everything if I give him a chance.

She wasn't sure whether the decision was wise or cowardly, but the idea of pushing the boundaries of their agreement and taking more risks without further thought made her stomach ache.

She re-entered the cave, again twisting sideways so as not to dirty herself on the stone. Three paces in, she paused, then turned slowly.

The cave's other entrance was wide enough to admit a bear, but she'd seen Beau squeezing himself through the cabin door enough times to know he'd never make it out this way.

So he left through the wider entrance before I got here, or he was never here at all and some other creature left that scrap of fur.

…Or he entered the cave as a bear and left it as something smaller.

The chill of the cave crept deep into her bones, and Sorra shivered hard.

There were plenty of stories where magical creatures disguised themselves to trick mortals or hide from enemies. The elven spy who took on the appearance of a cat and was only found out because he had to shed his feline skin to wash it in enchanted waters every night. Or Ranirahul, the knight who was trapped in a mouse's body by a cruel witch and was only set free when a princess learned his secret and spoke his true name.

And the goblin king who made himself look like a handsome man to win the heart of a human princess and take her kingdom for himself. Sorra had never liked that story, and the hairs on her arms prickled as she remembered how the soldiers in Cottsbridge had spoken of goblins at the Gate.

Sorra gave her head a shake and stepped deeper into the cave, searching it more carefully than she had before.

On a raised portion of the cave floor, she found the remains of a small campfire and an old blanket made from moth-eaten brown wool. There was nothing else—no clothing, no picked-clean bones to show that someone was taking meals there, no extra wood for the fire.

But someone has slept here, and bears don't need blankets.

As she walked by the little pool at the back of the cave, something beneath its surface caught the light of her candle, flashing like a stray sunbeam. Sorra crouched, then drew in a sharp breath as she made out the shapes of a handful of copper and silver coins. Not a great treasure, but certainly a strange thing to find in the middle of an otherwise unremarkable mountain cave. She rolled up one sleeve and reached in to collect the coins for examination.

There was nothing odd about them. They were Andonian currency, simple and common, and there weren't enough of them to buy much.

But when she looked back into the pool, she found that she'd missed another small pile. She reached for those as well. Then she blinked, and more coins appeared in their place.

"Magic." Her whisper filled the cave. She reached for more, setting the coins she drew from the water down on the stone beside it. When she was finished the pool looked exactly as it had when she'd discovered it, containing a single pile of bright metal, and the rest remained where she'd put them.

Sorra frowned at the mess. It seemed strange that someone with the magical skill to create a never-ending supply of money wouldn't conjure more efficient gold ones, or even banknotes. The weight of the less-valuable coins ensured that no one could carry too much treasure out of the cave.

She dropped a few back into the water, watching as they sank and glinted back at her.

It wouldn't do to leave them, then. Beau—or whoever else might use the cave—would see the excess and guess at who had been playing with their magic. Sorra stuffed the coins into the pockets of her dress, weighing her down but leaving the pool looking as she remembered finding it.

A breeze threatened to douse her candle, and Sorra backed away from the pool. Time was passing, and she didn't dare let Beau catch her in the cave. All she'd collected was an idea and a few vague suspicions, and she couldn't let him know she'd been here until she'd decided what to do with them.

She left the cave the way she'd first entered and followed Beau's faint trail through the forest, trying not to get lost in her thoughts and finding it impossible to hold them off.

Beau had a source of human currency. If the road beyond the cave did lead to a town in the valley, he could use it to buy supplies there.

There was more magic at work than he'd told her, and not only in his past. It was a part of his present—and therefore hers—in ways he didn't want her to understand.

When she reached the cabin, Sorra emptied her pockets into a bowl that she shoved deep under her bed, hiding the only evidence against her. Then she lay staring up at the ceiling as conflicting thoughts fought on the battlefield of her mind.

I should have taken the road.

I shouldn't have followed him at all.

I should have fled the other way while he was distracted.

I should trust the arrow.

I shouldn't ignore the blessing.

She rolled over on her side and fought the urge to scream.

Patience, she reminded herself. *As long as he thinks I've let go of my mistrust, he has no reason to harm me. There will be other nights, as long as I'm careful about how I play whatever game this is.*

The fact that she hadn't gotten lost, caught, or eaten by a mountain lion felt like a small victory against her blessing.

She hoped Davina would be proud.

CHAPTER SIXTEEN

Sorra dressed the next morning and glanced at the clock, then looked again, frowning. She'd slept late, and Beau hadn't wakened her as he usually did when he had gifts to offer.

Maybe he forgot to go. She hurried to the door, though the heaviness in her gut betrayed fears that went far deeper.

The door wouldn't open.

Sorra pushed again, then threw her shoulder against it, but the door remained firmly closed.

"Please, no," she whispered, and banged both fists against the unyielding wood. "Beau!"

A harsh scraping sound from the top of the door silenced her.

Sorra backed away, trembling as the door swung open. The morning sun silhouetted Beau's familiar form, haloing him with gold.

Rage kindled in Sorra's gut, and she welcomed its warmth. Her fear remained, but anger felt like a measure of power where fear alone left her helpless. She dared a step closer to him and pointed at the door. "You need to explain yourself."

"As do you." There was no warmth in his voice. "May I come in?"

"No." Sorra matched his frigid tone, but the fire inside her burned brighter.

"Very well." Beau sat on the porch, leaving room for her to join him. Sorra stepped out, just to be sure she could, and stood facing him with her arms crossed.

Careful, she told herself. Anger might feel good, even righteous, but her temper had never done her any favours. It made her more impulsive and tricked her tongue into speaking truths she'd have been better off hiding.

And now would be the worst time to slip up. She'd been cautious of Beau in the past, but even last night it was only because of Davina's warning, the blessing's threat, and warning signs that a more foolish or generous person might have chosen to ignore. But now...

"You said I wasn't a prisoner." Her voice trembled. "You promised."

"You weren't. And you're not. You can still come and go as you please, most of the time." Beau spoke calmly, though there was an edge to his voice she'd never heard before, even when he was irritated with her. "I thought you'd chosen to be happy here. I've treated you well, I've done everything I could to convince you that I mean you no harm, and all I've asked in return is that you let my secrets rest where they must. I thought we'd reached an understanding and might be on our way to friendship or—" He paused. "Last night you proved otherwise."

Sorra caught her fists clenching. "You can't buy trust. Not with gifts or kindness or anything but honesty. If you'd only tell me why you can't tell me—"

"No." Beau looked into her eyes. "I am sorry. More than you can know. I've told you, I think, that I have reasons for keeping my secrets, for asking you to know me as I am and not as I was or will be."

Sorra bit back a sharp laugh. She wanted to scream, to hit him, to go back into the cabin and slam the door in his face. But none of that would get her what she wanted.

After three slow breaths she was able to unclench her fists. At five, her heartbeat slowed.

She turned to the door. There was no lock, but the rusted hasp stood open. The heavy bit of hardware had held the door shut all on its own, leaving her helpless inside until a bear's great paw swatted it aside.

He'd let her take the lock, and like a fool she'd let the matter slip her mind, not realizing how cheaply he'd bought a tiny piece of her trust.

She turned back to him. "I can't know you as you are, though, can I? Nothing feels true. You do and say what you think I want, which means you offer nothing of yourself. You're not becoming my friend, you're lulling me. Taming me."

And it's almost worked more than once, she thought, remembering his anxious pacing when he waited to see whether his first gifts had pleased her, his apparent kindness when she'd been unwell. A few slips of his mask to reveal the truth beneath it, or his best performances?

She nodded over her shoulder at the door. "And now you show me that you're willing to cage me. I did trust you at first, more than I should have. I let you take me away from my home and my sister and gave you control of my life with no idea of who you are."

"I saved you. I've been nothing but kind to you."

"And I'm grateful. But do you see how hard it is to trust you when you hold all the cards? I don't know why you brought me here, why you keep visiting when our shallow conversations can't possibly entertain you, or what you mean to do with me when this year is over. You offer me peace and safety for the moment, but how can I know it's not an illusion?" She paused to steady her voice. "Can you promise me that you are my happily ever after? That putting my faith in you won't harm me in any way?"

Beau looked away. "I don't want to hurt you."

"That's not what I asked." Sorra leaned a shoulder against the wall. She'd suppressed the urge to scream and fight, had made herself smaller and quieter just as she'd been taught to do all her life. Now, though the embers of her anger still burned hot and low, the absence of its flames left her feeling drained and defeated.

"It's not." Beau stood. He, too, seemed diminished somehow. "I can't offer you the answers you want, and I can't tell you why. I could make up a story that would explain everything." He chuckled sadly. "Maybe I should have right from the start, for your sake as much as mine. You might have been happier, but I didn't want to lie to you. I still don't. I suppose at this point you wouldn't believe me if I offered you simple answers to put your mind at ease."

"Probably not."

Beau nodded. "You broke my trust last night when you followed me. I see that I've broken yours by threatening to remove what little freedom you have here, and I apologize for that. I acted in anger. I swear I won't do it again."

But you could, Sorra thought. He could tear her arms from her body if he wanted and there would be no higher court where her soul could accuse him of breaking their agreement.

"Perhaps we might put the past, including all of this, behind us," he said. "We could begin again."

Sorra almost laughed. She'd wished so often for a chance to leave her past behind. But she'd wished for a destiny she had some control over, not a life of locked doors she was forbidden to open, never knowing whether beauty or danger lay beyond.

Perhaps he was like Ranirahul, trapped as an animal until the princess learned the truth and spoke his name. It seemed possible, sometimes, that he was a victim of magic just as she was, that there might be a fair reason for his secrets.

But if actions spoke truth where words might lie, he'd revealed something about himself when he locked her in the cabin. Breaking one promise weakened the foundation of every other.

Either way, the answer was to learn the truth, and to do it before he found another way to keep her in the dark. Not to follow him, but to go where he'd gone. His magical coins could pay for bread and clothing, but they might also buy information.

He would be angry if he found out. Sorra didn't care. The guilt she'd felt the previous night for going against his wishes had burned clean away.

Her fingers clenched into fists again, and she hid them behind her skirt. She could keep calm. But not for much longer.

She cleared her throat. "I need time to think," she said, allowing her suppressed anger to creep into her voice, turning a request into a demand. "Give me the day to walk the woods alone and assure myself of my freedom. Show me that you trust me enough to do that without you shadowing my steps, and then we can talk about how we might fix this mess."

"You won't run away?"

Sorra's gut twisted. "No. I suppose breaking our agreement and leaving you would be dangerous for me."

"More than you know. Not only for you, but for…" He trailed off and coughed gently. "It's best for everyone that you see this through."

Another non-answer, but one that hinted at how dire the consequences of breaking an agreement with a magical creature could be —and one she didn't dare question further. Her insides knotted with regret over not negotiating the unstated price before she bargained for her escape.

"Be careful not to wander too far," he added. "There are worse things than me out there, and I can't protect you if you go alone."

Beau descended the porch steps and stuck his head beneath it, pulling it back with the basket in his jaws, half-filled with goods. He set it gently on the ground. "I brought what you wanted."

"Good." Sorra didn't move. "Come back at sunset, and we'll talk."

He frowned but nodded. "Sunset, then."

Sorra didn't retrieve the basket of baking supplies until she'd lost sight of him in the woods. He'd gone uphill, which served her well even if she couldn't be sure he wouldn't double back to follow her.

She slammed the door behind her, then set the basket down on the table and muffled the frustrated scream she'd been holding in.

The emotion was a relief, and she clung to it.

Whatever he said, whatever she wanted to be true of the creature who seemed to be her destiny, the rules of the game had changed.

Maybe he had only locked her in during a fit of anger and regretted it as she so often did her own rage-fuelled actions. But he still held all the knowledge, and therefore power over her. The latch on the door was a reminder that her access to food, to shelter, and even to fresh air depended on him. She might take the axe and hack it off, but he'd find another way if he wanted to.

Even if he was good, even without the threat of the blessing hanging over her, a person would be a fool to offer anyone so much control when he might change his mind the next time she displeased him.

The careful balance between the danger of acting and the danger of waiting had shifted.

She knelt beside the bed and pulled out the bowl she'd stowed her stolen coins in. They were still there, real and solid. A cloth bag that had once held sugar served as a coin pouch, and she set that, a candle and matches, and a spare sweater in her knapsack.

She stood on the porch for several minutes, waiting and listening. When she was as sure as she could be that Beau wasn't watching, she hurried into the woods, not allowing herself to look back.

CHAPTER SEVENTEEN

The forest looked different in daylight, but Sorra soon found the cave and its store of magical wealth. She set her candle down at the edge of the water, then took as many coins as she could carry before she continued on.

The old road's condition improved as she walked downstream. Though covered by leaf litter and pine debris, it had clearly offered a convenient route up the mountain at one time. It promised civilization, and the idea that others had once walked here lifted Sorra's spirits.

She hadn't realized how lonely she was, or how desperate for the sound of human voices.

Her pace picked up until she was almost running, barely paying attention to the silver river outracing her on her right or the deep forest on her left. She slowed when she ran out of breath but didn't stop. The forest was larger than she'd realized, and there was no time to waste.

The sky darkened with heavy clouds, and a light drizzle soon turned to heavier rain. Sorra ducked her head and kept walking.

She was beginning to think the forest was enchanted to be as unending as the supply of coins in the cave when the tree cover thinned, revealing a proper village huddled next to the water.

A thrill ran through her as she walked past thatch-roofed homes made of grey stone and found a town square bordered by several modest shops built in the same style, identified by the signs swinging in the breeze over their doors. None had words written on them, but the carved pictures were easy enough to understand—a loaf of bread with two stalks of wheat crossed over it for the bakery, a pig with an apple in its mouth for the butcher, and one showing a barrel, a rake, and a spool of thread that likely indicated a general store.

There was a steepled structure at one corner that might have been a temple of some description, a smaller building with wine bottles on its sign, and more houses with little yards and gardens. A far larger and finer home at the edge of town appeared to still be under construction, awaiting the last of its elaborate windows and a proper front porch. It looked like one of the fancy new city houses Aurelia had described so evocatively in her letters, all sharp angles and dark wood instead of the weathered stone of the older buildings that stood nearby.

The rain seemed to be keeping people inside, and Sorra supposed she should be glad of that.

Two wanted posters had been pinned to a large board at the edge of the square. One warned of a soldier who had deserted his position at the Gate, hinting that he might be dangerous, but not half as terrible as the consequences of not turning him in. The other, posted low on the board and drawn in a childish scribble, described someone called Daniel the Dimwit who had apparently stolen a doll and would be punished if it wasn't returned.

Sorra smiled, relieved. The soldiers might have mentioned her when they passed through on their way to the Gate, but at least her distinctively marked face wasn't posted for all to see and remember as she asked her questions.

The general store seemed like a promising place to start.

A bell clanked miserably over the door as an overwhelming mix of smells hit her—flour, spices, dust, something floral, something sweet. She blinked, forcing her eyes to adjust to the low light. As they did, the shadows around her coalesced into mannequins wearing dresses much like the ones Beau had brought her, a display of gardening tools, and what appeared to be a pile of wool sweaters being sorted for the coming winter.

"Hello?" she called.

A middle-aged woman poked her head out from behind one of the mannequins. Her pale hair was piled on top of her head in a messy knot, but she was respectably dressed in a stylish blouse and wool skirt. "Good morning! Or is it good afternoon?" She looked closely at Sorra's face, appearing bemused but not unfriendly. "Where did you come from?"

"Oh, here and there. Your town is lovely. And what a fascinating shop!" Sorra picked up one of the sweaters, a rough thing knit from yarn dyed a yellow that reminded her of the contents of diapers she'd changed when she'd minded Mrs. Alberton's infant twins. "Beautiful."

"Do you need anything in particular?" the clerk asked. "If you're heading back out on the road, we've got any supplies you could want."

Her comment reminded Sorra a little of old Abraham at the Ambling Goat, whose first question when anyone requested a room was when they'd be leaving. It almost made her miss his ridiculous face.

Almost.

"I'll be off soon," she said, and reached into her pocket for a few coins. The clerk followed her movements, then smiled.

"That's one of my dresses, isn't it?"

Sorra looked at the mannequins and pretended to be surprised. "I suppose it is! You make them yourself?"

"I do."

"Do you remember selling this one a few weeks ago?"

The clerk's smile faded. She tucked a stray wisp of hair behind one ear. "Not sure. I sell so many."

Sorra reached for the shopkeeper's hand and set the coins in her palm, then added a few more. "That's for you. All I want in return is to know about the customer who bought the dresses, and maybe some other things over the past few weeks."

The clerk backed away, clutching the coins tight. "The man who bought those isn't anyone we're supposed to talk about."

Sorra's attention caught on the word *man* like a fish landed on a hook. "Please," she said, and held out another handful of coins. "No one will know we spoke about him. It's important."

The woman blew out a long breath between tight lips, then nodded and reached for the coins. "I don't know much," she said. "It's probably not worth all this."

She didn't offer a refund, though.

"Anything you can tell me," Sorra said. "Quickly."

"He's made arrangements with several shops, going back quite a while now. We leave things for him at the edge of town, he picks them up in the dead of night and leaves payment. Good customer, especially in these past few weeks. Buying dresses is new. He had to wake me to ask for those directly, along with several other items. He's never done that before."

Sorra's blood pounded in her ears. She felt certain the bell over the door would clank any second, breaking their fragile sense of secrecy and ruining everything. "So you've spoken to him?"

"Not exactly. He leaves his orders in writing and did the same that night."

"What does he look like?"

The shopkeeper frowned. "Couldn't tell you. No one's ever seen his face. He wears a black cloak with a deep hood."

A shadow passed the store's dusty window. Sorra stepped closer to the clerk and pulled her behind the gardening display. "And you're sure he's human?"

The blood drained from the shopkeeper's cheeks. "Excuse me?"

"Could his cloak hide non-human features?"

"I suppose. I don't know what one of them would be doing down here, though."

"One of who?"

The door opened hard enough that the bell didn't have a chance to object before it flew across the store to hit the floor with a sad clunk. "Marie?"

The shopkeeper grabbed Sorra's arm and shoved her into a storage room. "Right here, Ethan. Be with you in a moment."

"You had any visitors?"

Marie held a finger to her lips. Sorra nodded and stood in the storage room, trying to keep her breath silent.

"Visitors?" Marie asked, sounding entirely natural. "Not so far. Be nice if someone dropped by to help me with these sweaters. Adelaide was especially optimistic this year about how many we'd be selling for her." She paused. "Something wrong?"

A sigh. "Gerald thought he saw someone he didn't know passing through the square. Probably just his imagination after those foolish books he's always reading, but I thought I'd ask."

A few seconds of silence followed before Marie spoke again. "Did you need anything else? A sweater, perhaps?"

"Not today." The door closed, and Sorra let herself relax.

Marie appeared a few seconds later, her eyes hard as glass. "Head out the back. You were never here, right?"

"No, never."

Before she could ask another question Sorra found herself in a narrow alley with the shop's side door closed behind her. The lock thunked home, hard and final, as Marie's words echoed through Sorra's mind.

Don't know what one of them would be doing down here.

Stuart had said that goblins never made it past the Gate, but what if he was mistaken? Sorra couldn't imagine why one would take the form of a bear or why he'd need her to promise to stay with him instead of just carrying out his terrible plans, but it might explain everything that had happened since she'd loosed the arrow.

She crouched, biting the skin at the edge of her thumbnail as she tried to fit the pieces together.

If Beau himself was coming to collect supplies, he wasn't a bear when he visited town.

And he always came in the middle of the night, exactly when he refused to stay in the cabin. As if whatever he was hiding happened every night, and he had no choice in it.

She couldn't know why he changed at night. It didn't matter, really. What did matter was what she was going to do about it.

Following him again wasn't an option, and not only because he'd be alert to it now. She'd meant to see where he went, not realizing how dangerous it could have been. If she'd seen his true form, he might have killed her.

Sorra didn't think she'd ever been so pleased about her own failure, but she still needed to do *something.*

Fleeing was an option. She had a good head start, and if he kept to his word, he wouldn't know she was gone until he arrived at sunset and didn't find her in the cabin. But then what? If he were a goblin, with magic enough to conjure coins from nothing and change himself into a bear, he might be capable of tracking the woman who had broken her end of their bargain. He'd made it clear this morning that there would be consequences if she ran.

He'd said it was better for everyone if she stayed. Did that mean she'd be putting her family in danger if she broke their agreement? Cottsbridge?

All of Andonia?

Maybe this is what the blessing was warning about, she thought, and leaned back against the wall as a wave of nausea passed over her. *Maybe this is how I destroy everyone, by fleeing to save my own hide.*

It was the same impossible situation she'd faced since she'd begun to suspect he wasn't quite what he seemed.

If he's good, it's safe to run, but better to stay.

If he's bad, Andonia might not be large enough to hide me from his punishment, and we might all be in danger.

She poked her head out from behind the building. The square was empty again. It clearly wasn't safe to approach the baker, the butcher, or anyone else involved in Beau's financial dealings.

Her gaze landed on the tavern, and an idea sprouted.

The only time he'd come close to accidentally revealing any of his secrets was when he'd been half-asleep. He hadn't risked a nap in her presence again, but she'd seen drink do the same to people at the Ambling Goat, stripping them of their inhibitions and laying their hidden parts bare.

He'd said he chose not to drink, not that it didn't work on him. If she could talk him into imbibing, she might get a glimpse of his true self, the one he hid behind his restrained courtesy. Maybe he'd let loose and call her a scatterbrained, no-good failure, but at least then she'd have something honest from him. Maybe he'd spill a sad tale of being an ugly man who had bought a flawed potion to change his appearance, and she'd be able to assure him that she didn't care as long as he had a good heart.

And if it was something darker, she'd have to be prepared to do whatever it took to keep him from following or from harming anyone else as revenge when she fled.

The thought terrified her, but it wasn't half as horrifying as the idea of letting the blessing win when the stakes felt so high.

Sorra calculated the value of the coins in her knapsack as she made her way to the tavern, sticking to the shelter of buildings, ducking under windows as she passed.

She wished Grace were there to tell her more about how a bear's body worked, but even without her, Sorra knew a few useful things. Alcohol had worked its magic on pigs after they'd escaped from her care and got into the ale in Olaf Engleson's barn. A bear was far larger, but surely not so different from a pig or a person. It would simply take more to loosen his tongue, and maybe a bit of trickery to get it done before he excused himself for the night.

Her stomach clenched. Being sneaky and devious came naturally to her, and the need to let those skills lie dormant had been forcefully impressed on her from an early age. She saw how Beau's desire to bury their differences might be used to convince him to have a few drinks, and how that might lead to her finding out how dangerous he really was.

She also knew these weren't the actions of a good person. Her sisters would have found a better way.

But this is the only gift I have. Maybe it'll finally be good for something.

Sorra sighed with relief when she found the tavern empty save for a clean-cut fellow polishing heavy drinking glasses behind the bar and a younger woman sweeping the opposite side of the room. Chairs were set upside-down on the few tables, and the floor was cleaner than she'd ever seen the one at the Ambling Goat.

She hurried to the bar, flashing her brightest smile. "A friendly face at last!"

He returned the smile, and she caught his gaze dropping to the bodice of her dress before returning to meet her eyes. "Hard thing to find around here some days."

"As I've learned." She didn't dare ask about Beau for fear of being tossed out. It likely wouldn't do any good, anyway—as far as she knew, he'd never bought anything here. "I guess you don't get many visitors all the way up here."

"Not many visitors, not much attention from the outside world. Except for soldiers, of course. And the builders that come in to work on Alistair's new house, but they'll be gone soon." He set the glass he'd been polishing on the bar. "I guess most folks will be happy about it, even with them leaving that monstrosity behind."

Sorra didn't particularly care about visitors or houses, but she was happy to offer friendly conversation after weeks without human contact. "Rich man?"

"He is now. Did a favour for the king, got a generous reward for it, and now we have a new blight on the landscape." The bartender winced. "Sorry. You probably didn't come in to ask my opinion on houses. Unless you're a distant relation who's come to admire Alistair's, in which case I should still offer an apology."

Sorra laughed. "No apologies necessary. Just between us, I also think it's horrible. I did come here on a mission, though. I'm with a group of soldiers from down south who are doing a bit of surveying on the mountainside."

The young woman looked up but continued her sweeping. Sorra didn't care if she listened, as long as she didn't start asking questions. "They've been hard at work and need a bit of relaxation and fun. Their supervisor's away, and..." She shrugged. "I'm looking for a supply of drinks for a party."

The bartender raised his eyebrows. "Just you and a bunch of soldiers? Is that safe?"

"I can take care of myself." She leaned on the bar and lowered her voice, drawing him in. "All I need for tonight is a delivery brought up the side of the mountain. It's a bit of a jaunt, but I can pay you for your time as well as the alcohol if you'll bring it to the end of the road for me. I'll have the boys come down to carry it the rest of the way. I'll take anything strong enough to knock an ogre on its ass."

The bartender tilted his head to one side, appraising her again.

Sorra was glad to not know whether he was wondering about her and those soldiers.

"Go on." The young woman set her broom aside and came closer. She had a pinched face and a nose speckled with constellations of freckles. "I'll mind things while you're gone if she has the money to make it worth your while."

"I suppose I could make a delivery," he said. "How much do you need?"

Sorra considered Beau's size and how much it took to make a man a fraction of his weight fall drunk on his ass. She wanted Beau to remain lucid, but it was always best to be prepared. She set her knapsack on the counter, letting the coins jingle dully within. "How much can you spare?"

CHAPTER EIGHTEEN

The rain had stopped, but that didn't make the trip back up the road comfortable. Sorra sat next to the bartender on the seat of his cart, hands resting on her knees, not touching him save for when the cart jostled over the warped road and forced contact.

He'd introduced himself as Pat but hadn't seemed inclined toward conversation. That had been fine with Sorra.

Pat pulled the big chestnut horse to a stop at the end of the road, just shy of where Sorra had stepped onto it that morning. "Good enough?"

"Certainly. I'll holler for the men, and they'll be here quick as anything."

She hoped that would serve as a warning as well as an assurance, if one was needed.

"Good." He climbed down and went to the back of the cart to unload the boxes.

Sorra stepped down to the road before he could offer his hand to help, hoping he'd be back in the driver's seat and on his way without further conversation. Instead, he stood next to the horse, stroking its nose.

"Everything been normal here since you arrived?" he asked.

"Normal?"

"You know. Regular. Safe. As expected."

Sorra tensed. "I suppose so. There's not much that's a real threat to a dozen men who know their way around a sword. Why?"

"No reason. Just be careful is all. Maybe draw straws and have a few stay sober tonight. Swords aren't much good if everyone's passed out in pools of their own vomit, you know?"

The horse pawed at the ground and snorted. It seemed eager to leave.

Sorra searched the bartender's eyes, but they gave nothing away. "Is there something besides wild animals up here? Or someone?"

"Not that I know of. But just in case, here." He pulled a blue glass bottle from his pocket and handed it to her. "Old family recipe. Sobers you up in a snap, and it'll help shake off the sickness tomorrow morning. Not much there, but you only need a sip if you want your wits about you."

Sorra held the bottle up to the light. "How much?"

"No extra charge for you, miss." He climbed into the cart and turned the horse toward the village. "Even if there aren't monsters in these woods, I know how men can be. Take care."

"You as well," she said, though he couldn't possibly have heard her over the clatter of wheels already carrying him away. It always pleased Sorra when people offered pleasant surprises. It didn't happen nearly often enough for her liking.

She pocketed the bottle and moved the crates away from the road, though she doubted anyone would come by and find them before she returned.

There was no sign of Beau at the cabin when Sorra dug out the old wooden sled she'd discovered in the shed not long after her arrival.

The sled didn't make the trip from the road easy—every step was a struggle, especially where the runners caught on ridges of exposed stone that broke through the soil of the forest floor. Sorra cursed with every bump, but in less than an hour she had ten bottles of cheap but strong spirits labelled 'Bristow's Fire' stowed in the cupboard. She also had plenty more of Beau's coins, which she'd stopped to collect from the cave on her way back to the cabin. Beau hadn't said anything about the ones she'd taken before, so it seemed safe to assume he wouldn't notice another loss.

Sorra sat at the kitchen table and pulled the cork from one of the dark brown bottles, sniffed, and wrinkled her nose. The stuff inside smelled like it would burn straight through the wood floor if she spilled any.

It would do, though, if she could convince Beau to join her for a friendly little party.

~

Sorra sat on the porch steps with an open bottle hidden behind her skirt, her hair damp from the bath she'd taken after supper. Beau hadn't shown himself yet, and the fear that he wouldn't come was nearly as terrible as the fear of what could go wrong if he did.

The sun had vanished over the treetops in the west, leaving the sky bathed in a vibrant glow Sorra wished she was in a mood to appreciate, when the great bear lumbered out of the woods. He paused before he reached the steps, scratching at the ground. An anxious movement, perhaps, but all Sorra could think of was the damage those claws might do to tender human flesh.

The urge to let things lie returned, stronger than ever. It was a more dangerous choice in the long term, shutting the door on any chance that she might thwart the blessing or her own dark destiny, but for the moment it was undeniably safer.

"Good evening," he said.

"Hello."

He came closer, and Sorra observed him with new eyes. Whatever he really was, the transformation into a bear was impressive. Even knowing it wasn't natural, she saw no flaws in his form or his movements. If he'd never spoken to her, she wouldn't see him as anything but a large and healthy animal, beautiful and powerful and dangerous.

They watched each other for a few moments.

"Did you have a pleasant day?" Beau asked.

"I don't know if pleasant is the word. I did a lot of thinking, though. And walking. And I had an idea about how we might make a fresh start."

She didn't try to sound excited. Too drastic a change of mind or heart would put his guard up.

"I'd very much like to hear it."

Sorra looked down at her fingers, which worried at the fabric of her skirt. "The first thing is for me to apologize for following you last night. You've been so kind to me and have only asked for privacy in return. The not knowing has been driving me mad, the questions buzzing like bees in my head, but… Well, I'm sorry."

"Thank you. It's another impasse, isn't it?" he asked. "Like with the arrow. You want answers. I can't offer them and can't even say why. We both have our reasons, and we can't both have what we want."

"True. But last time we did both get what we wanted, once I took the risk of trusting you not to murder me and you trusted me not to slit your throat while you were laid out like a nursing sow on that forest floor."

Beau gaped at her. "You considered that?"

"Certainly not." She smiled. "My point is that trust is the key. That requires openness. Honesty." Beau opened his mouth to object, and Sorra raised a hand to stop him. "Not about your past. Not about mine, for that matter—me speaking about my old sins and misdeeds was what set us off on the wrong foot. What we need is a fresh start, with both of us being honest about who we are, here and now, knowing we might not like what we see in each other but finding a way to make things work without pretending to be what we're not."

Beau nodded slowly. "You may be right. And I owe you an apology as well. My actions this morning were…" He paused. "I was wrong. I acted badly. And I'm sorry."

"All right," she said, not offering forgiveness but acknowledging his apology as he had hers.

"All right," he repeated. "How do we make things right, then?"

She pulled the dark glass bottle out and took a sip of its watered-down contents. It was still strong, and she coughed as it burned her throat.

Beau's eyes narrowed. "Where did you get that?"

"It was a long walk. Did you know there's a village down the mountain?"

"Is there?"

Sorra's stomach tightened. Clearly his interest in a fresh start wasn't going to lead to true honesty without a little help.

So be it, then.

She stood, bottle in hand. The heavy iron lock in her pocket settled against her thigh, and she turned so he wouldn't see its movement. "Come inside."

She went into the cabin, leaving the door open behind her. Orange light filtered through the window coverings, but she lit the lamp against the coming night.

Something nagged at her mind—something she'd forgotten. But everything was as it should be, as far as she could tell.

"I know you said you don't usually drink," she said. "But I brought you a little something. It's sort of a tradition where I come from. We toast new beginnings and special occasions. We share a little wine with friends as we warm our hearts in each other's company. It shows we trust each other."

Beau pushed the door closed against the darkening forest, swiping with one paw. "You shouldn't have wandered so far."

"I know." Sorra folded her hands behind her and tried to look penitent. "I hope you're not angry. I swear I didn't say anything about you to anyone. I just wanted to see where the road went. I considered staying for a drink and a little human company, but I didn't want you to think I'd run off forever. Then I thought maybe, since you're my only friend, I'd bring a few bottles back here instead. It was probably a stupid idea."

"Not stupid." Beau stepped closer. "I understand what it is to be lonely. To miss what's familiar. I trust you're not hoping to get me drunk and make me spill my secrets?" There was a smile in his voice, but a sharp look in his eyes.

Sorra laughed, ignoring the chill that crept up her spine. "Look at you! This stuff is pathetic. I'm on my second bottle and I'm barely beginning to feel anything. I'd guess a bear could drink a bathtub full of it before it'd even make you stumble. I only miss the ritual of it, the reminder of home. A few drinks to toast our fresh start, a little conversation as our true selves, and then you can be on your way."

Most of that was a lie. Sorra considered herself an experienced drinker, but the lone sip she'd taken from her watered-down bottle was already buzzing through her veins. It was potent stuff, and she'd need to be careful if she wanted to keep her wits about her and stay in control of what could quickly turn into a dangerous situation.

But its strength buoyed her hopes that her plan might work if Beau sampled the stuff at full strength and in higher volumes than he realized.

"Your second?" he asked. "How many did you carry back with you?"

"Four," she lied again. There were two by the sink and one in her hand, but seven more open under the bed, waiting to be swapped out when he wasn't looking.

Or so she hoped. Her plans rarely went the way she wanted even when she had plenty of time to prepare, and this whole situation had been rushed and uncertain. The blessing would trip her up, but perhaps not before she learned something that would help her understand Beau and what sort of destiny he was leading her to.

And if the answers revealed that she should stay, she'd shove him out the door to sleep it off, no harm done.

She tried not to think of the alternative even as she glanced at the knife she'd left in easy reach on the counter. A lock, a knife, matches… options for an escape she hoped she wouldn't need.

Beau looked at the bottles, then at the one Sorra had sipped from, obviously considering her proposal.

For a moment she almost hoped he'd refuse, that she'd have no choice but to give up her plans. It was too much, too dangerous.

But giving up would mean spending the next year feeling as though she were going mad, second-guessing every kind word he spoke, guarding herself against being drawn into the kind of trouble that had tempted her all her life, waiting for the axe to fall the moment she let her guard down.

Almost anything was better than living like that. She was as good as helpless, and knowledge was the only way to protect herself.

She silenced her doubts and fortified her nerves with a sip of her drink.

Beau sniffed at the bottle, wrinkled his nose, and nodded. "A little wouldn't hurt."

Sorra thought again of her panic when he'd locked her in the cabin, the nightly disappearances, the hint he'd let slip of pain to come, and the answers she'd never get about any of it.

Be brave. Be clever. Be strong, just this once.

"Good," she said. "Shall we sit?"

Sorra collected a deep bowl, a tin cup, and Beau's bottles of drink from the kitchen, then spread a blanket on the floor next to the bed as though she were laying out a picnic. She sat with her diluted bottle of drink at her side so she wouldn't mix it up with the others.

"Can you drink out of this?" she asked as she poured a solid serving from one of his bottles into the bowl.

"I think I can manage." He sat on his bottom and took the bowl in his forepaws, balancing it with clumsy movements as he brought it closer to his mouth. "The bottle would do as well."

"But would be far less civilized." Sorra poured herself a drink and raised her cup. "To... whatever this is. A new chapter of our companionship."

"To whatever this is," Beau rumbled, and drank. He looked into the bowl, frowning. "This is weak?"

"The effect, not the taste. If it's too much for you..."

"It's fine." He sipped again, then emptied the bowl. "Not terrible once you get in there, is it?"

"Not at all." Sorra refilled his bowl, emptying the bottle as much as she could without making it obvious how much was gone. "Where did you go today? I didn't see you on my walk."

"Farther up the mountain. Staying out of your way."

When he raised the bowl to his mouth again, Sorra switched the half-empty bottle for a full one, then poured him another serving before he'd seen the bottom of the bowl.

She steered the conversation to light topics, nothing that would put his guard up. They spoke of her favourite music and how it had filled the house until Aurelia moved away. She told him a few stories she remembered from her childhood, then used words to paint amusing portraits of the people of Cottsbridge for him, carefully editing out her own part in any of their foul moods or misadventures. He drank slowly but steadily, and she topped him up frequently to keep him from seeing the bottom of the bowl, switching out the half-emptied bottle again when he wasn't looking.

It was fun, aside from the trickery. Beau laughed at her jokes, and she laughed harder when he slapped his knee like an old man. It was a good start, but it didn't feel like answers quite yet.

"That one done yet?" he asked. "It seems bottomless."

Sorra emptied the third bottle into the bowl and set it next to the bed, near the shadows where the two half-emptied ones hid. "It's gone now. Congratulations. Shall I open your second?"

He clearly wasn't feeling the effects yet. He looked over his shoulder at the clock. "A little more, and then I'll be on my way."

Something tickled at Sorra's mind again, but she didn't try to catch it. Her thoughts were becoming fuzzy from the drink she'd so badly underestimated, and she knew better than to risk distraction.

Beau had gone through most of another bottle before he began to list to one side. He leaned against the bedpost and stared at Sorra, his head wobbling slightly.

Sorra squinted at him. Something was wrong.

"It's not the end," he said. He scratched his chest, then looked down at his claws as though he'd never seen them before.

"What?" Sorra shook her head to clear it. She desperately wanted a sip of the bartender's remedy but didn't dare take one when Beau was watching.

"When you said about your un-blessing, you said your sisters had bright futures but your story felt over."

Sorra leaned in closer. "And?"

"I wanted to say a lot of things about that, but I couldn't, you know? I can't tell you that it made me angry when you said it. And I can't tell you why." He pointed a paw at her, clearly intent on doing exactly that. Sorra scrambled up onto the bed and sat with her legs crossed beneath her skirt. He watched, but his paw still pointed at the space she'd vacated.

"Why?"

Sorra held her breath. This was what she'd planned and hoped for—loose thoughts, loose tongue, a way past his walls that would tell her whether she could trust him with her present and the path to her future.

He laughed, wild and deep, and flopped onto his back. The bed vibrated from the impact. "Gods. If you knew what you have in your soft little hands."

Sorra crawled to the end of the bed and peered down at him. "My hands? The ones that ruin everything they touch? The ones everyone is safe from now that I'm here?"

"So what?" He rolled over and planted all four feet carefully on the floor, then glared at her. "So your sisters have destinies and happy endings and pretty fates." He spoke each word with disgust. "So you didn't get one and all that arrow led you to was this. So you're a mistake who should never have been born."

Sorra gripped the footboard tight and drew in a sharp breath. *"So what?"* She glared back at him and tried to catch hold of her scattered thoughts. She thought she was supposed to be careful, to not be encouraging a fight, but he'd dug his claws straight into old wounds. "You think that's nothing?"

"I think that's everything!" he roared. Whatever concerns he'd had before about letting her see his anger, drink had chased them away. "You have a warning about what you might become, but you don't have your life laid out for you. You don't have responsibilities hanging over you like an executioner's axe. You have freedom."

"Until you bar the door again."

He ignored that, lost in the unfettered thoughts he'd obviously been holding back. "You could go anywhere. Do anything. Change your name. Lose your name and be no one if you wanted. Do you have any idea how precious that is?"

Sorra's anger melted away as she understood that he wasn't talking about her at all. "No. Tell me."

"I can't. You know I can't. But it makes me angry. For you. *At* you, but I can't say that without..." He rolled onto his side. "I should go."

Sorra didn't answer.

"All my life is," he muttered, "is responsibility and executions. I mean, expectations. But you? You could do anything. But you won't. They made you afraid of... you. They taught you to guard your own prison, didn't they? And now you're scared to be anything."

Sorra's chest tightened. He was a stranger who knew nothing, but his words cut her.

"Because I can't help but do harm if I try to do anything at all," she said. "Because it will go wrong no matter how good my intentions are." She crouched beside him and looked into his eye. It looked strange and unfocused, even compared to a few minutes before. "I'm not even sure those are correct most of the time."

"That's not my point." His eye closed. "You're a force. You're alive."

"You're not making sense."

"I am. Your story's not written for you. You could go charging through the world like a hurricane, overturning vice and virtue in equal measure. Or not equal, but what of it? The world needs shaking up is what it needs. I need it... shakened. But you'd have blown yourself out in that little town and changed nothing at all. What time is it?"

Sorra didn't answer.

I didn't give him enough to do this to a bear.

He was fine a few minutes ago.

Cold dread flooded her body. She knew she should be glad her plan was working, but that was exactly the problem. Nothing in her life ever went this smoothly unless it was leading her to disaster.

He rolled his head to see the clock. "I'd've sworn it was later. What was I saying?"

Sorra followed his gaze. Nearly ten. Later than she'd realized, but not so bad.

Her heart stumbled, and it took a moment for her dulled mind to catch up.

She wound the clock every morning to keep it from slowing.

She was proud of the habit, and of never missing a day once she'd realized how the clock slowed in the evening if she did.

Today was different.

I forgot.

It's late. Late, late, late.

Suddenly she didn't want to know what happened after he left her each night, and no part of her wanted to see whatever monster he was about to become. It was too much, too easy, too dangerous. If he left now, he wouldn't need to find out that she'd tricked him.

All could still be forgiven, maybe even forgotten.

She shivered as she felt the blessing's cold breath on the back of her neck.

"Beau? You have to go. Come on."

He growled, and she scrambled away. Then it happened again, and she realized he was snoring.

"Shit." She paced the room, keeping well away from him, then picked the blanket up off the floor and draped it over him.

"I'm sorry," she whispered, though he wouldn't hear. "I didn't know this would happen. You're so big, and you really only drank two bottles. I don't know how I got it so wrong."

She pulled the bartender's remedy from her pocket and sipped, gagging at its bitterness. Her head cleared, and she silently thanked the bartender and wondered whether he'd considered selling the stuff outside his small town. He'd make a fortune.

Beau groaned and snorted in his sleep.

I'll leave, she decided. *He'll be fine, and I won't need to lie when he asks what I saw.* She doused the lamp, leaving the cabin in darkness as she collected her bag.

She had a hand on the door when his snores fell silent.

"Beau?"

There was nothing. No movement, no snuffling breath. But even in the thin moonlight from the windows she could see that the shape under the blanket was smaller than it had been moments before.

Run, she thought, and reached for the lock in her pocket to imprison him while she fled. *If he's changed, he's more dangerous than ever.*

Or he's dying.

With her mind clear, she understood her mistake. She'd given him enough drink to loosen a bear's tongue, but enough to kill a smaller creature. It had taken hold quickly because he'd begun to change, and now her accidental poison would finish its work if she let it.

She'd gotten what she wanted, but it had gone too far. Alcohol wasn't a truth potion, but she thought what he'd just said, garbled as it was, had been a glimpse of everything he'd been holding back. And those hidden thoughts, even if they came mixed with anger, were about her potential and his desire for her freedom. Even if he was leading her to a terrible destiny, he wanted better for her.

There was good in him, even if it was mixed in with lies and misunderstandings and danger.

Whatever he was, she didn't want him to die.

She dug through her bag for the candle and matches she'd taken to the cave. It took two tries for her trembling hands to strike the match and light the wick. Panic gripped her as she crept closer, cautious at every step, trying to remember what the goblins in stories looked like, bracing herself for the worst. Scaly skin. Claws. Sharp teeth for tearing flesh.

Instead, she found a man lying on the floor with her blanket covering him up to the middle of a sculpted back. He'd rolled onto his front as he changed, leaving his face pressed into the floor.

Not a goblin.

He might still be a villain, but there was only one way to find out.

"No dying," Sorra told him, and rolled him onto his back. He was quite handsome, with a strong nose, well-formed lips, and bronze skin that would probably look sun-kissed even in the depths of winter. Thick, dark hair reached nearly to his shoulders, but only a shadow of a beard showed on his jaw. Older than her, but not enough to have lined skin or grey hairs.

Under other circumstances, she'd have liked to look for longer.

She placed a hand behind his head, tilted it to open his mouth, and poured the rest of the remedy down his throat.

A minute passed.

Too late, she thought. *Or too little.*

She tried to think of a time when she'd made a worse mistake, hoping it would offer some comfort, and came up empty.

Maybe I can keep him breathing until he changes back. He'll never have to know I saw—

His eyes snapped open. They were the same deep, warm brown as they'd been when he was a bear.

They were also sharp and lucid as they widened in obvious horror.

"Sorra," he whispered. "What have you done?"

CHAPTER NINETEEN

Beau stood, shaking, and wrapped the blanket around his waist. "You've seen me."

"Yes." It hadn't been a question, but it seemed rude not to answer.

"Right." He looked at the clock again. It had stopped entirely. "You did this on purpose?"

Sorra backed away, ready to run for the door if she needed to. "No. At least, not the clock. I meant to get you drunk. I thought—that is, I didn't know who you were. Are. I thought the arrow might have led me to all the badness the blessing warned about. I thought if I could relax you a bit, I could know you."

Beau laughed as though his mind had crumbled, then he stumbled to the bed and sat on its edge. "Of course you did."

His voice had changed, but it still held some of the depth of his ursine tone. He kept laughing.

Sorra's cheeks warmed, though she wasn't sure why she felt ashamed. "It's not as stupid as it sounds," she said, edging closer to the counter so she could grab the knife if she needed to defend herself from a madman or a witch. "I had no reason to believe you were good aside from you saying so. You might have been a goblin."

He calmed himself, then rested his face in his hands. To Sorra he looked like he might be trying to keep from falling apart. "I'm not laughing at you. I'm laughing at... I don't know. Destiny, maybe.

151

Myself, for being such a fool. She knew what she was doing. I didn't stand a chance."

The apprehension that had shadowed Sorra since the first hint of her success now wrapped itself around her shoulders like a shawl of ice. "I don't understand. What's happening? Who are you?"

It seemed for a moment that he wouldn't answer. Then he lifted his head and smiled sadly. "No harm in telling you now, I suppose." He stood, blanket held tight to his waist, and bowed slightly before sitting down again, hard, like he didn't have the strength to stay upright. "Beauregard Alphinex Regus Tolineau, at your service."

Sorra considered locking him in and leaving after all. He was calmer now, but clearly not entirely sane. "What kind of a name is that? It sounds like one of the ridiculous ones they give royal folks."

"So it is," he said. "It's funny. You chose my name from nothing, and you chose so correctly that I feared it would lead to you realizing I was the heir to Andonia's throne, the prince who disappeared at the end of the great curse."

"I could have told you not to worry about that. Nobody in Cottsbridge cares enough to memorize the names of a bunch of princes, even if they go missing. We keep busy enough with our own gossip."

"A small mercy." His shoulders slumped. "If you'd guessed who I was, this would all have ended much sooner than it has. Not that it matters now."

Sorra used the candle to light the lamp again, hands shaking, then moved closer to get a better look at him. Even in his state of undress, even looking utterly defeated, there was something regal about his bearing. It was still possible this was a trick, another layer to some devious plan, but every word he spoke felt true in a way Sorra couldn't define.

The prince. Not a goblin.

It didn't make sense, but she was accustomed to feeling out of her depth. The only things she felt sure of were that she'd done the wrong thing and that he was in pain.

She sat beside him on the bed, resting her fingertips lightly against the back of his forearm. He was real, his skin warm, the fine, dark hairs softer than his fur had been. "What doesn't matter?"

"I don't really know where to begin." He looked down at his hands as he spoke. "I was raised to serve Andonia. My studies, my social calendar, my amusements… all of it was designed to shape me into a king. I knew what my life was to be. Then the curse came and nearly destroyed my country—*our* country—with famine, plagues, storms, floods, droughts."

"I remember," Sorra said softly. "I was only a child, but folks in town blamed it on me until it became clear that even I couldn't cause that kind of chaos."

"No. It took someone far more powerful to manage that."

"Who?"

It had been more than a dozen years since the end of the curse, and to the best of Sorra's knowledge no one outside the palace in Embercliffe knew who or what had caused it, or why it had ended as suddenly as it had begun.

Beau looked up, then tilted his head as though he were listening for something. "Gwelain."

Sorra scoured her memory for the name and came up empty. "I don't know her."

"Nor do I, really, even after more than a decade as her prisoner. She's the queen of the goblins, though no one in Andonia remembers her as that or as anything else now. To make a long story short, she—do you know the stories about Queen Linnea?"

He asked without implying that he anticipated ignorance, and Sorra was almost as grateful for that as she was for the fact that she could offer something. "Her I do know. She died a few hundred years back after ruling for centuries. She carried the blood of the Bright Ones in her—the magical folk who lived here before us. She was beautiful, just, and wise, or so they say. She kept magic in Andonia after her people left, and she invited humans here from every nation to build a new one. After she died, there was less magic in Andonia, but they say the land remembers her."

She didn't remember many history lessons, but the ones about Linnea had burrowed into her mind and made a permanent home there.

"Very good," Beau said, sounding like a gentler teacher than Sorra had ever known in Cottsbridge. "Her body held magic even after her death, and in that way she continued to care for Andonia. The royal mages drew from her power to serve the king who followed her. It was strongest in her heart, which was stolen not long after her death."

"And no one knows who took it," Sorra said, then understood. "It was that goblin queen?"

"It was. It took Gwelain a long time to learn how to control it and longer to decide what to do with her stolen power. She was old even then, though, and knew how to be patient. It was our bad luck that she cursed Andonia in our time. She wanted the land for herself and used Linnea's magic to weaken us and force my father's hand. He wouldn't give her the crown, but she settled for the next best thing."

Sorra shivered. "You?"

He nodded. "There was no other way. Instead of an engagement to some princess from another country, I was promised to Gwelain and sent to live in her lands north of the mountains, which she had erased from every map and every memory generations before."

Though she felt entirely sober, Sorra's mind stumbled drunkenly in the onslaught of information. Goblins in the Forgotten Lands, just as Stuart and the other soldiers had said, and all of it forgotten thanks to Linnea's stolen magic. A curse no one would ever forget caused by a queen whose name no one in Cottsbridge had ever heard.

A lost prince not so lost after all. It was like a bedtime story that hadn't yet found its happy ending.

"So no one remembers her? Or knows where you went?"

"My father does." Beau held out his left arm to show her three parallel lines marked on the underside of his forearm. They looked as though they'd been swiped on with an artist's paintbrush loaded with black ink. "This magic marks me as heir to Andonia's throne, and when my father dies, it will change to prove my identity as its true king. It's been a reliable security measure for generations. Now it unfortunately lets Gwelain be sure my father hasn't named a different heir, which he'd certainly do if he forgot their fragile terms of peace."

"So you were made her prisoner to keep the rest of us safe?"

Sorra pulled her feet up onto the bed and rested her chin on her knees. "That's terrible."

"That's duty." Beau pulled one hand down his face. "From my first breath it's been my responsibility to serve my people. I thought it would be as their king. As it turns out, it was as a sacrifice of sorts. Andonia lives, and Gwelain seems content to uphold her end of the agreement as long as my father doesn't provoke her and I don't cause her trouble."

"And if you do?"

"Then she's free to finish what she started. I'm the dam holding back her flood of destruction. All I can do is hope my father finds a way to defeat her before these lines become a crown." He turned his arm over, hiding them. "I wish I could speak with him. Help him. Do anything but sit and rot in her damned castle."

He spoke without obvious anger, but Sorra felt enough for both of them. She held it in, not wishing to make things worse, but it blazed through her.

No wonder he envied the freedom of a commoner like her, even one with the potential to cause so much harm. She had choices, though she'd spent her life having them slowly stripped away. She was free now, as he had never been.

"And how did you manage to find yourself back in Andonia as a bear with an arrow in your bum?"

That made him smile, which pleased Sorra more than she'd have thought possible in that moment.

"I thought I was so clever," he said. "I challenged Gwelain for a chance to win my freedom. It angered her, of course. I've never pretended to be pleased about our arrangement and kept putting off signing the marriage contract, but I didn't dare risk breaking my oath by trying to escape. But she likes games and wagers. She agreed to set me free if I could find someone who'd make a better wife than she would—someone willing to love me as I could never love her. I would not be allowed to meet this person as myself, or as a prince, or any such thing. If I could convince this unknown someone to marry me without knowing who I really was, Gwelain said she wouldn't stand in the way of true love."

His brow furrowed, and for a moment he reminded Sorra of the bear she'd nearly befriended.

"I suspected she might alter my appearance so no one would recognize me," he said. "I didn't realize she'd change me so much as to make a joke of the whole thing. I spent a year as a bear, becoming myself for several hours each night whether I wanted to or not, knowing I'd lose the wager if anyone recognized me. Then you came speaking of destiny, and I thought you might be the answer. A woman like a storybook heroine, trapped by an evil guardian, destined to fall in love with the prince in spite of his monstrous appearance and end his captivity. It seemed so perfect that I had to try."

Sorra looked away. "I'm sorry I wasn't what you needed. If I'd just accepted my destiny and stopped trying to be so smart, if I'd believed what you wanted me to believe, I guess I would have been a hero." A tear slipped down her cheek, and she wiped it away. "I did warn you that you'd get hurt. Even when an arrow of destiny led me to a happy ending, I ruined it by trying not to let it ruin me."

"Please don't apologize." Beau reached for her hand, and she let him take it. His skin was warm, almost feverish. "You did nothing wrong. I'm the one who owes you the apology. You deserve so much better than to be a casualty in all of this."

Sorra drew in a hard breath. "You said that before, when you were half-asleep. That I deserve better, that you didn't want to hurt me. Why?"

"Because I would have saved myself by breaking your heart. I couldn't have had a commoner as my queen, so once I'd earned your love and won the wager, that would have been the end for us." He looked into her eyes, searching. "Please understand. I didn't know you when I agreed to all this. I had a vague idea of a commoner who would be glad to save Andonia, who would be compensated for my necessary trickery with wealth and security and position for the rest of her life. It seemed like a simple equation when I agreed to Gwelain's terms—one broken heart for the fate of a nation."

Sorra gently pulled her hand away from his. "I suppose it would have been a small price to pay."

"No." Beau spoke firmly, and with anger Sorra thought wasn't meant for her. "The moment I began to see you as a person and not as a necessary sacrifice, it complicated everything. I've hated myself more with each day that's passed since then. Your life has taught you not to trust or love too easily, and I intended to build a false foundation for you to offer me exactly that before I revealed the truth and ripped it all away. You'd have had money and a home and whatever else you wanted as your reward, but you deserve so much more."

"But it's still a small price. It's only me."

"Sorra." His voice twisted through her, warm and lovely. "You are as precious as any noble or king. It shames me that I didn't realize it before I dragged you into this. I always knew a king's duty was to serve his people, but I was never encouraged to know them. A king who would sacrifice an innocent subject for the good of all—for the good of himself, even if he thinks that's the same thing—isn't fit to be king at all." He sighed. "I'd like to blame the time I've spent in the company of goblins, but it was still my choice."

"You were desperate."

"True. And desperation is no excuse. My only consolation is that this never could have worked. I thought Gwelain's cruelest trick was changing my form, but that's not what doomed this to failure. It was the secrets her terms demanded. You were right to mistrust my motivations and to uncover my secrets, and I'm sorry if I made you think otherwise."

"Great." Sorra sniffled and wiped her nose on her sleeve. "The one time I'm right is exactly when being right ruins everything."

"You didn't ruin anything that deserved to be preserved." He waited for her to meet his gaze before he spoke again. "As I said, Gwelain knew what she was doing. I'm glad you didn't let me prove myself no better than her."

Sorra lay back on the bed and stared at the rafters. A few seconds later, Beau did the same, clasping his hands on his chest. "It's funny," he said. "If you'd been the person I needed, I might have been able to make myself into a monster for the sake of later becoming a good king. But if you'd been her, if you'd been docile and accommodating and demanded nothing, I'd like you and admire you less than I do now. You're quite extraordinary."

Sorra turned on her side, propped up on one elbow. "You don't have to say kind things anymore."

"I know. That's why I can." The lamplight reflected in his dark eyes as he met her gaze. "At first, I tried to be nice to win you over. I thought I understood who you were—prickly, defensive, sour, not very good at pretending to be otherwise, and the perfect obstacle to my plans."

Sorra scowled half-heartedly at him. "That's both accurate and hurtful."

He smiled again, creasing the skin at the corners of his eyes, and Sorra wondered whether a person could become addicted to the sight. "Perhaps. But once I let myself see past that, to understand why the worst thing I could ask of you was blind trust, I saw you differently. Your pain and confusion, but also the flashes of joy you kept close to your chest, your sharpness, your humour, your determination to keep fighting when I would have given up. You're not like anyone I've ever known. I wish we'd had more time, and that we'd met under better and more honest circumstances."

"Me, too. Though I guess you wouldn't have liked me much if you'd been a pampered prince instead of a bear. I can't imagine someone like that trying to soothe a commoner's cramps."

"You're probably right. Maybe my unfortunate circumstances have had a positive effect on me, after all."

He sat up and rolled his shoulders back, stretching. Sorra stayed where she was for a few seconds longer, reasoning that there couldn't possibly be anything wrong with enjoying the view even in the midst of disaster.

After all, small scraps of joy were sometimes the only thing that kept a person going.

Then she forced herself to sit up.

"Can we pretend this didn't happen?" she asked. "You go back to being a bear, I'll agree to marry you, you'll win the bet. I won't tell anyone what just happened if you won't."

"I'm sure she knows already," he said. "She has ways of hearing whatever she wishes to. She's probably laughing at me now, as I'm sure she was when you told me about your chaos blessing. I suspect I'll be gone by morning, taken to suffer the consequences of my defeat."

"Which are?"

"Nothing you need to worry about, now or after I'm gone."

He sat up straighter, steeling himself for what would come. Not death, surely, if Gwelain wanted him to inherit the throne, but a body could suffer quite a lot between his present state and death.

Sorra's jaw clenched painfully as she considered the unfairness of it all. Here sat a perfectly good prince who, if his more honest actions as a bear and his regret over his treatment of an insignificant subject reflected his true nature, might have made a fine king. When she imagined what could have happened if there had been no secrets, if there had only been himself as a talking bear who eased her pain and loneliness, who brought her trout and enjoyed her pies without shaming her for the burnt crusts, she thought she could have loved him. Not as she would a human, with physical attraction and all that came with it, but...

But there was never a chance.

She looked him over, taking in his human form. The physical change was astonishing, but the way he spoke hadn't changed, or the way she felt in his presence when he was most himself. Even discouraged and heartbroken he carried himself with the strength he'd had in another body, as though even the weight of a nation on his broad shoulders wouldn't break him.

He was beautiful in his sadness. She wondered what he'd be like if he were happy and free, and how it would feel to make him laugh.

"Where is this goblin queen's castle?" she asked. "Besides north in the Forgotten Lands."

He turned to her, surprised. "Why?"

"So I can rescue you."

He smiled at that. Not with hope or true happiness, but it was something. "That can't be done," he said. "In the old days many knights and heroes tried to steal Linnea's heart back from Gwelain. None of them ever returned to Andonia. But I do appreciate you wanting to try for my sake."

"Because no one else has?"

Beau's breath trembled, but his expression didn't change. If he felt anger or bitterness, he hid it better than Sorra usually managed. "Gwelain was careful about the terms of the agreement. My father can't send anyone after me or after Linnea's heart without shattering the peace he negotiated. I can only hope the time I've bought him is enough."

"You don't know?"

"No. Communication is forbidden. Will you promise not to tell anyone what I've told you? No letters. No visits. If my father gets word of any of this, it will be the end of his truce with Gwelain."

"Of course."

It all made sense in a terrible, logical way, but Sorra hated the king for abandoning Beau. If she deserved better than to be a pawn in a game against a wicked queen and her stolen magic, so did he.

She turned to face him, her toes brushing against the blanket that covered his thigh. "You must know something about where her castle is, though, if you've lived there for so long."

"East of the sun and west of the moon," he said.

"Is that the postal address?"

He smiled again, this time revealing straight, white teeth. "Perhaps. It's the only answer anyone has ever given me when I asked. I've never travelled to or from Gwelain's castle except by magic. She prefers that uninvited guests not be able to find her."

"So that's it?" Sorra didn't mean to sound angry but couldn't help it. "You're going to give up and accept that you're doing more good waiting than you could fighting?"

"I have no choice. If I run, the curse will return and whatever plans my father has made in my absence will be worthless." He sounded as though he'd reminded himself of it many times. "The only way I can serve Andonia is by doing nothing."

"Right." Sorra punched the mattress. It was silly and childish, but she had to do something. "This is ridiculous. The arrow led me to you for a reason."

"It did, but I don't think it's so you can die on an impossible rescue mission." He brushed his fingers down the left side of her face, tracing the edge of her birthmark. "You were born for a reason. You may not have your sisters' gifts, but you have your own, even if no one has cared to help you find them. You're more clever and interesting and beautiful than you think."

Sorra laughed. "It's been a while since you've been around humans, hasn't it?"

"Long enough to clear my mind." His jaw tightened. "You are meant for greater things than you could have found in your old life, and now you're free to turn away from Cottsbridge and its backward thinking. Will you promise me that you'll live a life that pleases you? I'll happily face my fate knowing my sacrifice is keeping you from harm, knowing you are pursuing a better life than you'd have had without my small part in it."

"I'll try," Sorra said. "It won't be easy as a wanted criminal. I told you the man I was accused of killing was a soldier on his way to the Gate?"

"You did. And I believe you'll find a way forward." He was still watching her, taking her in with human eyes that perhaps saw more than he'd noticed as a bear. Her cheeks warmed.

"May I kiss you before I go, Sorra?"

She liked how he said her name. Gently, like it was a thing of hope and not a warning of future sorrows. "Of course."

He moved closer, cautious and hesitant. She leaned forward to meet him, sinking into the warmth of his lips as they touched hers, breathing in the clean, wholly human scent of his skin. His hands cupped her face, holding her close, and she adjusted her position on the bed to allow herself to move freely, brushing her tongue over his lower lip, trailing a hand down his chest. Every movement stoked a liquid fire in her.

It was better than she'd hoped. Perfect in its uniquely tragic way.

"How long did you say we have before she takes you?" she asked, her lips barely leaving his.

"I don't know. I'd guess until we fall asleep."

Sorra trailed her lips over his jaw and his throat, revelling in his racing pulse. Desperation filled her—not pure lust, and certainly not anything like true love, but a mix of sorrow and rage and longing and regret. A hot tear rolled down her cheek, and she brushed it away before he could see.

There would be time for that later.

She tried not to think of goblin queens or royal destinies, letting herself sink instead into the sensations of his hands on her body as she shed her dress, his lips against her skin, his breath in her ear, whispering her name like a blessing.

His destiny would take him soon enough. For now, he was entirely hers.

CHAPTER TWENTY

$\mathbf{W}$ hen Sorra woke, she was alone.

Sunlight shone through the fabric at the windows, bathing the room in dim light. She'd been alone every morning since her arrival, but now the cabin seemed lonelier. Emptier. The bartender's potion had worked to chase away the morning-after sickness as he'd promised, but she still felt heartsick and hungry.

And a little sore after the night's exertions, but that was nothing to complain about. Holding off sleep had proved impossible in the end, but trying had been delightful.

And now there was nothing. She had tried to avoid the mayhem that followed her like a dust cloud after a herd of cattle, and all she'd done was call it to her more quickly.

Of all the times for Davina's advice to lead me astray...

But it hadn't. Davina had been right—Gwelain's tricks when she'd set Beau up for failure proved that it was a terrible idea to trust magical creatures. Her good advice had only led Sorra astray because she had thought Beau was the enemy.

Even when I'm right, I'm wrong. Even when I'm clever, I'm a fool.

She forced herself to sit up, then wandered naked to the kitchen. There were still a few bottles of that wretched drink left, and they'd dull the hurt for a while.

She raised a bottle to her lips, then set it down without drinking.

Nothing good would come of that. And she'd promised Beau— she couldn't think of him as Prince Beauregard—that she'd try to have a good life when he was gone.

She could still numb herself later if she changed her mind. For now, there were decisions to be made.

She tried to focus on them as she visited the outhouse, stoked the fire, boiled the kettle, and prepared a cup of the contraceptive herbs that Davina had insisted she bring along. One less worry, which only left a hundred more.

Sorra was a wanted criminal, and that wasn't going to change. The cabin was a safe place for now, though, and once Cottsbridge had settled down and learned to enjoy her absence, she might send a coded letter to Davina saying she was all right. Maybe Davina would join her, and they'd go on to better things despite the bounty the crown might already have placed on Sorra's head.

But it would be a long time before contact would be safe, and longer before she'd risk Davina's safety for the sake of her company. The thought of spending long days and evenings without even an overly reserved bear for company made her stomach turn.

Now that she knew Beau's secrets, she felt she could happily have spent a year with him in this cabin even if she never saw his human face again, but it was too late.

You did nothing wrong.

Beau's words. She supposed he was right, but that was how things went. In trying to avoid disaster she'd run into its arms. Not only for herself, but for Beau, who might have had a chance to escape if he'd met a different sort of woman in the woods.

But there had been no one else there to meet him. Only Sorra and her arrow.

Her destiny, which he'd insisted wasn't going to end here.

That, at least, was a pleasant thought. The cabin felt not only empty now but haunted by her mistakes and a goblin queen's cruel laughter. The worst thing she could do would be to stay long enough to get used to it.

Sorra finished her drink and washed the cup, then packed her things—clothes, knife, food, blankets. She didn't know where she intended to go, only that she couldn't stay at the cabin.

She pulled the bowl out from under the bed and counted the coins she'd stowed there, tossing each onto a jingling pile on the floor. It wasn't a fortune, but it might be enough for the supplies she'd need on the road, for food, for a cheap room.

And if the cave's magic still worked, she'd have as much as she could carry.

She was free. She could go anywhere, be anyone, try to escape her old identity and start a new life, grabbing onto scraps of happiness wherever she could for as long as possible in some large city. Queen's Run, maybe, where the strangers who bought the arrow had come from. Drinking, dancing, moving on when the blessing caused trouble.

It sounded like a good enough place to start, but something tugged at Sorra's mind like the arrow had before she'd loosed it, urging a different direction.

A few weeks ago, she'd have jumped at the chance to leave Cottsbridge behind with money in her pockets, but it no longer seemed like enough. Not when Beau was suffering unspeakable punishments in a castle east of the sun and west of the moon, somewhere in a land Andonia had forgotten.

But *she* hadn't forgotten. Every word Beau had spoken the night before was burned into her mind, playing over and over.

Gwelain was careful about the terms of the agreement. My father can't send anyone after me or after Linnea's heart without shattering the peace he negotiated.

King Ranthorn had bargained his son away for peace. Now he couldn't send anyone against Gwelain, and since she'd made the world forget her, no one had known to send themselves.

Until now.

Until me, the girl doomed to ruin everything.

It would have been funny if it hadn't been so horrifying.

Sorra dressed, hauled her knapsack onto her shoulders, and stepped out of the cabin. A blue jaybird sat on a low branch in one of the pines, watching her.

"I can't go after him," she said. "It's a stupid thought, right? This can't be my destiny."

The bird cocked its pretty head to one side.

"He said himself that it was impossible. A castle no one can find in a land no one knows anything about that's probably full of goblins and any number of other monsters. A jealous queen with Linnea's magic in her hands. He said knights and heroes had lost themselves on their quests, and I'm certainly less qualified than either. I'm destined by my blessing to *not* be a hero." Sorra paced the yard. "I mean, look what just happened. I've ruined everything for everyone. I—"

She froze in her tracks.

"Maybe that's it, then. Maybe this is what the blessing warned about, and now the debt of my birth is paid."

It was wishful thinking, but she couldn't dismiss it.

"What would I do if the blessing was gone? Or if I thought Beau was right and I could do better if I had the chance?"

The jaybird flapped away, apparently bored by the questions that had set her heart pounding.

"What if my greatest destiny is to find my way free?"

There was something to the idea, and she wished she could talk it through with Davina. She would understand it all better.

Sorra resumed her pacing, but when she reached the edge of the woods she didn't turn back. The shadows of the trees cast shifting patterns on the ground as she walked, lost in her thoughts.

"I know he's not my happy ending," she muttered, speaking just loud enough to keep her thoughts travelling in a straight line. "He's a prince and the heir to the throne. Even if I somehow saved him, it wouldn't lead to us being together."

She knew perfectly well what the previous night had been. She'd been there for his last moments of freedom, and it was natural enough that he'd want a bit of pleasure and human affection. It had been situational. Temporary. They'd both known it.

But there had to be more to her destiny, something beyond a night's comfort and the end of Beau's wager.

"And him saving me from hanging isn't it, either—there has to have been an easier way for the arrow to accomplish that. So why this? Why him?"

She tried to imagine what might come of it if she somehow did save him. Certainly not Beau back in her arms, but there would be rewards.

She remembered the big, ugly house being built by a man who'd done a favour for the king and had been showered in gold.

"Maybe this is my door to the better life Beau said I deserve," she said. "Surely King Ranthorn would offer me a pardon for a crime I didn't even commit and a reward I could use to start a whole new life for me and Davina."

She allowed herself to imagine it—her somehow succeeding where others had failed, rescuing Beau, returning him to his rightful place.

Being applauded and adored by people who mattered more than those who'd made her life so miserable.

Finding some way to be a hero instead of a barely competent excuse for a town villain.

No one, least of all Sorra herself, had expected anything of the sort from her, but there was something in her that wanted to try. Maybe a great destiny was out there waiting now that she was free to search for it.

Maybe the arrow had pointed to a happy ending, after all.

Her steps slowed. "It's entirely unlikely. Small attempts at significance have led me to enough trouble."

The jay let out a jeering shriek from somewhere in the forest.

"Good point." Sorra sighed. "If I go after him, there's a good chance it'll end in disaster. But if I don't try, I'll certainly die in either infamy or obscurity, and probably very soon. So why not try to be a hero for once and see if anything has changed? At least it's a direction."

With that undoubtedly foolish decision made, Sorra headed deeper into the forest, her mind filled with familiar dread and the fearful prospect of hope.

PART II

CHAPTER TWENTY-ONE

The village hadn't changed.

The fact of its sameness shouldn't have come as a surprise to Sorra—it had, after all, been only a day since her last visit—but it felt wrong that these people should be going about their lives as though the world hadn't tilted on its axis in the middle of the night.

The sun shone on the grey stone buildings, the thud of hammers echoed across the square, and the scent of warm bread hung thick in the air around the bakery. Sorra kept her eyes on the ground in front of her, one hand pressed to the pocket that held the handful of coins she'd picked up from the cave on the way down the mountain.

No more had appeared to replace them this time. Whatever magic Gwelain had been using to provide for Beau during his time away, it was gone. Between that fresh, if small, supply and what Sorra had collected the day before, she guessed she had enough for the supplies she'd need, but it wasn't nearly what she'd hoped for.

She bypassed the bakery, though her stomach protested, and stood facing the general store and the tavern. Supplies would be essential, but given the way their first meeting had ended it seemed possible the shopkeeper would bar the door. Information was important, too, and Pat the kindly bartender was at least a friendlier place to start.

Sorra opened the tavern's door slowly, then paused at the sound of conversation.

"…that boy of yours be back soon, then?" Pat asked.

"No." A woman's voice. "Even with the new ones gone up, Johnny's stuck for a good while yet."

Sorra pushed the door open a little wider, lighting the floor with a bar of sunlight as she stepped inside. Pat and the girl who had been sweeping the floor on Sorra's last visit looked up from the bar, which was covered by loose papers and a thick ledger. The girl wore a blue dress that was a little too long for her, its sleeves rolled up to her elbows, and she'd wrangled her hair into a messy braid.

Pat's eyebrows lifted in surprise. "Hello, again. How was your party last night?"

"Your potion served me well. Thank you again." Sorra wondered how far she could push the stranger's kindness, how much it was safe to reveal. Her first impulse was to confess everything and ask what he'd charge to take her to the Gate, but there was too much she didn't know about this village and its people.

Pat smiled politely. "Did you need something else?"

"No more drinks. But we're headed to the Gate now before we go home. I was wondering whether you could tell me what to expect there."

His eyes narrowed. "Your men don't know?"

"They've never been there. I thought since you live nearby you might know what it's like. Who's there. What lies beyond, whether there's a way through." Sorra paused. "That is, whether we should worry about anyone getting through from the north."

Pat glanced at the girl. "Tarla, why don't you go see about lunch?"

She crossed her arms. "It's too early."

He didn't answer, and the two locked gazes like dogs considering a fight. Then Tarla shrugged. "You're the boss."

Pat watched her go, then returned to his papers, sorting them into piles. "My sister," he said. "I probably can't tell you much she doesn't already know, but the less she thinks about the Gate, the better."

"She has a fellow up there?" Sorra asked, piecing together the scraps of conversation she'd overheard.

"She does. I'm afraid neither of us can offer you much advice, though. Soldiers coming back are tight-lipped about the Gate and whatever they've seen up there, and most of us around here don't care to ask questions. I know the Gate lies a good distance away, but I'd guess you'll be there by morning if you can keep up a good pace once you leave here. I've heard it lies in a deep and narrow pass. Might have heard there was a bit of a fortress tucked in there, but I'm not sure why I think that." He squeezed his eyes closed and shook his head. "Strange magic up there, and they carry it back with them. Some men hold on to memories for a while, some seem to forget everything before they get here. I once saw a man with half of his left arm missing, bandages still bloody, and he couldn't tell me how it happened. Or wouldn't, maybe, but I think he was already forgetting, and happy to do it."

"I see."

It wasn't anything different from what she'd heard at the Ambling Goat when the soldiers were frightening the new recruit with their returning memories, but now it seemed more real, more possible. There was a goblin queen somewhere up there who was doing everything she could to avoid receiving visitors, and this strange magic was a part of it.

Pat nodded politely, then returned his attention to his papers as though the Gate didn't interest him at all. Maybe that was a bit of magic, too.

There was his sister, though. If she had a connection to a soldier at the Gate, she'd have plenty of reason to keep her eyes and ears open.

"Thank you for your help," Sorra said as she backed away from the bar. "All of it."

Pat looked up and flashed a distracted smile. "Take care. And see whether you can convince your men to stop in here for a drink or two on the way back. I could use the business."

Sorra nodded, though her passing this way again seemed like a remote possibility at best.

As she stepped onto the street, Sorra narrowly avoided a collision with Tarla. The girl's hands were empty, and she made no move to enter the tavern after Sorra stepped aside.

"No luck with lunch?"

Tarla shrugged one shoulder. "I told him it was too early. You're really going to the Gate?"

"That's the plan." Sorra glanced over her shoulder and lowered her voice. "Could we speak in private?"

Tarla's brow furrowed. "Sure."

She led Sorra down the alley beside the tavern, which opened onto a path bordered by a rickety wooden fence that wouldn't do much to keep drunk patrons from falling into the river rushing by on the other side. Tarla stooped to pick a daisy from among the wildflowers growing around its posts, then leaned on the fence and looked out over the river.

Sorra stood beside her and tried to take up an equally relaxed posture. "I didn't mean to eavesdrop, but I overheard you saying you know someone at the Gate."

Tarla smiled down at the daisy as she plucked its petals one by one and released them to be carried away by the river. "Johnny, yeah. His bunch stayed here longer than most, fixing the bridge before they went up. Gave us time to get to know each other."

"Have you seen him since?"

"Nah. They don't give them time off, or at least they don't let them travel until their time at the Gate is up. Just letters." She turned to Sorra, one eyebrow arched. "Why?"

"I wondered whether you could tell me whether his letters have said anything about what's on the other side, whether he's been there, what he might have seen."

Tarla laughed under her breath. "He couldn't tell me anything if he wanted to. Letters get read by the higher-ups, incoming or outgoing. Not much room for embarrassing declarations of love when a fellow's worried about his superiors teasing him, but we get by." When she'd plucked the last petal, she threw the flower's bare stem into the river. "Why do you ask?"

"Just curious. The soldiers I'm with don't know much, so I thought I'd ask around since I was in for supplies anyway."

"Ah." Tarla tilted her head to one side. "And where are they? The soldiers, I mean. I've never met any who wouldn't insist on stopping at the tavern for a quick nip." She didn't make it sound like a challenge, but Sorra's shoulders tensed.

"Waiting for me at the road. I should get back to them." Sorra adjusted her knapsack's straps and stepped away.

"Wait." Tarla scuffed at the ground with the toe of her worn leather shoe. "I didn't say I don't know anything, I just said Johnny hasn't told me anything. I pick things up here and there. I'm observant, like. And I know the trick of remembering what doesn't want to be remembered."

"Such as?"

Tarla leaned back against the fence. The joints creaked, and Sorra feared it would dump the girl into the river. "Such as tales of groups of heroes who passed through here more than a hundred years ago. They never came back, or so the stories say. And they were the last ones to go into the Forgotten Lands. Know why?"

"No."

"Because going through the Gate is illegal. They catch anyone trying it, into Andonia or out…" Tarla drew her thumb across her throat. "I'm not even supposed to go up to visit Johnny, they're that strict about it. Maybe if I went with you and your soldiers, though, it would be all right. Think I could tag along?"

Sorra hesitated, and Tarla smiled. There was something shrewder about her than anything Sorra had seen in her brother.

"Don't worry, I'm not going to tell anyone," Tarla said. "But if you were asking about what's on the other side because you want to get through—and I don't think that's advisable, mind you—I might be willing to help."

"How? Not that I'm planning anything of the sort. I'm just curious."

"Yes, and I'm sure your soldiers are curious, too." Tarla flashed another sly smile, but it faded quickly. "You could deliver a letter to Johnny for me. It won't get you anywhere, but delivering it would give you a reason for showing up. I could say in the letter how you're a new friend, and that he should talk to you over a meal before he sends you back. I can't tell him plainly that you want to get through, but we've gotten good at hinting, and you can tell him the rest yourself. I can't say for sure he'll help, and even if he gets you through, you'll never make it to the Forgotten Lands, but it's better odds than you'd have without our help."

Alarm bells rang in Sorra's mind.

"That's very kind of you," she said. "I don't often meet people who make such generous offers to strangers. Is it that difficult to get a letter delivered?"

Tarla's freckled cheeks flushed pink, but she didn't look away. "It is. But I was thinking perhaps I'd also tell Johnny about how extremely generous you've been, leaving me coin to save for when me and him get married. If that happened, he'd be more likely to help. And I guess I might think of a few more things you need to know before you go up there."

"I see."

Sorra leaned on the fence and watched the sun flashing on the water, calculating how much money she had left. She needed to hold on to as much as she could for supplies and lodgings and anything else she might need on her journey, but coins would do her no good if the soldiers at the Gate arrested her for trying to sneak through.

The girl might be taking advantage. But the alternative was to move ahead knowing nothing, and ignorance had never worked out well for Sorra.

"There's no other way to get north?" she asked.

"Not one."

"And why do you say I wouldn't find the Forgotten Lands? Assuming I was looking for them. Which I'm not."

"'Course not." Tarla frowned, though not at Sorra. "I'm not sure why I said that, to be honest. It's one of those hard-to-remember things. Like I have this whiff of an idea, but when I look straight at it, it's gone. The trick is to think of something else and catch the memory out of the corner of your mind, then say it aloud before it's gone. I suppose I could try to remember if only I were motivated..."

Sorra sighed and dug a few coins out of her pocket. "See if this helps."

Tarla wrinkled her nose at the offering, but the coins vanished into a pouch on her belt. "Give me a moment." She hummed a gentle tune under her breath, then stopped suddenly. "You can't get there by trying to get there."

Sorra stood up straighter. "What does that mean?"

"Damned if I know. It's just…" Tarla's voice trailed off, and she sighed. "I don't know. Must've heard it somewhere. Is that enough to change your plans, or do we have a deal?"

Sorra rested her face in her hands. Everyone in her life these days seemed determined to plant more questions and doubts in her mind when all she wanted was answers.

I can still change my mind if I get there, she reminded herself. *One step at a time is progress, even if the road ahead is dark.*

"I'll need one other thing," she said. "How well do you know the woman who runs the store?"

"Marie? Well enough."

"Good. Will you put in a good word for me before you go off to write your letter? Our last conversation ended on an awkward note."

"Might be possible." Tarla grinned. "We do love to see a stranger who's willing to generously support the local economy."

For Beau, Sorra reminded herself. *For one last chance to be better than anyone expected.*

"Fine," she sighed. "How much of a contribution should I make to your wedding fund?"

Less than an hour later Sorra waited at the edge of town, counting far fewer coins among her possessions and having lost her silver bracelet in the bargain, but with the addition of a sturdier backpack, a bedroll and a flimsy tent, a small lamp and spare oil, matches waterproofed with wax, a new hunting knife, a water skin, a warm coat, and as much food as she could carry. She'd also purchased a pale cosmetic cream that the shopkeeper swore would cover her birthmark. Sorra wasn't sure it would be enough to hide her identity if she bumped into any of the soldiers she'd met in

Cottsbridge, but it, like Tarla's letter, would at least improve her odds.

It didn't seem likely that the hideous yellow sweater she now wore would do the same, but the shopkeeper seemed to be drowning in them and wouldn't let Sorra go without taking one.

She had only been waiting a few minutes when Tarla jogged up the road and handed her a letter sealed with red wax.

"There you go, miss. Don't speak to anyone but Johnny about your questions, right? He's trustworthy, but I wouldn't trust any of the others with my drink, let alone my life. He'll be the young fellow with hair so pale it's just about white. Hard to miss."

Sorra tucked the letter into her coat pocket. "Anything you'd like me to tell him when we meet?"

"No. Only something I need to tell you." A grave expression shadowed Tarla's thin features. "Don't stray from the road. There's funny magic around here, and it only gets funnier as you go north. If you leave the road, maybe if you so much as look back, you'll get turned around and find yourself elsewhere. Could be back here, could be some southern town, could be anywhere except headed toward whatever's up there." She looked past Sorra at the empty road and the fields beyond. "I suppose your soldier companions knew about that, though."

Sorra gave her a tight smile. "Of course. I'll remind them when we meet up, just in case."

Tarla rolled her eyes, then spun and raced back toward the village.

Sorra checked the position of the afternoon sun to be sure of her direction and headed north, telling herself she had nothing to fear from magic, funny or otherwise.

It was a lie, but lying was the only way she could keep her feet moving.

CHAPTER TWENTY-TWO

Sorra kept the sun to her left until it set, not daring to step off the road for anything. When she needed to eat, she nibbled on the hard cheese she'd bought at the general store. When she felt thirsty, she drank the water strapped to her knapsack, and when that ran dry, she went without, not daring to descend to a fast-flowing stream that beckoned her with its musical babbling.

The temptation to leave a marker and step off the road to test Tarla's advice was nearly unbearable, but Sorra carried on in spite of it, in spite of legs that grew sore from walking uphill, and in spite of the invisible companion she imagined sitting on her shoulder, whispering in her ear.

Goblins.

Magic.

A queen who cursed a nation.

Heroes have failed.

You will fail.

It was the same voice she'd heard before at low moments, but clearer and louder. She couldn't shut it out, but she could keep moving forward.

Sorra chose a high mountain peak and kept it in her view even when it became nothing more than a black point set against the stars. When the sky clouded over and she couldn't see even that, she kept her eyes on the road, walking close to its edge and making sure the grasses and bushes nearest to her stayed on her right side.

As her energy flagged, it took what little optimism she still had with it.

This was another mistake.

You're going to feel foolish when you fail.

"At least that will be familiar territory," she said. Maybe the circumstances of her birth meant that failure was inevitable, that chaos would always walk beside her like her shadow, that she would never be great or even good like her sisters no matter what her intentions.

So be it.

"Beau was right." She spoke quietly, but doing so made it easier to focus on her own voice and not the other, less welcome one. "I could make doing no harm my life's greatest goal. Or I could try for better, knowing I'll probably fail. At least that's doing something. At least it's living. If I don't, I might as well die right here and be done with it. If this is my greatest destiny, I can't turn my back on it yet."

The voice fell silent, leaving Sorra feeling more alone but a little more hopeful.

Hours later the sky lightened, its suffocating blackness fading to charcoal and then a misty purple as the sun fought its way into the sky, its light diffusing through the uniform layer of clouds overhead. It had been hours since Sorra had been able to convince herself that she wasn't walking in place, but there, just ahead and barely visible through the fog that lay over the road, stood two rocky slopes with a deep cut between them.

Soon, more details became clear. The pass was four times as wide as the road but had been blocked off by a wall made from logs standing on end. As she walked closer, Sorra realized they must have once been the trunks of trees taller and broader than any she'd ever seen, some with bases as large as the cabin she'd left behind. They created an imposing barrier and made the massive door of iron bars set into the wall look laughably small by comparison. Torches burned on either side of the door, leaving whatever lay beyond it in shadow.

The faint scents of smoke and burnt food touched the air, but the world was silent.

Wooden platforms jutted out from the sheer cliffs that formed the sides of the pass, dizzyingly high and accessible only by way of zig-zagging wooden staircases that rose out of the fog bank. The mountains stretched to the east and west, with no other pass, path, or passage to the other side in view.

There didn't seem to be anyone standing guard on the wall, but if there were lookouts on the platforms, they'd probably seen her already. She stopped for long enough to smear a fresh layer of make-up on her face, and as she approached the entrance, she reminded herself that coming to the Gate was stupid but not technically illegal, as long as no one caught her trying to pass through.

But they could kill you and no one would ever know.

"Or they could offer me breakfast and a place to nap," she whispered, and pulled up the hood of her coat to cover her hair. "I'll explain that I've brought a letter for Johnny and go from there."

The voice had no answer for that, which satisfied Sorra.

She stuck her head between two of the widely spaced iron bars that made up the entrance gate. Beyond them, a short, dark tunnel led through the wall and into the fog on the other side.

"Hello?" she called. "Is anyone there?"

Nothing. No voices, no movement. The hairs on the back of Sorra's neck prickled.

"Anyone?" she called again, but more quietly, suddenly afraid of who might answer.

She looked down at her feet, still stubbornly pointing north as they'd been all night. Before she could think her way out of it, she removed her knapsack and passed it through the bars, did the same with her heavy coat, and then squeezed her body through.

Terrible security, she thought, then remembered that any threat they needed to hold back wouldn't be coming from the south.

Still, someone should have been standing guard.

She put her coat back on, then her bag, and stood in the darkness of the tunnel.

What next, brave adventurer?

Before she could answer, a creaking noise reached her from

somewhere ahead, notable only because of the silence that surrounded it.

Sorra's breath came shorter and shallower as she made her way toward the yard she could now make out at the end of the tunnel, a wide space flanked by wood-plank huts huddled against the mountain walls on either side. The shapes were still indistinct, shrouded in fog so thick it seemed like a heavy cloud had settled in the pass. Two small fires burned low somewhere not far ahead, glowing in the haze.

She stepped out of the tunnel and tripped over a pair of outstretched legs.

"Sorry! I didn't—" She stopped, her voice and breath stolen as she realized there was no face to offer an apology to. Nothing above the waist at all save for a dark puddle of blood spread over the flat stone floor of the pass.

Sorra's heart hammered as she forced herself to lift her gaze. The upper body, still dressed in a rumpled soldier's jacket, lay some distance away, its innards trailing out to point back at the legs it had left behind.

A violent spasm seized Sorra's body, but there was nothing for her heaving stomach to eject as she turned away. The nausea passed, leaving her dizzy and sweating.

There should be an alarm. Someone must know. Someone must have seen.

The sun cleared the mountains, brightening the yard and cutting through the fog, turning the vague shapes of buildings into things more solid and real. Sorra made herself focus on them, on the black pot hanging over one of the cookfires and the faint smell of burnt stew.

On anything but the mutilated corpses of Andonian soldiers that littered the yard.

The creaking noise continued. Sorra followed it, turning to her right, finding a high wooden scaffold with three naked bodies hanging from it, swinging in the nearly non-existent breeze.

The cruel voice had fallen silent, and Sorra's other thoughts became muffled and distant. She stepped forward, more out of habit than decision, and vaguely considered the idea that whoever had done this might still be around.

The battle was over. The soldiers who guarded the Gate had been soundly defeated. But it would be dangerous to assume the enemy was gone.

Hide, she told herself. *And be quiet.*

There was still no sense of panic, but the thought got her feet moving toward the half-open door of a building to her left. Her steps wove drunkenly through the yard as she avoided pools of blood and splayed bodies, some with gaping chest wounds, others with their throats torn out in ragged chunks, some missing arms or legs or heads. A few had died from clean wounds made by weapons that had been discarded nearby, but much of the damage looked like it might have been done by a pack of animals.

Or monsters.

As she passed, Sorra looked them over with a distant, clinical eye that frightened her as much as the bodies themselves.

She should have been horrified, but her emotions seemed to have been heaved out of her back by the first corpse. But her limbs trembled, and warm tears slid down her cheeks as though her body might be feeling what her mind couldn't.

She hesitated outside the long wooden building on the western side of the pass, then stepped inside when doing so felt safer than staying where she was. Lamps burned inside a barracks with rows of cots along the walls. More bodies on the floor, a few of them half-dressed as though they'd been roused from sleep to join the battle and hadn't quite made it. The air smelled of sweat and blood and human filth, but Sorra barely noticed it as she approached the body lying diagonally across a cot near the door. The soldier had a sword pushed through his chest and a look of confusion lingering on his youthful face.

His hair was like cornsilk, so pale it was almost white.

Sorra drew the letter out from her coat pocket and set it in his hand, then sank to the floor with her back against the wall.

No wedding for poor Johnny.

With that thought came a deep ache that cracked the dam holding back the terror that now flooded Sorra's mind and body.

Her trembling hands felt like ice as she pressed them to her mouth to hold back sobs that might alert an enemy to her presence.

Dozens of soldiers, all dead. She wondered how many of them had passed through Cottsbridge and stopped for a drink at the Ambling Goat, what kinds of lives they'd left behind, how many of them would be missed and mourned.

Her breath came quicker and shallower until she was gasping for air, crushed beneath the weight of the horrors that surrounded her.

She wasn't sure how much time passed before the flood slowed and she lifted her head, wiping away tears she feared might never stop.

Nothing more had happened. No one had called out to other survivors or come through to hunt them down and finish them off. She'd arrived after the end of the battle, after the end of everything for the men of the Gate.

She got to her feet and walked into the yard. Her legs had stiffened and her muscles ached from her night of walking, but her thoughts couldn't run free while she sat still. The air was warming with each passing minute, and the stomach-turning smells of death hung heavier in the air than they had before.

The bodies still swayed at the ends of their ropes on the scaffold opposite the barracks. They'd looked human enough at a glance, but now, with the fog nearly gone, there was something wrong about them.

What caught her attention first were the long tails hanging behind bare legs. One was thin and tufted at the end like a cow's, one scaled like a black snake's. The other ended in a scarred-over stump close to the creature's backside.

And then there were the legs themselves, which ended in feet that weren't quite like any animal's that Sorra had ever seen—long like a dog's hind feet but scaled, not furred, with bird-like toes ending in vicious claws.

Clawed hands, too, though two of the creatures had ground theirs down to the quick, or had it done for them.

The bodies appeared largely human otherwise, but swollen, their skin mottled with settled blood. The faces, too, might have looked almost human, though their open mouths revealed sharp teeth where they weren't hidden by the creatures' swollen, lolling tongues.

Sorra stumbled to the ground, where at least the mutilated corpses were human.

The soldiers in Cottsbridge had said goblins didn't look like they did in stories, where they were always smaller, with thick muscles and green skin.

"Is that why they attacked?" she asked one of the human bodies at her feet. "Because you killed those goblins?"

That didn't seem right. If the attackers had been avenging these creatures, they'd have taken the bodies with them, not left them to rot.

In any case, what was done was done, which once again left her with the question of her next steps.

Going back to the village seemed like the reasonable thing. She could report what she'd seen and get a message to the king about the Gate being vulnerable and unguarded.

She frowned, thinking of the locked gate at the Andonian side of the pass.

"They could have gotten through," she whispered. The attackers had defeated dozens of soldiers but hadn't swarmed down the road to continue their hunt on Andonian soil.

Because they couldn't. Not if they were Gwelain's goblins, and not as long as Beau was upholding his father's end of his deal.

A random attack, then? Or a warning?

And if it was a warning, who was it meant for?

She waited for the unwanted voice in her head to chime in with a suggestion, but it had never been good for much besides reminders of her worthlessness. There was no need for it to speak up now, when the enormity of her unpreparedness was staring her in the face, written in garish blood spatters and shards of broken bone.

Sorra made her way to the buildings on the other side of the yard, where an open stable housed the remains of three horses that had been stripped of much of their flesh.

So had the five soldiers who lay beside them, their skeletons dressed in little more than blood and a few entrails.

The attack was a warning for King Ranthorn, surely. A reminder of the fragility of the truce, or something more specific Sorra couldn't begin to guess at.

She looked over the wreckage in the stable and the yard, at bodies that had once held human souls.

The other possibility—that Gwelain had heard her conversation with Beau, knew she was coming, and had left this gruesome gift to turn her away—was almost too horrible to contemplate.

They'd have waited to attack me if that were the case, she thought. *A ruthless queen wouldn't leave a warning when she could just as easily see her enemy dead, which means this has nothing to do with me.*

There was some comfort in the idea, horrible as it was.

She stopped next to the body of a dark-haired soldier, lean and sharp-featured, recognizable even with claw-marks slashing across his face. She remembered him playing cards, accusing Stuart of cheating. The one beside him, too—the dealer who had told the story about her sisters. One of them might have killed his roommate and started the chain of events that had led Sorra to finding them here, but she still couldn't imagine that either had deserved to die this way.

Anger stirred within her, and she welcomed it. If she'd been in Cottsbridge, she'd have tamped it down for fear of it burning out of control, but there was no one here she might harm with it.

It felt right to let it rage as she considered the situation she'd stepped into.

A land erased from memory. Massacred soldiers. A queen so powerful a king had offered his heir as a sacrifice to appease her.

Any wise person would turn back. Such a person might be heartbroken to leave a good prince to a terrible fate, but she'd understand that he'd face it no matter what she did.

"The question is whether I want to be wise." Her voice rang out across the silent courtyard, and from somewhere beyond the northern wall, a crow answered with a harsh, rasping caw.

The king would learn of this soon enough, either when a fresh crop of soldiers came or when his army's commanders didn't receive some expected communication. Security might be increased as a response to the attack.

But no one would venture into the Forgotten Lands, even if they knew how to get there. No one would pursue justice, and nothing would change for Beau, except that the king might weep with gratitude for his son's selfless sacrifice that kept Gwelain's violence from spilling into Andonia.

As far as Sorra was concerned, the king could stuff his gratitude up his ass far enough that he choked on it.

The wise thing would be to forget all this, to let Gwelain's message stand. This was the business of kings and queens, not inexperienced young women from a town most of Andonia had probably forgotten.

But if she didn't try to do something, no one else would. Gwelain had made sure of it.

Sorra gritted her teeth. "I'll be damned if I let you win, you royal bitch."

A wide gate stood open at the north end of the pass, offering passage into whatever dangers lay beyond.

It was too easy, and obviously foolish.

Maybe that's why destiny chose me, she thought as she filled her water skin at the well. *No one else would be stupid enough to do this.*

Sorra left the dead soldiers and continued north without looking back.

CHAPTER TWENTY-THREE

Sorra left summer behind her at the Gate. Snow fell in light flurries that dusted the road and melted in her hair. Still, she grew warm as she walked, and before long she'd opened her coat to reveal the hideous yellow sweater beneath.

The pass opened into pine-and-brush forest that pressed close against the downward-sloping road on both sides. There was no wind, and the snow piling gently on rocks and branches gave everything a feeling of sameness no matter how Sorra scanned her surroundings for some way to mark her progress. There was no direction without the sun, and no time. The mountain peaks to the south might have provided comforting perspective, but she didn't dare glance back.

She didn't know whether Tarla's warning about keeping her eyes ahead still applied, so she followed the rule as well as she could, even when a branch snapped somewhere deep in the forest to her right. If her focus or her feet strayed, she might find herself in Cottsbridge, waking as if from a dream, or on the smoggy streets of a large southern city where smokestacks belched filth into the sky and no one knew their neighbours' names.

And then there was Tarla's other piece of advice—*you can't get there by trying to get there.* Put together, they made an impossibility.

She kept walking, and under the overcast sky nothing seemed to change. Then, as she was contemplating removing her coat entirely so as not to build up a layer of sweat that would only freeze later, a crossroads came into view ahead. Sorra picked up her pace, pleased to have found some sign that she wouldn't be walking forever into this strange forest.

As there was no sign to indicate direction or what she might find down any of the three new roads, she kept going straight, hoping she was still heading north. The road tended as it had before—straight, snowy, with nothing to distinguish it from the one she'd been following for what felt like hours. When she came to another crossroads, she was ready to walk straight through again until she noticed the shadow of footprints dusted over by a thin layer of snow. They passed from the road to her left and continued on to her right, leaving faint trails behind the heels where the traveller's boots had scuffed along.

Perhaps they're as tired as I am, Sorra thought, and backed up to see her own footprints, which left similar trails.

Not similar. The same.

Same footprint. Same stride. Same scuffs.

She hadn't stopped. She hadn't turned, and neither had the road. She was certain the gentle downward slope of the mountain hadn't changed, but somehow she'd looped to the west and come back to the same crossroads again.

That only left one road to try if she didn't want to turn back to the Gate. She continued down the untracked road, more alert to her surroundings than she'd been before.

She soon came to the crossroads again. More snow had fallen, but the footprints were there, barely visible.

Sorra gritted her teeth and charged up the road to her left. All it earned her was a fresher view of the footprints when she returned to the crossroads.

Several sets of hers now, and another had joined them. Not boots, but the sort of footprints that might be left by a massive bird of prey, with long toes spread wide, each punctuated at its end by a hole where the tip of a curved claw had sunk into the snow.

A solid line traced between the footprints where a long tail had dragged along the ground.

Sorra fought to breathe as she remembered the scaled legs and vicious claws of the creatures hanging at the Gate. Her imagination offered her the image of one of them following her—not as it would have looked in life, but a bloated, mottled corpse with its dead tongue hanging from between teeth that could rip her throat out in a single bite if it chose to offer her a quick, merciful death.

She carried on, following the strange footprints, hoping she'd catch a glimpse of her pursuer from behind so she could turn and run down another road.

The crossroads again, now with more and fresher footprints—hers and the monster's. She told herself it was only one girl, only one monster, but still imagined a second goblin joining the first, sniffing the air.

Or maybe stepping off the road to wait for her to pass.

Tears traced down her cheeks, cooling as they reached her chin.

I don't want to be a hero.

Panic seized her. She held tight to the straps of her knapsack and ran, her breath coming in short gasps.

Moments later scuffling footsteps came up behind her as her nightmare pursuer sacrificed stealth for speed.

Sorra didn't look back before she changed course, stepping off the road and into the trees, darting between trunks and veering around patches of low, leafless bushes that grabbed at her skirt as she passed. The heavy knapsack swung every time she changed direction, throwing off her balance.

The sounds behind her grew louder, and she caught the raspy breath of something that was drawing closer with every step. A mad, barking laugh rang out deep in the forest ahead, freezing Sorra's blood. Seconds later something moved between the trees to her right, quick and agile.

She veered to the left and let out a scream of fear and frustration. A fallen tree blocked her path, too tall to run around before the goblins would catch up. She climbed, grabbing onto branches and digging her boots into the wet bark, but the weight of her pack pulled her toward the ground. With a grunted curse, she slipped the straps off her shoulders and left the knapsack—her food, her water, her blankets, and most of her coin—behind, then dug her fingers into the rough bark and hauled herself over the tree, landing hard on the other side. Free from the extra weight, she ran faster than she ever had before, feeling like the only solid thing in a world that blurred around her. Her lungs burned and her breath came in ragged gasps, but her blood still flowed in her veins, and all she knew was that she wanted to keep it that way.

I want to go home, she thought. *Back to the Gate. To the smoggy city. Anywhere in Andonia where goblins can't follow.*

The ground under her feet disappeared, and Sorra pitched forward, grasping at nothing as she plunged toward a roaring river she hadn't heard over her own panicked breath.

CHAPTER TWENTY-FOUR

The frigid water burned the exposed skin of Sorra's hands and face as the current dragged her down into frozen darkness. She opened her eyes and clawed at the water to drag herself toward the light above, but she was too heavy.

Instead of fighting the river, she fought her coat, which the current had caught like a sail. Her chest screamed for breath, and Sorra battled the urge to take in water and let the adventure end.

She freed one arm, and the river did the rest, grabbing on to the heavy wool coat and dragging it away from her, carrying in its pockets the last of her coin. A dark shape appeared ahead. Sorra shielded her face with her arms as she slammed into a boulder, already too numb from the cold to feel anything. The river pushed her over it, and her head broke the surface.

Sunlight shone around her, and the air was blessedly warm as she sucked in a breath before the water pulled her under again. The air made her stronger and cleared her mind. She kicked off her boots and, freed of their weight, she surfaced again, forcing her unfeeling arms and legs to paddle her clumsily into the shallows where long grasses provided handholds she used to drag herself out of the water.

She stood and stumbled forward, but her legs wouldn't hold her up. The ground met her more gently than she might have expected, with a thick bed of fallen leaves that gave off a pleasant, earthy odour as they crumbled beneath her. She lay on her chest, her cheek pressed to the earth, too tired to care about goblins or princes or anything but the bliss of each aching breath.

The unfamiliar forest felt like a world entirely separate from the one Sorra had left behind—warm, richly fragrant, alive with bird-song, and safer than any place she could remember.

At least I'm somewhere, she thought. She didn't care where as long as the magic or the river had carried her far from Gwelain's doorstep, goblins, and endlessly repeating crossroads.

Adventure was grand only as long as it was shiny and new. When it became bloodstained and dangerous and horribly real it hardly seemed a thing worth fighting for. She hadn't properly considered the cost, and it was beyond clear now that she wasn't qualified for heroism or anything like it.

Someone else will have to save Beau. She rolled onto her back to look into the sunlit leaves above her. *The king can't send anyone to do it, but I haven't made any foolish agreements saying I can't find someone else to take on a quest.*

Dying in obscurity would be sad, but at least a person might get some sleep while doing it. And letting go of the idea of a pardon wouldn't be too hard—the odds of her earning one had been ridiculously slim to begin with.

They were reasonable ideas, and probably ones she should have thought of before she'd made the mistake of leaving the cabin. They didn't bring relief, though. Only a familiar sense that she'd failed, that she wasn't enough, that she never could be.

He told me not to try.

But I wish he could know that I did my best anyway. I wish I could see him one more time before someone else saves him and he goes back to being too important to bother with people like me.

Sorra let herself rest until sleep threatened to take her, then forced herself back to her feet and took stock of her situation.

The goblins were gone. So were her supplies, her coin, her boots, and everything else. It felt unfair, but she doubted complaining to the gods, the birds, or anyone else would change anything.

Dead leaves crunched under her squelching socks as she started into the forest.

She hadn't walked far when the sound of a baby's cries reached her. Her stomach clenched at the sound, but she followed it to a shack with wood slat walls and a sway-backed roof. Its porch had collapsed, but a woman sat on a wooden chair among its ruins, her eyes closed, apparently lost in sleep even as the wailing inside the shack continued.

"Ma'am?"

The woman, whose plain brown dress and white bonnet seemed comically old-fashioned to Sorra, opened her eyes slowly. The pale skin around them was lightly traced with lines. "What?"

"Are you all right?"

The woman stared at her, and Sorra realized she must look frightful with her damp clothes, shoeless feet, and tangled hair. She plucked a dead leaf off the front of her horrid yellow sweater and let it fall.

"Who're you?" the woman asked. She still seemed half-asleep. "You new?"

"I suppose so. Ma'am, is your baby—"

The woman waved a hand dismissively at the open doorway behind her. "You a hero, then?"

Sorra felt as though an invisible cockroach had skittered up the back of her neck. "Pardon?"

The woman leaned forward, her hands still folded in her lap. "Are you a hero, or are you lost?" She spoke slowly, as though Sorra might be incredibly stupid.

Sorra looked around again at the shack and the unfamiliar forest. "Where are we?"

"Not a hero, then." The woman sighed. "Where were you headed?"

Sorra smiled as pleasantly as she could. "This might not make sense to you if I'm too far off course, but I was looking for the Forgotten Lands."

"Huh. Is that what they're calling it now? Well, guess you made it."

Sorra's heart leapt, and her stomach sank.

The woman leaned to one side and spat on the ground. "My condolences."

The baby continued to wail as Sorra gripped the damp fabric of her skirt, trying to ground herself.

You can't get there by trying to get there.

Finding the Forgotten Lands had been the last thing on her mind when she'd run from the goblins, but thanks to them, she'd done the impossible. If such a thing had happened to one of her sisters or a person in a story, Sorra would have called it good luck.

Given her history, she felt like a fly landing at the edge of a spider's web.

But the road ahead was open, even if everything beyond her next step was buried in shadow.

One foot in front of the other, she reminded herself. *Eyes ahead.*

"Thank you," she said. "I don't suppose you know how to get to the castle."

The woman settled into her chair again. "No more than anyone knows, no more than I care to. You should go."

"But I don't know where I'm going."

The woman closed her eyes and didn't answer.

"Ma'am? Why did you ask if I'm a hero?"

"Who else has ever come here?" The woman shrugged. "You don't look like much to me, but I thought you might still be better than the one we've got now."

"Who do you have?"

The baby let out a long wail, and the woman grumbled as she stood and climbed through the open doorway into the cabin. The crying faded to a hitching whimper as she emerged and lowered herself to the ground clutching a baby wrapped in a dirty blanket.

She held it out to Sorra. "Here, lost girl. Help me with this burden for a time."

Sorra took a step back. "I can't, I'm sorry."

The baby looked blankly up at her, its face still red and damp with sweat.

Its mother set her jaw and nodded. "Guess maybe you are a hero, then. They never offer the sort of help a person really needs. Go on, then. The fellow you're looking for is usually up the road somewhere, or was last I heard. Been a while. Could be dead for all I know."

"I wasn't actually looking for—" Sorra said, but the woman climbed back into the cabin, hauling herself up with her free hand while the other held the baby, and slammed the door behind her.

"—anyone specific," Sorra whispered.

The idea of a hero was promising. Beau and Tarla had both said none had come here for more than a century, but perhaps they'd left descendants, or maybe this place had its own heroes who might be willing to take a quest off her hands.

The forest seemed colder and more menacing now that Sorra knew where she was. She'd escaped the goblins by running straight into their country, and for all she knew they were still following her trail.

An overgrown path led away from the cabin, and Sorra followed it to a road much like the one she'd left behind in Andonia, made of flat stones set into the ground. To her left, it ran straight through the forest. To her right, it disappeared in a broad curve, obscuring her view of what lay beyond.

Sorra went right. The deceitful road beyond the Gate had seemed straight but had led her astray. At least this one was honest about its turns.

The forest ended not far past the curve, opening onto grain fields bathed in hazy sunlight. A white farmhouse and a red barn beckoned, promising human company, water, food, and a place to rest. Sorra convinced her legs to keep walking.

When she stepped off the road and into the dirt yard in front of the farmhouse, she found that the setup wasn't quite as pretty as it had seemed at a distance. The white paint on the house was cracked and peeling, several planks were missing from the walls of the barn behind it, and the little vegetable garden next to the house was overrun with weeds between rows of yellow squash. A few musty haystacks slouched at the edge of the yard, but there was no sign of animals that might make use of them. There wasn't even an old dog left to guard the front door, which only added to the disused atmosphere of the place.

The pump near the barn was spotted with rust, but daisies

bloomed beneath the dripping spout. Sorra ran to it, suddenly overwhelmed by thirst, and pumped until cold, clear water flowed. There was no cup and no bucket, so she gathered it in her hands between pumps and brought it to her mouth. She hadn't realized how parched her lips were until water touched them, and she thought she might drink until she exploded.

Someone cleared their throat.

When she looked up, an old man with leathery skin stood between her and the house, staring at her from the shadows beneath his broad-brimmed straw hat.

"Hello." Sorra remembered again how frightful she must look and offered her friendliest smile to make up for it. "I hope you don't mind me drinking your water."

He didn't say anything, but his lips moved rhythmically, like he was sucking on his teeth behind them. There was no expression on his face otherwise, no sign of whether he was angry or frightened or completely indifferent to her presence.

A small boy, perhaps three years old, wearing nothing but sagging trousers held up by suspenders, wandered out of the house and picked up a stick from the ground. Without looking at Sorra, he made his way to the side of the yard, where a brown chicken lay dead in the dirt. The child hitched up his pants, sighed like an adult about to begin a long day at work, and began poking the corpse's eye with the stick.

Sorra's stomach tightened, though she wasn't sure why. The man was odd and the child was strangely incurious about their visitor, but perhaps they were only a little dull.

"You have a lovely farm," she said.

The farmer glanced at the house and the barn, then over the fields, blinking as though awakening from a dream. "I suppose."

The child kept poking at the dead chicken, indifferent to their conversation. Something about it all made Sorra want to scream.

"Could you—" she began, but stopped when the farmer's eyes widened. He wasn't looking at her, but beyond her, up the road to where a cloud of dust had appeared beyond a field of ripe corn.

"Go," he rasped, and shooed her toward the barn. "Get up. Hide."

She didn't argue. In a few paces, she'd reached the barn, her exhaustion forgotten as she climbed a rickety ladder onto the floor of a low hayloft that bowed under her weight. She crouched next to a wide hole in the wall, able to see and hear what was happening in the yard below but, she hoped, hidden from whatever had lit a fire in the old farmer.

The little boy shuffled around the chicken, placing it between himself and the road to watch as the dust cloud came closer.

Two finely dressed men wheeled their horses into the yard and leapt to the ground, leaving their mounts to snort and paw at the dirt as the riders strode toward the farmer.

They moved strangely. Not like men at all. As they came closer, Sorra saw that their legs were too long, bent in too many places as they walked on long, clawed toes that flexed and gripped the ground with every step, their dark scales collecting dust from the farmyard. Though they went barefoot, they wore fine but old-fashioned suits, one with a peacock-blue vest and the other bright emerald under their black jackets, and long tails swatted at the air behind them.

Goblins, Sorra thought, and pressed her hands to her mouth to muffle the sound of her breath. She'd imagined them naked, as the dead bodies had been, prowling about like vicious animals. These creatures appeared civilized, intelligent, and far more frightening for it.

She tried not to think of the mutilated soldiers at the Gate.

The one in blue strode toward the farmer, who cringed back, stepping in front of the child.

"Taxes," the goblin said, grinning to expose jagged teeth. His face appeared unnervingly human save for its greyish hue and unusually heavy jaw.

"No," the farmer said, his voice trembling. "Please."

The creature's grin widened theatrically. "It doesn't have to be you. The child would do as well."

The boy looked up at them, wide-eyed, the chicken forgotten.

"No," the farmer said again.

The goblin darted forward, knocking the farmer into the dirt, and grabbed the child's arm. His companion let out a wild whoop and laughed as the boy struggled. This one had a longer face, and his coppery complexion glowed against the green of his waistcoat and the stark white of his high collar.

Sorra remained frozen, torn between the urge to help and the knowledge that it would do no one any good even if she tried, watching as the goblins dragged the boy toward their waiting horses.

"Halt!"

Not the farmer's voice, but another, coming from somewhere past one of the slumped haystacks.

Not past it, Sorra realized. *More like inside it.*

A tall, lanky man stood, shaking off the fallen hay that had blanketed him. He was dressed a little like a knight out of an old story in a silvery cuirass over a dark shirt and fitted trousers, but instead of a helmet, he wore only steel-grey hair that stuck out in every possible direction. Any other armour he might have once possessed was gone. Beyond that, the overall effect was greatly diminished by the fact that bits of hay still clung to his sleeves and stuck out from his overgrown beard.

Sorra prayed this wasn't the hero she'd heard so little about.

He stumbled drunkenly as he raised his sword.

"Away!" he called. "Unhand the boy, or you'll be the ones paying taxes." He paused. "To me. In blood."

The goblin in blue reached beneath his jacket and pulled out a pair of gleaming knives, but his companion held out a hand, motioning for him to wait.

The goblin's scaled tail lashed like an irritated cat's. "Are you interfering, old man?"

The knight, if he was such a thing, held his sword level, pointed at the goblins. "Taxes," he repeated, as though that settled the matter.

Hardly a stirring speech in Sorra's opinion, but the goblin set the child back on the ground.

"This is becoming tedious, old man," said the second goblin, hissing his words slightly. "You could stop hiding in haystacks and making empty threats if you'd quit being an ass and accept our benevolent queen's generous and inevitable terms."

"Generous?" the knight roared. "Off with you, and tell her I will never bend!"

The goblin in blue bared its teeth at him. "Perhaps not now," he said. "But soon enough."

They both mounted their horses, turned, and rode off. The knight sheathed his sword and, without stopping to speak to the farmer, stumbled off in the opposite direction, holding his armour-plated stomach with one hand and shielding his eyes against the sun with the other.

He wasn't what Sorra had imagined when she'd thought about handing Beau's rescue off to someone else. Still, he'd done something good. Heroic, even, and it didn't seem like he was a friend of Gwelain's.

Sorra watched as the child ran to his father, who had gotten back on his feet during the strange standoff. She expected tears of relief, an embrace, a shout of thanks to the knight.

Instead, the boy passed by the farmer, crouched beside the dead chicken, picked up his stick, and resumed his poking, though now with his gaze lifted to watch the road, more wary than he'd been before. The farmer picked up a bucket from beside the house and went to the pump as though nothing had happened.

Sorra climbed down the ladder and ran to him, her dirt-crusted socks slapping on the hard-packed dirt.

"Thank you for not saying anything about me."

The farmer lifted his gaze to meet her eyes, blinked twice, and frowned. "Leave before you upset everything."

Sorra raised her hands in surrender and backed away. He seemed to forget her as soon as she was out of sight and went back to pumping water until the bucket overflowed.

By the time Sorra reached the road, the knight had disappeared.

CHAPTER TWENTY-FIVE

Even with the farmer and the strange child behind her, Sorra's nerves didn't settle. She passed another farm as quiet as the first, its fields overflowing with a mix of vegetable crops that appeared to be thriving despite the weeds threatening to choke them. The only evidence of past care was an old-fashioned plow that had been abandoned not far from the road, rusting as the soil slowly swallowed it.

A flat meadow came next, perhaps attached to that same farm. The black-and-white cows grazing on the long grasses and wildflowers didn't raise their heads as she passed, and their movements felt strange, though Sorra couldn't tell why. She'd left them behind before she realized it was their tails, which lay still and limp, and their motionless ears. In such pleasant afternoon heat, they should have been beset by flies that they'd flick away with their tails or unsettle with a twitch of their ears, but they'd seemed unbothered.

Back in Cottsbridge, the mosquitoes and black flies that came out in the summer were such a common annoyance that Sorra hardly thought about them except for when they ruined her sleep. This place should have been the same—flies pestering the cows, clouds of nearly invisible insects above the road making the most of their short lives—but when she peered over the rickety wooden fence into the meadow, she didn't see even a fat bumblebee sampling the clover.

She told herself she was mistaken, that there had to be bees if there were crops growing, but she couldn't shake the unease that had settled deeper into her mind, setting her senses on edge.

It was several more minutes before she realized she hadn't felt even a faint breeze since she'd emerged from the river or heard a bird chirping. Tiny details, but it gave a sense that she was walking through a painting where the artist hadn't quite captured reality.

As she followed the road over the top of a low hill, a small group of women came into view, walking toward her. They all wore faded, dusty dresses and large bonnets that shielded their faces from the sun. One of them led a docile brown cow, and another had a half-grown girl clinging to her skirt. They didn't speak to each other, and none of them smiled or offered a greeting as they passed. Only the child met her gaze, and Sorra wished she hadn't— the girl's eyes were sunken and haunted, the eyes of an old woman who had seen far too much for one lifetime.

Sorra was afraid to speak to them, and once the shuffle of their footsteps had passed, the road was silent, as though they'd never been there at all.

The road continued downhill toward what was either a small town or a large village, the in-between kind of place that might declare itself to be either. There was no sign to offer welcome or provide its name before Sorra reached a stable where a few thin horses rested beneath an open shelter. The faint, familiar odour of animal waste touched the air, not quite covered by the more pleasant scent of the pink and purple lupins that stood straight as soldiers next to the fence around the stable's yard.

There were no humans, so Sorra went on.

The country road became what looked to be the main street of the town, lined with two-storey wooden buildings painted in shades of yellow, pink, lilac, and mint. They were better kept than the farm had been, but the air of disuse lingered even when she saw people coming and going from shops and houses, their steps slow, their gazes distant until they landed on her. Some watched her pass with narrowed eyes or open curiosity, but none of them offered an opening for conversation.

She'd have to speak to them, though. There was still no sign of her potential hero, and no one who seemed like a more promising prospect in terms of finding help.

The people's clothing was as old-fashioned as what the woman in the forest had worn. The dresses had excessively large sleeves and strangely layered skirts, and the few well-dressed men who walked the street looked downright ridiculous in their short pants and tall stockings. They were like people from a schoolbook, and anyone dressed in their fashion would have drawn stares and whispers even in Cottsbridge, which Sorra knew from Ingrid's letters was hopelessly backward in matters of style. But here, she was the one who stood out, and she wished her clothes were at least clean and pressed so maybe these people wouldn't stare.

A big green house with an exuberant garden filling its narrow front yard caught Sorra's eye. A trio of old men in yellowing white suits sat in a row on its broad porch, occupying rocking chairs that creaked gently with their movements. One smoked a pipe, one drummed his fingers against his leg, and the other stared into the distance without moving.

Each sported a beard so long it seemed his face was trying to grow roots to the ground, as though they'd been planted in those chairs for decades.

Sorra stepped onto the porch and stood with her hands folded in front of her, trying not to tug nervously at the hem of her sweater. The fellow with twitchy fingers glanced at her, then away, returning to whatever had been occupying his thoughts. The one with the pipe watched her with no more interest than he might have shown if a robin had landed on the porch railing.

"Good morning," Sorra said.

"Eh?" The old man spoke with his teeth still clenched on his pipe.

"I said good morning." She spoke a little louder and enunciated more clearly.

"Eh?"

Sorra sighed. "Have you seen a man in armour walking by?"

The smoker leaned back in his chair and resumed his rocking.

"Do you know the—"

"Eh? Eh?" He looked past her as he repeated his question over and over.

Sorra left the porch, her skin crawling like she'd walked through a spiderweb. The voice followed her down the street, never changing volume or inflection.

A woman with grey-streaked hair tucked under a white cotton cap was watching. She didn't offer an answer to Sorra's question but held a finger to her lips and nodded up the road before hurrying away.

Everyone else seemed to have vanished from the street while Sorra's back was turned, but she caught a flash of movement at a ground-floor window before its yellowing lace curtains fell back into place.

She walked on, wondering how long it would take for the bare whisper of footsteps against complete silence to drive a person mad.

The road soon met another at an intersection with a large tree stump at its centre. There was no clear reason for it to have not been pulled out, but a sign hanging above the door of a stone-walled building on the corner announced it as "The Lucky Stump Public House."

Sorra considered the state the old man had been in when he'd burst forth so heroically from the haystack. There seemed to be a good chance he'd gone into the local pub to resume the previous night's activities. If not, it might still be the sort of establishment that had comfortable seating where a person could rest for a while, maybe after she did some cleaning in exchange for a bit of food, and where she might ask questions of a bartender or cook.

It looked like a nice enough place, with old fieldstone walls and diamond-paned windows. The sun reflected off the warped glass, denying any chance to see what lay beyond. But the door was unlocked, and Sorra stepped inside.

She paused, blinking, as her eyes adjusted to the pub's dim interior. She'd known finer establishments than the Ambling Goat existed but hadn't realized just how much better they could be. Everything struck her as posh, from the dark wood of the bar and the wide plank floor to the burgundy velvet upholstering of the armchairs set at round tables. The same fabric covered the benches at booths under the windows. A large stone fireplace took up most of the wall opposite the bar, with more seating clustered near it. Overhead, a pair of fixtures held rings of unlit candles that would illuminate the glass teardrops hanging from them. The place smelled of clean soap, lemon, and the leather of the barstools.

The pub's only patron sat on one of those stools, his sword leaning against the bar, his head resting on his arms. He seemed to be asleep, one hand clutching a crystal glass.

Sorra's stomach twisted as she took the stool next to him. She knew she should be glad to have found him, but it was hard to muster hope that he'd be any help to her in his current state.

The knight opened one bleary eye and glared at her.

Sorra nodded at his drink. "What do you recommend?"

"Leaving."

As friendly as everyone else in these lands, then.

He still wore his cuirass, though it must have been terribly uncomfortable. Up close it was clearly old, its silvery surface scarred and dented. The shirt beneath was no better off, threadbare at the elbows and mended in several places with different coloured threads. His trousers might once have been black but had faded to an uneven grey, smoky in some parts and the sooty in others, and the leather boots that reached to his knees looked as battered as the armour.

But his sword had been cared for, its polished blade reflecting the dim light from the windows.

An engraving on the pommel depicted a bird in flight with a tiny rose clutched in its claws. Sorra's chest tightened as the image connected with something deep in her memory—the same design embossed on the leather cover of a book that had belonged to her father. It had been the first book she'd ever read about Queen Linnea, and the one she'd been most heartbroken over when Corinne had sold off the family's tiny library.

"Nice sword."

He grunted and closed his eye again.

She leaned in closer. "Did it belong to one of the heroes who came looking for Queen Linnea's heart?"

The old man lifted his head slowly. "Belongs. What do you take me for if not a knight?"

Sorra looked him over. He'd lost most of the hay that had been stuck in his beard but hardly looked prepared to slay a dragon.

"I take you for alive. The heroes sent by old kings are all rotting in their graves by now."

He snorted. "You must be new in these lands."

"I am."

"Are you?" The knight looked at her again more carefully, from her hair to her socks, his gaze lingering on her hideous sweater before returning to her birthmark, which he examined more openly than anyone with manners ought to. "How long?"

"I only arrived today," she said. "Not long before you came bursting out of that haystack. Who were those creatures?"

"Bah." He sipped his drink, nearly emptying it. "I don't care when you got here. How long since our good queen's heart was stolen?"

Sorra tried to remember. The stories in her father's little book had been about Linnea's life, not her death. What little Sorra had heard about what came after—Linnea's untimely death, her heart being stolen, her magically preserved body resting beneath the castle in Embercliffe—had seemed as legendary as her life, and she hadn't studied history in school for long enough to learn dates.

"I don't know," she said. "A few hundred years since she died, at least."

The knight's ruddy cheeks paled. "I see. Hardly feels like more than..." He trailed off and laid his head back down on his arms, muffling his voice. "Feels like a thousand some days, but I'd've guessed no more than a century since the night she left us."

She waited for him to reveal that he was joking, but there had been no lie in his voice, and nothing but regret written in the deep lines on his face.

Excitement kindled in Sorra's body, making it hard to sit still. "You're saying you're one of the heroes sent to retrieve her heart?"

"The last party sent out, to the best of my knowledge." He turned his head toward her, but it seemed to be too much effort to lift it again. "And I'm the last one here, which makes me the last of the last."

"But how, after all this time?"

The knight blinked at her, his eyes bleary. "You really did just stumble in here, didn't you?" He let go of his glass for long enough to press his hand to his forehead, which she supposed was aching badly. "It's Gwelain's magic. She wanted to win over the humans in these lands she'd stolen, so she offered them what all humans want —safety from natural death. No fear of starvation or disease, no ageing. I could have told them not to take her offer, but they jumped at it. Cut all ties to Andonia and pledged themselves to a goblin queen in exchange for her shutting Lord Death out of her lands."

Sorra shivered as she thought of the dead-eyed women on the road and the child at the farm. "They're all as old as you?"

"Mostly. They could work, but few do. They could still play songs and tell stories, but it's grown old for them. Every day's the same for most of them at this point." He looked down into his glass. "For most of *us*. Nothing changes most days. If someone gets taken by the goblins for their bloody taxes, someone else ages up to take their place. But that's all. No other births. Nothing to die of, nothing to live for. The melancholy got to them faster than you'd think, but like I said, it feels like a thousand years some days. Ten thousand." He belched gently. "The fields grow, the rivers flow, but the people's souls have gone sour and life has lost its flavour. Gwelain can't give without taking. Can't speak without lying, as far as I can tell."

Before Sorra could say anything else, he knocked on the bar three times. A curtain hanging behind the bar shifted, and a man with bushy blond sideburns stepped out, eyeing Sorra suspiciously as he refilled the knight's drink. He didn't speak before he left them again.

"Why are you here?" the knight asked, speaking into his glass.

Sorra wasn't sure how much to tell. She didn't exactly trust him, but the fact that he disliked Gwelain so strongly helped a little. Honesty, then, but only as much as she was sure would serve her.

"I'm on a quest of my own," she said. "I mean to rescue the

prince Gwelain holds captive in her castle. Do you know where it is?"

He scowled at her. "You're alone?"

"Yes."

"Where's your sword?"

"I don't have one."

"Magic?"

"None."

"Hmm. A prince, you said?"

"I did." Sorra's stomach sank. "You hadn't heard about him? He's been here for a dozen years."

"No." The knight drew a long, slow breath. "As I said, I recommend leaving. You can't save him or anyone. We searched for decades and never found the castle. She doesn't want it to be found."

Sorra folded her arms on the bar, mirroring his posture. "I'm not leaving."

"Fine, settle in. Not on that stool, though. Go find your own place to rot." He closed his eyes.

Sorra wasn't sure whether she felt more annoyed by his refusal or fascinated by the way he seemed like a knight from a children's story who had been awakened from a centuries-long sleep, determined to drink his way back into oblivion.

A grumpy, drunken knight, but he was still the only person she'd met so far who might be able to do what she surely couldn't. Interest would get her further than irritation, so she pretended not to mind his rudeness even as she fought the urge to slap him awake.

"I'm not ready to give up yet," she said, louder than was necessary. Her voice made him wince, and she didn't regret it at all. "You seem like a capable fellow who once knew about this sort of thing, and who might know his way around these lands." *If you ever got off your bar stool,* she added to herself. "Surely a new quest is better than wasting away here."

The knight sighed. "Even if I could get you to the castle, which I can't, it wouldn't do you any good. Nothing changes here, no matter how hard you try. The only question is how long it takes you to accept it."

Sorra's cheeks warmed. A lifetime of being talked down to and dismissed hadn't made it any easier to take, and this former would-be hero was certainly in no position to treat her like she was stupid. "Is that why you gave up?"

Life came into his eyes as he glared at her. It was unpleasant, even frightening, but it made him more real, more present.

And possibly more useful. For a moment she caught a glimpse of a man who might have been someone, once.

"I haven't given up," he said, his voice low and hard. "Linnea's heroes swore an oath to remain loyal until the end. We must remain so if we wish to serve her in whatever lies beyond death. But the heroes are gone, save for me. And hope is gone with them."

"It will be different for me." Sorra tried to sound more confident than she felt. "I'll find the castle, with or without you."

He laughed quietly, and the anger drained from his face, leaving him tired and old and nothing more. "You poor child."

Sorra's fist came down on the bar before she had a chance to consider whether it would get her what she wanted. "I need help, not mockery."

He waved one hand at her, unbothered. "It's not mockery. I'd only forgotten what hope looked like. It surprised me." He sipped his drink again, set it down, and rested his forehead in his hands. "You'll get over it soon enough."

Sorra snatched his drink and finished it. It burned down her throat, warming her pleasantly, leaving its rich, unfamiliar flavour on her tongue.

"That was mine," he grumbled.

"So order another. Or get off your ass and help me find the castle like you were supposed to a hundred years ago."

He reached for his empty glass. "You're not here for Linnea. I'm not here for a cast-off prince. Leave me be."

Sorra stood and threw the glass across the pub, shattering it against the fireplace. As crystal shards rained onto the floor, she snatched the knight's sword from where it rested against the bar. It was lighter than she'd expected and easy to lift. She darted back before he could reach for it.

He stood and turned, straight-backed and scowling. "Give that back."

"Why?" Sorra raised the sword and pointed it at him, as he had at the goblins. "It'll do more good in my hands than yours. Maybe I'll find the prince *and* the heart."

The knight roared and lunged at her. Sorra ran for the door on the back wall, hauled it open, and stepped into a sunny, fenced-in yard. The knight stumbled out after her, one hand raised against the sun. He seemed alert, though, even more than he'd been when he'd faced the goblins that morning.

"My sword," he said, and held out an unsteady hand. "Please. It's all I have left of her."

Sorra set the sword's tip in the dirt. "I'll give it back if you'll promise to help me."

His lips pressed into a tight line beneath his overgrown moustache. "Scoundrel. How do you expect to accomplish anything with this kind of behaviour?"

"I got you off your stool. That's not nothing."

He narrowed his eyes at her, not trying to disguise how he was once again studying her birthmark. Then he looked toward the sky and held his hands out, palms facing the clouds. "Tell me this isn't the mystery you spoke of, my queen," he said, his voice pained.

He didn't seem to receive an answer, but when he looked back to Sorra, it was with a mix of disappointment and resignation she was all too familiar with after a lifetime of being herself. "Make your demands."

At least I've got his attention.

"You say you're helpless because nothing changes here," she said, wishing for more time to think before she spoke, "but I'm a change, standing right here before you. You believe you can't continue your hunt alone? Here I am."

The knight rubbed the back of his neck, frowning. "Are they really sending underfed little girls on quests these days?"

Sorra squared her shoulders. "I'm a strong, healthy young woman, and I'm here, aren't I?"

"For what that's worth." The knight sounded unimpressed, and Sorra didn't think that would change even if she explained how much she'd already gone through to get to him. "You don't look at all prepared for this, and I'd say the same if you were a skinny *boy* with no weapons, no armour, no magic, and no companions. Who sent you?"

"No one except my destiny. An enchanted arrow led me to this quest." Sorra wanted to lie and tell him someone had thought her competent, but that would lead to questions she couldn't answer. "Gwelain cursed Andonia when I was a child. The king let her take his heir in exchange for her ending the plagues and droughts and everything else, but if he sends anyone after the prince or Linnea's heart, she's free to attack us again. I sent myself, and I mean to see it through."

She'd let herself imagine she could turn back if things got too bad but realized as she spoke that doing so had never really been an option. This was her destiny, and if she didn't save Beau, it seemed no one else would.

The thought terrified her more than it had back in Andonia.

"I see." The knight's brow furrowed. Not in anger, but in deeper thought than he'd seemed to give anything else so far. "Perhaps things are changing, after all, and the time the visions foretold has come. The question is whether this will lead to our victory or to disaster."

Sorra didn't offer an opinion. He seemed to be talking to himself, and not about anything that increased her faith in his competence or sanity.

His eyes sharpened. "Are you a person of good moral character? Are you wise and clever and capable? Have you made it your aim in life to help others no matter the cost to yourself, and have you pledged to behave in a manner that reflects the ideals of a true hero?" He glanced at the sword in her hand. "Your recent actions notwithstanding, obviously."

Sorra hesitated. A person of good moral character would probably tell the truth about her birth blessing and beg for his help anyway, but he clearly didn't want to take up a new quest with anyone but a real hero by his side. Telling him she was born to be the very opposite would probably send him back to his barstool, and she couldn't afford to let that happen.

And if I'm escaping it, it doesn't matter at all.

"I'd like to be," she said, "if that's the kind of person who can get this done."

"Hmm."

She offered the sword back to him, hilt-first. "You said you'd searched for the castle. Is that where the heart is?"

"We believed so."

"Then we want the same thing, if for different reasons. We can help each other. Surely joining me is better than doing nothing."

He didn't seem convinced, but he accepted the sword and rested its blade across his hands instead of using it to drive her off. "You'll need to become a proper hero for this to have any chance of working, and commit yourself to my quest above your own, to Linnea above this prince of yours. If you are the Mystery—" He sighed. "Even then, we're at least two short."

"The Mystery?"

He nodded. "Of all the heroes Linnea saw in her visions surrounding the return of her heart, only four ever came close to being named—the Might, the Mind, the Magic, the Mystery. Not those words in her original tongue, of course, but close enough. Others came along on these quests, but there were always those four. 'Marked by birth or marked by life,' so at least that much fits you."

Sorra touched her cheek. Nearly everyone in Andonia probably had a birthmark or a collection of scars, but she wasn't about to say so if he thought a bit of wine-tinted skin was a sign he should join her.

"It does fit," she said. He wasn't making much sense, but that could be sorted out once he sobered up.

"Were you born at night?" he asked.

"I don't know." Her sisters would have remembered, but Sorra's birth had been too painful a subject for much discussion over the years.

Her answer didn't seem to please the knight. "It would be better if we could be sure. All of the four had to be born during the day, you see. I was the Might in my own party."

"I could have guessed," Sorra said, nodding to his armour, which had Linnea's songbird and rose engraved over his chest. She wanted to ask more about his past and these visions he kept mentioning, but then he might suggest stepping back inside for a few drinks. They'd sit, they'd talk, and another century might pass.

All that mattered for now was getting him to step forward again, even if it meant going along with his talk of visions and pretending to be a hero. She could always tell him the truth about herself and her blessing later, but she couldn't take a secret back once it was spilled. She'd made that mistake on her first night with Beau, and it wasn't one she meant to repeat.

I'm not a hero, but if I can act the part for long enough, maybe it won't matter.

I can't do this on my own.

"Two short," he muttered again. "No Mind, no Magic."

"You've got me now," she said. "That's double the heroes you had an hour ago. Who's to say the others aren't out there waiting for us? The prince I've come to rescue has a sharp mind. He can't act against Gwelain directly, but he must know things that would be helpful."

"We'll see about that," the knight grumbled, but Sorra thought his eyes betrayed a spark of interest.

"Will we?"

"Perhaps. What's your name, young lady?"

"Sorra. And yours?" She resisted the urge to return his courtesy by calling him 'old man.'

"Tullian." He bowed slightly.

"Very well, Tullian." She tried to sound heroic. "I accept your offer. Train me enough to get me ready for what lies ahead, and we'll begin the hunt for the castle, starting wherever you left off. We'll find it, steal back the heart, free the prince, and save Andonia."

His moustache twitched, perhaps with the hint of a smile. "As simple as that, eh? Very well." He pushed his way through the gate, and Sorra followed. He seemed to be heading back the way they'd come, toward farmland and forests.

"Wait!" she called. "Could we start with a rest? And a good meal? Perhaps a bath?"

Tullian seemed about to object, then raised one arm and sniffed himself.

"Agreed," he said, adjusting the trajectory of his brisk march to continue deeper into the village, leaving Sorra scurrying to keep up.

CHAPTER TWENTY-SIX

"Could you tell me—"

"No."

"But I only want—"

Tullian spun to face her, his armoured form haloed by the sunlit leaves of the thick forest they'd been pushing through. "You'll have all the answers you want soon enough," he said, scowling. "I see patience isn't one of your heroic virtues."

"Not usually." Sorra fought the urge to glare back at him. Their time at the inn had been the most pleasant part of her journey so far—two hot meals, a bath, a soft bed to sleep in until Tullian had ordered her up, dressed, and on the road before she'd finished rubbing the sleep from her eyes.

Perhaps it had only been enjoyable because he'd locked himself in his own room to rest and, she hoped, make his plans. His sober self was as rigid and harsh as his drunk self had been, and his clarity only made it worse.

He's all I've got, she reminded herself, and gestured for him to keep walking.

At least he looked a little more promising now that he'd bathed, trimmed his beard, and tamed the grey hair that was now more mane than mess. Even if she still couldn't see him as a hero she could imagine that he had once been one, and his purposeful steps offered direction she wouldn't have had on her own.

But his sobriety had brought on a desire for secrecy she hadn't expected given his willingness to talk about Gwelain the day before. All he'd said was that they were going somewhere safe and that it would be best not to speak until then. That made it his direction, not hers, and though she told herself his way was almost guaranteed to be better than any she chose, she chafed at the knight's refusal to tell her anything.

The sun had begun its westward descent before they reached a building in the middle of the forest. Its stone walls looked badly neglected, their pale mortar dried and crumbling. Its wooden roof was halfway rotted and sprouting long grass, and its few windows were shuttered tight against the elements.

Tullian didn't stop before he pushed through the door. The hinges let out a piercing creak, but there was no lock to slow him. Sorra waited to see whether the walls would collapse before she followed him in, wrinkling her nose at the musty air.

Cracks in the roof let in rays of light that illuminated a single, cluttered room that came into clearer view as Tullian opened the shutters and turned a crank attached to one of the building's support posts, raising a roof panel that let in air and light even as it shed scraps of wood onto the floor.

Nine bunks were stacked three high against the far wall. Each was long enough that a tall man like Tullian could have stretched out in it, but so cramped vertically that he'd get a hard knock on the head if he sat up without thinking in the morning. Not much more room than the inside of a coffin, and the greying sheets hanging from the bunks reminded Sorra of ancient shrouds.

The rest of the room was less haunting and more interesting. A simple kitchen area with a filthy wash basin had been built into the corner to the left of the door, but there was no stove—only the remains of a fire pit surrounded by a low stone wall and the panel in the roof above that would allow smoke to escape. Six simple wooden chairs sat around the pit.

Everything else seemed at first glance to be a random assortment of items spread over tables of varying sizes, but as Sorra wandered the room, she began to pick out the organization of it all.

On one table, maps. On another sat a pile of books piled so high it was a wonder the table—and whoever had carried them this far—hadn't collapsed under their weight. Weapons hung on the wall between the kitchen and the bunks, and on the table below them lay jumbled piles of metal and leather armour, along with bows, arrows, and more weapons that might have been in the process of being repaired or cleaned when the place had been abandoned.

And it had certainly been abandoned. Though the walls had done a fair job of protecting the building's contents, everything was coated in a fine layer of dust, and some of the maps and book pages had been warped by moisture. Moths had made a fine meal of the blankets and the few items of clothing that hung from a wash-line in the corner.

"Can I speak now?"

Tullian looked up from the pile of maps he'd been scowling at. "It seems you can."

Sorra gritted her teeth. "I mean, can you tell me now what we're doing here? Or what this place is?"

Tullian looked around the room as though he hadn't really taken in its current state. "A safe place. Or it was. Should still be." He motioned for her to follow him the few paces to the door, where he touched a row of symbols carved into its wooden frame. "Do you know anything about magic? Do people still use it in Andonia?"

"Some do," she said. "The king's mages do it legally, but not for the benefit of anyone like me. There are witches who risk losing their heads if they're caught using it without the king's permission. I haven't met many of them, either."

In truth there had only been one, and for only a few minutes under the bridge the night she'd fled from home. As far as Sorra knew, magic was not only dangerous, but difficult to learn, and anyone with any skill in it would be stupid to settle in a place as useless as Cottsbridge.

Tullian didn't appear shocked by her ignorance. It seemed he'd settled on expecting nothing from her, and a part of Sorra was glad they'd moved so quickly past the possibility of his hopes for her being raised and dashed.

"These are symbols of protection," he said. "Gwelain employs a human mage who listens by magic and whispers everything he hears into her ear. One can never be sure that he's listening, or that he isn't. Does she know you're here, and why?"

Sorra's stomach squirmed. "I think so. I got away from the goblins that were chasing me, though."

"At least that's something. She knows the visions as well as I do, and if she thinks there's any chance you're the Mystery, she'll be trying to prevent our meeting. If she asks questions at the pub or the inn, she'll know we've met and be terribly angry about it." He smiled, obviously pleased at the thought. "And she'll have her mage listening, but he can't spy on us here. These protections are solid, as are the ones carved into the trees we passed outside, but be sure not to say anything you wouldn't want her to hear if we stray too far during your training."

Sorra looked around the dim, cluttered room again, this time with a growing sense of dread. "We're staying here?"

"Of course. The forest will provide the food we need, and this building will be our shelter." Tullian raised one eyebrow. "Is that a problem?"

"No. I don't suppose we'll be here long, anyway, if we want to find the castle or Linnea's heart."

"We'll see." Tullian shuffled through the maps and set one on top of the pile, then motioned for Sorra to come closer. The paper was rippled at the edges by age and moisture, but most of the beautifully drawn lines were still clear. It was strange to see a map with the northern mountain range at its bottom and unfamiliar shorelines extending up from the top of what most folks in Andonia considered the northern extent of the land mass.

"Marthis?" Sorra asked, pointing at the word printed at the top right-hand corner of the map.

"Of course. Once Andonia's northernmost province, now its own country. Have you not studied geography?"

"A little." Sorra tried not to sound defensive. "Things have changed since your time. Gwelain has made most of Andonia forget these lands exist. They've been erased from maps, memories, and records. There's only one pass through the mountains, and—" Sorra looked again at the map. "It looks like there are more here."

There weren't many, but there was a clear gap in the range west of where the Gate would lie, and another not far from the eastern shore.

Tullian nodded. "Gwelain has incredible magic at her disposal. She closed off her lands, or very nearly. This forgetting would be one more way of protecting herself and the heart. If no one remembers these lands exist, no one will come after her or it. Except you." He set the map aside and turned to Sorra. "This prince you're searching for—you said he's been here for a decade?"

"A little more than that. Beau said Gwelain's curse ended because she intended to marry him and claim the throne that way."

"Of course she did. She never changes." Tullian smiled grimly. "But then how did you meet him and begin your quest?"

"Gwelain let him return to Andonia because they'd made a wager about him being able to find a human wife, but he was a talking bear when we met, and he couldn't tell me who or what he was, so…" Sorra judged by the knight's incredulous expression that she wasn't making as much sense as she'd have liked. That was the problem with stories where magic was involved. It seemed to erase straight lines and logic entirely. "I loosed an arrow that was supposed to lead me to my greatest destiny. It landed in his backside."

Tullian frowned, but he said nothing.

"He couldn't explain it all to me under the terms of their wager," she continued, "but once he'd lost, he told me about Gwelain and these lands and all he knew about where her castle might be. He said, 'east of the sun and west of the moon.' Does that mean anything to you?"

Tullian set the maps down and paced the centre of the room. His legs were long enough that it was only a handful of steps each way before he met beds or the front door.

"Nothing," he said. "Perhaps worse than nothing."

"What do you mean?"

Tullian rubbed his fingers in circles over his temples. "What is east of the sun?"

Sorra looked down at the map. "At sunrise, nothing. At sunset, everything."

"And what is west of the moon?"

She pictured a clear, starry night, which she'd never appreciated as much as Beau seemed to. "I don't know. It moves through the sky."

"Correct. It's a joke, isn't it? The castle is everywhere, or perhaps nowhere."

Sorra waited for him to tell her she'd been stupid to think otherwise, but he didn't.

"Beau wouldn't have mentioned it if he didn't think it meant something," she said, though she couldn't even be sure of that when he hadn't meant for her to follow him. "He did say it would probably be impossible to find him."

"And yet you came." Tullian clapped a hand to her shoulder, hard enough that she flinched. "You're not what the scholars anticipated when they studied the visions, but there may be hope for you yet. Let's get you armed and see what else you're hiding."

Sorra smiled, though cold doubt snaked through her guts.

I'm doing better, she told herself. *I'm escaping my blessing. If a hero is what it takes to get Tullian back to searching for the castle, then him believing that's what I am is the best thing for both of us.*

Tullian went to the table of armour, and Sorra turned to the one covered in books. Some were written in a language composed of strange letters, but there were a few she could read, though the old-fashioned handwriting slowed her considerably.

On the first page of a slim volume bound in cream-coloured leather someone had written "Visions." The pages that followed had been written out in clear lines, but the margins were packed with cramped notes in a different hand.

Words Tullian had spoken the previous day caught her eye.

"North, south, east, west," she read aloud, and Tullian turned. "Might, Magic, Mind, Mystery." She looked up. "This was Linnea's vision?"

"One of many." Tullian set down the sword he'd been examining and motioned for her to hand the book to him. She did, and something strange passed over his expression as he looked down at the page. "Our good queen was plagued by them over the course of her lifetime. Waking dreams, she called them, when she spoke of them at all."

Sorra's heart fluttered. "You really knew her, didn't you?"

"As well as I could, though not for nearly long enough. Every well-kept secret written in this book came before my time." He flipped back to the first page, careful not to damage the fragile paper. "She saw all of it—the discontent among her people, her death, her power being stolen and how it might be returned to Andonia, but she rarely remembered details when she came back to herself, and what scraps she did remember she recorded in the old language."

"What was she like?" A dozen questions bubbled to the surface of Sorra's mind all at once. "Where did she really come from? Were the Bright Ones real? What about Gwelain? And are goblins—"

"Hush." Tullian looked as though she might be giving him a headache. Sorra was familiar with the expression. "We have more immediate concerns—the visions, our quest, your training. If you want stories to satisfy your curiosity, you'll need to earn them."

Sorra tried not to scowl. Linnea's history seemed entirely relevant, especially where Gwelain came into it, but she held her tongue.

Tullian set the visions aside and reached for another book, this one so well-used that pages had come loose from the binding. Sorra reached for it, but he held it away. "This isn't for your hands. But look."

The pages were covered in handwriting written in the same unfamiliar language as other books in the room, the words long and strangely accented.

"Selim's notes," Tullian said, his voice taking on a rough edge. "He was our Mind, and he made his notes on the visions in Linnea's old language. He said it was an entirely different way of thinking and knowing."

"Can you read it?"

Tullian closed the book and laid it gently down on the table. "It's a terribly complex language. Layers of meaning that shift like the tides, according to Selim. Requires extensive study to understand it, and even then it's slippery and imprecise if you don't have the mind and the heart for it. Selim said the average human trying to comprehend the Bright Ones' language is like a dog trying to understand the writings of Donchanel and Berrouac. A joke, of course, but there was some truth in it."

Sorra smiled and nodded as though the names meant anything to her.

Tullian gestured toward the symbols at the door. "The condensed form often used in magic is even more difficult, or so Selim said. The rest of us were glad to leave that sort of thing to our Mind and our Magic, but now I wish I could know what he wrote in his secret notes."

Sorra's fingers itched to reach for the book, though she'd be able to make even less sense of it than Tullian could. Something about its age and its mysteries appealed to her, or perhaps it was the idea that all the answers they both needed might be in its pages. Tullian set it aside, his eyes distant.

Then he reached for the book of visions again. "Linnea tried to speak about her waking dreams with her advisors before her coronation, but no one believed in them. They thought of her as an extraordinary woman by then rather than a lesser goddess. Even she wasn't convinced they were true prophecy. Then her death and the theft of her heart proved their warnings true, and finally the scholars began the difficult task of translating her writings." Tullian opened the book and brushed his fingers lightly over the pages. "We have so little. A terrible fire destroyed the original writings before translations could be completed, and even what we have is somewhat poetic and, therefore, hard to interpret. But this is our surest guide to victory, and our most valuable warning against defeat. If you're ready to learn, I will teach you what I can. And when I'm sure you are one of the heroes destined to defeat Gwelain, we will proceed with our quest."

Sorra looked down at the slim volume. As fascinating as it was to meet someone who had met and known her favourite legendary queen, she didn't like the idea of her next steps being guided by something so flimsy.

But Tullian was watching her, waiting for an answer that would please him, and Sorra sensed that her journey would end immediately if she didn't say it was a wonderful idea to blindly follow incomplete writings based on half-remembered dreams and translated from a language humans could barely understand.

She forced a smile and took the book from him. "I'm ready."

"Are you?" Tullian looked down at Selim's notes again. His voice had become thick and rough. "Are you prepared for the dangers we'll face?"

Sorra's smile faded. "I think so."

"Better to know, and to go forward with your eyes open. Come with me and bring the visions with you." Tullian strode to the door and stepped into the woods without further explanation, leaving Sorra with little choice but to follow.

CHAPTER TWENTY-SEVEN

Tullian didn't speak as he led Sorra through the woods, and she didn't dare ask questions even when she spotted the protective symbol carved into an ancient oak. He stopped before a strange tree with a trunk that twisted from the ground, bearing twin branches raised like the arms of a dancer in motion, its wooden back gracefully arched.

Tullian reached for the trunk, his hand shaking until he planted his palm against its greyish bark.

"Selim," he whispered, and his next breath caught at the top of his inhale as he held back what Sorra thought might have been a sob. "I'm sorry it's been so long."

Sorra stepped closer, and her own breath caught in a choked gasp.

The tree had a face. Not carved into it, but a natural one formed from the pitted surface of its bark. What she'd taken for a knothole was a mouth opened in a scream, and twin scars above it were eyes closed in pain or terror.

It wasn't dancing. It was writhing, or had been before it was frozen into this position.

"This is Gwelain's work," Tullian said, and cleared his throat. "This is her cruelty. For more than a hundred years she and I have maintained an uneasy peace. You and I are about to upset that balance, so it's only fair you know what happened to the last man who threatened it."

Sorra waited as he wiped his eyes. When he turned to her, she pretended not to see the redness in them.

"Selim was a brilliant man," Tullian said. "He almost wasn't chosen as our Mind—he was too much a scholar of the world, chasing whatever knowledge caught his fancy instead of following any one course of study. But I knew him well, and I convinced those in charge that his breadth of knowledge would be useful."

"That seems wise," Sorra said, unsure of how else to offer comfort.

"It did seem that way, and he was eager to come. Selim was faithful to the end, even when it was only the two of us left. Then he insisted on pursuing an idea he couldn't let go of. He wouldn't tell me anything about it or where he was going when he left one night—said it was too dangerous, that he'd only tell me when he was sure he was right. He returned with his eyes shining as if some discovery had lit a fire in him, but before he could tell me anything, Gwelain silenced him." Tullian's expression hardened as he touched the tree next to its tortured face. "There are worse fates than death. He's still alive. Still aware and still suffering, if I know her cruelty as I believe I do. If we'd both been a little less wise, he might have stayed in Andonia and lived a better life, if a shorter one."

Sorra tried to imagine a fate like this—to be aware but silenced and restrained, forever unable to move forward or change anything.

"Can we help him?"

"Not yet." Tullian slid his hand down the trunk and turned to her. "But when Gwelain is defeated, her enchantments will be broken. Selim and I will serve Linnca in the lands beyond life as a reward for our faithful service. The question is whether you wish to risk a fate like his, or whatever other torments Gwelain might have in store for you. Consider it carefully while I hunt up something to eat. You'll know where to find me if you still think my quest is your destiny."

He marched back toward the hideout without another word, leaving Sorra alone with his tortured companion.

She rested her palm against the bark, which felt warmer than it should have even under the summer sun.

"I'm sorry for your suffering," she said, in case Selim could still hear.

The tree creaked like an old wooden floor. It might have been her imagination, but she swore she felt movement beneath the bark like a slow, steady pulse.

Sorra pulled her hand away.

The tree frightened her in a way the soldiers' bodies at the Gate hadn't. They, at least, had been unaware of their own fates, and their suffering was over. This was so much worse.

"I didn't come here to save you," she whispered. "But even if I'm not the hero Tullian has been waiting for, we're going to finish your quest. I won't let him stop again."

The wind blew, rustling the tree's branches in an answering whisper that made no more sense to Sorra than the words in Selim's secret notes had.

She ran for the safety of the hideout before the urge to flee could take root and change her mind.

The hideout was empty when Sorra returned, but Tullian soon entered with a skinned rabbit in hand. He didn't seem surprised to find Sorra there and only nodded to her before getting to work building a fire in the dusty old pit and setting the meat over it.

His calm, unhurried actions set Sorra on edge.

"What's next?" she asked.

"Supper."

"Of course," she said, trying to sound as calm as he did. If this was a lesson in the heroic virtue of patience, she wanted it to be over as soon as possible. "But you said there were things I needed to learn before we could get on with our search for the castle and the heart."

"And your prince, yes. Bring me the book. The visions are the foundation of everything we do, and the place where you'll begin your training."

Tullian sat next to the fire, and Sorra pulled another of the dusty chairs closer so she could see the pages as Tullian turned them.

"Four quest parties were sent out over the course of the decade following the theft of Linnea's heart," he said, not reading from the pages. "When it was certain that one group had failed, another would be formed and sent out, always with someone fulfilling each of the roles represented in Linnea's vision of her heroes in the hopes that they'd be the ones she'd foreseen. The Might was usually a knight, or at least someone strong and skilled in battle. The Magic was always a trained mage, though each had a different specialty. The Mind would be a scholar of some sort."

"And the Mystery?"

Tullian grimaced. "I never cared for that bit of uncertainty, myself. Linnea's surviving writings made no attempt to clarify who that unknown factor might be. I suppose any of those sent along with us to cook or carry or to do anything else could have turned out to be the Mystery, but the official candidate was..." He trailed off as he searched his memory. "Always a man of good character and great potential, but not in the same way as any of the others. A nobleman, a hunter... I can't remember the third, but the one I knew was no one, really. A good man from the provinces who seemed like nothing more than the ordinary sort of person Linnea had so loved. The hope was that he'd reveal some great talent at just the right moment."

Sorra glanced at the coffin-like beds and their empty shrouds. "Did Gwelain kill them all, other than Selim?"

"She couldn't." Tullian flipped with practiced ease to another page, and Sorra read the few original lines to herself, ignoring the notes added to the margins.

Should the queen's sworn champion die by the enemy's order or intention, on that day shall Gwelain meet her end.

She read it three times to be sure she understood.

"You're protected?"

"To an extent. You saw yourself that Gwelain is able to find creative ways around it." Tullian turned the roasting meat, which was already filling the hut with a rich aroma that made Sorra's mouth water. "She must have learned about the visions from whoever stole the heart for her, or from the first quest party before she could make the mistake of killing any of them. It would have been a great advantage if we could have kept them secret. As it is, she knows as much as I do. She takes the visions seriously and is careful not to risk spilling the blood of Linnea's potential heroes."

"Then what happened to your Mystery and Magic, or the groups that came before you?"

"We're only protected as long as we're pledged to the quest and faithful to it, and the truth in our minds and hearts is clearly shown by magic." He pushed his sleeve up his right arm, revealing a mark on his skin that reminded Sorra of the one branding Beau as heir to the throne but in the shape of Linnea's songbird. "We were all marked, from the chosen heroes down to the lad who tended to Selim's books. When members of my party gave up one by one, this mark vanished and there was nothing to keep Gwelain from hunting them down. I don't suppose any of them made it back to Andonia. Not all of them simply gave up, but—" He stopped himself, jaw clenched tight, and tugged his sleeve down. "She didn't kill any of them while they were faithful to the quest. If she had, the vision would be fulfilled and this would all be over."

Sorra watched the fire, listening to the sizzle as fat dripped into the flames. "So when you stood up to those goblins yesterday…"

"They wouldn't have harmed me, no." Tullian hung his head. "There's heroism in doing good in small ways, but it entails little risk for me. Any monster under Gwelain's control knows not to harm me, so we do our little dance—the goblins threaten the people, her other creatures stir up trouble, I stand in the way, nothing changes. Or if I'm not there, taxes are collected."

"But that means she can't touch us while we search for the castle, right?"

"She won't hurt me. And she won't risk hurting you if she thinks you've taken the oath."

Sorra bounced to her feet, too excited to stay still. "I'll pledge to the quest now. I'm ready."

Tullian poked at the sizzling rabbit meat. "You will not, and you are not. Look." He wiped his finger on his trousers and turned the page in his book. "Most of Linnea's visions were of things that will certainly be, and a good number of them have already come to pass, but our victory is not guaranteed. She saw two outcomes after the theft of her heart—one where Gwelain is defeated, and one where she is victorious. Look here. *When the hero pledged to Linnea bows to the goblin queen and becomes her creature, then will the door be opened so that our greatest enemy may come to power, raining misery and destruction upon Andonia.*"

Sorra sat again and took the book from him.

"The mages insisted we be marked as loyal to the quest," he said. "It showed us who was faithful, who had given up, and most importantly who was planning to betray our cause. Without that warning, Gwelain might already have claimed her traitor and her victory." He glanced at his sword, so quickly Sorra almost missed it. "But it showed Gwelain who among us could be the key to her victory as well as who she could safely eliminate because they'd renounced the quest. As of today, I am the only potential traitor. She's tried to win me over with offers to end tax collection forever if I'll bow to her, but I've held out. As long as I do, she can't win."

Sorra looked down at the page again, her gaze lingering on the words *misery* and *destruction*.

It wasn't written about her, but she hated how it echoed the warning of her birth blessing. She knew she'd never betray Andonia but was glad she hadn't told Tullian about the fate she hoped she'd left behind.

"Can I still be the Mystery from the vision if I haven't taken your oath?" Sorra asked.

"I believe so. The identities of the heroes are entirely separate from the visions regarding potential outcomes." Tullian removed the rabbit from the fire and stood with his back to her at the table near the wall, carving the meat with a long hunting knife. "All I know for certain is that Gwelain believes her traitor will be marked as one of us. Until I'm sure you're truly *adonthai*—the word for hero in Linnea's tongue—with courage and strength enough to resist whatever Gwelain might tempt you with, I can't take that risk. Outside these walls we'll speak as though it's done, and she won't know otherwise. If it's meant to be, I will see some sign that I should swear you to this quest. Don't be too eager, though. Once you're marked, you could become the sacrifice that leads to our victory. You're safer for the time being if I'm the only one who can die for our cause."

Sorra swallowed back the lump in her throat.

Tullian carried two plates back to the fire and handed one to Sorra. "You'll have to use your fingers."

"Thank you." Sorra ate, too lost in her thoughts to notice the flavour of the meat, then cleaned her fingers and paged through the rest of the visions. There was a warning about the mage Tullian had mentioned—*Gwelain's secret strength and secret weakness, the key to her rise and her fall*—as well as some vague details about the heroes and their quest.

Marked by birth and marked by life.
Born not under the light of the moon.
Mind, Magic, Mystery, Might.

Nothing seemed to be in order, with terrible visions about Linnea's death coming after the one about the traitor and before a short note saying the heroes would follow 'the humble path,' whatever that might mean. The visions surrounding Linnea's death and the theft of her heart were clearer, but worthless now that they'd come true.

It was so little, but Tullian obviously treasured every word.

"I'll become whatever I need to be to see this through," she said, and closed the book.

Or at least I'll act the part, she added to herself, hoping it would be enough.

"I'm sure." Tullian set his plate aside and went to the armour table. "For Linnea's sake, we'll see what we can make of you. Here. Killig's armour should fit you. He was our mage. Slight fellow."

Sorra examined the armour he held out to her—a cuirass styled much like his own but made from thick leather. She glanced at Tullian's again. It looked heavy and uncomfortable, yet he continued to wear it more than a century after he'd stopped searching for the heart. What dangers could it protect against when Gwelain and her goblins couldn't kill him?

The songbird on his breast caught the sunset light from one of the hut's windows.

It protects him from despair, Sorra thought. *And from the danger of him abandoning his queen.*

It was a constant reminder of who he was, even if Andonia had forgotten him and his quest.

Tullian motioned for her to raise her arms and slipped the armour over them, then fastened it at the side. It was heavy and uncomfortable, but he seemed satisfied with the armour, if not with the person wearing it.

"Good enough for now," he said. "Set that aside, take care of your needs, and choose a bed. We start work early tomorrow."

"And we'll find the castle soon?" Sorra asked, her voice muffled as she struggled out of the armour.

"When I'm sure you're meant to find it," Tullian said, turning away. "Until then, we train here. Make yourself at home."

He left the hut, taking the dirty plates with him.

Sorra sat on the edge of one of the lower bunks, sending up a flurry of dust, and rested her head in her hands.

Beau might be suffering unspeakably after his return to Gwelain's castle, and every day that passed without searching for him would be torture. There was no reason they shouldn't take the maps and set out immediately, except for the visions and Tullian's ideas about heroes and worthiness.

But maybe this is the way out.

Maybe I do get to be a hero after all.

"I've made it this far," she whispered, and yawned. "I can survive a few days of hero training if that's what it takes."

CHAPTER TWENTY-EIGHT

Tullian's sword came down, swinging toward Sorra's face. She raised hers to block as he'd instructed, and the impact vibrated through her arms. As her sword fell, the knight's whipped back around, faster than she could track, and stopped just short of her throat.

"You've lost your head," he said. "Again."

Sorra turned her back as she picked up her sword so he wouldn't see her face—not the sweat that she worked up when he hardly needed to put in any effort at all, not the tears that blurred her vision every time she failed, and certainly not her gritted teeth as she bit back a sharp retort. Those angered him, and only made the corrections come harder and faster on her next try.

She'd told herself she could bear anything for a few days. But days had turned into a full week, and another, and with each hour that passed, the pressure inside her built. She'd wakened this morning feeling as though she might explode if something didn't change.

So far, nothing had.

Their training space was, as usual, the clearing directly outside their hideout—a tiny plot of land that had become Sorra's world. Physical training outdoors, studying and cooking and contemplation indoors, venturing only as far as a nearby river when she wished to bathe.

She bathed more than Tullian thought necessary. Except on two blessed occasions when the old knight had walked to a nearby town for supplies, the stream was the only place she could be sure he wouldn't be watching her with a critical eye and a heaping serving of advice on how she could be more like him.

Courageous. Honest. Wise. Honourable.

Insufferable.

But she carried on, collapsing into bed each night with the thought that perhaps tomorrow she'd be good enough. The trouble was that there were so many ways to fail.

She trained every day with sword or dagger or bow, learning how to move in the leather armour she wore over a threadbare black tunic and trousers, ignoring how poorly it fit her no matter how she adjusted the fastenings. Her body grew stronger, but her arms still ached after an hour of swinging her sword about, and Tullian never let her quit before they'd been training for three.

At Tullian's insistence, she pored over dry commentaries on the visions, cursing Selim and whoever had helped him carry a small library along on a quest to a foreign land. She never got to read or hear the stories she wanted about Linnea or Gwelain, which Tullian still said he'd share when she was worthy of them.

She studied harder than she ever had in school, but displeased Tullian with questions that demonstrated a lack of understanding she wasn't sure how to overcome if not by asking questions.

And there were smaller failures for him to pick at—her hair falling in her face during fights when it should be more firmly tied back, her shoulders slumping when she walked, her rabbit snares not being set in exactly the right place, her tongue being too loose when she didn't have anything useful to say.

Tullian rarely found her words useful, so resigned silence had become her habit as she reminded herself that she needed his help no matter how painful it might be.

The only respite had been the few days of rest he'd allowed her when her body had put her through its monthly tortures. He'd even brought her a little wine to dull the pain, and it had taken the edge off his sharp comments when he'd felt it had disappeared too quickly.

He hadn't taken a drink, himself. The drunk she'd met in the pub had burned away, leaving behind nothing but a shining example of what she herself would never be.

"You're not paying attention to your stance," Tullian said behind her, interrupting her bitter thoughts. "You're focusing on your arms and drawing no support from your legs or the ground beneath you. You're grass when you should be an oak, and it makes it easy to cut you down."

Sorra kept her back turned as she found her breath, telling herself to let his words flow over her, to use them if she could and release them if she couldn't. Linnea's heroes had to be patient.

But what for?

Sixteen days since they'd met, and they hadn't begun to search for Gwelain's castle. Beau was there, being punished gods knew how for his failed attempt to leave her, and here Sorra stood, sweating and broken down and utterly useless.

Her fingers tightened around the hilt of her sword. They were stronger than they'd been when she started her quest. Her mind felt sharper, at least when it wasn't overwhelmed by ideas translated from an archaic language and written in nearly indecipherable handwriting. She was trying her best and was doing a fine job at faking the humility and obedience he wanted, but it wasn't enough.

And it never will be, because it's not about me at all.

Tullian had left his drinks behind him, but he'd found a new excuse to not move forward.

It's him. It always has been.

And nothing will change as long as I play along.

With that thought, a strange feeling settled over her. Anger, but quieter than she was accustomed to, and with it a sort of peace.

Sorra turned to face Tullian. "When are we going to leave to search for the castle?"

She'd asked many times over the past few weeks, but this time she watched him without expectation of what she'd see and hear.

Tullian smiled, though he didn't seem amused. "You need to be more patient."

"And you've been too patient." Sorra told herself to stay calm. It didn't work. She'd contained her chaotic impulses for too long, and for better or worse, her next words would change everything. "You've had over a hundred years to keep searching. Maybe if you'd found it sooner, we wouldn't have lost so many to the curse and Andonia wouldn't have lost the heir to its throne."

Tullian stiffened. "You have no idea what you're talking about. I was alone."

"You're not now. So I'll ask you again, when will we start searching for the heart?"

"You're not ready."

Sorra's gripped her weapon tighter. "And when will I be ready?"

Tullian couldn't have missed the bite in her tone, but he answered calmly, returning ice when she breathed fire. "When you are worthy of the quest. When you are patient and selfless as a hero should be, seeking the heart for Linnea's sake or Andonia's, not because you're infatuated with a missing prince."

Sorra hoped the redness already present in her overheated skin hid her blush. She hadn't shared every detail of her time with Beau, but Tullian had clearly filled in the gaps for himself. "I'm not saving him for my own sake."

She'd reminded herself many times that dreaming of a story-book ending was a waste of time, that she was not doing this for herself.

But somewhere deep inside it felt like a lie, and she hated the foolish part of herself that imagined him loving her.

Focusing her anger on Tullian was far more comfortable than reflecting on that. She tapped the point of her sword on the ground. He scowled, as she'd known he would.

"I don't think I can be good enough for you. I don't think you want me to be." She twisted the hilt, grinding the sword's point into the dirt as she held his gaze, unafraid of the cold rage she found there now that she'd discovered a crack in his heroic exterior. "I think you've crawled out of your drunken haze and found a new excuse for not moving forward. I think you're scared, and I think you're hiding behind Linnea's visions so you don't have to continue your quest."

"Bah." Tullian turned away with a dismissive wave of his hand and walked toward the path that led to the river.

Sorra followed. "What, then?"

He spun on her, his face twisted with what Sorra at first took to be anger. When he spoke, though, his voice cracked with something else. Fear, yes, but more than that.

"Of course I'm scared! You speak as though this were a game to you, but it is my life—and Linnea's life, and her death, and her chance to be at peace knowing her heart is serving her people. The fate of a nation rests on my shoulders."

"Our shoulders."

Tullian laughed. "Oh, yes. I was doing my part, refusing to become the traitor Gwelain needs to ensure her victory. I could do nothing else on my own, so denying her was enough. But now, you. Perhaps a chance to do something more meaningful than holding my ground, but even if that's true, it's the last chance I'll get." His shoulders dropped, and his expression went slack. "Linnea's last chance. Andonia's last chance. If the only help fate has offered me can't understand that we must make each of our steps perfect so we don't fail, what hope is there?"

"I've studied the visions as you asked. I've memorized them."

Tullian nodded, his chin low, defeated. "And I know how you see them—as a relic. An ancient queen's mad ravings. An old man's ridiculous obsession."

"Not entirely." She did think he was too fanatical about the visions, but his pain had doused her anger. She wasn't sure what to do without it.

Tullian squeezed his eyes shut. "I can't fail her again."

"What do you mean?"

"It doesn't matter."

"I think it might."

He sheathed his sword. "I've tried to be what this quest needs, to be an example and inspiration to you. The truth is I'm..." Tullian sighed and sat on the forest floor. "I told you I knew Linnea. I was one of her personal guards. I loved her, I suppose, as well as a mere human can love someone like her, but even I didn't take her visions seriously enough. I was meant to be watching her door the night she died, but I wanted to attend the—" He paused. "You know, I can't recall what festival it was. It seemed important at the time. Jervis offered to take watch alone. He wasn't the best of us, but I didn't see the harm in leaving him in charge for one night. I went. I drank. I slept. And I awakened to word that the queen was dead."

No wonder he never wants to tell stories about her, Sorra thought, imagining the weight of his guilt.

She sat next to him and rested a hand on his arm for a moment, unsure of how to offer comfort to someone who might feel ashamed of needing it. "You couldn't have known."

"Linnea knew, though. Not the exact date or time, and she herself may have doubted the visions, but she believed she needed protection from Gwelain, and she relied on us for it. On me." He smiled sadly. "Perhaps her death was inevitable—the visions are clearer than you think, and we've seen plenty of them prove true already. But it shouldn't have happened on my watch."

"I see." Sorra polished her sword on the hem of her tunic. Tullian's mage companion had enchanted their weapons to remain sharp, but she regretted abusing it. "Is that why you weren't chosen for the first quests?"

"I didn't think myself worthy. Then the others failed, and I realized this might be my chance at redemption, so I offered myself when few others dared to try." He rested his hands on his lap, palms up. "Look at me. I was younger when I set out, though perhaps too old even then. The quest wore me down, took everything. I aged here, until Gwelain made her bargain with the foolish people of this land. Perhaps I'm afraid of finding out for certain that I can't win this. That I'm only a foolish old man and not the Might from her visions after all."

Sorra offered him a tentative smile. "You're the last hero standing. That has to be worth something."

Tullian winced. "Not much of a hero. I failed her once. I don't dare risk failing her again, and that makes me a coward."

Sorra breathed in the warm, still air of the forest, taking in the silence that cloaked it like a spell waiting to be broken.

"Thank you," she said.

Tullian turned to her. "For what?"

"For being human." Sorra stood and brushed the dead leaves off the back of her trousers, then sheathed her sword and offered both hands to pull Tullian to his feet. "I've been thinking that it's impossible to live up to the standards of this *adanthee* idea—"

"*Adonthai*," Tullian said, more gently than he usually corrected her. "Heroes."

"Right. And I've been thinking that I can't possibly be the Mystery because I won't ever be that kind of person no matter how hard I try. But if even you can't live up to it after being chosen for this quest, after fighting so hard and resisting the temptation to give up for so long, then maybe no one can. And maybe we just need to get off our asses and do something anyway." Sorra smiled as she remembered Beau's insistence that the world needed her to turn it upside down. "Trying and failing has to be better than not trying at all."

Tullian rubbed a hand down his face, tugging at his beard. "We're risking so much."

"I know. But things are changing, and waiting isn't an option anymore. I'm scared. I sometimes wish that enchanted arrow hadn't led me to this, or to you. But if you can stop trying to be perfect, and if you can stop trying to make me perfect, maybe together we can try to be good enough."

Tullian's shoulders slumped, and Sorra resisted the urge to correct his posture. "There may be truth buried under your crude phrasing. I only wish there were some way of knowing that the time was right for the visions to prove true."

"Maybe there will be signs if we take the first steps on our own," Sorra said. She didn't know whether she believed that but suspected Tullian would see even mundane events as signs when he was ready to.

"Perhaps." Tullian started back toward the hut, and Sorra fell in beside him. "I think it's time you joined me on a trip to the village. The walk will do you good, and it will give you a chance to understand Gwelain's world better."

Sorra suspected it would also give him a new setting to judge her progress in, but that didn't matter. Something was changing, and for the moment that was all she needed.

~

The village of Renfield—marked by a sign so faded that Sorra had to run her fingers over the carved letters to feel them out—lay an hour's walk to the north of Tullian's hideaway. It resembled the first town Sorra had visited, at least on the surface, with its painted buildings, air of general neglect, and the old-fashioned clothing of its citizens. The people plodded about as the others had, but something about them felt different.

Sorra stopped in the centre of the broad, dusty street, letting Tullian pull ahead by a few paces before he stopped and turned back. She wasn't watching him, but had her eye on a trio of girls between the ages of perhaps six and ten, each dressed in a faded blue dress, each with her dull blonde hair styled in twin braids that hung limply on her shoulders. Two turned a frayed rope for the smallest to jump listlessly over as they all mumbled a half-hearted chant, pausing only to switch places so the tallest girl could take a turn heaving herself over the rope. The rhyme started again, steady as the grinding of a machine, quiet enough that Sorra had to strain to make out the words.

"Stranger sellin' goods come to town, come to town,
Sellin' herbs, sellin' rags, sellin' seed.
Says to Mama, 'buy some sage, buy some rope, buy some thyme,'
Mama laughs, 'We got all the time we need.'
How many years 'til the clock runs down?
One, two, three, four..."

The girl in the middle continued her lead-footed jumps, never missing a beat, as the counting went on.

Of course they don't stumble, Sorra thought. *They've probably had over a hundred years of practice.*

Every day the same. Sorra had thought her life in Cottsbridge was unbearably dull, but she'd grown and changed, and so had the world around her in small ways. This was another kind of monotony entirely.

Tullian stood next to her, watching the girls. None of them

looked at their audience, each seeming determined to ignore everything but the next turn of the rope.

Everyone else ignored them, too, though two armoured people carrying swords should have drawn the eyes of the faded and dusty townsfolk.

"It's torture for them, isn't it?" Sorra asked, keeping her voice low enough that only Tullian would hear.

"It is. Most people I've met here are shadows of who they were, or who they might have been." The old knight spoke without emotion, stating facts he'd had too much time to grow accustomed to. "They exist for no reason except that they have no choice. I've seen women endlessly pregnant, infants who have watched a century pass without understanding a scrap of it. Fields go untended because they'll produce crops no matter what, and even if they didn't, no one would starve. There's no purpose. No pleasure after this much time. I suspect their dear goblin queen stole their joy and hope as part of their deal, even if it's not a term I can imagine them agreeing to."

Sorra watched the girls for a little longer, noting how the chant stopped again at one hundred—not because the girl had missed a step, but because it seemed part of their ritual to switch.

"And they never take another way out?" Sorra's belly squirmed as she spoke the question. "That is… I assume the goblins taking taxes means death. That's an ending. But the farmer seemed afraid, even before the goblins turned to his son. And so many have held on. Haven't done the job for themselves, I mean."

Tullian looked down at her. "Would you take that way out?"

Sorra shrugged. "I can't say. I'm not them, am I? But I guess I couldn't fault them if they found their own way out of this life."

"Nor I. But they can't." He turned to walk up the street, and Sorra followed. Townsfolk stood in silent groups, walked with their gazes set on the horizon, or sat watching the empty sky. A woman on a bench outside the general store passed an embroidery needle through fabric over and over, not seeming to notice or care there was no thread trailing behind to mark its passage.

"Death is barred from these lands, remember?" Tullian glanced back at the children. "When these people are lost to taxes, their bodies are sacrificed, but their spirits don't go to Lord Death and the lands beyond life."

Sorra shuddered. She'd never been entirely certain what became of a person after death, but she'd always hoped something better came after the suffering of this world. "What, then? Are they wandering spirits?"

"Worse. You've heard of blood magic?" Tullian punctuated the question by spitting in the dust and didn't wait for Sorra to answer. "The goblins likely feed on the sacrificed bodies, but Gwelain's mage uses the tortured spirits to feed his power."

"The mage from Linnea's visions?"

"I believe so." Tullian's voice took on the lecturing tone Sorra had come to dread over the past few weeks, but for once he was speaking on something that held her attention entirely. "Human witches make a physical sacrifice of their own pain and blood to open themselves to magic, but only the worst of them go on to take the same from others, or to burn souls up for the sake of their own power. Gwelain's mage is human, and according to the visions he's a powerful threat. I have no doubt what becomes of the spirits Lord Death can't collect from these lands, whether the body is lost through accident or intentional harm or taxes."

Sorra's breakfast rose in her throat, and she swallowed it back. "But if we took the heart from Gwelain, this would end?"

"It would. All of this is based in her fragile, stolen power."

"Good."

"Now, no more of this talk until we return to safety." Tullian's steps slowed. "It's said that speaking the mage's name calls his attention so he can listen in, but I prefer to speak as little as possible of him even in general terms. I don't doubt these folks will inform someone we were here and be well rewarded for it, but—"

"None'll tell." The voice that interrupted Tullian was like stone, and when Sorra turned toward it she found a man just as rough sitting in the dirt, his hair grey as slate, his eyes like flint. He used a weathered cane to struggle to his feet, waving away the helping hand Sorra offered. He glared at Tullian. "You haven't been around to protect us from the increase in taxes, but I guess folks're still angrier at the goblins than they are at you."

A small group of pedestrians slowed behind Tullian, obviously trying not to look like they were listening to the conversation.

The old man nodded his chin at them. "Minding their own business. As if that'll make the queen leave us alone."

"What increase?" Tullian asked.

The old man's already tiny eyes disappeared into his wrinkles as he squinted up at the knight. "Where've you been? Don't know whether it's the same everywhere, but we've seen more goblins 'round here in the past few weeks than we saw in the year before."

"Not just the goblins," said one of the women who stood behind Tullian. Her voice was hesitant until one of her companions took her arm as if to silence her. The speaker pulled away, stepped closer, and spoke more firmly. "Last few times they came 'round it wasn't for simple taxes. Usually they just drag folks away, but now they're chasing us down, trampling us under their horses, breaking bones and leaving folks to suffer, doing their worst to anyone who tries to hide or fight. Last few times, they brought the queen's hunting dogs."

"That's horrible." Sorra imagined packs of hounds baying and snapping as they chased people down the street, or perhaps dark-coated, wolf-like dogs that ran faster than any human.

Tullian stood straighter and looked over the people in the street. "I thank you for the information," he said, his voice firm. "I assure you I will do whatever I can to see the harassment ended."

The old man let out a jeering "yeeeeeh," and wandered away, joining the woman who had spoken and the others as they resumed their trek up the road.

Tullian waited until they were gone before he spoke again. "This isn't about taxes. Gwelain has offered many times to end her attacks on the people if I'll come to her side. It seems she's growing desperate for a traitor."

"Of course she is," Sorra said. "She has Beau and her path to the throne, but she doesn't have you."

Tullian's brow furrowed as it did when difficult thoughts crowded his mind. "But she's had him for years. Something has changed."

"Maybe it's because you've changed. Even if she doesn't know for sure where we are, she knows you're not where you should be, that you're not doing what you usually do." Sorra wasn't sure whether the chill that came over her was fear or excitement. "Maybe she's afraid."

"Or she knows something we don't." Tullian pulled both hands through his thick hair, smoothing his brow into a more relaxed pattern of ruts and creases. "I suppose we should leave the area so there will be no reason for Gwelain to continue her attacks. I only wish…"

"What?"

Tullian shook his head. "Nothing. When we get back, we'll discuss—"

A scream cut him off, and Sorra reached for her sword. The sound felt inevitable, as if some part of her had been listening for it from the moment the old man had mentioned increased taxes.

The studied placidity left the townsfolk's faces. Most carried on as they had been, but with more panicked expressions or with tears in their eyes. Several darted into houses or shops, but all movements ceased as a piercing howl split the air, sending bolts of ice through Sorra's veins.

Another howl joined the first, and a third, as the pack stalked up the street. Even from a distance, Sorra realized that her imaginings had been terribly wrong, that she'd been stupid to think a goblin queen's hunting dogs would be anything less than monsters.

Three dogs, but the smallest was the size of a cart pony, the largest as big as a draught horse.

Shaggy coats, grey as fog, fur standing on end from shoulders to upraised tails.

"Hide," Tullian said. "They won't hurt me."

He didn't say *you're not ready*, but Sorra heard the echo of his repeated hesitations and corrections, and she agreed whole-heartedly.

But she stood firm and rolled back her right sleeve, revealing the songbird Tullian had painted onto her skin in black ink before they'd left the hut, praying as she did that the monsters would know what it meant, terrified that they'd somehow sniff out the lie.

One of the dogs lunged at a pedestrian, who screamed as the beast's teeth sank into his arm.

Behind the dogs, someone laughed, loud and high and excited, and a goblin on a black horse rode into view. His laugh stopped short and he grinned as he saw the two heroes.

Sorra decided it didn't matter whether she was ready. She drew her sword.

CHAPTER TWENTY-NINE

The goblin let out a sharp whistle, calling the dogs back to his side. He wore a dark hunting jacket and cream-coloured breeches, but his bare talons rested lightly on the stirrups until he dismounted, swinging gracefully to the ground with his reptilian tail arcing behind him. Though his rosy skin was patched with scales, Sorra was again struck by the way these creatures seemed both monster and human, which made them more monstrous in her mind than if they'd looked like the goblins from stories.

"They're testing us," Tullian muttered. "Show no weakness."

Another whistle and the dogs fell in behind the goblin, snapping at humans who continued about their business—not running, not speaking, as though ignoring the threat would hide them from it.

"Tullian," the goblin said, stopping outside of sword range. "We thought you'd fallen into a pit and left us for good."

"What luck that would have been for you," Tullian said.

The goblin glanced at Sorra and frowned at the mark on her arm, then looked back to Tullian. "You could end this, you know. Any time you wish. Our good queen would be pleased to negotiate."

"Tell her this will end, but not on her terms," Tullian said. The change in him compared to the last time he'd faced goblins was remarkable. The old drunk had disappeared, and in his place stood a true knight, confident and strong.

The goblin smiled grimly. "Your choice." He snapped his fingers, and two of the dogs attacked, one returning to the poor fellow who had collapsed behind them, the largest of them chasing a red-headed woman into a house, howling and throwing itself against the door when she slammed it shut. The wood splintered under its weight but didn't break.

The goblin mounted his black horse to watch as Tullian charged into the fight.

The third dog, the smallest of the three, prowled toward Sorra, growling and sniffing the air. Thick ropes of drool hung from its grizzled jowls, and its eyes were red as blood.

Sorra stood as Tullian had instructed, firm and balanced. She adjusted her grip on her sword and held it ready to attack, checking with her other hand to be sure her dagger was still at her waist.

Show no weakness.

"You can't hurt me," she said. "And I won't let you hurt these people."

The dog didn't stop its approach, either not understanding or, worse, not believing. Up close, Sorra picked out more details of the creature's strange body—ivory spines protruding from the raised fur of its hackles, teeth so sharp they cut into its lips and darkened its saliva with blood, claws that looked to be made of sharpened iron. Sorra's legs trembled, but she forced her arms to remain steady.

"Kill me," she shouted, with far more confidence than she felt. "See what happens to your mistress then."

The dog snarled and leapt. Sorra lashed out with her blade, her muscles forgetting all of their training as she imagined those teeth sinking into her throat, proving her a liar and ending her quest for good. The beast's musky stink surrounded her as it brushed by, knocking her off balance, unharmed by the poorly timed swing of her blade.

Relief surged through Sorra as she realized Tullian's trick had worked—the dog understood the marking, or perhaps the goblin had instructed it not to risk killing her. She was safe, at least for now.

But the dog hit the ground running, and instead of turning to test Sorra further, it headed straight for the trio of girls who had stopped their chanting and huddled together wide-eyed as the beast drew closer.

Sorra glanced over her shoulder. Tullian was still fighting the larger dog, his back to her.

She cursed under her breath and ran for the girls.

After a few steps she almost forgot her fear and barely heard the shouts from onlookers as the girls ran for the nearest house, where an older woman held the door open for them.

Two of them made it to the porch. The smallest girl fell behind, and the dog's long legs carried it quickly enough to cut her off from the others. It stood between her and the house, its growl like rolling thunder.

Sorra pushed herself to run faster. There was no time to think about what she should do, and in the absence of thought her body remembered the movements and positions she'd repeated to the point of exhaustion. Her grip became more natural, the sword an extension of herself.

The girl tried to run, and the dog followed, snapping at the back of her dress, catching and tearing the fabric.

Playing with her.

The dog lunged, pinning the girl to the ground, and she screamed. Sorra's shout sounded thin and childlike to her ear, nothing like the battle-cry she'd intended, but the dog turned its head as she plunged her sword into its back. Its skin was tougher than she'd expected, and the blade barely broke through before one of the spines on the dog's back sliced into the side of her right hand. She tried again, aiming for the thick meat of the creature's thigh.

The cut went deep, but it was nothing like a mortal wound.

The dog twisted away. Sorra lost her grip on the hilt, which had quickly become slick with her own blood, and the dog paced away with the sword protruding from the muscle behind its hip.

"Go on!" Sorra shouted, echoing the sharp tone people in Cotts-bridge used to command their dogs. "Leave it!"

It ignored her and leapt at the girl, who had curled into a ball, her arms protecting the back of her head as claws ripped through her dress, leaving a line of bloody gashes like whip-marks.

Sorra lunged for her sword, but the dog kept its hindquarters out of reach.

"The throat!" Tullian yelled. Sorra glanced at him, hoping he was finished with the others and on his way to help, but he was caught in a standoff with the biggest dog.

The other one lay dead, surrounded by mud where its blood had soaked into the dusty street.

The monsters can be killed, then.

Sorra threw herself at the dog, using her body weight to upset its balance. She crouched over the whimpering child, reaching for her dagger as the dog lunged again.

The beast collided with her, pinning her and the girl to the ground before she'd pulled the blade free of its sheath. It snapped at Sorra, snarling hot, stinking breath as it wrestled her aside, intent on harming the girl she aimed to protect.

The next few moments were a blur as she pushed against the underside of the dog's jaw with one hand, wrestling, grabbing the fur of its throat as she tugged her dagger free of its sheath. The girl fought, too, kicking and screaming. The dog roared and snapped, its jaws closing on Sorra's left forearm as she thrust it between the dog and the girl. The pain barely registered, nor did her own movements as she plunged the dagger into the monster's throat and tore it open, releasing a flood of hot, thick blood.

The dog released her and stumbled sideways. Sorra climbed to her feet, guiding the girl behind her, and watched as the dog stumbled and collapsed, her sword still sticking out of its hind leg.

Sorra's breath came in hard, sharp gasps as she looked down at herself. The creature's blood, which coated her from head to waist, was the green of pond scum, and the blood that flowed from her own hand and injured arm stood out bright red against it.

The ink mark on her right forearm had been smudged in the fight, and she rolled down her sleeve to cover it.

She stalked toward the goblin, who was watching with amusement as the big dog teased Tullian, leaping out of reach each time he approached it, threatening a bystander whenever Tullian turned away.

"Hey!"

The goblin turned, baring his oversized teeth as Sorra raised her left arm to show her injuries.

"Your queen's beast did that. Do you think she'll be pleased when you tell her?"

The goblin's horse danced nervously beneath him. He whistled, and the surviving dog ran to his side. They raced away, leaving the townsfolk to deal with the bodies they'd left behind.

Only monsters, though.

The girl ran to the porch where her sisters and the older woman waited, and the four sank to their knees, holding each other. The man Tullian had rushed to defend earlier was on his feet, cradling his injured arm with his other hand, very much alive.

Sorra's knees shook, but she forced herself to stay on her feet.

"Inside, all of you!" Tullian called, and the people obeyed, leaving them alone in the street. He watched Sorra carefully for a moment, then caught her under her arms as her legs gave way.

"Don't forget to breathe," he whispered. "Don't allow weakness to take you now that the fight is over." But he let her lean on him until her heart settled and she was able to walk.

"I killed it," she said.

"That you did." Tullian led her back to the fallen dog and pulled her sword free. "With a little more training, you might learn to hold on to your weapon through the entire battle, but you did well enough. If Gwelain meant to test you, I'd say you passed."

The praise was faint, but Sorra caught the pride in his voice.

A door creaked behind them, and Sorra turned to find the oldest of the three girls approaching with a narrow roll of white cotton in her hand.

"For your wounds," she said shyly, and pointed to a water pump beside the house. She plodded back to the house as soon as Sorra relieved her of the gift.

Tullian helped her wash the wounds and wrapped her arm and hand. The torn flesh was still bleeding, and the pain was making itself properly heard now that the excitement had died down.

"Come," he said. "We'll buy supplies another day. We have things to speak about, and you need to rest after we do a better job of knitting you up."

Sorra didn't object and didn't speak as they walked back to the hideout in the woods. The sun warmed the air and dried the blood on her skin, leaving her sticky and uncomfortable and smelling as bad as any of the dogs. But Tullian led her straight to the hut instead of to the river to bathe.

He didn't speak until the door closed behind them.

"He'll be listening now," he said. "That mage. No chance they don't know where we are after that, so we must be extra cautious in our speech outside these walls."

"Of course." Sorra waited, hoping he was going to say it was time to leave, not wanting to make him feel she was forcing the decision.

Her impatience ached as badly as her wounds.

He looked her over from her gore-soaked hair to the sword she'd carried in her hand the whole way back, not wanting to dirty its sheath with the blood that had dried on the blade.

"I'll clean it," Sorra said.

"I'll do it for you this time," he said, and took the sword. He set it on a table, though, and turned his back on it. "You did well today, Sorra. You lack skill, patience, bodily strength, and so much else that I might demand of you, but you showed the seed of heroism I've been praying to find in you. Selflessness. Acting on another's behalf even at risk to your own life. When we left this place today, I was unsure of whether you could be one of Linnea's heroes. These wounds are the sign I was waiting for."

Tears stung Sorra's eyes.

No teacher had ever praised her so sincerely or given her a chance to prove herself worthy of it.

He'd never have given her a chance if he'd known about the blessing, but maybe that was all right. She'd come further in the past few weeks than she'd ever thought possible when she lived under its shadow.

Maybe I can become another person entirely—not the Sorra who was cursed by her family's blessing, but the hero her old self was never meant to be.

She blinked back the tears before Tullian could see them. "If that means you're ready to continue your quest, I'm glad to hear it.

I have plenty more to learn on the way, though. One fight against a snarling pup hasn't proved me just yet."

It didn't feel like something her old self would have said, but it suited the new Sorra and her seed of heroism.

Tullian beamed. "You're the Mystery, sworn or not," he said. "Humility suits you."

Sorra looked away. "Thank you."

"We should leave soon," Tullian said. "No sense putting it off. We'll get our weapons in order, gather our things, stop for supplies on the way…"

"And a bath?"

Tullian chuckled. "Three baths for you, I think." He handed her the cracked old bar of yellow soap that had been in the hut long before their stay. "Go. Clean those wounds well and return refreshed. We'll eat, we'll rest, and tomorrow the real adventure will begin."

Sorra gathered fresh bandages and a blanket to dry herself with, then walked to the river, leaving Tullian humming an off-key tune to himself.

She'd never seen him so happy. He seemed excited and sure of the path ahead even if he still had no clear idea of where to look for the castle.

A seed of heroism wasn't much, but his critical eye had seen it in her. A seed could grow into something far greater if it had the right soil, the right care.

Her old self couldn't hope to save Beau or steal back a heart, but her old self also couldn't have killed a monster. Maybe Tullian was right. There would be hard work ahead, and great challenges. But beyond them, great rewards.

I've changed, she thought. *If I keep on like this, anything is possible.*

She promised herself she'd get properly to work on her new self as soon as she'd washed the stink of victory from her skin.

CHAPTER THIRTY

Sorra took her time at the river, first washing her clothes and spreading them over nearby bushes to dry in the sun, then cleaning the gore and dog fur off her armour before turning her attention to her body and the blood that had dried in her hair.

She'd used up the last of the soap before she was done, and though the water chilled her, she stayed submerged in a deep pool for as long as she could, scraping her nails over her skin to be sure the smell wouldn't cling to her.

By the time she'd dried herself in the sun and walked back in her damp clothing, carrying her armour under one arm, it was nearly sunset. Smoke rose from the hole in the hut's roof, carrying the scent of rabbit stew. It wouldn't be *good* stew. Tullian hadn't bought any spices on his previous trips to the village, and he tended to compensate by over-salting the meat and foraged vegetable matter. Still, her stomach growled.

Several bags sat by the door—leather saddlebags, two knapsacks made of thick canvas, and a small assortment of weapons Tullian hadn't yet found room for. His cuirass lay on top of the pile, polished and shining. He stood next to the fire, stirring the contents of the iron pot hung over it, his brow furrowed and his gaze unfocused.

"You've kept busy," Sorra said, testing the waters. He seemed ready to leave, but there was a fair chance he was in the process of thinking himself out of it. For once, she didn't think badly of him for his hesitation. Now that the bags were packed, the dangers they might face on the road seemed clearer and closer.

"No point delaying once the decision is made." He didn't sound entirely certain, but Sorra's chest tightened with a mix of anticipation and fear as she took a bowl of stew and sat by the fire.

The old knight didn't speak again as they ate, and after the meal was finished, he sat and scowled some more.

"Should we discuss our plans?" Sorra asked. "It won't be safe to talk once we've left this place."

Tullian blinked hard, as if coming out of a trance. "We leave in the morning and will return to the village for supplies, including a pair of horses." He paused. "You can ride?"

Sorra offered him a weak smile. "Haven't done it much, but I'll get the hang of it."

The truth was that her night spent travelling to Beau's cabin accounted for most of the hours she'd spent riding any sort of animal, but she'd always got on well with horses.

Tullian stood, stretching out his back before making his way to the table of maps. "You'll have to. The good news is they're as hardy and as complacent as the humans in these lands."

He held up a map, tilted toward the firelight. A wash of faded red ink covered much of it, accompanied by pale blue in a few small patches and swaths of purple where the two overlapped.

"There's nowhere in these lands that hasn't been searched," Tullian said. "The red shows where my own group journeyed during our time here. The blue was covered by a previous party— the ones who built this shelter. They'd vanished before we discovered it, but they left notes and a few maps, all encoded with magic. I've re-covered most of that ground, but there are a few areas left we might explore."

Sorra took the map and stepped closer to the fire to examine the notes in the margins. The script was small and hard to read, but it was written in the common tongue.

"Selim's notes," Tullian said without Sorra asking. "He kept his own records in the old language, but he never gave up hope that the rest of us would take an interest in his studies, and occasionally wrote for us in a language we could understand. I've packed another book of notes he made on our travels—ideas about what had once existed where we found only ruins, stories about festivals held when these lands belonged to the Bright Ones, that sort of thing."

Sorra handed the map back to him, and Tullian rolled it carefully and set it with their things.

"It's not much to go on, is it?" she asked.

He smiled grimly and sat next to the fire again, his legs stretched out in front of him, crossed at the ankles. "It never was."

"What will we do when we find the castle?"

Tullian chuckled.

Sorra sat next to him, unbothered. "*When.* There's no room for *if,* especially if you think this is your last chance."

"I suppose not." Tullian sobered quickly. "I don't know for certain. I believe the heart is there, that its presence is both the reason Gwelain hides the castle so well and the reason she rarely leaves it. She'd need to be close to the heart to draw from its power."

"Of course," Sorra said, though she had no idea how such things worked.

"But I don't know what the castle looks like, or where she might hide a heart within it, or how it could be guarded. We'll need to find a way in so we can search."

"And then we'll creep around like mice, hoping no one finds us?"

Tullian's gaze cut sideways, and the amused glint in his eyes caught Sorra by surprise. "No. We'll stay as guests."

Sorra stretched her legs out, matching his posture, and folded her hands on her stomach as she waited, sure she wouldn't need to prod now that his confidence in her had loosened his tongue.

"I don't know what the customs are in your time," Tullian said, "but in mine, the old ways held, passed down from the Bright Ones to Linnea. In the old times, if a subject presented him or herself before the throne, the ruler was bound to welcome them as guests. To treat them well, to offer hospitality, to do them no harm. To do otherwise was not only a break with tradition that would cause many to question a ruler's strength and legitimacy—it would leave a king open to the sort of ill luck even near-immortal creatures fear. If we can make it to her throne room before she stops us, we'll be safe."

"And you really think Gwelain will hold to that?"

Tullian watched the flames for a moment, then nodded. "She's doing everything she can to stack the odds in her favour, so she won't risk bad luck unless we push her to it. Beyond that, she craves legitimacy. If you want evidence of that, look at the path she's apparently chosen to taking Andonia—not finishing the work she began with this curse you spoke of, but using it as leverage to take Linnea's throne and rule over her people. She'll hold to her grandfather's law."

Sorra drew her heels up onto the edge of the chair and rested her arms on her raised knees, staring into the dwindling fire. "She wants to negotiate with you. What if you pretended to be interested in that—would she invite you to the castle? If you could keep up the ruse long enough, it would buy us some time."

Tullian smiled sadly. "You must think very little of me if you believe I'd miss such a simple solution. Even if I could convince her of my interest, she wouldn't bring me to the castle. She'd meet me elsewhere."

"You're sure?"

"It's what she did when she tempted one of my close companions to betray us. I followed him to their meeting. There was no castle."

"And your close companion?"

"He didn't live long enough to offer Gwelain her victory." Tullian spoke matter-of-factly, but Sorra caught a waver in his voice that wasn't usually there.

She had no desire to ask for details.

"So we find the castle, get to the throne room, you offer to negotiate while we enjoy her hospitality, then we..." She trailed off and dropped her voice to a whisper. "Kill Gwelain and take the heart?"

"No." Tullian turned fully toward Sorra, drawing his legs around to sit sideways on his chair. "Listen carefully."

Sorra had never seen him so focused, sharp as a blade as he looked into her eyes, confirming her attention.

"Everything I know about magic came from our mage, from Selim, or from the greater wisdom of the scholars and mages who sent us after Linnea's heart," he said. "I believe what they taught me, and you must take every word just as seriously."

"I will," Sorra whispered.

"Gwelain doesn't simply possess our queen's heart in a physical sense. She has a magical bond with it that gives her control over its power, a connection no one but Gwelain herself can sever. It would be very difficult to kill her—the Bright Ones and creatures like them are able to use magic to protect themselves in ways humans and half-humans cannot. But even if we could, we wouldn't dare. As long as the connection exists, Gwelain's death would cause the destruction of Linnea's heart."

Sorra's mouth went dry. "And then Andonia would lose its magic?"

"I don't know. The truth is I wouldn't care if it were only that. But Linnea's spirit is bound up in her heart. If we kill Gwelain, we destroy what remains of our good queen's soul."

"I understand. So you plan to steal it back?"

"It's the best idea we had." Tullian spoke dully. "It wouldn't be a true victory, though. Gwelain needs to be close to the heart to draw on its power, so taking it away and hiding it would weaken her. But until she released her hold on it, the heart would be of no benefit to anyone else, and we certainly couldn't return it to its proper resting place where she might steal it again. There would be no return to the grand old magic Linnea left to the mages after her death."

"That would be all right, maybe. As long as we were safe."

Tullian frowned. "I believe another path will show itself if we keep our eyes open, one that leads to her heart and her soul resting at peace in Andonia. If this prince of yours is as clever as you think, perhaps he's our Mind and the key to what comes next."

"I hope so." Sorra's cheeks warmed. She'd been trying not to think of Beau, but the idea of actually finding him, seeing him again, hearing his voice, brought a flood of memories and anticipation.

"You care for him," Tullian observed without obvious judgement.

"I do, but it doesn't mean anything. He's not… it's not like that."

"Be careful, regardless." Tullian closed his eyes and settled more firmly into his chair. "It's good to have a strong purpose, and even a specific one. But affection blinds us, and it can cause good heroes to make bad decisions."

Sorra doubted Tullian was speaking from personal experience. When faced with the prospect of a potential traitor he hadn't let personal bonds keep him from doing what was needed for the sake of his quest.

"I'll remember," she said. "Thank you."

He wasn't wrong to think she needed the warning. Her own quest had become much larger than it had been when she'd set out, but Beau was still the heart of it no matter how many times she told herself he wasn't.

But if I understand a weakness, I can overcome it.

Exhaustion crept into the edges of Sorra's mind, weighing down her thoughts and her eyelids. Tullian didn't look much better off, but he also didn't seem to have any intention of leaving the fireside to turn in early.

"We should get some sleep," she said.

"Go ahead. I'm not quite ready."

"You'll get a crick in your back if you nod off in that chair."

He smiled but didn't move.

Sorra lay on her side on the same bunk she'd been sleeping in since her second night at the hideout, when she'd moved higher to put space between herself and the rats she'd heard on the floor the first night.

She knew she should sleep, but she couldn't shake the thought that she'd forgotten something important, something that needed to be done before they started out. Then, like a bubble rising from the depths of her mind, an idea broke the calm surface of gathering sleep.

One more history lesson, and one she suspected she'd finally earned.

"Tullian?"

"Hmm?"

"You're so sure about Gwelain's desire for legitimacy. You've said she hasn't changed, and you have no doubts about her belief in the visions or her desire to follow them. You speak like you know her well and going way back."

Tullian sat up, shifting the shadow he cast on the hut's wall. "I've hardly seen her in person," he said. "We've only exchanged words through her goblins. Everything I know about her came from Linnea. Old stories, but carried unbroken in the memory of one who heard them directly, or was there herself." He paused. "All of it has truly been forgotten?"

"As far as I know." Sorra yawned. "Tell me about her, please. If I'm going to be useful, I need to know our enemy. Not just about her, but what drives her, and why she hates Linnea. Why she's doing any of this."

Tullian grunted. "Your mind wanders when I offer lessons."

"Because you tend to drone on without letting me help you make them interesting."

Tullian scowled at her, but she caught a twitch of amusement at his mouth. "If you'll watch your tone, I'll do my best to entertain. Just this once."

CHAPTER THIRTY-ONE

"I'll do my best to tell it as Linnea would have," Tullian began. "The story came to me in pieces over dozens of conversations, but the parts should all fit together well enough in the end."

Sorra lay on her back, eyes closed to better focus on Tullian's voice—on the true history of the quest, of Gwelain, and of the queen she'd always loved, told by one who had known her.

A pleasant shiver traced her spine.

"I've told you these lands were once part of Andonia," he said, "but before that they were called Duatheseronis—at least, that's the closest my human tongue can come to saying it. It was the land of the Bright Ones, who in later legends were called faeries or *grounthrais* or a hundred other things by humans who never knew them. Their magic was incredible, their beauty legendary. Their extended family included lesser creatures, weaker and uglier, but to the noble Bright Ones they—and humans—were little better than animals.

"The Bright Ones lived lives that would seem impossibly long to us. Births and deaths were rare. They lived for beauty and pleasure, and when a child was born no one considered paternity too deeply."

Sorra's imagination filled in the gaps between the scant details Tullian's story provided. Andonia, but not as she knew it. No smog-choked cities, maybe no cities at all. Forests, gardens, everything bursting with magic. She imagined the Bright Ones as beautiful people, tall and strong, then added delicate wings to them and smiled at the image.

It was probably wrong, but it made them real to her.

"Gwelain was born to the daughter of King Oresthetes and raised within that culture of beauty and luxury and excess, but in time she decided it wasn't enough for her, and she set her sights on her grandfather's crown."

"Did she try to kill him?" Sorra asked.

"Naturally. She failed, and as punishment Oresthetes revealed to all what he'd never told her privately—that her father had been a goblin, one of those lesser members of the extended family tree. The knowledge shamed Gwelain. Not as if her father were a pauper, but as if she'd discovered her mother had taken a toad as a lover. And everyone knew."

The images behind Sorra's eyelids showed the scene in the crisp lines of a woodcut illustration. The king sat on a silver throne, his open-roofed palace filled with his beautiful subjects, all of them jeering. Gwelain, looking much like the goblins Sorra had recently encountered, stood with her back turned to them as if bracing herself against a cold winter wind.

"The second part of her punishment was crueller still." Tullian's voice had taken on a rolling, soothing cadence entirely unlike the one he used for lectures. "Gwelain had wished to rule over the beautiful, sophisticated Bright Ones. Oresthetes made her queen of the goblins instead and sent her to live in the swamps and forests among her new subjects.

"I suppose he expected her to die of shame or return humbled if she ever dared face his court and its gossip again. Instead, she embraced her role and tried to teach her goblins to look and behave like the Bright Ones. She won their loyalty, and she loved them as well as she could. According to Linnea, they loved her in return."

"Did she use them to try to take the crown again?" Sorra asked.

"No. Though Gwelain possessed magic like the Bright Ones, the goblins were never able to wield it and wouldn't have stood a chance against Oresthetes and his army. She only returned home once, wearing a crown and escorted by a dozen of her hideous subjects, to ask that they be recognized and elevated to a proper place in society.

"The Bright Ones laughed her out of the palace, but she smiled like she'd won some victory as she walked away."

The Gwelain in Sorra's mind changed, standing straight and tall, wearing a crown of bones set with flashing jewels, her head held high. She'd taken an insult and turned it into a source of pride, becoming a true queen to spite those who mocked her, turning what they saw as her weakness into power.

Sorra couldn't help admiring Gwelain for that, just a little. She knew all too well what it was to be discarded as unworthy, to be denied a place among the people she'd grown up knowing, though she'd never earned anyone's judgement as proficiently as Gwelain had.

She decided she wouldn't reveal that glimmer of empathy to Tullian.

"Does that help you understand?" Tullian asked.

"I think so. But where does Linnea come into it?"

"I'm getting to that," Tullian said gruffly. "It starts with the humans, I suppose. Our kind had infested other lands, but the Bright Ones rarely let humans set foot here, and at first only as servants. There were some who proved themselves worthy, though, and raised their status greatly. One was called Andon, a young man who was born among the Bright Ones and the first to use magic as they did. Not as naturally or as proficiently, but it made him a pet to the king and the nobles. They taught him, he impressed them, and in time one of the king's granddaughters had his child."

Sorra's eyes snapped open. "Linnea."

"Obviously. Linnea was a new kind of creature, as bright and charming as her father, as beautiful as her mother, and as naturally gifted in magic as any of the Bright Ones. She grew up as one of them but was fascinated by the humans she met. Good humans, impressive humans. The Bright Ones would have no others among them."

Sorra imagined it easily. A child with bright, golden hair and rosy cheeks, dressed in white skirts flowing behind her as she ran through lush gardens, watching intently as humans scrubbed the floors and tended the fields.

A blessed child, beloved by all.

Sorra's guts twisted. She'd always been fond of Andonia's legendary queen but understood how Gwelain might have resented a child so favoured when she herself had been overlooked, perhaps even rejected by the king before she knew why.

Speculation, she told herself. *Don't let your imagination spin storms out of lamb-clouds.* But she couldn't help wondering whether Gwelain's attempt to kill the king and take his crown had been prompted by more than shallow ambition.

"Oresthetes decided to show his favoured great-granddaughter the truth about humans so she might know to distance herself from them. He took her to human lands and showed her the worst of them. The journey convinced him that humans were as stupid, cowardly, and cruel as he'd always believed, and he decided it was time for the Bright Ones to leave this world behind forever.

"Linnea took a different lesson from their journey, and she made a proposal."

"Andonia," Sorra whispered. She knew the story, or thought she did, but silenced herself so Tullian could tell it as he knew it from the queen herself.

Tullian's voice warmed as he spoke of Linnea, though Sorra didn't miss the way it broke every so often. "She believed the wickedness of the human world was the result of history and circumstance, not of their true nature, and that humans could and would do better if they were given a fresh start in a land where no humans were wealthier or more powerful than others, where everyone was provided for. Her greatest hope was that they might finally have room to find their goodness."

Sorra sighed. *If only.*

"Oresthetes laughed," Tullian said. "He might have forced her to leave this world with him if Gwelain hadn't also seen an opportunity. She wished to stay behind with her subjects, believing they deserved a chance to rule once those who had so despised them were gone. She would truly be queen then, not just of swamps and goblins, but of everything her grandfather had claimed as his own.

"Maybe it was to spite Gwelain, maybe to allow his dear Linnea's experiment to fail so she'd see the truth. Whatever his reasons, Oresthetes decided to give his lands to Linnea. She sent letters to every nation, inviting settlers who would cut ties to the old places and begin fresh here. All were welcome if they would pledge to peace, to hard work, to responsibility for themselves, and to caring for their neighbours. There would be no nobility, no hoarding of wealth or power."

Silence filled the hut for several long breaths before Tullian spoke again. "It didn't work."

"I know," Sorra said, her voice thick. "I wish it had."

"Do they still speak of her fleeing her coronation?" he asked.

"They do, but not about the visions that made her do it. We still have a city called Queen's Run. They say that's where she was caught."

"Caught?" The disbelief and disgust in Tullian's voice forced Sorra to bite back a laugh. "Our good queen was not dragged back like a fugitive. Linnea chose to return when one of her subjects convinced her they needed her." He grumbled something under his breath. "Caught. Imagine."

Tullian reached for the charred stick he used to tend the fire. Sparks drifted toward the rafters as he prodded a blackened log that collapsed into the ashes, reducing the flames to a dull glow. "Andonia in my time was not entirely what she wished it to be, and I imagine it's only worse now. Even so, she'd want us to save it. That's how she was."

Is, Sorra thought, thinking of the queen's soul still tied to her disembodied heart.

"Gwelain kept to these lands north of the mountains after the Bright Ones left, and she didn't cause trouble at first," Tullian continued, his voice growing slow and sleepy. "Linnea's magic was far stronger than hers, and the people who lived here had no complaints. There was no warning before Gwelain made her move except for Linnea's visions, and by then—by my time—they rarely troubled her. Our queen seemed so strong, so eternal, but she was still halfway human, and that was enough to leave her vulnerable."

"Poison, you said?"

"Magical poison delivered on the blade her killer used to stab her in the gut. He got in disguised as a servant delivering her supper." Tullian stood and poked the glowing coals in the fire pit. "I usually carried her evening meal in myself, and no one got past without me accompanying them."

He didn't say *but I wasn't there*, but Sorra knew he was thinking it. She supposed he did any time he thought of her.

"Who was it?" Sorra asked.

"We don't know. I have my suspicions—there were plenty who wished to see the queen replaced by a human who might see the benefit of nobility, accumulated wealth, and power in the hands of a 'deserving few.'" Disgust dripped from his voice. "All that matters is Gwelain found someone. Whoever it was, he cut out Linnea's heart and her eyes, and he made a clean escape."

The hairs on Sorra's arms stood on end, and she shivered. "Her eyes?"

"It's somehow worse, isn't it?" Tullian grunted as he climbed into his bunk. "He didn't take them, just destroyed them. There was a purpose to Gwelain ordering the theft of her heart, the seat of her power. But to blind her helpless body? That's spite. That's all it is. Sometimes I think that's all Gwelain is in the end—spite and envy."

Sorra's skin crawled. She'd heard about Linnea's heartless body lying beneath Embercliffe, but she'd never had to imagine gaping holes where the queen's eyes should have been closed in eternal sleep.

"Gwelain sent her goblins to start a war," Tullian said, "thinking humans would be lost without the queen's magic, but she underestimated us. Most, maybe all, of her subjects died before she admitted defeat."

Sorra frowned. "The goblins?"

"Hmm? Oh, yes. The ones you've had the displeasure of meeting aren't the sort she's descended from. She calls them goblins, but they're really what she wanted goblins to be. They're her creations, made by transforming humans into her new nobility. Prettier than the old goblins and more appreciative of her lifestyle. If any of the old ones remain, I'd guess they're happy to be left alone as she plays with the new toys Linnea's power helped her create."

Sorra's thoughts raced to catch up. She didn't doubt what Tullian had said, but it turned everything sideways. In her imagination Gwelain became uglier, lumpier, more like the goblins from stories.

A true monster keeping a prince as her prisoner.

"Is that enough?" Tullian asked. "Do you understand her now?"

"I think so," Sorra said. "You're confident in her desire for legitimacy because it's what she's always believed she deserved. If she marries onto the throne of Andonia, it will be a perfect victory, spitting in her grandfather's face. Killing his darling Linnea was a deep wound, and taking her throne will be the salt she rubs into it."

"Especially if she can force your prince to name her as his legal successor," Tullian added. "Not just queen as co-ruler then, but ultimate authority, with the ability to do whatever she wishes to the people Linnea so loved. Power no one can take from her. But her plan remains uncertain. She's tried to take Andonia at least twice without a traitor and has failed. The surviving visions don't tell us why she needs one, so she's feeling her way forward just as we are."

And as aware of time running out as we are, too, Sorra thought. *I hope that troubles her. I hope she's afraid.*

Tullian's breathing became deeper and more even, and Sorra thought he'd fallen asleep. Then his voice cut through the silence.

"But listen well, Sorra, and remember this even if you learn nothing else from this story. If your king hadn't sacrificed his son, Gwelain would have let the curse run its course, destroying Andonia and everyone in it, legitimacy be damned.

"Gwelain wants what was given to Linnea. But if she can't possess it completely, she'll be nearly as pleased to burn it to the ground."

CHAPTER THIRTY-TWO

Sorra had rarely camped out under the stars. When she had, it hadn't been by choice, but because she was hiding from the unintended consequences of her own actions. Such occasions hadn't left her with much time to enjoy the situation.

Tullian had spent more than his share of time on the road, though. He'd been as trapped as any other human in these lands and, for a time, had taken advantage of his inability to succumb to age, hunger, or disease, searching harder than ever for the heart as his companions fell away, one by one. He knew what to pack, what to watch out for, and how often they'd need to rest the horses.

So, in spite of the relentless pace they kept as they passed through the Forgotten Lands over the course of nearly a fortnight, Sorra had found herself enjoying the journey more than she'd expected to. They trained each morning, and though Tullian was as demanding as he'd ever been, he seemed more willing to offer encouragement along with corrections, and his methods suited Sorra better now that he'd stepped down from the pedestal he'd tried so hard to place himself on.

They'd left the farmlands behind and travelled broken-down roads through ancient forests where people had built villages among the branches, hiding and refusing to come down to speak to the strangers. They'd crossed a blank place from the old maps and found a swamp shadowed by trees with roots that arched out of the water like ladies making their way through a puddle, their leafy skirts held high.

Today they'd searched an abandoned city of crumbling stone, braving the suffocating silence to see whether Gwelain had built a new castle among the ruins her people had left behind. The structures seemed far older than they should have. Tullian said it was because everything had crumbled when the Bright Ones left, taking the magic that had sustained it all.

But though the journey was more pleasant than Sorra had anticipated, a thunderhead hung over her, darkening what joy and wonder existed in this unfamiliar world.

They'd found nothing useful. Not a sign, not a word, and certainly not the castle itself. Every sunset reminded Sorra that they'd failed again, and she awoke every morning with new determination to find the castle, free Beau, and steal back Linnea's heart.

Sunset had come again, and they'd camped among the ruins. The campfire crackled and the horses snorted drowsily as Sorra carefully turned the pages of the book of visions.

Tullian set his sword aside. He hadn't used it that day or any other, but he polished it every night. "I suppose you have every word memorized by now," he said. "Unless you hope to frighten the poor book by glaring at it like that, you might consider saving your eyes by reviewing in your memory."

Sorra hadn't realized she was glaring. She set the book aside and used her fingers to smooth the muscles of her forehead, which refused to relax on their own.

He was right. She knew the visions by heart, and not only because he'd ordered it. She hadn't become as ensnared by them as Tullian was, but she was beginning to understand why he felt as he did. The visions told a story that was being written around her, but not one with a definite ending.

The trouble was that they raised more questions than they answered, hinting at solutions that burned away like morning mist when she examined them too closely.

Sorra lay back on her bedroll and rested her arm over her eyes, blocking the firelight, but found herself too wound up to rest. She sat up again and resisted the urge to pick up the book. "It's not enough, is it?"

"The visions? I agree that if we had all of them, they might provide a more complete picture, but—"

"No." Sorra knew she was about to speak something like blasphemy but hoped he'd forgive it. "Do you ever wonder whether we'd have been better off without the visions? We have only part of the story, and so little of it gives actual instructions. *The heroes' journey begins where their broken queen's ended,* fine. Clear enough. But even that raises questions. Can I be the Mystery if my journey started at a cabin in Andonia, or back in Cottsbridge when I loosed the arrow?"

Tullian raised one thick eyebrow. "You've joined my quest, which began in the bedchamber where Linnea died, as they all did."

"But it's like that with everything—the visions we have are so vague that it's impossible to use them as a map, and I doubt we'll realize any of them have been fulfilled until the dust settles. Does that mean it would all happen anyway? Or did she know so many of them would be lost and she saw the outcomes based on the ones we do have, in which case we have no choice but to use them as we can? And what about this?" She gestured loosely at the fire, the ruins, and Tullian himself. "If I'm the Mystery she saw, the other quests were doomed to fail. Yours was doomed to fail, too, so you could sit there pickling yourself until I showed up. So what does that say about anything else? Did I really make any of the choices that led me here? Did you? Did Linnea, or anyone?"

Tullian nodded thoughtfully. "You're speaking of destiny."

"Obviously!" Sorra stood, unable to sit still any longer even if her aching muscles begged for rest.

Tullian watched her frantic movements with interest. "You've gone from not caring to thinking too much on the subject. I understand. It happened to me, as well."

"And what did you conclude?" Sorra asked, hoping his answer would somehow leave her freer than it had left him. "Are we making choices, or are we fate's puppets?"

"My conclusion was that it doesn't matter." Tullian shrugged. "The twin outcomes Linnea foresaw are proof that nothing is set in stone—Gwelain may win, or we may defeat her. If Linnea foresaw the end of our quest or any step along the way, it's because she knew what our choices would be, not because we don't have a choice."

Sorra groaned. "That doesn't help. That means I could choose to walk away right now, which would mean the visions won't come true at all. What then?"

Tullian smiled so calmly it made Sorra want to hit something. "Are you going to walk away?"

She gritted her teeth. "No."

"Then that's the choice you're making, and the one she foresaw."

It would have been bad form to scream, so Sorra let her frustration ricochet through her brain until it faded.

Tullian got stiffly to his feet and placed his hands on her arms. "We have a small measure of guidance. Better yet, we have warnings about the dangers we'll face—the mage, Gwelain's need for a traitor, the potential for her to take control of Linnea's lands as well as her heart. Use what you can, watch for signs we're on the right path, take care not to make bad choices, and then trust the visions."

Sorra narrowed her eyes at him. "You're not the Tullian I met in that pub. Or at the hideout in the woods."

"I hope not." His gentle smile tightened, and the care lines around his eyes seemed etched deeper than they'd been a moment before. "Pray to your god or gods if it helps and try to get some sleep. I'll take first watch. That is my choice, as it was my choice to pickle myself for all those years—a choice I believe Linnea foresaw, but that I also believe was mine to make."

He released her, patting her shoulder in what might have been an attempt at comfort before he sat on his bedroll again.

Sorra lay with her back to the fire, one arm crooked beneath her head. The sky was dark and salted with stars so bright that even the firelight at her back couldn't erase them.

She'd expected her chaotic thoughts to pick up where they'd left off. Instead, she found herself thinking of Beau—not Prince Beauregard, but the bear she'd seen out the cabin's kitchen window, his wide, furry bottom planted on the ground, his nose pointed at the stars. She wondered whether he could see them from wherever he was now, and whether he liked them as much when he looked at them through human eyes.

I'll find you, she thought, then turned her thoughts to prayer as Tullian had suggested, not wishing to travel too far along the mental path marked by clawed paw prints. As she had for so long, she spoke to Linnea, barely moving her lips and making no sound, doubting it would do any good.

"If you're still here," she began, trying not to imagine what it would be like to be a spirit trapped in this world, "please help us. I don't know how to do this. I almost wish it *were* all settled, that it wasn't a choice, that I could know for sure the arrow had led me to Tullian's victory."

She stopped herself.

There might be comfort in believing everything was predestined. If the story had been written before her birth, she wasn't responsible for Beau losing his bet with Gwelain, and it couldn't have been otherwise. If her blessing had made things go bad for herself or anyone else, none of it had ever been her fault.

Comforting, indeed.

But destiny felt like an excuse, an easy way to make both failure and victory meaningless for the sake of never having to be wrong.

"No," she whispered. "I've spent my life having decisions made for me. If my future is in my own hands now, Linnea, make me strong enough to become the version of myself who makes the right choices, and to set things right when I go wrong. Let me be enough."

There was no answer save for the crackling of the fire, but Sorra found that the prayer had eased her mind. Still, sleep seemed as distant and unreachable as the goblin queen's castle, and Sorra tried to be content with watching the stars.

CHAPTER THIRTY-THREE

The fact that she and Tullian were crossing territory he'd already searched undermined Sorra's enjoyment no matter how she tried to appreciate the beauty of dirt roads winding through sun-dappled forests. Excitement came only from possibility and hope, and there was none of that in the areas marked in red on Tullian's map, especially when they were passing within a day's journey of the town where they'd met.

"We'll find the castle along the eastern coast," Tullian said with confidence he was clearly forcing for her benefit. "Who's to say she hasn't built her secret home in the rocky cliffs, or on an island revealed only when the tide recedes?"

"Anything is possible." Sorra didn't bother to inject cheer into her voice. She thought Beau would have mentioned it if he'd seen the ocean outside the castle, but she didn't wish to cut the thread of hope she and Tullian were so desperately clinging to.

The sun beat down, and she wished she could roll her sleeves back to let her skin cool. But Tullian had dropped the idea of marking her arm with Linnea's songbird when he saw how easily it smudged. Word of her marking had surely reached the queen already, though, and long sleeves would let any scouts or spies assume she was protected until she reached the safety of the throne room.

But heavy cloth and the weight of her armour left Sorra longing to escape the atmosphere of her own body.

Distant laughter floated through the air, drawing Sorra from her mental haze. She wasn't sure at first that it *was* laughter—it had been some time since she'd heard any.

Then it came again.

"Tullian, stop. I heard something."

He slowed his horse, his hand positioned to draw his sword. "Danger?"

"I don't think so."

Tullian frowned, but he dismounted, motioning for Sorra to lead the way. Dead leaves crunched beneath her boots as she and her docile chestnut mare wound their way between the trees.

Splashing sounds soon joined occasional bursts of excited laughter. Sorra's heartbeat quickened. It wasn't only that sounds of human happiness had been absent for so long—it felt like something more significant, though she wasn't sure why.

The source of the noise became clear when she reached the edge of a rocky cliff. A sparkling pond spread out from its base, its water clear enough that Sorra could see the stones and mud at its curved bottom, like a bowl set into the forest floor.

A group of people had gathered at the far shore to swim, to splash each other, to lie on the rocks at the water's edge. Sorra guessed they were her age, at least in appearance, or maybe a little younger. One of the boys hollered as he swung on a long rope from the branch of a tree, his voice echoing until he let go and splashed into the middle of the pond.

Another boy took a brown-haired girl by the hand and led her deeper into the forest.

Goose-pimples rose on Sorra's arms.

"They're having fun," she said, not bothering to whisper. The vibrant young people were too far away to hear.

Tullian watched them as he might observe a flock of vultures that showed up outside his window—curious but wary.

"Were the people like this the last time you came through?" Sorra asked.

"I suppose they were. But everyone was back then, before Gwelain's gift of supposed immortality showed its pale and sickly side." He turned away, leading his horse back toward the road.

Sorra hesitated, casting one last look over the happy souls below, then followed. "Shouldn't we talk to them?"

"We'll waste time finding a path down. There's a town nearby, though. We'll see whether this merriment has spread that far. If I recall correctly, there was a fine new inn at the edge of town the last time I passed through. Good meals. Soft beds." He cast a glance over his shoulder, his eyes sparkling with uncharacteristic amusement. "That is, if you're interested in that sort of thing."

Suddenly the charms of sleeping under the stars seemed a bit thin, and at the thought of a real bed, the sore points in Sorra's back and legs awakened, begging for the comfort she'd been denying them.

She grinned. "You know, I think you might be able to persuade me."

~

Afternoon was stretching toward evening when Sorra and Tullian reached the largest town Sorra had ever seen.

She knew it would be nothing compared to the great cities of Andonia, but the densely packed rooftops spreading beyond its sturdy walls gave her a thrill all the same.

The forest had been cut back, leaving the dusty hillside descending toward the town's walls bare. No one called out to stop them as they rode through the open gates.

The road, which had been nothing but a stretch of dusty, packed dirt, became neat cobblestone that changed the horses' slow hoof-beats from dull thuds to pleasant clops. Small homes built from pale stone crowded up against the street. The buildings became larger, though no less tightly spaced, as Tullian led the way deeper into town.

Though the houses might have been as old as the ruins where they'd spent the previous night, their walls had been maintained beautifully, showing signs of repair where the stone didn't quite match the original. Words and symbols in the old language that had been worn away in the ruins were clear and fresh here, though they meant no more to Sorra than their weathered shadows had.

No one greeted them, and no one peered out of the windows they passed, but sounds drifted through the empty streets from somewhere ahead—faint at first, then growing bolder and clearer.

Music. Laughter.

Sorra felt as though her heart might burst.

The road ended at a grand square surrounded by shops, every storefront, lamppost, and roofline festooned with bright banners and ribbons. It was enough to draw Sorra's attention away from the people, but only for a moment.

The town might not have been more densely populated than the villages elsewhere had been, but here the people had all gathered together, giving the square a sense of lively bustle Sorra had rarely experienced. People glanced at Sorra and Tullian as they passed, curious and bright. There was something about them that put Sorra on edge—something she associated with that first thrill she'd felt at witnessing the fun at the swimming hole in the woods.

Everywhere Sorra looked, something new begged for her attention.

A brass band dressed in red-and-white striped shirts, playing a raucous tune.

People dancing to their music, skirts flaring, feet stamping, drinks sloshing.

Clothing that still struck her as odd and old-fashioned, but brighter and fresher than she'd seen elsewhere.

Two young men sitting at the edge of the fountain in the centre of it all, their heads tilted toward each other, oblivious to the splashing water and the swirling crowds.

Sorra slowed her horse, wishing to take it all in. But Tullian rode on, barely seeming to notice the wonder that surrounded him, and she had no choice but to follow.

The music faded as they left the square behind them, but it was soon replaced by another bright melody drifting from the open window of a single-storey house a few blocks away. Flowering vines grew up its walls, and Sorra spotted a bountiful vegetable garden through the open gate to its back yard.

There was no one outside, and Sorra leaned toward Tullian to speak. "What is this place?"

"Historically? One of the towns occupied by the Bright Ones." He reached into one of his saddlebags and pulled out the well-worn leather notebook filled with Selim's historical and geographical notes. "Here we are, Gauldraith—sounds like an old name. Summer homes. There was a festival back before humans lived here, held on the grounds where the inn now stands, and this town grew up nearby to serve those who travelled to attend." He cleared his throat to read. "'Suspect that humans must have occupied the town before or immediately following the Bright Ones' departure as buildings lack the signs of deterioration that occurred elsewhere when the Bright Ones withdrew their magic. May indicate they left behind their human servants and the others who lived among them.'"

He tucked the book carefully back into its place and urged his horse forward.

The streets wound through Gauldraith, narrowing and widening, passing by little cottages and larger homes, shops, and an open-air theatre where performers juggled flaming bottles on a round stage.

"It's strange, isn't it?" Sorra asked. "Not like anywhere else."

Tullian didn't answer until they'd ridden slowly past a middle-aged couple sitting on a stone bench surrounded by roses.

"It is. What do you make of it?"

Maybe he'd only asked as a test of her mental sharpness, but Sorra let herself hope that he believed her insight would be of some value even if he'd already come to his own conclusions.

The streets narrowed again, and Sorra dismounted to lead her horse. Tullian did the same, and they walked in silence as Sorra tried to put into words what she already knew somewhere in her bones.

No one dies of old age in Gwelain's lands, so no one grows up to take their place. Unless...

"Taxes," she whispered, though there still didn't appear to be anyone listening in. "If people around here were being taken by goblins more frequently than elsewhere, they'd be a younger population, living more like people with natural lifespans." She thought back to the square, to the music, to the wild gleam in the dancers' eyes. "Grabbing harder at life, maybe, knowing what's coming."

"Could be," Tullian said, though without the excitement Sorra felt at the idea. "It could also be that they've simply found a way to hold on to joy and meaning."

"But say it was taxes, for the sake of argument. The increase would have to have been going on for generations to change things this much. What if there are more goblins around here who want to be fed? Or what if this is the most convenient source of souls for Gwelain's mage to feed his magic?"

Tullian shot her a warning glance, though she hadn't spoken the mage's name. She couldn't because he hadn't told her, and that was just as well.

"It's possible," he said. "Except that we searched this area thoroughly."

"A long time ago."

"Certainly." He frowned, then nodded. "We'll stay long enough to ask questions, but we must be careful. If you're right and this place is for some reason a favourite of Gwelain's, the people might not be as eager to see her brought down as they are elsewhere. They might try to please her with reports on our presence, especially if doing so might spare their hides. Or if she might reward them by making them into her little monsters."

The thought of anyone wanting to become like the goblins turned Sorra's stomach, but she supposed a way out of the cycle of birth, taxes, and worse-than-death might appeal to some. So might living in a castle, or being favoured by a queen, no matter how cruel she might be to those she loved less.

Tullian paused at the edge of another square that looked much like the first, though the music was different and the people seemed far more inebriated.

"I may be wrong, though," Sorra said. "If people were constantly being taken for taxes, they'd all have moved elsewhere by now."

"Perhaps not. The destruction of one's soul is a high price to pay, but when the other option is to move to places like the ones we left behind…" Tullian left the thought unfinished as he led his horse around the edge of the square.

A young man who had been dancing an off-kilter jig fell on his backside, drawing a chorus of laughter from his companions.

It's true, Sorra thought as she watched him dust himself off and resume his dance. As horrifying as it was to consider the idea of a soul's destruction, there were worse fates. She'd heard of religions that threatened eternal torture for anyone who didn't submit to the will of their gods, and that would be worse than not existing. And in this life Gwelain had condemned her subjects to an existence not of pain and fear, but of the absence of joy and purpose far beyond what the years alone could have inflicted on their spirits. Nothingness would surely be an improvement.

She'd spent her life grabbing on to pleasure and beauty and comfort where she could, knowing things could be worse tomorrow. The only difference was that these people knew exactly what bad end awaited, so they chose to live shorter but lovelier lives than others, never existing for long enough for Gwelain's magic to poison them into the husks that folks became elsewhere.

An unfair choice, and one that made Sorra hate Gwelain just a little more than she had before.

She can't create anything good. She poisons everything she touches. Even beauty is an illusion that hides horror beneath. Tullian had told her as much, and Sorra thought she finally understood.

There was no wall at the north end of town, only a gradual thinning of the buildings until they reached a spot where the forest had begun a campaign of tentative regrowth along the sides of the road.

"Why would there be an inn so far outside of town?"

Tullian glanced at her and shrugged. "I suppose the festival grounds were a convenient spot to build one back when humans were still travelling these roads. The real question is whether it will be open now that most of them are keeping to their own towns and their own unchanging lives."

Sorra let herself hope for the best. The people seemed like ones who would venture outside of town for a nice meal and even a night away from home, though perhaps not so far that they had to face the grim reality of what older folks in Gwelain's lands had become.

The inn sat well back from the forest road on its eastern side. Unlike the buildings in Gauldraith, it was built from long, sturdy logs, but that was where its similarity to Beau's cabin ended. The inn stood two floors tall, and when Sorra counted the doors opening onto the balcony over its wide porch she guessed there must be a dozen rooms upstairs.

The front doors stood open like the offer of a welcoming embrace.

Tullian rode ahead, following a broad, perfectly circular path of pale stone set between the road and the inn. Sorra followed more slowly, reaching out to brush her fingers over the tops of the neatly shaped boxwood hedge that formed another circle at its centre, with more smooth, white stone within.

Circles within circles, perfectly spaced. A ring of ornate black lampposts bordered the outer edge of the path, and though the sun wouldn't set for a while yet, a grey-haired man in a simple but well-made black suit stood on a short ladder to light them one by one.

Sorra approached the porch, only half-noting how strangely the smooth stone dulled her horse's hoofbeats. The inn itself had grabbed her attention with scents of roasting beef and freshly baked bread wafting out from the open doors, accompanied by the sweet tones of a stringed instrument playing somewhere inside.

A spark of joy lit inside Sorra as she imagined an evening of music and good food—maybe even dancing if Tullian couldn't think of some reason to call it unbecoming of a hero. The inn made the Ambling Goat look like a rotting dung heap, and the food had to be better.

She didn't want it. She needed it.

"Wait here a moment," Tullian said. "I'll see about rooms."

Sorra left the horses hitched to the post by the stairs and wandered back toward the road, too giddy with excitement to stand in place.

As she walked, she noted the design of the path, which was in better condition than any of the roads they'd travelled. Wedges of pale stone had been set into the ground so perfectly it appeared at first glance to be one massive piece of white-grey rock, unbroken except for where the ring of hedges had been planted at its centre. Shadows remained of designs that had once been carved into the stone, but time and travellers had obscured anything but the hint of their existence. Sorra shivered as she imagined the Bright Ones at their unnamed festival, engaged in strange rituals and celebrations no human had ever witnessed.

She caught up to the lamplighter at the edge of the road.

"Good evening," he said. "Will you be joining us for supper?" His voice was smooth and somehow too pleasant.

Sorra smiled. "I hope so."

She meant to complete the circle to return to the inn, but a battered wooden sign on the western side of the road caught her eye. Its paint had faded almost to invisibility, making the words impossible to read. An overgrown path led into the trees behind the sign, and when Sorra squinted she spotted a building lurking deep in the shadows. Stone, but dilapidated in a way that surely would have horrified the residents of Gauldraith. She would have thought it abandoned if there hadn't been a faint glow shining beyond its glassless windows, barely a flicker at this distance.

She turned to the grey-haired lamplighter, who smiled at her with his step stool in one hand. His face was unlined, making him younger than she'd thought at first glance—not an elderly fellow, but one gone prematurely grey.

They're all young, she realized. She hadn't seen a single elderly person in Gauldraith, or even a shock of grey hair until now.

Perhaps the goblins take the older ones for taxes as part of the deal. A beautiful life, but a short one.

She decided not to ask. Instead, she pointed across the road. "What's that place?"

He glanced at the sign without any apparent interest. "The Hog and Keg. An inn back in the time of the Bright Ones. Its owners have tried to keep it going over the years, but it hasn't been popular since we built this place. You don't find the best sort of folks there, if you find anyone at all."

Something tickled the back of Sorra's mind. "Yours is newer and better."

"Absolutely." He smiled, friendly and welcoming. "May I escort you inside? Supper should be ready just about now."

"Sorra!" Tullian stood on the porch, waving.

"I won't interrupt your work," Sorra said. In truth, she didn't like this fellow—not his good suit, not his friendly smile, though she didn't know why she wished to get away from him. "Thank you."

She hurried back to the inn, skirting the edge of the drive to avoid stepping on the faint carvings in the stone.

Tullian leaned on the porch railing, looking more relaxed and contented than Sorra had ever seen him. "Two rooms," he said, beaming. It was a strange thing to see. "Hot baths. Soft beds, if only for one night, and at an excellent price."

Sorra stepped onto the porch and looked past him. A wide staircase faced the doorway, welcoming weary travellers and inviting them to their temporary resting places. To the right, a huge wooden desk where a round-cheeked woman stood smiling at her guests. To the left, an open room full of spindle-backed chairs around tables where the most delicious food she'd tasted since her arrival in these lands would surely be served.

She wanted it as badly as she'd ever wanted anything in her life.

And she couldn't step forward. The tickle at the back of her mind had become an itch, drawing her thoughts to the book of visions.

"What is it?" Tullian asked.

Sorra swallowed hard. *Don't say it,* she thought. *Don't ruin it.*

"*To find her heart, the queen's heroes must walk the humble path.* Are we supposed to enjoy this sort of thing on our journey if we're following Linnea's visions? There's another inn right across the road. Two paths. And this isn't the humble one."

The wrinkles at the corners of Tullian's eyes deepened as he smiled. "Very good. Keep that in mind when sacrifices are required later, but for now know that my friends and I stayed at the other place on our last visit here. We chose humbler paths any time we could, literally or figuratively, chasing that clue as wide and deep as possible. The Hog and Keg is a dead end, but you and I will take another look at it in the morning if you wish."

That should have been the end of it. Sorra wanted it to be, and she quickly realized why.

"I want to stay on this side of the road," she said. "Which means I shouldn't. My old self would already be up the stairs and in that hot bath, but I'm not supposed to be her." She felt, wholly irrationally, as though she might cry. "I want to sleep here, but I want something else even more. I probably won't gain anything but a sore back from a bad bed and loose bowels from undercooked meat, but if I don't try the humble path tonight, I'll never stop wondering whether I should have trusted the visions."

Tullian looked down at his boots and sighed.

"You don't have to come," Sorra added. "Just give me a few coins, and in the morning you can laugh at me."

The old knight cast one more longing glance into the inn, then descended the stairs with heavy steps. "I can't let you go alone. Last time we passed through they were serving some rough customers over there."

"I've handled those sorts before."

"I believe you. But still."

They led their horses past the lamplighter and across the road without further discussion.

The humbler of the two inns was even worse up close. A faint whiff of something rotten hung over the moss-speckled ground outside, and the wooden steps bowed under their weight as Sorra and Tullian climbed them. Another wooden sign hung flat against the stone wall above the door, etched with the image of a drunken pig passed out over a barrel, and the shutters that flanked the windows hung at imperfect angles that made them look nearly as intoxicated.

The air inside was little better, smelling more of sour ale than of delicious food. Someone had decorated the mantel over the cold and dingy fireplace with a collection of dust-covered copper pigs. Though the tables that ran the length of the room looked polished —possibly by the elbows of the two mangy men who turned to glare at the newcomers—Sorra's boots stuck to something sticky on the unwaxed pine floor that she didn't care to examine more closely.

Tullian hung back, perhaps waiting for her to change her mind.

He wasn't the first to have his plans derailed by her stubbornness, and Sorra supposed he wouldn't be the last, assuming she survived long enough to torment someone else.

A young man who looked like he'd just walked twenty leagues in a hurricane stepped out from behind a swinging door, wiping one index finger on the front of his shirt and leaving a wet smear that Sorra tried not to stare at.

"Are you the innkeeper?"

"Suppose I am."

"Do you have any rooms available?" she asked. "Two, if possible. And we'll need food."

Someone chuckled, but when Sorra looked toward the tables the men seemed to be ignoring her.

The innkeeper sniffled. "You can pay?"

"I can," Tullian said.

"Fine. Might have one room. You can fight over the bed." He looked from Sorra to the old knight and shrugged. "Or share it. Just don't break it." He accepted a silver coin from Tullian, disappeared back through the doorway, and returned with two bowls of watery soup and two slices of bread on a tray that he set on the table, well away from his other patrons. "I'll see about your accommodations, then."

He left them, presumably to find the key or to remove an existing guest who wasn't paying him in silver.

Sorra studied the men at the table, wondering at their condition. It seemed unlikely that they'd drifted here from elsewhere, but they did seem older in some way. Maybe they'd survived long enough for the shine to go out of the world and for the bright young people at the other inn to become an irritation.

Even grabbing desperately at life's pleasures might grow tiresome after a while.

The heroes sat facing each other. Sorra picked up one of the bowls and offered it to Tullian.

She knew she'd probably made a stupid decision based on too

many readings of the visions, but going back on it now would wound her pride too deeply.

"I can imagine worse places to spend a night," she said, as much to drive away her own disappointment as to help him with his.

"Is that so?" Tullian sipped his soup and grimaced. "If that's the case, your imagination is far better than mine."

CHAPTER THIRTY-FOUR

"Should we ask about the goblins?" Sorra sipped her soup, then slurped it down as quickly as she could, hoping to fill her belly without having to taste the foul brew. She regretted it when she tried to bite into her bread. It was like gnawing on a rock, but she didn't dare ask Tullian whether she could dip it in his soup to soften it.

"Not just yet," he whispered. He hunched over his bowl, his posture similar to those of the men at the other end of the table, but he couldn't blend in with them. Not when he was new here, and certainly not when he wore armour and carried a sword. "We'll want to tread carefully. No speaking directly of goblins or castles or queens."

He didn't need to say that she should therefore stay out of it. Eager as she was to help, she was also painfully aware of what a mess she was inclined to make of things.

Sorra cast a glance sideways but couldn't tell whether the men were trying to listen to their conversation. One had a strained look about him, but that might only have been the soup's fatty lumps of meat worrying at his guts.

She went to the window to make sure no one had stolen the bags from the horses, who would need to be tended to soon—it didn't seem this fine establishment offered such services. Then she walked the perimeter of the room, searching for anything she could feign interest in while she eavesdropped on Tullian's conversations.

The only obvious attempt at decoration in the room, besides the dusty copper piggies on the mantel, was a faded tapestry hung on one wall that depicted a hog lying on its back with a wooden keg resting on its four hooves, a stream of piss-yellow ale flowing into its open mouth. The piece was clumsily executed, but it had a certain hopeless charm to it.

She lost interest quickly and moved on. Tullian was still finishing his soup and hadn't moved closer to the other men, so Sorra made her way to the fireplace. It was built from the same stone as the rest of the building, but someone had crafted a fine mantel from a single piece of hardwood. When Sorra used her sleeve to wipe away a layer of grime, the wood had a warm, golden glow. Its outer face was skilfully carved with a vining branch across its centre, bookended by crescent moons.

Sorra's mouth went dry as she touched one of them, pressing her finger into the depression that marked the dark part of the moon.

She hadn't spoken of Beau's clue to the castle's whereabouts since Tullian had dismissed it, but she'd thought of it often. *East of the sun and west of the moon.* It meant nothing—surely the clue, if it was a clue, had nothing to do with the mantel on the fireplace of a run-down inn from the time of the Bright Ones.

And yet...

Tullian had moved down the bench and sat closer to the other men. He didn't appear to be speaking with them. Nothing to hear there, not much to observe.

But there were wooden window frames to examine, so Sorra crossed to them as casually as she could manage, telling herself not to get excited. Her chest tightened as she noted gouges where something had been hastily and imperfectly erased by someone who couldn't bear to mar the beauty of the mantel, or perhaps hadn't cared enough to bother with its destruction.

The tip of a crescent moon still showed at the edge of one of the gouges.

A tiny thing. Probably insignificant. But then, why remove them?

Tullian might have thoughts on it, but he wasn't to be disturbed.

She went to find the innkeeper. Tullian had said not to ask about the castle or the queen, but she couldn't see any harm in asking about the history of the inn.

She found him in the kitchen stirring a pot over a fire that appeared to be gasping its last breaths.

"Excuse me?"

"Hmm?" He looked up from the soup, which no one was lining up for seconds of. "Oh. You want your room key?"

"I do, yes. But I was also wondering who built this place. The details are lovely."

"You mean the tapestry? My wife did that. Name was Henrietta."

His voice was irritating and unpleasant, but still better than the fellow across the road with his smooth smile and welcoming tones.

"It is quite unique," Sorra said. "I was more curious about the carvings, though. The ones on the mantel?"

The innkeeper grunted. "That was there before us. Why?"

Sorra shrugged, pretending not to notice how his little eyes had narrowed. "They're pretty, that's all."

The innkeeper's lips tightened, and he took the pot off the fire. "We don't have a room available after all. You and your friend had best be going."

"Perhaps after another bowl of your delicious—"

"Now." He grabbed her by the arm and hauled her out of the kitchen. Sorra twisted away, repulsed by his touch.

"I'm going." She brushed the wrinkles from her sleeve. "I'll see myself out."

The innkeeper followed close, leaving no room for her to stop and examine anything else. He stood in the doorway until she'd stepped off the porch and into the orange light that bathed the yard, then moved aside to let Tullian follow.

The knight glared at the innkeeper when he passed, and just as hard at Sorra as he descended the steps. The door slammed behind him and a lock thudded home. Seconds later the innkeeper reached out through the vacant windows and slammed the crooked shutters closed as well.

"Guess everyone else is staying the night," Sorra said.

It didn't seem like an especially good thing to say, but something needed to break the silence that accompanied Tullian's disappointed scowl.

"What did you do?"

"Nothing! I only asked about the inn. There were moons carved on the mantel and scratched out on the window frames. I thought —" She sighed. "I didn't ask about anything important. Or I thought I didn't." She looked over the inn again. "Why would he kick us out if the moons didn't mean anything?"

Tullian continued to look unimpressed. "Because you're so good at making friends?"

"No." Sorra stepped back onto the porch and made her way to the closed-off window. "Look."

The wooden shutters hadn't fared well over the years. Moss had grown on the surfaces that now faced outward, settling deeper into the crescent moons carved into the wood. "What do you make of that?"

"I think there are probably celestial symbols carved into a thousand mantels, doorframes, and shutters all over these lands," Tullian said, but his expression had softened. His hands trembled as he reached for the wooden sign hung high above the door, knocking it back against the wall with his fingertips before he pulled it free and dropped it to the ground.

Sorra held her breath as she looked at the crescent moon carved into the stone above the door. Something was written above it, but not in the language of humans.

Her skin prickled. "This place used to be called something different."

Tullian, too, seemed unable to look away. "The Waning Moon, perhaps."

"The humble road led us here." Sorra's body vibrated with excitement. "The Bright Ones didn't gather here for just any festival. It was a lunar celebration of some sort, wasn't it?"

Tullian glanced back toward the other inn and the circle of

stone that might have sat there for a thousand years or more—a full moon set into the ground, its surface now disrupted by hedges that reshaped it into a stone path.

"I don't know," he said. "Selim's notes didn't say."

The sun was setting behind the Hog and Keg, barely visible over the tops of the trees that obscured Sorra's westward view as she circled to the rear of the building. "What's over there?"

"Dense forest." Tullian followed, leading their horses. "There's nothing else. No roads, but we searched the area anyway. Thoroughly."

"At what time of day?"

"I'm not sure, but if I searched through Selim's notes—"

Sorra didn't wait for him to check before she mounted her horse.

"Sorra." A warning note had entered Tullian's voice. Sorra ignored it.

"This forest used to lie west of the moon at the festival grounds," she said, her voice high with excitement as she pointed toward the setting sun. "For the next few minutes, it also lies east of the sun. Do you see? One part of the clue is about a physical location, the other is about time. The castle is there, but we have to go now."

Her horse, perhaps picking up on her excitement, pawed at the ground and tossed her head.

Tullian's eyes widened. "You may be correct. We need to approach this carefully—we'll find somewhere else to rest tonight, make our plans for what comes next, and try it tomorrow. The sun will set again when we're prepared for what's to come."

"And by then someone will have warned Gwelain that we're on our way."

Tullian paled visibly in the dying light. "It's too easy. I don't like it."

Sorra steeled herself and turned her horse to the west. "Hundreds of years, dozens of lives lost, and a signpost from the visions we nearly missed isn't *too easy*."

"Sorra, wait."

She knew she was supposed to obey him, that he knew better, and that disobeying was what her old self would do.

But she also knew that Tullian was afraid, that sometimes the Might needed the Mystery to drag him in the right direction, and that she would see this through whether or not she was truly one of Linnea's heroes.

She would find Beau if she rode west, but the time to act was slipping like water between her fingers.

Sorra rode as hard as she could into the darkening forest, ignoring Tullian's shouts until they disappeared behind her.

CHAPTER THIRTY-FIVE

Branches whipped at Sorra's face. She ducked behind the horse's neck to keep from being knocked off, letting the mare choose her course and correcting it only to keep the sunset ahead of them between the trees.

"Sorra!"

She didn't look back to call out and tell Tullian she couldn't stop. Tarla's warning about the road to the Gate still hung heavy in her mind, and she feared that letting her focus stray from her path would make her lose it entirely.

Her horse stumbled and slowed, and Tullian caught up.

"Sorra, we can't—" Tullian said, then fell silent as the horses broke free of the thick tree cover and their hooves clattered over a road paved with flat stones.

"No roads in these woods?" Sorra shouted.

"There weren't!" There was madness in Tullian's voice, joy or terror, or maybe both. It didn't matter to Sorra. She only cared that he was no longer trying to stop her.

They rode until the sun burned as nothing more than an ember between the trees.

We're too late, Sorra thought.

But as the sun vanished, the forest that had surrounded them ended at the edge of a meadow dotted with pale flowers and quick flashes of light from glow beetles. A river flowed across the meadow, molten gold in the lingering light, and beyond it rose the white spires of a castle.

The horses slowed as they approached the slow-moving current and splashed across, wetting themselves to their knees. Sorra let her horse pause for a taste of water but never took her eyes off the castle.

"This wasn't here before?" Sorra kept her voice low and quiet, but she supposed it would do no good if Gwelain and her mage knew they were coming.

"None of it." Tullian urged his horse on at a more cautious pace. "We scaled the hills to the west for a fuller view of the land, and there was nothing here but forest. I suspect that even if we'd looked at sunset, we'd have seen nothing because the starting point was wrong." He drew in a long breath and nodded. "Well done."

Sorra tried to ignore the tumult raging in her stomach—excitement, pride, and terror at what might wait for them when they reached the castle.

"Where the journey begins is as important as where it ends," she said. "Linnea told you as much when she said your quest needed to start where she died."

"Our quest," Tullian said, so quietly Sorra wasn't sure he'd meant for her to hear.

The castle was more beautiful than Sorra had expected, and stranger. The solid, pale mass of its main body was taller than it was broad, its foundation rounded instead of square. A half-dozen towers reached up in graceful curves, giving the impression of a patch of bleached seaweed frozen in its underwater dance.

As far as Sorra could tell, there wasn't a straight line on it anywhere.

"Should we stop talking?" Sorra asked.

"I don't know. Odds are that the one who might be listening lost track of us long ago, which means he might not have his attention on us here and now. On the other hand, word may have come that we were in the area. They could be watching from the windows."

Sorra waited for him to think it through.

Finally, Tullian nodded. "If he's listening now, we're already at a disadvantage that silence won't improve. Speak quietly if needed, give nothing away, and watch for signs of what we might be walking into."

As they drew nearer, lights appeared in the oval windows that dotted the castle's walls and towers.

With each step, Sorra's fear grew, overtaking her excitement like weeds choking a garden. Tullian was certain they'd be safe once they reached the throne room, but that seemed farther away now than it had before they'd found the castle.

There will be soldiers waiting. And when they see I'm not marked...

But there were no goblins outside the castle, and no parapets for them to watch from with their bows or spears ready to kill an imposter.

The road ended at a courtyard with walls that curved around it like an embrace, high where they met the castle's mother-of-pearl walls, sweeping low to touch the edge of the road where it passed between them.

A ramp arched from the paved courtyard toward a pair of twin doors set high on the side of the castle, closed against the night.

Sorra and Tullian stopped outside the courtyard, waiting and watching, but the doors remained closed.

"I don't suppose knocking would do any good?" Sorra whispered.

"No," Tullian said, speaking only a little lower than normal volume. "It's dishonest to keep potential guests away from her throne room, but I expected no better. We could probably camp out here for a decade and not be invited in so she doesn't have to offer hospitality. Still, we'll wait just behind the wall and see whether anyone comes to ask about our business."

"That's it?"

Tullian sighed with dramatic flair Sorra hadn't thought him capable of. "Nothing else to be done. Everything will be locked up tight if she's intent on keeping guests out." He motioned for her to lean in close as he drew his horse up next to hers. Though he whispered into her ear, Sorra had to strain to make out his next words. "If you-know-who heard that, he'll be focused on listening near the entrance while we find another way in."

It was a flimsy attempt at trickery, but any plan that might delay a meeting with Gwelain seemed like a good one. Tullian might be all right even if he only made it to the basement or the dining room—he was the only hope Gwelain had of the traitor she so desperately needed, and if he demanded hospitality in exchange for his willingness to negotiate, what choice would she have?

But if Sorra were caught before Gwelain was bound by tradition and superstition against harming a guest, Tullian's pleas might not be enough to save her from imprisonment or death when Gwelain found her unmarked and therefore not protected by the visions.

Tullian nudged his horse to a walk, circling clockwise around the castle's foundation.

Sorra cast one more glance at the twin doors. Even without the sun to illuminate their detail, they were things of beauty, forming a delicate arch that ended in a point where they met at the top. Intricate golden filigree curled vine-like around circles of smoky violet glass that ranged in size from something like a serving platter to one as large as a dinner table.

No shadows showed through the glass to hint that there was anyone waiting on the other side.

Sorra patted her horse's neck and urged her to follow Tullian's. The poor creature was winded after the hardest run Sorra had ever asked of her, but there would be no rest for either of them yet.

Tullian stuck close to the windowless lower walls, and he didn't speak again as they made their way around the castle. Its foundations didn't form a perfect circle, but dipped in and pushed out on their way to forming an uneven oval shape.

Sorra judged that they'd gone halfway around the castle before she decided to dismount and lead her horse. The grass was thick and pleasant beneath her boots, and it felt good to stretch her legs. Tullian joined her without comment, and they continued on.

They rounded a curve that jutted out on the castle's eastern side, forming the base of one of its towers. A patch of warm light stretched across the ground, and Sorra's steps slowed. The wall was lower here, bulging out where the side of the castle bowed in, leaving space for an open yard they would have passed by without notice if not for the light shining out from its arched doorway.

Sorra left her horse behind and crept closer, her back pressed to the wall, hugging the shadows until she could peer through the opening. The garden beyond was brimming with vegetable beds, berry patches, and compact fruit trees, all lit by lamps that hung on either side of a wooden door leading into the castle. A young woman sat on a three-legged stool at the outer edge of the lamp-light, plucking apples from a basket on the ground and slicing them into the glass bowl she held on her lap.

Her hands were covered in cuts and smeared with drying blood. She winced as the blade sliced her finger again but didn't stop cutting.

Tullian looked in over Sorra's shoulder, then motioned for her to fall back.

"A servant," Sorra whispered.

"Probably."

"She'll be able to open that door."

Tullian said nothing. Sorra tried not to interrupt his thoughts but couldn't help herself. "Did you see her hands?"

"I did. I suspect she did something to displease her queen."

"And therefore might be willing to help the people who could free her and everyone else?"

Tullian closed his eyes. Breathed. Opened them again. "Perhaps, if she has enough hope left to outweigh her fear of further reprisals. Wait here, and say nothing. I'll see whether another opportunity presents itself ahead."

Sorra waited as he passed the opening in the wall, skirting the patch of light, then disappeared into the gloom. She clenched her fists to feel the pinch of her nails digging into her palms and counted slowly in her mind to ground herself.

And she watched the girl, who showed no sign of being aware of anything but her painful duty. Not listening for voices, not watching the doorway for signs of movement. Not at all like someone who was expecting unwelcome visitors.

Sorra had counted to three hundred before Tullian returned, shaking his head. He hesitated, seeming to come to a decision, then spoke.

"Can you handle this in an appropriate manner?" he whispered.

"That girl is not our enemy. If anything, she's one in need of our protection. We can't trust her yet, but—"

"But don't harm her, I know." Sorra straightened her shoulders and tucked a loose strand of hair behind her ear. "I'll go. I'm less frightening than you'd be."

It seemed like he wanted to say more, perhaps to launch into a lecture or a detailed explanation of how he'd approach the problem, but whatever it was, he kept it to himself.

Sorra stepped into the garden alone.

The girl leapt to her feet, spilling sliced apples into the dirt.

"It's all right," Sorra said, her hands held out to show she meant no harm. "Do you live here?"

The girl glanced at the door, but she didn't try to run.

Sorra smiled at her and walked past. There was no knob or latch on the door, and it didn't move when she pressed against it. She hadn't expected it to.

She looked at the girl again, who was watching her warily.

"Are you a servant here?"

The girl nodded and bent to scoop the scattered apple slices back into her bowl, then sat and reached for another whole piece of fruit from her basket. She cut into it, but the dull knife slipped, slicing into her finger again. She popped the finger into her mouth to suck the blood off, then went back to work.

Sorra crouched in front of her, making herself small and unthreatening. She wished she'd left her armour with Tullian.

"Is anyone listening to us now?" she asked, knowing she wouldn't be able to trust any answer but hoping the servant would at least speak.

"I don't think so." The girl's voice was gentle. "My skin doesn't feel like it's trying to crawl off my neck like it does when he's listening, and he's probably resting up for tonight's feast. You're not safe, though, whoever you are. You'd best leave while you can."

Her hands didn't stop moving, and she didn't look at Sorra as she spoke.

Sorra looked down at the apples. "Do you have to cut all of those tonight?"

"And every night." The girl made another slice that looked more difficult than it needed to be. Her fingers were covered in old scars under the fresh cuts. "I displeased our good queen, and she rightly decreed that this should be my punishment. It's an enchanted blade, you see, made to bite my flesh as I deserve. And for every apple I cut, another appears."

As Sorra watched, the servant's words proved themselves true. She didn't see another apple appear on top of the pile to replace what was taken, but as the girl worked, there never seemed to be less fruit in the basket.

"You can't use another knife?"

"No one will give me one. If they do, our queen may do worse to them. It would only be fair and just."

Sorra removed one of her daggers from her belt and took an apple, slicing it easily into even sections that she dropped into the bowl. The girl watched as she cut another, and then a third. Sorra held the dagger up to the light, letting the girl admire it.

"It's not made for kitchen work," Sorra said, "but it's sharper than yours. Even if the apples keep coming, it would save your fingers. I could give it to you, but I'd need something in return."

"What?" The girl's whisper was so soft Sorra barely heard her. "I can't let you in."

"Of course not." Sorra tried to sound like she hadn't hoped for anything of the sort. "But do you know the prince who lives here? Handsome fellow. Human like you and me."

"Of course."

Sorra cut another apple. The fruit was perfectly ripe, and its juices wet her skin. "Is he well?"

The girl's brow furrowed. "As well as any of us."

Hardly a comforting thought. Sorra imagined Beau's hands covered in cuts. His whole body, maybe, if Gwelain thought he deserved a worse punishment than this girl had earned.

"Do you know where he is now?"

"Probably in the library, taking in the quiet before the feast." The girl bit her lower lip and winced. "Not that I pay attention to his comings and goings. She'd take my eyes if she thought I did, and rightly so."

"I need to speak to him. If you can't let me in to do that—"

"I can't."

"Then all I need is for you to take a message to him." Sorra spoke calmly and carefully. The girl was like a doe in the woods, braced to flee if she scented danger. "Do that and I'll give you my knife. Just tell him the girl with the arrow is in the garden, and don't let on to anyone else that I'm here."

The servant watched as Sorra cut two more apples and took another.

"Just the message?"

"Just that. I won't tell anyone you did this, and if all goes well, there might be a way to free you from your punishment forever."

The girl reached out a trembling hand and took the dagger from Sorra, hid it in the pocket of her apron, and went to the door. She glanced back, then pressed her hand flat to the pale wood. The door opened, then closed tight behind her.

"Well?" Tullian stepped into the garden. "I couldn't hear your conversation, but it seemed intense."

"She's going to tell Beau we're here," Sorra said. "She seemed sure no one was listening, and that Beau would be alone when she found him. I don't know what he'll do with the information, but he's the only person here we can trust."

Tullian glanced at the door. "We're trusting her."

"She's not a friend of Gwelain's. If she goes straight to the queen out of fear, I won't blame her, but I think we can hope for better." Sorra dropped the apple slices in the bowl, which was no fuller than it had been when she'd entered the garden.

"Let's hope so. If not, we've just done a fine job announcing our arrival." Tullian took two apples from the basket and carried them out to the horses. He didn't return, perhaps thinking it best not to frighten the girl with an apparent ambush.

The last dim hint of twilight disappeared and the sky transformed into a perfect blanket of stars. Sorra kept cutting apples with her remaining dagger. She had nothing else to occupy her and felt better with a weapon in her hands.

Finding the girl might be luck, or it might be a trap. Sorra wanted to hope it was the former, but a lifetime of living with her blessing made it difficult. When the door opened again, she leapt to her feet, prepared to face a goblin army.

Instead, her heart twisted in her chest as Beau stepped into the garden, dressed in a simple white tunic and brown breeches much finer than what Sorra and Tullian wore. His face was exactly as she remembered save for the neatly groomed beard he'd grown during their time apart, and her heart leapt at the sight of him. She didn't move until he spotted her and closed the distance between them in three long strides, laughing quietly with disbelief.

"You came," he said. Before she could answer he pulled her into a long, deep kiss that made her forget what she'd meant to say, or that she'd meant to speak at all. "What are you doing here? How did you find me?"

She pulled away without letting go of the grip her hand had found on his arm. He was solid and real, his resonant voice as pleasant as it was in her memory. "We need to get to the throne room without being seen."

Tullian stepped into the garden and bowed low. "Prince Beauregard, I presume."

Beau nodded back. "And you are?"

"Tullian," Sorra said. "He needs to get in, too. We're on a—" Tullian frowned and shook his head. "Can you get us into the castle?"

Beau looked at her as though she might have lost her mind. "We're not going back in there. I'm lucky to have sneaked out at all —no other servant has ever risked opening a door for me. This is our only chance to escape." He took Sorra by the hand and stepped toward the darkness beyond the garden wall.

She planted her feet without considering why.

Beau looked back at her, wounded. "Didn't you come to set me free?"

"I did." She looked him over. He didn't seem worse off for his return to the Forgotten Lands, but something was wrong. Not with his face, which remained quite pleasing, or his body, which she could imagine all too well beneath his plain but well-made clothes. She imagined fleeing with him, her personal quest fulfilled even if it meant abandoning her promise to help Tullian complete his.

He'd never properly sworn her to that quest, anyway. It wasn't truly hers, and with Beau gone Gwelain would lose her chosen path to Andonia's throne. It wouldn't be the victory Tullian wanted, but things would go back to what he had chosen for himself before Sorra had come to disrupt everything.

But she didn't move.

She forced herself to think before she spoke, to absorb the indefinable wrongness she so wished to ignore. "What about your duty?"

Beau looked away. "You were right. My father was wrong to make the deal he did with Gwelain. All we're doing is delaying the inevitable, and I'm no good to Andonia as a prisoner. But I'm the key to her plans. Without me, she has nothing." He placed his fingers under Sorra's chin and lifted it until she met his gaze. "She'll force me to marry her, and I can't face that. Not when we could ruin her plans and be free together. Not when I'm in love with you."

Sorra drew in a sharp breath.

It was better than anything she'd wished for when she set out from the cabin, the perfect conclusion to everything she'd already fought so long and hard for.

But it was wrong.

Even if he cared for her, Beau was too damned reasonable to call it anything like love after so little time together. Beyond that, the Beau she'd known was constant, consistent, and solid enough to border on boring even when he seemed to be something as miraculous as a talking bear.

…And loyal to his people no matter what it cost him. His escape would foil Gwelain's plans, but it would also break the treaty that kept her from cursing Andonia again.

Sorra looked deeper into his eyes. They were the same beautiful brown she remembered. Everything down to the faint freckle above his left eyebrow that she'd noticed deep into their night together was perfect.

She wanted him as much as she'd ever wanted anything. Her old self screamed for her to take him, to let Andonia burn, to accept that the blessing could end in their happiness.

But it was wrong.

She swallowed back the tightness in her throat. "You would abandon your duty and all you stand for? You'd break the treaty… for me?"

He smiled, so warm and lovely that Sorra thought she might melt. He leaned in to kiss her again. "Of course."

"Then you're not the man I came here to save." Sorra spoke before his lips could touch hers, before she could let herself believe in this tempting new version of fate. Her dagger was still in her hand, and she pressed its tip to his throat. "Show me how to get into the castle. Now."

"Sorra!" Tullian's whisper was so loud she wasn't sure why he bothered.

"Take us inside," Sorra said, keeping her own voice to a threatening murmur, "or I swear I will slit your throat." She glanced at Tullian. "This isn't Beau."

"I can see that."

When Sorra looked back, the illusion was already fading, leaving a stranger standing where a prince had seconds before. He was the right height but thinner than Beau, with a patchy blond beard barely covering his weak chin. His bulging green eyes were wide with fear.

But he'd sounded right. He'd felt right. The thought made Sorra angrier as she remembered how this pathetic creature had worn Beau's lips, how his thin arm had felt so much stronger under her hand than it really was.

"Who are you?"

"Just a servant, I swear." His chin quivered. "Please. I can't take you inside. She'll kill me."

"And I'll kill you if you don't." She pressed harder, drawing a bright drop of blood.

She didn't know whether she could kill but thought she might manage it if she let her temper slip its leash.

"Sorra," Tullian said again with a warning tone.

Sorra ignored him. "Did the queen send you?"

"N-no. I was granted this illusion under orders to use it and lead you away if you ever found your way here." The servant licked his cracked lips. "Sally came to me, said it was time. I'm supposed to take you to a spot in the woods and see whether you have a marking on your arm. Then Sally and I were going to tell the queen when we were sure we deserved a reward and hadn't earned punishment." His voice wavered. "Please. If the queen finds out I failed her, I'm done."

Sorra's cheeks burned as she imagined what might have happened if she'd fallen for his ruse—their entry thwarted, her lack of protection exposed, all because she'd chosen not to doubt an impressive but ultimately fragile illusion.

She was angrier at herself than she was at the servant, but there was plenty of rage to go around.

"You will take us to the front doors," she said, loud enough so the mage would hear if he happened to be listening. "Then straight to the throne room."

Sorra forced the servant ahead of her—not out of the courtyard, but toward the door in the castle wall. He let out a choked sob but didn't shout a warning or beg for mercy as he pressed his hand to the door. It swung inward, and Sorra released him.

"Go," she whispered, and he fled into the darkness, away from the castle.

Sorra peered into a short hallway lined with wooden crates and baskets of vegetables, illuminated only by the light shining through the open doorway at its end. If there was anyone waiting to attack, they were well hidden.

Tullian stalked toward her, his cheeks red and his eyes bright. "Those were the actions of a villain, not a hero," he said, pointing after the servant.

"She sent an imposter out to lead us away. To kiss me and win me over. She's cheating," Sorra snapped, still burning with rage, her more heroic self forgotten. "How are we supposed to win if she's allowed to lie and cheat while we have to play fair?"

Tullian's nostrils flared as he drew himself up to his fullest height and finest posture. "We might have persuaded him to help us if you hadn't acted so rashly. We'd have come up with a false story about how we got in, and having him on our side might have been the key to our success." He poked a finger against the leather that covered Sorra's chest. "You've brought us far tonight, but it will do us no good if your recklessness ruins everything."

Sorra ground her teeth together and forced herself to breathe. "I promise I'll work on that in the future," she said, as calmly as she could. "For now, we needed a way into the castle, and I found it."

Tullian leaned in close. "The fact that something worked does not make it right, and we must be at our best if we wish to see this through. The visions clearly state that the quest requires heroes, and you're behaving like a cutthroat. Good always wins in the end."

Sorra stood aside to let him enter the castle first. "I hope so," she whispered to herself. "But breaking the rules still seems a lot more efficient along the way."

CHAPTER THIRTY-SIX

Muffled voices, accompanied by the clanks of pots and pans, reached Sorra as she sidestepped through the cluttered passage. The scent of roasting meat hung thick in the air, and the aching pit of her stomach reminded her of how unsatisfying her last meal had been.

Tullian's silhouette filled the doorway at its end, tense and alert as a rabbit in a fox's den. He turned his back on the voices to follow a gently curved hallway in the opposite direction, motioning for Sorra to follow.

She glanced both ways before she stepped into the brighter and more open space, then paused after a few steps, intrigued by the strange light that shimmered against the pearlescent walls—not firelight, but pure, gentle sunlight, cast by orbs that floated inside lamps shaped like silver birdcages. Sorra placed her palm near one. There was no heat, but when she closed her eyes, she felt as though the summer sun touched her skin.

"Sorra."

She followed, her footsteps silent on the thick lilac carpet that ran the length of the hallway. A staircase at its end led upward, following the curve of the castle's outer wall to the level of the front doors—and, Sorra hoped, the throne room.

A grand, open arch on the wall to their right opened onto a dining room with a soaring ceiling, easily three times the length of the town hall back in Cottsbridge. Four long tables ran most of its length, while another sat on a raised platform at its far end, each draped with gauzy white fabric and set with silver dishes. Glass vases overflowed with fresh flowers in shades of violet, pink, and blue, and vines of pale ivy trailed across the tables. A chandelier made from raindrop crystals reflected the same sunlight cast by the lamps in the hallways, casting bright shards of light on the walls.

A woman stood at the far end of the room, her back to them, carefully poking a blue hydrangea into a floral arrangement. She moved methodically, her eyes downcast, oblivious to the opulent beauty that had stolen Sorra's breath.

Sorra grabbed Tullian's arm to draw his attention and nodded at the human.

He shook his head, as Sorra had suspected he would. The girl in the garden had proved that a servant's fear could outweigh any desire to help those who might remove its cause.

"The front door should be straight ahead," he whispered, "and I expect the throne room close to it. Almost there."

The atmosphere of the castle clung to Sorra, curling tight around her body. It wasn't dampness or cold or anything else she could put a word to, and whatever it was might not have been off-putting on its own. But it was there, a strange tingle, too warm and too cold at the same time. A part of her wished she could peel her skin off just to be free of it.

The absence of obstacles was strange, too. It was possible that her ruse had worked, that the mage had ordered Gwelain's guards to gather outside the front door, but that would have been the definition of *too easy*. The idea that even now no one knew they were coming, that no one was waiting to leap out at them before they could make it to the throne room, seemed even less likely.

The thin set of Tullian's lips told Sorra he felt the same.

We've come this far, Sorra thought, but that was where the idea ended—a statement that offered little encouragement even as her feet carried her forward.

Her apprehension should have blinded her to the beauty around her, but Sorra's eyes drank in every object she passed—tapestries in pale tones, ivory tables topped with golden statues, shining suits of armour with jewels set into their engraved surfaces, and towering vases of exotic flowers. But she kept up with Tullian and stayed silent, knowing that things were probably about to go terribly wrong but not wishing to be the direct cause of any such disaster.

Tullian held up a hand as he paused at the junction of their hallway and another running crosswise to it. Rumbling voices reached them from the passage to the left, and Sorra's stomach cramped. Tullian backtracked to twin suits of armour and hid himself behind one with his back pressed to the wall. Sorra did the same, mirroring him, but couldn't resist peeking.

Two goblins stalked past the junction, their movements strange thanks to their tiptoe gait and long, taloned toes. One had rose-red skin from his round head to his scaly feet, and a long, rat-like tail that dragged on the ground. His companion, an ivory-complexioned creature with no tail at all, bore features so sharp they looked like they'd been carved from stone. Both wore armour of the same shining silver as the suits she and Tullian hid behind, though far less ornate.

Neither appeared to be carrying a weapon, but their claws and talons looked like they could do the job. Sorra remembered the injuries to the soldiers at the Gate, gobbets of flesh torn away from the bones beneath, throats opened by claws or fangs. Her heart fluttered, and pale clouds crowded the edges of her vision.

"Onward," Tullian said softly once the goblins had passed.

As they passed a series of closed doors, Sorra braced herself for each to burst open, anticipating the scaly arms and vicious claws that would drag her into darkness, but all remained firmly closed. When she glanced backward, the hallway seemed to stretch forever behind her.

Then, finally, the carpet widened to cover the floor of a massive rotunda. Twin staircases curved up its wall to their right, framing a tall doorway beneath a round balcony. Opposite the staircases stood the doors Sorra had examined from a distance outside. The shimmering light of the chandelier hanging high above revealed minor imperfections in the glass circles, gradations of colour and minor inclusions that hadn't been polished out when they were shaped into subtly convex discs.

Not glass, but amethyst.

Tullian stepped ahead, his attention on the open doorway between the stairs. His focus hadn't wavered once, as far as Sorra could tell, and he remained oblivious to the beauty that surrounded him.

"There," he said, his voice tight. "I can see the throne room at the end of this passage."

A rough voice called out behind them—not in words, but in a startled growl followed by the muffled thumps of feet against carpet.

Sorra didn't look back. She couldn't afford to be more frightened than she already was, so she focused instead on the promised safety of the throne room.

Tullian was taller than Sorra, his strides longer. He reached for her hand, hauling her along faster than her legs wanted to go. Still, the footsteps behind them caught up quickly, accompanied by hard, rasping breaths and the rattle of armour. Sorra stepped into the throne room, eyes wide and breath heaving as she absorbed what she could at a glance.

Not an empty room, as it should have been if everyone were preparing for a feast, but occupied by a small crowd of goblins in pastel-hued ballgowns and suits. They stood in two groups, leaving an aisle of black and white diamond-patterned floor clear between them. The twin thrones visible at the far end of the room were both occupied.

A woman in a white gown sat in one, her dark hair topped with a jagged white crown.

Gwelain.

The shock of finally laying eyes on the goblin queen should have kept Sorra's mind from anything else, but her gaze locked on Beau. He sat beside Gwelain, his eyes widening as he leaned forward. Everything else—the queen, the goblins, the black sky visible through the domed glass ceiling overhead—turned vague and insignificant as she met his gaze.

Then something collided with her from behind, and all she could see was the rough, callused hand the goblin pressed to her face to keep it from hitting the floor. She landed hard on her right arm and grunted as her left was twisted behind her. She struggled and kicked, though the weight on her back left her helpless.

The room erupted into a deafening hum of overlapping conversations, cheers, and laughter.

The goblin twisted Sorra's head to one side, facing Tullian. He wasn't fighting, though he'd bared his teeth in what might have been pain or anger.

He'd said Gwelain wouldn't hurt him as long as he didn't cause trouble and that she had to treat both of them as guests if they reached her throne room. Sorra forced herself to be still, though everything in her raged to keep fighting.

"We are residents of Marthis," Tullian said, his voice muffled by the clawed hand that pressed his face to the floor. "We have come peacefully to seek an audience with its queen, who is required to welcome us as stated by the old laws, if she believes herself worthy to observe them."

"Release them, faithful servants." Gwelain's voice filled the room, rich and gentle, with a hint of amusement covering something darker. The goblins fell silent.

The guard who had tackled Sorra growled in her ear, then hauled her roughly to her knees, facing the thrones.

"Rise," the queen said. Sorra obeyed and looked up to meet her enemy.

Gwelain wasn't human, but she also wasn't what Sorra had expected.

She was beautiful.

The queen's skin was bone-white, dusted with gold that highlighted her sharp cheekbones and high forehead. Her chin came to a dainty point, but jutted out in a delicate underbite that left a hint of her long lower canines protruding, pressing into the soft pink swell of her upper lip. The hair that flowed over her shoulders was as black as Sorra's, but it shone with the iridescence of a starling's feathers in the summer, emerald and cobalt where the light caught on its gentle waves. Her white gown hugged her curves, and the skirt parted like curtains to reveal gilded talons and scaled lower legs that shone like mother of pearl.

Even at a distance the queen's eyes flashed bright gold. They were focused on Tullian, and Sorra risked another glance at Beau, seeking whatever comfort he might offer to shield her against the terror that pounded through her veins. He looked strong and healthy and wore finer clothing than the servant impersonating him had—cuffed leather boots, fitted breeches, and a cobalt-blue waistcoat and a long jacket with gold piping at its wide lapels over a crisp white shirt. Old-fashioned clothing, but it suited him as well as it did his surroundings. The prince, if it was really him, sat straight-backed, gripping the arms of his throne tight, staring straight ahead, every trace of surprise or any other emotion erased as he looked pointedly away from Sorra.

Her stomach churned, the horrid food from the Hog and Keg threatening to pay a visit to the castle's spotless floor, but she held it down and forced herself to breathe and focus on something else.

Anything would be better than seeing the face she'd dreamed of for so many nights frozen in a disinterested mask.

The other goblins were less lovely than Gwelain but might have had their own beauty if not for the way they looked at the humans with a mixture of hunger and disdain.

Sorra decided that observing them was not better and turned her attention back to their queen.

"Forgive my guards for their enthusiasm," Gwelain said. "They are so very protective."

The guards both snorted, horse-like. Sorra watched over her shoulder as they stalked back to the doorway and took up positions on either side of it.

Gwelain folded her golden claws on her lap and smiled benevolently at the humans who stood before her. "I've been expecting you, of course." She narrowed her eyes at Tullian, though her lips still curved with amusement. Then the queen turned her gaze on Sorra, leaving her feeling like a mouse frozen before a snake. "You're the Andonian girl, aren't you?"

Sorra nodded, too frightened to speak.

"Good." Gwelain rested her hand on top of Beau's, her claws stroking the backs of his fingers. "We'll skip introductions, then. I believe you've met my husband."

CHAPTER THIRTY-SEVEN

The room froze. Sorra's thoughts, her breath, even her heartbeat seemed to cease entirely, their existence incompatible with the words the goblin queen had just spoken.

Then one of the goblins snickered behind her. The sound spread through the room, blooming into whispers and murmurs before a sharp look from Gwelain silenced them again.

But she, too, seemed to be holding back laughter.

"Beauregard," she said, leaning closer to him. "You were to end things."

He turned to Gwelain, his movements smooth and natural. "I told her not to follow me."

"Indeed. We should have known it wouldn't be enough." Gwelain smiled down at Sorra, but a cold glint remained in her golden eyes. "This is terribly awkward. When I told him to go out and have his little adventure before the wedding, I didn't imagine the consequences would follow him quite this far. Did you think he needed rescuing?" She pressed her lips together, barely holding back a laugh. "And that you were the great hero who would do it?"

Sorra couldn't answer. There *was* no answer. She had thought exactly that, but when Gwelain said it, the idea sounded more ridiculous than it had even in her darkest moments. Her head swam as she struggled to remember why she'd come.

Beau watched her, his expression offering nothing. Then in an instant he relaxed, smiled, and slipped his fingers between Gwelain's, clasping her hand from beneath.

"Let her be, my queen," he said. "She's only a poor girl from an isolated village. She was taken up by the spirit of adventure, and it carried her farther than anyone intended. Send her home and there will be no harm done."

Gwelain tilted her head gently to one side. "I could do that. Of course, I'd have to wipe her memory clean of all this. Would you like that, Andonian girl?"

Sorra felt the weight of every eye in the room on her, save for Tullian's. He was watching Gwelain so intently that Sorra wondered whether her decision mattered to him, or whether he'd heard the question at all.

She looked to Beau instead. He was still smiling as though he pitied her.

But she remembered the night in the cabin when he'd told her about his sacrifice, losing his future to end the curse, and remaining heir to the throne only so Gwelain would maintain peace in hopes of marrying the future king. He'd seemed defeated, heartbroken to have lost his chance at freedom, and dismayed by the unspoken consequences of losing the wager.

Not torture, but marriage.

His amusement now didn't seem like an act, but his despair then hadn't seemed like one, either.

She'd need to choose which she believed.

And the only way I'll ever know is if I stay.

"I have nothing to go home to," she said. "And my destiny, for what it's worth, is here."

Gwelain waited for the wave of laughter that followed to die on its own, then motioned toward the doors. "Go, all of you. Varek, Corvin, you may remain." She turned to Beau. "I'll see you soon, love."

Beau nodded, and without another glance at Sorra he left, exiting through a door to the right of the thrones while the others filed out the way Sorra and Tullian had entered, taking their clicking talons and sharp whispers with them. Sorra wanted to run after Beau but supposed that would be the worst thing she could do.

Gwelain's guards closed the heavy wooden doors and stood at attention, glowering at Sorra and Tullian.

The only others who remained were two figures dressed in black, revealed by the crowd's departure. One was a goblin who appeared more monstrous than Gwelain's other subjects, with a jaw that protruded farther than the queen's, exposing vicious lower canines. His heavy brow and moss-green skin reflected what Sorra had always imagined a goblin to be, though he was taller than most humans and had a full head of thick, dark hair brushed behind his pointed ears. There was a sharp intelligence to him that cut through Sorra as his gaze landed on her, and not a hint of the gossipy excitement the rest had carried from the room with them.

Sorra tried not to shudder.

The other was human. He appeared to be about Tullian's age, for whatever that was worth in a place frozen in time, but the years had been far less kind to him. His grey hair did a poor job of covering the mess of scars on the side of his head where his ear looked to have been torn off, and the scars extending over his scalp and down his throat made Sorra think him lucky to be alive at all. The only lovely thing about him was the emerald pendant that hung on a long gold chain around his neck, shining against his black cassock.

Her mage.

He didn't look like much, but Linnea's warnings had been clear. This scarred, scowling old man was one of the greatest dangers they'd face in the castle.

When Sorra turned back to Gwelain, the queen's smile had faded.

"Your destiny, then." She tapped her chin with one claw. "A good enough reason to come here, and to stay. But what about you, Sir… what was your name?"

"Tullian, Majesty."

"Yes. Why have you come to me now?"

The knight and the goblin queen watched each other, silently feeling each other out.

"I've come to speak to you about your offer, Majesty."

Gwelain chuckled. "Let's not lie to each other just yet. We both know you aren't likely to change your mind at this late hour."

"Yet you continue your attempts to persuade me." Tullian stepped closer to the throne. "I've noted the increasing frequency of taxation over the past decade, but until Sorra's arrival, I hadn't considered why you'd wish to put more pressure on me. I recently learned about the prince and your plan to take the throne of Andonia through him."

"And?"

Tullian's posture relaxed into one of defeat, though not dramatically enough to mark it as a lie. "And it's a fine plan, Majesty. I see that your victory may come with or without my cooperation but have realized that I might still protect Andonia by placing limits on your victory—assurances regarding your future treatment of humans, maintenance of the land, and other such things. It's not the outcome I desire, but if the alternative is your unchecked power over Linnea's lands, I may have no choice."

A good act. Sorra hoped it would be enough.

No one spoke. It seemed that no one breathed as they waited for Gwelain's response.

"Do you doubt the visions, then?" the goblin queen spoke softly but with intense interest. "They speak of my rise to power or my absolute defeat, not of middle ground."

Tullian cleared his throat. "Rise, yes, but power may be held in check. And we're missing so much of the visions, Majesty. I can't know what other outcomes Linnea might have seen, and therefore I can only do what I believe she'd want."

"Oh? And I foolishly assumed you'd come intending to steal my property."

Tullian stiffened. "Linnea's heart belongs to the people of Andonia. My feelings on that have not changed. But if the alternative—"

"Yes, yes." Gwelain silenced him with a wave of her flashing claws. "Linnea is dead. Her heart is no good to her, and no good to anyone if it's not in capable hands." She looked to Sorra. "I don't know what he's told you about me, but I didn't kill Linnea. She died at the hands of her own people. She was standing in the way of what they called progress. I call it greed, myself. They wanted a more human mind on the throne." Her voice was smooth, her cadence as musical as a lullaby. "I only liberated the heart from them. It will be returned to Andonia in my hands and in my time. Do you understand?"

Sorra blinked hard, trying to clear the dreamlike sense of unreality that stole over her mind. "I think so."

"Good." But Gwelain didn't sound pleased. "You've fully sworn yourself to his foolish quest?"

"I have," Sorra said, though she wasn't sure whether bluffing mattered anymore.

"Show me your arm, then."

"I—" Sorra looked to Tullian.

"Never mind. Your hesitation is answer enough." Gwelain rested her chin on one gently curled fist. "I suspected you weren't protected, but I had to be sure." She snapped her fingers and nodded to the guards. "Reaver, remove her head."

Tullian stepped in front of Sorra, then drew his sword. Sorra drew hers as well, but she could barely feel her hands and nearly dropped it.

The buzz of panic in her mind made everything seem distant and strange.

"What about the laws of hospitality, Majesty?" Tullian demanded. "Have you abandoned the old ways so easily? Would you dare to invite ill luck at such a critical moment?"

"Not at all." Gwelain rose and moved closer, talons clicking against the floor. She stood before them, taller than Sorra had expected, her lips pursed in a strange smile. "I'll call you a guest, brave and foolish knight, while we negotiate your terms. I still don't trust your intentions, but if you're going to cause trouble I'd just as soon have you do it where I can see you. But perhaps you've forgotten that I am bound to extend hospitality only to citizens of my lands. You've been here for long enough that I'll call you one of mine if you wish. But her? This Andonian child who thought she could steal my dear prince's heart?"

The rose-skinned guard who had tackled Tullian earlier strode closer, gripping a two-handed axe, and Gwelain stepped back.

"No protection as a citizen," she said, shaking her head in mock sadness. "Not one of the sworn heroes Linnea's visions work so conveniently to protect. No reason for me to let her live."

Sorra fought to breathe as the guard raised his axe. Tullian lunged at him but came up far short, unwilling to leave Sorra exposed, and the goblin laughed as he sidestepped the swing and set himself up to attack again.

It's a game to him, Sorra thought as the goblin bared his teeth at her in a mocking grin.

And to her.

Gwelain wasn't looking at Sorra, but at Tullian, daring him to make his next move.

Tullian cursed under his breath and stepped backward, forcing Sorra toward the corner of the throne room as the other guard approached her exposed flank.

She corrected her grip on her sword and tried to make space for herself to fight, but everything she'd learned about swordplay seemed to have vanished from her mind.

Tullian glanced over his shoulder at her. "I pledge myself to my queen, Linnea, and to the quest to return her heart to Andonia. Say it! And mean it."

Sorra stared at him, her mind a blank, willing herself to understand. "I—I pledge myself to my queen, Linnea, and the quest to return her heart to Andonia."

"I swear my life to standing against her enemies," he said, his voice breaking.

"I swear my... my life... to standing against her enemies." Sorra stumbled over the words as she tried to understand what she was promising.

Tullian held off another half-hearted attack. "My days, my nights, and my own heart are hers. If I fall, may it be in her service."

There was no time to think about right or wrong or whether Tullian would offer this protection if he knew about her blessing. There was only an axe meant for her neck and the certainty that there was no other way she'd live to see the quest through.

Whether Beau was the humbled prince she'd met at the cabin or the dismissive jackass he now seemed to be, her destiny had brought her here. If he was worth saving, it would be done through Tullian's quest. Even if she'd misjudged him, there were still others who needed Linnea's heart back in its proper place.

No more curses, here or at home.

Let me help. Let me be a hero.

"My days, my nights, and my own heart are hers," Sorra repeated. "If I fall, may it be in her service."

Gwelain held up one hand. A tiny smile played about her lips as her guard lowered his axe. "Let's see it, then."

Sorra trembled as she rolled up her sleeve, expecting to reveal nothing and prove her unworthiness. Instead, she found Linnea's songbird etched into her skin in dark, clean lines.

Gwelain stepped close to brush a claw over it, and Sorra flinched away.

The mage shuffled closer to Gwelain, his hands folded into his long sleeves, and she bent so he could whisper something in her delicately pointed ear.

"I haven't forgotten, Corvin. Thank you."

He bowed and backed away.

Corvin. Sorra was glad to know his name, if only so she could be sure never to speak it and draw his attention.

"I suppose I can't kill you now," Gwelain said, studying Sorra with cold interest, then turned to Tullian. "Let's dispense with the idea that you've come to negotiate—we all know you're here for the heart, and pretending otherwise makes us all look foolish. Still, you are welcome here as long as it serves me, and as long as you don't harm me or anyone else in the castle. If you do, I will be within my rights to cast you out. Beyond that, you will leave only when I permit it. Agreed?"

"Agreed, Majesty," Tullian said after a moment's clear hesitation.

"Hmm." Gwelain looked sideways at Sorra again, considering. "You're still not my subject, though, and therefore not covered by the old laws. I could imprison you if I wished. Even torture you as long as I could be sure it wouldn't kill you. But you'll find that I'm not the monster you may have been led to believe. I will treat you well as long as you behave yourself. Food, drink, fine lodgings, entertainment. Perhaps we'll become friends in time."

No, not a monster at all, Sorra thought, recalling the horrors the humans of the Forgotten Lands had faced for hundreds of years, but she did her best to nod. The execution order still rang through her mind, and she didn't wish to anger the queen again.

Tullian glowered at Gwelain, but she didn't seem to notice. She snapped her fingers, and the sound echoed from the walls. "Varek, have two rooms made up for our esteemed guests. Baths, clothing, anything they might need."

The green-skinned goblin bowed and stalked from the room.

"Wait here for now," Gwelain said, gathering her full skirt in one hand. "I'll send someone along shortly to show you to your rooms. You'll join us for our feast tonight, of course." She wrinkled her nose. "After a bath and a change of clothes."

The queen turned and glided from the room before Sorra could decline the invitation. Her mage and her guards followed, closing the throne room's doors behind them.

Tullian sank to the floor. Sorra sat beside him, all the strength gone from her legs. She didn't need the book of visions in her hand to know the significance of what had just happened.

Should the queen's sworn champion die by the enemy's order or intention, on that day shall Gwelain meet her end.

When the hero pledged to Linnea bows to the goblin queen and becomes her creature, then will the door be opened for Andonia's greatest enemy to come to power, raining misery and destruction upon Andonia.

Tullian had protected her for the moment by swearing her to Linnea's quest, but he'd also opened the door to her becoming a sacrifice later.

And he'd made it possible for her to become the key to Gwelain's victory.

"You saved me." Sorra's voice came out thin and airy.

"Yes." The old knight rested his head in his hands. "Tell me I made the right choice."

"You did, I swear. I would never betray Linnea. Or Andonia. Or you, for that matter."

Tullian pulled in a shaky breath. "I believe you," he said, sounding like he at least wanted to. "It might have been better to let her kill you, but I couldn't."

Sorra winced and was glad he didn't see. He wasn't wrong. He'd killed before to keep a potential traitor out of Gwelain's grasp. He believed she was a true hero and worth protecting, but he'd feel differently if she'd told him about her blessing.

And now that it's done, he can never know.

She tried to tell herself it was for the best, that they'd only come this far because she'd kept her mouth shut, but it didn't make her feel any better.

"Do you think this was her plan all along?" she asked, when it was clear he wasn't going to speak again. "Did she only shut us out so we wouldn't realize she was drawing us in?"

What she really wanted to know was whether every lucky break and fortunate turn of events since she'd left the cabin had really been the blessing working to guide her here, but the sinking of her stomach was answer enough.

I wasn't escaping at all.

But it's not over yet. It can't be.

"Perhaps." Tullian climbed unsteadily to his feet and held out his hands to help Sorra up. She accepted, though she'd have been happy to rest a little longer. "But what's done is done, and there's no stopping what we've put into motion. The Might and the Mystery have come this far, and we may yet encounter the Mind and the Magic."

Sorra didn't ask whether he'd swear them to the quest, too.

He was trying to convince himself he'd done the right thing by saving her life, but she was sure he wouldn't make the same mistake again.

CHAPTER THIRTY-EIGHT

A woman in a petal-pink dress and a white apron bustled into the throne room, her lips pursed with distaste as she took in the disheveled pair of heroes.

She pushed her glasses up her beaklike nose and turned on her heel. "This way," she said, hurrying out without waiting to make sure they were following.

Sorra and Tullian exchanged a glance.

"This way, I guess?" Sorra whispered.

Tullian sighed. "After you."

The woman waited at the bottom of the left-hand staircase opposite the castle's front doors, one hand resting on the polished banister.

"Quickly, please."

Sorra's legs protested as she climbed the stairs and followed the woman down the hallway at the top. Windows in one wall overlooked the throne room's ceiling, but from the outside the domed glass appeared fogged, revealing only a hint of light from below. Above, the night sky sparkled.

"Your rooms are ready." The woman spoke as briskly as she walked, each syllable clipped and sharp. "Baths, beds, clothing for tonight. You'll remain there until I return to escort you to the feast."

"What if we—" Sorra began, but fell silent as their guide spoke over her.

"You'll remember that you're guests here. Behave and speak respectfully. Queen Gwelain likes things to look pleasing, smell pleasing, act pleasing." She shot a pointed look over her shoulder at Sorra. "You'll want to get to work on all of that right away to make up for your first impression."

Sorra's cheeks warmed. "Will I?"

"If you're partial to keeping your hide intact, I'd advise it."

Everything from the pastel-hued carpets to the gentle curves where the white walls met the arched ceiling were spotless, and when Sorra breathed deep, she identified the faint, clean scents of lavender and lemon on the air. Paintings in gilded frames hung on the walls, perfectly spaced and perfectly elegant. It was a castle that should have belonged to a kindly queen from a bedtime story, not a murderous goblin witch, and might have felt like something out of a beautiful dream if not for the nightmarish events unfolding within it.

Sorra kept her gaze fixed on the servant's pink skirt as she climbed a spiral staircase into one of the castle's towers, but the turns made Sorra's head spin by the time they stepped into a narrow room at the top with cream-coloured wooden doors opening off it on opposite sides. The servant pressed a hand against the door to the right just above the silver latch, then opened it and motioned for Sorra to enter.

Sorra wanted a chance to speak to Tullian privately, to assure him again that she'd never bow to Gwelain and perhaps to figure out their next steps, but the servant didn't seem inclined to leave.

Besides, Corvin was probably listening.

In spite of Gwelain's sugar-sweet words, Sorra wondered whether she'd climbed the tower only to be dumped in a dungeon cell. She sighed, relieved, as she stepped into a pleasant, if strangely shaped, bedroom.

The largest bed Sorra had ever seen sat against the far wall of the semi-circular room, its intricately carved headboard flanked by windows with their velvet curtains drawn tight. To the bed's left, a stone fireplace occupied a large portion of the wall, its roaring fire already burning to warm anyone who wanted to sit in one of the two armchairs that faced it, their backs to the door. An oak wardrobe faced it from the other side of the room, near a gleaming claw-footed bathtub filled with steaming water that smelled of flowers and something that took Sorra a moment to place—oranges. She hadn't tasted one since she was a child.

The colours in the room were all darker than those in the rest of the castle—oak floors like polished honey, forest-green velvet uphol-stering the chairs, and a round rug under the bed patterned in swirling shades of blue that shifted subtly like light warped through water.

The room was finer than anything Sorra could have hoped for, but it was the dress laid out on the bed that drew and held her attention. It was the rich blue of the summer sky, made from dozens of layers of fabric so fine that each would have been translucent on its own. No one had left undergarments to go with it, but the fitted bodice looked supportive, if daringly low-cut.

It was the loveliest dress Sorra had ever seen, or even imagined.

Tullian peered into the room after her.

"Don't wear it," he said, nodding at the dress. "Don't let her tempt you into thinking you belong here."

"No danger of that," Sorra said. She traced her fingers over the skirt, which felt as soft and airy as it looked.

"Armour," Tullian said, more insistently. "For your body and your thoughts, never mind making a good second impression. Woman, let go!" The latter was directed at the servant, who was tugging at his arm. He huffed out a breath and stepped away, and the door closed behind him.

When Sorra tried the latch, she found the door locked.

So I am imprisoned, she thought. *At least it's a nice cell.*

Still, she tried again, pressing her hand against various spots on the door as the servant had on the outside, then shoving with her shoulder.

"It's no good."

Sorra's heart stumbled at the rasping voice, which spoke from somewhere near the fire. A figure in black rose from one of the chairs.

The green-skinned goblin.

He looked even more monstrous in close quarters where Sorra

could focus on everything from his pointed ears to his long, scaled toes and the talons that tapped softly against the wood floor as he moved closer.

Sorra pressed her back to the door. There was nowhere to go.

He stopped beside the bed and bowed slightly. "Forgive me. I thought I should introduce myself, as my mother neglected to do so."

Sorra swallowed hard and tried to find her voice again. "Gwelain?"

"Queen Gwelain," he said, correcting her more gently than Tullian usually did. "You'll want to remember that, and to call her 'Majesty' at every opportunity. You've neglected to do so a few times already. She won't always be in such a forgiving mood." He moved a few steps closer, his gait smooth and graceful, his hands clasped as unthreateningly as they could be while bearing such large claws. His suit was styled much like Beau's had been, with a fine waistcoat and a long jacket, but the embroidered details at its lapels and cuffs were nearly lost in its uniform darkness. "My name is Varek. Welcome to my humble home."

"Um… thank you." Sorra aimed for a gracious tone but found it impossible to sound like anything but a frightened mouse. "It was good of your mother to invite us to dinner."

"Do you think so?" He smiled without any humour. "Well. Now that we're introduced, I suppose I should leave you to bathe and dress."

"Of course." Sorra stepped away from the door, but he didn't move toward it.

Varek released his hands to his sides, but his regal posture didn't relax. "I shouldn't be here," he said, more quietly. "I want to ask about your true plans, but it would be foolish to think you'd share them with me."

"It would," Sorra said, though she suspected she might be insulting him by agreeing. "Did the queen ask you to do this? I thought Tullian explained himself quite clearly, even if she didn't believe him."

"A fine speech it was, too. But no." He laughed bitterly. "She doesn't know I'm speaking with you, and I'd appreciate it if you kept it that way."

"Oh? I thought her mage could hear anything."

"No one hears what happens in this room." Varek bent and turned back one corner of the rug next to the bed, revealing a symbol formed from curving lines carved into the floor. "My magic isn't significant compared to what the queen currently controls, but I know how to use what I have. I've placed this protection against anyone listening by magic. If you want to keep secrets from my mother, I wouldn't speak of them beyond that door."

Sorra crossed her arms, frowning. "That's generous of you."

"Hardly. Removing one of Gwelain's unfair advantages serves me at least as much as it does you. I am taking a risk, of course, but it's only dangerous if she finds out." He didn't sound overly concerned. "If you're at all clever you'll make sure she doesn't."

"Why does it serve you?" Sorra asked.

Varek didn't answer. That was no surprise—it would be as foolish for him to trust her as it would for her to place any faith in him.

She took her eyes off him for long enough to study the symbol carved into the floor. It looked like the ones at Tullian's hideout in the woods, but that didn't mean anything. Gwelain had probably told Varek to spin a convenient lie about magical protection so her enemies would speak openly about their plans where Corvin would know to listen.

It was insulting, even a little clumsy in its obviousness, but Sorra supposed being underestimated by the goblins might be an advantage.

"Have you considered destroying the heart?" Varek asked.

Sorra tried to smile. "I thought you weren't going to ask about our plans."

"I said it would be foolish to expect an answer, not that I wouldn't ask."

He didn't sound like he was joking, but it reminded Sorra so much of her own approach to questioning Beau at the cabin that she almost smiled. "I'm really not the one you should be asking. Tullian would know better than I do."

Varek lowered his gaze. "I'll assume the answer is no, then." Sorra had thought he wanted reassurance that the heart would be safe, but he seemed disappointed. "It could come to that, you know. Not a question of it ending up in Gwelain's hands or yours, but hers or none at all."

"I don't want it in my hands."

Varek smiled, his eyes shining. Though it revealed more than she liked of his huge lower teeth, it was the first genuinely pleasant expression Sorra had seen on a goblin, and she wished she didn't feel as though his amusement was at her expense.

"That's good to know," he said. He stepped toward the door, then turned back. "Don't trust her. Don't trust anyone."

"All right." Sorra chose her next words carefully, knowing it might be wisest to say as little as possible but unable to resist the urge to prod. "I suppose that means I shouldn't trust you either."

"That's your choice. In my experience, trust inevitably leads to disappointment. I do hate to be disappointed." Varek's heavy jaw muscles flexed. "As does my mother."

"She's disappointed in you?"

"She is disappointed by almost everyone." He cleared his throat gently. "Well. I suppose I'll see you at the feast, then."

He pressed a hand to the door, then pulled it open.

"Wait."

He paused in the doorway. "I can't leave it open for you. If I did, she'd figure out I'd been here. Give it time. She may give you more freedom if you prove you deserve it."

Varek stepped out and closed the door behind him, leaving Sorra alone in her lovely prison.

She resisted the urge to slam her hand against the door, unsure of whether her visitor deserved her frustration. In the space of a few minutes he'd frightened her, offered her a warning she didn't need, made her wonder whether he'd only offered it to win her over, and left her unsure of whether their brief conversation had changed anything at all.

There was something strange about Varek that went beyond his monstrous appearance, and it took a bit of thinking before she decided he was too still. A human would fidget or twitch, or if not, it would be obvious that they were disciplining themselves not to. He simply *was* still, aside from a few shifts in his facial expression and purposeful movements. Everything about him was intentional and controlled.

That wasn't a reason to dislike him, but it didn't warm her to him, either. For the time being it was clearly best to take his advice and include him in the circle of those she wouldn't trust. Even what he'd said about having reasons to help her, his apparent desire to see the heart destroyed, and the indications that he might not have a loving relationship with his monstrous mother could all have been a convincing act.

As for where Beau fell in regard to her circle of trust, she decided to remain undecided until she could speak with him.

Sorra dipped a hand into the bathwater, which was still hot enough to turn her skin pink. It had been weeks since she'd had a proper soak in warm water, and though she kept her eyes and ears open for signs that anyone might be spying, she didn't hesitate for long before stripping down and slipping into the water. She sank in up to her neck, then examined the black songbird that had appeared on her forearm. A symbol of hope, and a warning of danger. Its appearance didn't make her a true hero, but it would be a constant reminder of how much would be lost if she failed.

I may not deserve it yet, but I will.

Her muscles relaxed. So did her thoughts, and they drifted toward Beau. He'd become the least of her concerns after Gwelain had sent him from the throne room, but there was plenty to consider, and none of it pleasant.

When he'd spoken of the consequences he'd face after losing his wager, she'd imagined physical torture.

But of course it would be marriage. Of course it would be the one thing he'd managed to keep from Gwelain that would put her a step closer to Andonia's throne.

Sorra dunked her head and scrubbed her scalp furiously, willing her useless rage to leave her body.

Either Gwelain had been telling the truth about Sorra being one last fling before their wedding, which seemed unlikely, or something else was making Beau behave so strangely. It could be another false version of him, but the shock on his face when she'd run into the throne room had been too real for her to think that was the case. He might be under an enchantment that made him believe Gwelain's lies, which would make it difficult to secure his help in rescuing Linnea's heart.

Or it was something else.

There was only one way to find out. Sorra wished it didn't involve facing Gwelain and all the other goblins who had laughed at her for following Beau all this way, but there was nothing to be done about that.

Someone knocked at the door. Before Sorra could answer, it opened. She slumped beneath the water, legs drawn up, arms crossed over her chest as the woman in pink stepped into the room.

"You're going to be late," the servant noted, casting a scathing glare at her. Her narrow frame and thin nose reminded Sorra of the herons that nested next to the river back in Cottsbridge. "Meal's beginning soon."

"I'll hurry," Sorra said. "I only need a minute to dry and dress."

The servant sighed. "You'll want more than that to make yourself presentable. Best if you missed the meal, anyway—I don't imagine your table manners would do anything to endear you to Queen Gwelain."

Sorra reached for the towel folded on the wooden chair next to the wardrobe. "Please, I can't be late."

"Miss." The servant spoke so sternly that Sorra winced and turned back to her, modesty forgotten. "You're better off not eating with the queen. Table manners aside, fine goblin food will be unfamiliar to a simple girl like you, and it's more polite to arrive late than it is to turn your nose up or be sick over such rich meats and delicacies."

She held Sorra's gaze, her eyes like slivers of flint. She was clearly trying to communicate something without using words she didn't want Corvin to overhear.

That, or she wanted to see Sorra further humiliated for some reason, but it seemed safest to play along. "You're sure the queen won't be angry?"

"Not if it's clear you used your time well. Keep scrubbing and brushing until I come to collect you."

"Thank you," Sorra said, not sure what she was meant to be grateful for but not wishing to make enemies. "What's your name?"

"Hannah. No point learning it, though. Someone else'll likely tend to you tomorrow. We all have jobs here and can't be wasting our time on guests."

She left, closing the door hard behind her.

Don't eat the food at the feast.

Don't expect to get close to anyone.

Look good enough that lateness doesn't matter.

And don't trust anyone—even the servants.

Sorra sank below the water's surface again before she let out a groan of frustration.

She dried herself and looked down at the dress that had been so carefully and temptingly laid out on the bed, then at the wrinkled clothes she'd left in a pile on the floor. The thought of putting her smelly old things back on seemed unfathomable, but Tullian had given clear orders.

Should have at least hung them up to let the wrinkles fall out while I bathed. It was really too late, but she supposed letting her clothes air out while she tended to her hair wouldn't hurt. She opened the wardrobe in search of a hanger and smiled.

More dresses hung inside, all of them far plainer than the one laid out on the bed, as well as tunics and fitted trousers in a range of soft, dark colours.

Gwelain—or more likely Varek, as he'd arranged accommodations—had given her a choice. It didn't feel like a test, but she supposed she might simply be too tired or stupid to see it as such. Either way, Tullian had been firm in his opinion.

He'd saved her life. The least she could do in return was to offer him every assurance she wasn't going to throw herself into Gwelain's service.

She cast one more longing look at the blue dress, then selected a tunic and trousers made from crimson fabric far finer than the items she'd discarded on the floor. Then, feeling foolish, she put on her armour as she'd done every morning of her time with Tullian and fastened her belt and sword to her waist. She tucked her sheathed dagger into her boot in case anyone decided to confiscate visible weapons at the door, then braided her hair.

She didn't feel beautiful, but she'd done as she'd been told. Her old self wanted the dress, but she hoped the new Sorra would instead be prepared for whatever might come.

After that, there was nothing to do except sit and wait for someone to take her to whatever awaited at the goblin queen's feast.

CHAPTER THIRTY-NINE

Music beckoned as Sorra followed Hannah past the throne room's entrance and down the hallway she'd travelled earlier—faint strains at first, swelling to a rich and intoxicating chorus of eerie strings underlaid with heavy percussion that made her feet itch to move. Her footsteps became lighter and more rhythmic as the melody trembled through her flesh, drawing her closer.

"In you go, then," Hannah said, stopping next to the open doorway to the dining room.

"You're not coming with me?"

"As I said, I have other duties." The servant offered no advice or reassurance before she stalked away, heading to the stairway and, presumably, the kitchens below.

Sorra steeled herself.

No way out but forward.

The first thing Sorra understood as she stepped into the dining room was that the goblins didn't just live in a different land—they occupied another world entirely.

The quiet, elegant dining room had become a crowded, noisy, sparkling riot. The tables, which were covered in used dishes and half-filled wine glasses, had been pushed to the sides of the room. A few goblins chatted and laughed around its edges, but most were occupied in a complicated dance that moved the crowd in a constant circle, though Sorra couldn't pick out any pattern or consistency to their individual movements. Some raised their arms in graceful arcs, others twisted their bodies and kicked their legs, but somehow it all formed a singular dance so captivating that Sorra had to squeeze her eyes closed and count to five before she could wrestle her attention to anything else.

Gwelain and Beau were seated at the raised table at the far end of the room, her watching the party with amusement, him staring out over the crowd with little interest. The elderly mage, Corvin, sat on Beau's other side, nodding off over his empty plate.

Sorra stepped back, hoping to remain unnoticed for as long as possible while she scanned the room for Tullian. Someone cursed behind her. She'd almost bumped into one of the human servants who bustled around the edges of the room, heads down as they cleared away dishes and replaced tablecloths.

"Watch it," he muttered, and went on his way, changing course to avoid two goblins who had squared off, their fists raised and teeth bared. Sorra edged away.

She couldn't see Tullian, but there was plenty to keep her eyes busy. Every goblin in the room wore clothing that was, if not attractive to her eye, at least colourful or elegant or daring. Feathers, gemstones, layers of skirts that looked like the petals of giant flowers, all in hues that paired perfectly with the castle. Some wore gorgeously tailored suits that looked like relics from times past with white lace at their throats, or stranger costumes of pale silk styled to mimic the silhouette of battle armour. One partygoer wore nothing at all.

Though she knew she shouldn't stare, Sorra found her gaze catching on every face and body it landed on. The dance carried a goblin with skin of petal pink past her, then others with complexions the blue of a forget-me-not, the grey of cinders, and tones of cream and bronze and brown that more clearly reflected what they'd once been—humans who had earned Gwelain's favour. It seemed their queen found variety pleasing. She'd gifted them with everything from horns to tails to, in one case, tiny wings that fluttered like a butterfly's above the low-cut back of a sheer, form-hugging gown.

Goblins, but more beautiful than the ones Gwelain's grandfather had given her to rule over. She'd kept their claws, though, and all had pointed ears and those strange, scaled feet that made Sorra think of dragons or eagles. Most of their faces and bodies were speckled with patches of scales or rough, knobbly skin. Some were bald as apples, but most sported thick, shining hair that they wore loose and flowing or in intricate knots and plaits.

Sorra touched the tight, plain braid that held her own hair in strict order, tempted to undo it and free her still-damp locks.

One of the goblins noticed her. Then another.

Not one of them spoke to her, even as they stared and whispered and laughed.

At that moment Sorra realized that no matter how much she owed Tullian, no matter how much it meant to him, she regretted not wearing the dress. She'd thought her armour would feel like protection as she stepped into a room filled with potential enemies, but as they cast smug glances at her and whispered to each other without looking away she knew for certain that trying to look like she belonged would have been vastly preferable.

Nothing would have allowed her to blend in, but she might have seemed less like a joke if she hadn't come to a fancy party dressed in battered old armour.

The goblins quickly lost interest in her. As they returned to the dance or filled their cups with a thick, red drink that flowed from a tiered silver fountain next to the head table, the crowd thinned enough that Sorra spotted Tullian standing in a distant corner. He raised a glass of sparkling liquid to her and wove his way closer.

Sorra glanced again at the head table. Beau still wasn't looking her way.

Tullian side-stepped a pair of goblins whose writhing dance seemed about to turn into something else entirely. He, too, wore his armour, but was still wearing his worn old things under it. His hair was damp and neatly combed back, though, and he smelled better than he had before.

Sorra wondered how long it had taken him to decide how thoroughly he could refuse Gwelain's overtures without being ruder than a knight ought to be.

"I was beginning to think you weren't coming," he said.

"Seemed a shame to waste a good bath," she said. "Have you been here long?"

"No. That horrid servant woman seemed disinclined to allow me to attend the meal."

Sorra glanced at the dripping red fountain. "Maybe with good reason."

"But you wore your armour instead of that ridiculous frock," Tullian said, clearly pleased. "They offered me the same. Not a dress, but something in the way of fancy party clothes. You made the right decision."

Sorra thought of how much easier it would be to hold her head high if she felt a little less like a child parading around in her father's clothes. "Does make one feel a bit underdressed, though."

"We're not here to impress anyone," he said, gentle but firm.

"I know." She wanted to tell him about her strange conversation with Varek, but it wasn't safe to speak. Instead, she nodded toward the head table. Corvin was nearly face-down on his plate.

"That's him, then. The mage the visions warned about."

"So it would seem."

"He doesn't look like much of a threat. Just a tired old man."

Sorra's skin crawled as Corvin looked up, his gaze suddenly sharp and fixed on her.

Tullian raised his glass to him.

"We'll need to be careful," Tullian said, leaning in to speak quietly into her ear, perhaps hoping the music and chatter would keep the mage from hearing. "If Gwelain speaks to you, be as honest as you can while giving nothing away, and try to direct her attention back to me if you can. Otherwise, observe and listen, learn what you can, and above all don't cause trouble. If you harm any member of Gwelain's household, you'll have broken the peace we offered when we arrived. She'll be free to imprison you or toss you out. We're guests here and will behave as such."

He didn't need to add *until I tell you otherwise*.

Tullian walked away before she could ask how she was supposed to learn anything when no one seemed inclined to speak to her. She'd need to try to talk to Beau, but it wouldn't happen at the feast, assuming he wanted it to happen at all.

So she stood in place, unsure of what to do with her hands, pretending she didn't notice the goblins staring at her.

Varek approached, still dressed in black and easy to pick out among the floral-hued crowd. He'd made an effort at glamour, though. The shoulders of his suit were covered in a thick layer of shining black feathers that continued down his arms, thinning toward his wrists. The goblin speaking to him, a creature in a lavender gown that matched her spiralling horns, laughed and leaned in to draw his attention to the considerable assets her dress displayed so effectively.

"Shall we go some place quieter?" she asked. Sorra strained to hear her over the music.

"No."

The goblin pouted. "Why not?"

Varek's jaw clenched visibly.

The goblin set her hands on her hips and raised her chin. "Out with it."

Varek's nostrils flared. "I don't want you. I find you vapid, irritating, and hopelessly predictable. The only arrangement that would suit me would involve gagging you or cutting out your tongue to keep you from speaking."

Sorra sucked in a breath and looked away.

"This is why no one likes you, Varek," the goblin said. She swept past Sorra without glancing at her, joined the dance, and pressed herself against the closest available partner.

Sorra waited for Varek to stalk away, but her stomach sank as he stood beside her.

"You'd have looked better in the dress," he said. "Lovely, even. At least by human standards."

"I think I would have, yes." When she turned to him, a faint smile touched his lips, but it faded quickly. "This is quite the party," she added, trying not to end the only chance she saw to obey Tullian's orders. "Are you not enjoying yourself?"

"As much as I ever do. Even celebrations become dull when one is expected to attend them so frequently."

Sorra nodded at the swirling confusion of the dance before her. "They seem to be having fun."

"They're fools who can't think of anything more meaningful than petty pleasures and whatever else their queen offers to distract them from the emptiness they'd find if they had nothing to entertain them but their own meaningless existence."

Sorra smiled uneasily. She had no desire to defend the goblins, but she could see why Varek might be widely disliked if he was always this sour and blunt.

He watched her, waiting for an answer, or perhaps another question. But Corvin would be listening. Even if he wasn't, she didn't know what to ask when she had no reason to believe Varek's answers would be anything but lies.

She was spared, though, when Gwelain raised one hand and waved at them, motioning toward the empty chair beside her. Beau was looking, too, though he seemed less pleased by Sorra's presence.

"That'll be for you, not me," Varek said. "Be careful, and mind your manners."

He didn't offer to accompany her, so Sorra picked her way around the outside of the room on her own, pressing herself against the wall when servants passed carrying heavily laden dessert trays that dripped honey onto the floor. The guards from the throne room stood next to the wall, and Sorra straightened her shoulders as she passed them.

One of them snorted like an angry bull, so close behind her that she felt his breath, warm and wet, on the back of her neck. She flinched, and he laughed.

But neither touched her, and she quickly left them behind.

Beau had his gaze fixed on the middle of the dance floor. When Sorra approached the table, he turned to her with a disinterested smile, but with something tight and sharp about his eyes.

"My dear, you must join us," Gwelain said, patting the empty seat next to her. "You've missed the main course, but I could have the cooks bring something out for you. We had the loveliest roast."

The head table's plates hadn't been collected. Gwelain's had a few bites of carrot left on it and a several dots of red sauce. Beau had eaten the vegetables but not touched the thinly carved, rare meat, which looked a little like pork. He made eye contact with Sorra for long enough to give his head a subtle shake before looking away again.

Sorra's heart skipped at the prince's acknowledgement even as her stomach soured as she wondered whether the questionable roast had anything to do with the goblins' taxes.

She hoped she'd see Hannah again so she could thank her for her veiled warning.

"That's very kind of you, Majesty," she said, and stepped onto the raised platform. "A few vegetables would be sufficient, though, or bread if you have it. Meat has been upsetting my stomach lately."

"Done." Gwelain motioned for a servant to approach and whispered something to her. "I'll have some wine brought out as well. Excellent vintage, flavour like you've never experienced, and wonderfully refreshing. Beauregard's favourite, I think."

He nodded, then looked away again as though bored by Sorra's presence.

Gwelain sighed. "You're being rude, darling. Leave us."

Sorra's chest tightened, but Beau seemed undisturbed. "Of course."

Corvin had pushed his plate away and laid his head down on his arms, apparently oblivious to Sorra's arrival. Sorra wished Gwelain would dismiss him as well.

Beau strode toward an archway on the opposite side of the room from where Sorra had entered. Sorra didn't let herself watch, though her eyes craved the sight of him. Gwelain knew what had happened between them at the cabin but reminding her of it seemed dangerous.

Gwelain turned more fully toward Sorra, resting her elbow on the table and her chin on her fist. Sorra expected her body to instinctively recoil from the queen's full attention, but there was something so warm in her golden eyes that she found herself relaxing instead.

"How are you finding things so far?" Gwelain asked.

"It's all quite interesting," Sorra said, searching for something nice she could say that wasn't a lie. "Thank you for putting me up in such a lovely room. And for the dress. I apologize for not wearing it."

"No need," Gwelain said, her voice low and confidential. "You're in a difficult position, torn between the knight's expectations and what you believe I want. He's meant to be your friend, but I hold the power here."

"Tullian is more of a mentor than a friend, I suppose, but yes."

Gwelain nodded. "Your attire is a true reflection of where your loyalties currently lie, and I appreciate that honesty. We'll see where you end up after you've spent some time here."

"Will we be welcome for long, Majesty?"

"That will depend on how useful you both are to me. And how things progress between us personally after our rocky start." The queen's expression turned sly. "I know every word that passed between you and Beauregard in Andonia. Every gasp and moan."

The hairs on Sorra's neck prickled. "I apologize, Majesty. If I'd understood—"

Gwelain waved one hand, shooing Sorra's apology away. "I was angry, of course, but I've had time to think things through." She chuckled and took a sip from her goblet, then wiped the red stain from her lips. "I can't be angry with you for being underhanded, opportunistic, ambitious, and selfish. Not when those traits could take you further here than they ever could have in your old life. We won't have a problem as long as you respect my marriage while you're a guest in my home."

"I—thank you, Majesty," Sorra stammered, unsure of whether she'd just been praised or insulted.

Gwelain tapped one claw against the side of her cup, out of time with the throbbing drumbeat and the dancers' movements. "I am curious, though. Does the knight know about that delightfully underhanded side of your soul? Or your so-called blessing?"

Sorra's throat tightened, but she remembered Tullian's advice— tell the truth, but give nothing away. She smiled and tried to sound confident. "I have no fear of my blessing harming him or Andonia. It has been far less troublesome since I left home, and Tullian has been helping me shape myself into a better person than I once was."

"I see," Gwelain said.

Sorra held her breath until Gwelain turned her intensely beautiful gaze away to watch her subjects dancing before her.

They'd formed a few concentric circles in a more organized dance than they'd attempted before, switching partners frequently, often pressing their bodies together or trailing their fingers over each other's exposed skin before breaking apart and spinning toward someone new. Something stirred in Sorra as she watched them—not a desire to join the dance, but the idea of such freedom came like a breath of cool, clean air.

The servant returned and set a plate of steaming carrots, turnips, and potatoes in front of Sorra, along with a tall, clear glass of sparkling pink wine.

But first, questions. Tullian wasn't there to tell her what to ask. Not about the heart, surely. Perhaps something that would display flattering curiosity.

"I hope it's not rude of me to ask, Majesty," Sorra said, "but I know so little of your lands or of goblins. Tullian told me these subjects of yours were once human?"

She speared a bit of carrot and potato on her fork, not sure whether she should be cautious about accepting food but too hungry to care. The vegetables had been soaked in butter and garlic, and it was all she could do not to fall on her plate like a starving animal.

"Indeed," Gwelain said, and sighed. "I adore them, of course. All were humans who had a special spark in them, who loved their dear queen so much they wished to become more like me. They are an homage to the creatures I was given to rule over so long ago, but they're not the same. The true goblins were smaller, more muscular. Skin like armour, jaws that could snap a man's arm in one bite." She spoke wistfully. "These ones are far prettier, but I do miss my black-hearted nightmares."

As though they'd heard and wished to defend their monstrous honour, two goblins in stunning dresses squared off near the centre of the room, their claws raised, snarling at each other as the crowd parted around them. The smaller goblin head-butted the taller under the chin, barely missing gouging her with her bull-like horns.

The soldiers stationed around the room looked to their queen, but she motioned for them to wait and leaned forward to watch the fight.

Sorra swallowed her food and set her fork down, not wishing to show poor manners by ignoring the entertainment. She wished they'd stop, though. The dance had been so much lovelier.

The taller of the goblins, who wore a green gown with a full skirt, touched a finger to her split lip, snarled, and launched herself at the other. The crowd cheered as the two darted and grabbed, slashing with their claws, snapping with their teeth when they could get close enough.

The goblin in green tore her skirt away, leaving herself naked from the waist down but free to kick and slash, opening a wound that stained her opponent's bodice with dark blood. The crowd cheered louder, and Gwelain nodded her approval. The fight went on, faster and harder and more chaotic, until Sorra couldn't track each movement.

When the smaller one let out a long wail and collapsed, Gwelain held up a hand to signal to her soldiers. Two grabbed hold of the winner and held her back as two others stepped in and picked the defeated party up off the floor, hauling her past the head table by her arms. One of her eyes had been torn out, leaving a gory hole.

Corvin snorted and mumbled but seemed content to sleep through the commotion.

"You see?" Gwelain sat back in her chair, satisfied. "They still have their charms, if not the same natural weaponry as their predecessors."

"Clearly."

Gwelain raised an eyebrow, apparently amused by Sorra's discomfort. "Most humans don't have it in them to want this kind of freedom," she said. "They want to be told what to do, to not have to take responsibility for the consequences of their actions, to be protected. My beautiful creatures understand their power and choose carefully how they use it. They are blessed, and they make their own destinies out of what has been given to them. We have laws, of course, but there's no wrong way to be a goblin."

"Fascinating, Majesty." Sorra took a sip of her wine. It was strong and made her mind buzz for a moment before the sensation flowed through her body as a faint hint of pleasant warmth.

She set it aside with some regret. It would be lovely to sink deeper into a drink like that, but it wouldn't be safe.

Gwelain leaned close, and her breath tickled Sorra's ear. "The place you were born isn't always the place where you belong. Keep an open mind during your time here and you might be surprised what you discover. And what you desire."

The queen stood and walked away, cutting a path for herself through the crowd, leaving Sorra with only her parting words.

The dance resumed, and no one seemed to mind the blood on the floor. The violence didn't appeal to Sorra, but she could imagine why some would be drawn to the idea of freedom, power, and being elevated above humanity.

Not me. But some people.

She searched the room for Tullian. He'd vanished, but Beau stood in the doorway she'd so carefully not watched him walking toward earlier.

He disappeared into the darkness beyond, leaving Sorra wondering whether he'd meant to be seen at all.

It didn't matter. If she wasn't going to get any more answers from Gwelain, she would have them from the one person who truly owed them to her.

She stood carefully, and when she was sure the wine hadn't gone to her legs, she pushed through the crowd to follow him.

CHAPTER FORTY

The noise of the party faded as Sorra hurried along the hallway, alert for signs of where Beau had gone. The lamps on the walls had faded to a warm sunset glow that made the white walls shimmer with shades of orange, but the castle's beauty felt colder than it should have. Paintings of heavy-bloomed roses and pastoral scenes framed in gold gave the impression of glacial cold, their blush pinks and lively greens offering nothing of the life and abundance they clearly intended to portray.

Undeniably breathtaking, but not quite right.

She glanced down the side branches of the hallway as she passed, but the castle was a labyrinth of lifeless beauty with not even a servant's silent movements or a goblin standing guard to assure her she hadn't stepped into an empty dream. Then, to her left, a flash of movement as Beau disappeared through a doorway.

Sorra jogged after him as quietly as she could, hoping he'd meant for her to follow but not wanting to alert him to her presence if he hadn't. Her stomach twisted as she considered what might come next, whether it might be further humiliation or the help she still hoped he might offer.

Or worse. No matter what she imagined, it could always be worse.

He'd left the door ajar behind him, but the room beyond was dark when Sorra pushed it open and stepped through.

She blinked as her eyes adjusted to the moonlight that shone through a pair of tall glass doors, barely illuminating a library with walls that stretched into darkness overhead. Each wall was covered in shelves, and each shelf packed with books, but Sorra didn't pause to examine them. All she wanted to look at was the broad-shouldered silhouette standing before the paned glass doors, his hands clasped behind his back.

He opened the doors and stepped toward the curved balustrade that marked the edge of a semicircular balcony, then placed his hands on it, leaning forward, his shoulders rounded, his head hung low.

Sorra approached slowly and took up a similar posture beside him. She kept her head up, though, to take in the slice of barely tamed wilderness before her.

She hadn't had any particular expectation for what she'd find beyond the library, but the enclosed garden still came as a surprise. It lay just a few steps below the balcony, surrounded on three sides by the castle's white, windowless walls, which seemed to offer complete privacy. A lower wall at its far end allowed a breathtaking view of the star-speckled sky.

Hundreds of glow beetles flitted through the air, their flashing lights dancing above a riot of overgrown loveliness. Rose bushes bowing under the weight of their white blossoms crowded against the walls, which supported thick ropes of climbing vines. The rest of the space was a lake of dark leaves dotted with pale flowers, some growing close to the ground, others straining toward the sky, leaving no visible path to the glass-smooth pond at the far end of the yard.

Sorra tried to find a word to capture her astonishment at finding such unexpected, silent beauty after the overblown exuberance of the feast, but before she could think of anything to say, Beau descended a short staircase that curved down into the garden. Sorra followed until he paused at the bottom, where the white steps met the edge of the dense greenery. He turned to her, his eyes softening into a hint of a smile that didn't touch his lips.

"After you," he whispered, and stepped aside.

Sorra hesitated, then took a step into the leaves, which grew as high as her knees. The plants parted, revealing a stone path that reached just a few steps ahead, leading her forward. Beau followed, and the garden closed in behind them, leaving them marooned in a patch of white moonflowers. He touched her arm and she turned to face him.

There was no trace of the humiliating pity he'd cast her way in the throne room, or the indifference he'd shown at the feast. It was as though he'd shed a mask, but she still couldn't quite read him. Lips parted, eyebrows drawn together, jaw clenched… she couldn't tell whether he was worried or angry or something else entirely, but she felt as sure as she could be that it was really him.

"You came for me," he whispered.

"I did. I'm not sure whether I should apologize for it."

He looked her over from her braided hair to her boots, and she wished again that she'd worn the dress that would have made her feel like a proper match for him, at least in this garden and this moment.

"I know it was foolish," she added.

"It was."

"You told me not to."

"I did."

"Are you angry?"

He looked away, following the path of a pale green moth that fluttered past. "I don't know what I am, but it's certainly not angry. I'm terrified for you. Shocked that you found me. More shocked that you tried at all." He turned his gaze back to her. "I keep wondering whether this is some trick of Gwelain's to torture me, to give me something else she can take when she needs to break me down again."

The way he looked at her—open, exposed, more vulnerable than he'd been even when she'd seen him naked and freshly defeated after he'd lost his wager—frightened her as much as anything else had that night.

She made herself smile. "I suppose she'd have made me look a bit nicer if that were the case. And if she wanted you to long for me, I'd probably have made a more graceful entrance."

His lips twitched, offering a hint of amusement despite the

worry that touched his eyes. "How would I have known it was really you if you hadn't blown in on winds of chaos?"

If anyone in Cottsbridge had spoken those words, they'd have angered her. He wasn't mocking her, though, even gently. There was something reverent in his tone that soothed her heart.

The problem was, now that she was here with him, alone in this moonlit garden, she wasn't quite sure what to do. She wanted to kiss him, which would surely be a mistake.

Tullian would tell her to ask him something useful. A terribly boring idea and the last thing she wanted to do, so it was probably the right thing.

She couldn't make her thoughts flow that way with him looking at her, though, so she walked toward the pond, letting him follow the path she made. It was easier to find words as they stood side by side, studying the tiny moon reflected in the water.

"Is it safe to speak here?" she asked.

"It's not truly safe anywhere." His voice was hard and bitter, but it still felt like sunlight flowing through her body. "I made sure he had plenty of the strongest wine with his supper to muddle his focus, but it's best to be cautious. Still, there's no law against us speaking, even if he hears."

He, she noted, not *Corvin*.

"So it's true, then? It's dangerous to speak his name?"

"Unless you want to draw his attention. We're here now. We should speak, but cautiously. And briefly."

Sorra touched her little finger against the side of his hand, and Beau turned to her as a glow beetle landed on her cheek. He brushed it away, then let his hand rest against her face.

Sorra placed her hand over his, drinking in the contact, afraid to want more. When she spoke, she kept her voice low, but it still seemed to fill the otherwise silent garden. "You didn't tell me marriage was the consequence of losing your wager."

"I didn't want to think about it at the time, or risk you getting word to my father. If I'd communicated anything so important to him, even indirectly, it would have broken his agreement with Gwelain."

Sorra searched his eyes. "Is it terrible for you?"

"It could be far worse." His free hand tucked a stray strand of hair behind her ear. "It's a marriage in name only, though that's a carefully kept secret. I sleep in my own room in the royal apartments, and Gwelain is happy as long as her subjects believe everything is perfect. I pretend to be enamoured, she pretends to have an enthusiastic marriage in every sense, the gossip is all envy. Peace endures."

Sorra let out a long breath. She hadn't let herself think about everything marriage might have entailed, but the relief that swept through her gave away how those gears had been turning in the deepest chambers of her mind.

"I hated saying the things I did when you arrived." He swallowed hard. "I hated humiliating you, implying that I'd used you. But if I'd told the truth, it would have made her look like a fool in front of her goblins. You're only alive because they think you're a joke."

Sorra's heart fluttered. "What truth?"

"That you so easily took what she knows she'll never have." Beau took her hand and pressed it to his chest so his heart beat strong and hard against her palm. "Why did you come?"

Sorra struggled to find the right words. "For Andonia. It deserves to have you as its next king, and you deserve better than this. And I hoped to earn a pardon for a crime I didn't commit. To try to escape my blessing. And now to help Tullian with his quest, though I didn't know about that when I left the cabin."

He cleared his throat softly. "Is that all?"

"I've tried not to let it be more than that." His pulse echoed through her body. "I can't have come because my life was worse without an uptight talking bear in it, or because I wanted to take back what I'd lost. Not when that bear is a prince, and I'm... me."

He leaned in and brushed his lips against hers. When she raised herself on her toes to meet him, he pulled her closer, deeper. For a few seconds there was only him, the warmth of his lips, the clean scent of his skin, the soft fabric of his shirt under her hands.

He pulled back slowly. "You *are* you," he said, as though the conversation hadn't been interrupted. "That's the problem."

Sorra blinked slowly, trying to regain her bearings. "You speak like you're not at all worried someone might be listening and reporting to her," she said, though she wished he'd never stop saying such lovely things.

Beau flashed a grim smile. "She knows my feelings, though I'm not sure she's capable of understanding them as they relate to you. Our agreement doesn't prohibit me speaking as I wish, provided she doesn't catch my words doing her harm. I doubt I've led you to think worse of her than you already did."

No danger of that, Sorra thought. It would have taken quite a lot to lower her opinion of the goblin queen.

"She'd be pleased to know how your presence tortures me," he said, "and to think how I might work as a distraction for you. She'll keep the peace as long as her subjects don't hear any of this, as long as we say our goodbyes now, and as long as we don't progress from pathetic speeches to you touching her property."

She looked down at his hand, which still rested above her hip, and hers on his arm. "You're sure he only listens?" she whispered. "He can't see?"

"I'm sure." Beau kept his voice quiet, too. "Varek told me as much on one of the few occasions he's agreed to speak to me."

Sorra pulled back. "He's trustworthy?"

Beau chuckled. "Inherently? Absolutely not. But he has no choice but to speak the truth. He angered Gwelain long before my arrival and that little curse was his punishment. I suspect she only meant for him to be unable to lie to her, but she was less certain of her new powers then. As it stands, he can't lie to anyone. Or rather, he can, but it results in an unpleasant and highly visible punishment. He didn't break out in boils when he told me about the old man only being able to listen and the task requiring his full attention, so yes. I'd bet my life on it."

Sorra didn't doubt Beau was himself, and now that she was sure of that, she couldn't bring herself to mistrust him. Beyond that, she'd witnessed Varek's unfortunate honesty on the dance floor and seen how it left him isolated and hated.

It seemed a fine reason for him to resent Gwelain, and to be curious about how her enemies might take away the magic she'd used to curse him.

And that meant everything he'd said earlier was also true—her bedroom was a safe place to speak. But it would be foolish to say as much if doing so might give away their only advantage.

Before she could think of a way to tell him without Corvin hearing, he smiled grimly. "I expect you came here hoping I'd help shift the odds in your favour."

"It had crossed my mind." Sorra picked up a smooth quartz stone from the ground and dropped it into the pond, sending out ripples that spread across its glassy surface.

They watched as the ripples vanished, leaving the water as undisturbed as it had been before.

"I don't know where she keeps Linnea's heart or how to take it from her," Beau said. "Even if I knew, I couldn't try to steal it myself and I couldn't help you do it. Not without breaking the treaty."

He spoke calmly, but Sorra caught the way his hands tightened into fists before he forced them to relax.

"Time is running out," she said. "She's married the heir to Andonia's throne. When your father dies, she's won."

"I suppose she has," Beau said, but shook his head slowly, contradicting his words.

Another secret, then, one he didn't dare speak if there was even the slimmest chance Corvin might hear. Sorra wanted to pry, but if she'd learned nothing else at the cabin, she'd learned to take his secrets seriously.

"I wish I could help you," he said, "but I can't. I'm sure it would please her to hear me say that, too." This time there was no hint he was anything but entirely sincere, and disappointment twisted through Sorra. "I can't know what my father is planning. All I can do for now is keep the promise I made before I left home, to do what was in my power to maintain peace and keep our people safe so he'll have time to make things right."

"That's it, then? You keep behaving like a good boy, waiting for others to act?" Sorra didn't mean to snap at him but couldn't keep the edge out of her voice. "We're here now. You could finally do something of consequence by helping us."

"And risk everything in the process." His obvious frustration lent a hint of a growl to his voice that made him sound like the bear she'd met in the woods. "Do you remember the hunger we faced during her curse? The sickness? The deaths?"

"I do." Cottsbridge had suffered as much as any other town.

Beau looked down at his hands as though disgusted by their uselessness. "I was raised to make judgements, to act, to rule. Instead, Andonia's fate rests on me doing nothing, appeasing our enemy, and having faith that others will do what I can't. I've hated every moment of it, but I've done my duty so my father can do his. He'll come through."

Sorra rested her hands on his. "I hope your faith will be rewarded," she said, unable to hide the bitter note that crept into her voice.

"So do I."

She wished she could offer more. He'd been raised for greatness only to have his future stolen from him, his strength made useless, and his purpose twisted so the only noble action he could take was to submit and obey. She knew what it was to feel powerless but could only guess how it hurt to crash into it from such a height.

No wonder he'd risked so much on a wager when he saw a chance to return home and join the fight. He'd willingly sacrificed himself for the sake of his people, but every day since had surely been a twisted form of torture even as he lived in physical comfort.

He seemed certain it would be worth it in the end. She wished she could be as sure.

There didn't seem to be much left to say. She'd come hoping Beau would be one of the heroes from Linnea's visions, but a hero who couldn't share what he knew wasn't much use.

Unless he only thinks he can't.

As she thought back over their conversation, she realized he'd offered her more than she'd realized.

Our agreement doesn't prohibit me speaking as I wish, provided she doesn't catch my words doing her harm.

It wasn't a question of harm, but of being caught. He seemed firm in his decision not to risk breaking the treaty, but if he could offer information without risk of her finding out what he'd done…

The mage only listens.

She held up one finger, drawing Beau's attention, then held her hand next to her face.

"I don't think we should speak again," she said slowly, hiding her lips as she spoke the word *don't.*

Beau raised his eyebrows. "I agree, we should not." He mimicked her, blocking the word *not.* "It isn't safe."

"It might be safer if we avoided each other completely." The plants parted to make a path as she took a step backward. "I'll be in my room until Gwelain calls for me."

He watched her hand's movements, and she hoped he got the true message.

It might be safer in my room.

Beau frowned, then nodded. "Sleep well tonight," he said. "I'm going back to the feast. The queen will be looking for me." He didn't block any words, but Sorra understood what he didn't say— he wouldn't be visiting her tonight. "I don't know what she has planned for you. The only advice I can offer is to keep her happy. Mind your manners, play along. If she lets you wander and you find yourself tiring of goblins you might consider visiting the kitchen. There are usually humans there who don't mind letting you sit as long as your hands stay busy. But don't try to leave the castle, and don't do anything to make her hate you more than she already does."

Too late, Sorra thought, remembering his lips pressed against hers, his arms pulling her close. They'd been quiet. Gwelain couldn't possibly know. It wasn't a risk they should take again, though, if she didn't want to end up like Tullian's friend in the forest.

Gwelain couldn't kill her, but that didn't mean she was safe.

Beau might decide it was too risky to visit her room, or to help at all. But hope fluttered in Sorra's stomach as he pressed one hand to his chest and bowed slightly.

At least, she thought it was hope. To be distracted by any other fluttery feelings would be a mistake.

"Goodnight, Sorra."

"Goodnight, Beau."

She meant to walk away. It was the responsible thing to do. The heroic thing, even.

Instead, she raced the few steps back to him and found her way into his open arms to lose herself in one last kiss.

No more foolish risks, she promised herself as she untangled her fingers from his hair and ran back up the steps to the library.

But she couldn't quite talk herself into regretting that one.

CHAPTER FORTY-ONE

Sorra lay on her back, staring into the eyes of the miniature goblin that perched cat-like on her chest, grinning as it huffed stale breath into her face.

"G'way," she mumbled, but couldn't make her limbs move to shove it off.

The goblin chuckled and the dream dissolved, but the heaviness didn't leave Sorra's chest as she struggled upward from the depths of sleep and forced her eyes open.

The room was bright, and Sorra squinted as she wiped a bit of drool from her cheek. She'd fallen asleep in her armour, which explained the heaviness in her dream, and the curtains were open, which explained the brightness.

But something was wrong.

She gave her head a quick shake to clear the cobwebs and swung her legs off the edge of the bed to wriggle her toes into the plush carpet, grounding herself in her current impossible reality.

A domed silver tray sat on the table next to the bed, glinting in the morning sunlight.

Sorra stared at it, then reached out to touch its shining surface. It was real, and it hadn't been there when she'd fallen asleep.

Wonderful. She rubbed the sleep from her eyes. *Everyone but me is free to come and go as they please.*

She'd sleep with her dagger under her pillow in the future. The intruder had clearly not meant her any harm, but Sorra felt naked at the thought of anyone sneaking in while she was asleep.

I hope I wasn't snoring.

Sorra unfastened the clasps at the side of her armour and shrugged out of it, wincing at the tender spots on her back where the thick leather had pressed against her muscles. As she turned and stretched, her gaze caught on a long, grey dress hanging on the wardrobe door.

A helpful intruder, indeed, but she felt no comfort at the knowledge.

At least there was breakfast, and that was always a consolation. Sorra lifted the silver dome, bracing herself for the suspicious pink meat she felt sure she'd find on offer, and smiled at the sight of fluffy scrambled eggs, toast, and bacon that steamed pleasantly, releasing the promising scents of fat and salt and yeast to make her mouth water. A little pat of butter had nearly melted into each slice of not-quite-burnt toast, and a tiny glass dish held a pinch of salt to be dusted over the eggs.

Sorra took up the silver fork and dug in, still sitting on the bed and leaning over the little table so any bits of egg that fell from her mouth would land on the plate.

She'd picked up a slice of toast and had it halfway to her mouth before she noticed the corner of a cream-coloured envelope protruding from beneath the tray. Sorra set the toast down and slipped the envelope out, hoping it might be a message from Beau but knowing it would have been too great a risk for him to send anything in with a servant.

A wax seal of shimmering gold held the envelope closed. There was no writing on either side, nothing strange enough to prompt the chill that came over her.

She studied the envelope a little longer as she took a bite of toast. It was still warm and buttery, perfect crunch giving way under her teeth, but the food had lost its flavour.

Go on, then, she told herself. *Don't be stupid.*

She slipped one finger under the wax seal and popped the envelope open, then pulled out a single sheet of parchment with a few lines of neat handwriting at its centre.

The pleasure of your company is requested
for this morning's performance in the Queen's theatre.

Nothing more.

A pleasant enough invitation if she'd trusted anything about her hostess or the situation, but Sorra bristled with apprehension as she wondered what entertainment she might find on a goblin stage.

She flipped the parchment over and found a hand-drawn map of her bedroom. A useless one, limited as it was, but detailed, showing an aerial view of its half-moon shape complete with sketched-in chairs by the fireplace, the bed, the tub, and the wardrobe.

A dotted line of the same black ink led to the door, but that seemed to be the end of the road. The envelope was empty. No further instructions, no more maps.

Sorra set the note aside. Breakfast had lost its allure, so she covered what remained and turned her attention to the dress hung on the wardrobe.

It was the grey of a summer thunderstorm, menacing but lovely. Sorra had always liked storms when they came along to break the oppressive heat of a midsummer day, driving folks inside whether they wished it or not, sending sheets of rain to pound against the rooftops, drowning out thoughts of anything else. She ran the soft fabric between her fingers and watched as the shadows deepened in its folds. It was lovely, but its dim and serious hue, or lack thereof, was nothing like the bright and fanciful gowns the goblins had worn the night before and seemed designed to let her fade into the background. Its high neckline and long sleeves would hide any hint of tempting flesh, and the heavy, ankle-length skirt was more suited to mourning than to dancing.

Armour was still an option. Tullian would have told her to wear it again. But Beau had said to keep Gwelain happy, and it might be easier to learn something useful if she made an effort to fit in.

Sorra shed her nightgown and slipped the dress over her head, then struggled to tie the sash neatly behind her without assistance. The dress fit perfectly, and despite its humble appearance was far from ugly. Its beauty was subtle enough, though, that Sorra wondered whether Gwelain knew about last night's conversation in the garden and had decided not to take any risks when it came to Beau's affections.

Sorra's face warmed as she thought of it—his kiss, his voice that reminded her so much of the bear she'd known, his heartbeat under her hand.

It had been a foolish risk. He belonged to the queen, and the fate of a nation depended on him remaining in her grasp, keeping her plans predictable until his father took action against her.

If they were going to speak again, it would need to be in safer surroundings.

Sorra found a pair of dust-grey silk slippers in the wardrobe and carried them with her as she used her toes to push the rug aside, revealing the marking Varek had shown her.

The goblin prince had been odd—so secretive, so guarded as he'd prodded her for information, as though he feared the consequences if Gwelain found out he'd been nosing about.

But his words had been clear, and Beau seemed to think she could trust them.

We'll speak here, and only when Gwelain won't know.

But first, the theatre.

Sorra's stomach clenched at the thought.

The slippers fit her feet far more comfortably than the worn leather boots she'd been tromping around the countryside in. But as she opened the door and stepped out of the room with her invitation in hand, she felt exposed in a way she wouldn't have if she'd worn her boots and battered armour instead.

There was no servant waiting in the hallway to guide her to the theatre, and no answer when she knocked on Tullian's door.

Halfway down the tower stairs she glanced at the useless map, then stopped to examine it more closely under the soft daylight of a lamp. The image of her room had disappeared, replaced by a circle filled with radiating lines that might represent the stairwell, with the dotted line circling it. When she reached the bottom and walked down the hallway, it changed again before her eyes, the ink melting away as though water had been poured on it, then reforming to direct her to the curving twin staircases near the castle's front door.

She still dreaded what might wait at her destination, but the map delighted her like a new toy would have when she was a child. She watched eagerly as she reached the top of the stairs above the throne room. The image faded at the edges.

Brilliant. Like—

The toe of her slipper caught on the hem of her dress, and she pitched forward, heart lurching as she grabbed at empty air before catching the curved golden railing. She clung to it until her heart stopped racing.

It's only magic, she chided herself. *Nothing to crack your head open over.*

She peered over the railing as surreptitiously as she could manage while she straightened her dress and was relieved to find that no one had seen her near-mishap. There didn't seem to be anyone about at all. If the goblins needed their beauty sleep after their night of debauchery and violence, Sorra was happy to leave them to it.

The map never showed her more than a tiny portion of the castle and seemed determined to be unhelpful to anyone wishing to learn Gwelain's secrets. None of the rooms were marked as anything other than blank spaces, and the dotted line, which brightened with a faint golden glow as she turned right near the dining room, offered her no options except to keep following it.

As a test, Sorra stopped in front of a portrait of Gwelain that imagined the queen with feathered black wings spread to shelter misshapen, monstrous goblins. The line on the map didn't change. When she stepped through an open door into a small parlour, though, it glowed red and the paper warmed in her hand.

"Not good for much, are you?" she asked it. The map didn't respond save to return to its previous state once she was back on course.

Its novelty wore off quickly, and Sorra's stomach squirmed as the line glowed brighter, seemingly delighted to have brought her closer to her destination and whatever Gwelain had planned for her.

The sounds of swords clashing reached Sorra as she passed a pair of open doors, and her heart climbed into her throat. The map led her to a narrower doorway not far beyond them. Sorra stepped through and made her way up a dark, enclosed staircase. The same noises reached her from above—metal on metal, now accompanied by murmuring voices.

Sorra steeled herself and continued up. The only thing more dangerous than accepting Gwelain's invitation would be to refuse it.

She reached the top and stepped into a theatre box like the ones her sister Ingrid had described in the letters she sent from Ember-cliffe. The little balcony, surrounded by a low wall of open silver filigree, sat on a side wall of the theatre, overlooking hundreds of empty seats on the floor below, offering a clear view of a stage with a rounded front. Two high-backed ivory chairs faced the stage, but Sorra hardly noticed them.

Tullian, dressed in his armour, stood at the centre of the stage, sword drawn as he faced off against a large goblin. A dozen others, all wielding swords, stood in a semicircle behind them, blocking any chance of escape.

Sorra froze in place, paralyzed by regret over her clothing choice but wondering how she might get down to the stage to help. She'd decided to backtrack to the theatre's main entrance before she noticed that none of the goblins were moving, save for the one facing the old knight. They were observing and waiting, and their furrowed brows displayed concentration or concern, not aggression.

And Tullian wasn't in trouble. He was in his element, grimly determined but not desperate or fearful as he swung his sword, stopping short of lopping the goblin's head off.

"A demonstration," Gwelain said, speaking over her shoulder. The queen leaned against the arm of her chair and turned toward Sorra, setting her profile into silhouette against the light from the stage. "Come closer. I won't bite."

Sorra took a moment to study the queen's impressive lower jaw and protruding teeth, then did as she'd been ordered, stepping around the chairs to face Gwelain as a new battle began on the stage behind her. She tried not to show her disappointment when she found not Beau, but Varek seated in the other chair, his chin propped on one hand, his expression unreadable as he glanced at her.

Both were dressed in black, though the dramatic cut of Gwelain's neckline left a broad swath of pale, shimmering skin from her left collarbone to the right side of her waist. Sorra wondered whether magic held the fabric in place, or some unimaginable feat of engineering.

"Leave us," Gwelain said. Sorra had taken half a step toward the staircase, drenched with relief, before she realized the queen wasn't speaking to her, but to her son. "Our guest requires a seat. If your manners are so poor that you won't rise for a lady and offer it to her yourself, you can go and be rude elsewhere."

"I don't really—" Sorra murmured, feeling she needed to object but not daring to contradict the queen at an audible volume.

Varek stood slowly and bowed, first to his mother, then to Sorra. The motion was the same, but there was something sarcastic about it when he faced her. "Enjoy the show," he said, and walked with heavy steps down the stairs.

Gwelain rubbed one temple with her long fingers, eyes closed. "Do you have children?"

"No, Majesty."

"I believe I might envy you. Sit."

"I didn't mind standing," Sorra said, and hastily added, "Majesty."

Gwelain smiled. "Let's set aside the formalities for today, shall we? They're necessary but grow so tiresome."

"Very well," Sorra said, and bit her lip to keep from adding the honorific she'd been warned to never forget. She sat stiffly, hands clasped on her lap to keep them from fidgeting.

A low table sat between the two chairs, set with sliced cheese, green grapes, and little bites of toasted bread and jelly. Gwelain snapped her fingers, and a young human servant appeared to whisk away Varek's silver goblet and replace it with another.

On stage, the battle continued. A new challenger was stepping up—the rose-skinned goblin who had nearly taken Sorra's head off the night before. He rolled his shoulders forward and back, clearly eager to take a shot at the knight. Tullian wiped the sweat from his brow and readied himself in the grounded posture that had become so familiar to Sorra.

Sorra leaned forward as the two circled each other, eyes locked, swords raised.

"Your knight is good," Gwelain said. "A little rusty, but impressive nonetheless. I asked him to put my best soldiers through their paces this morning to find their weaknesses. If there's anything he can teach them, I suppose that's how he'll earn his keep while the two of you are here."

"And what will I do to earn mine?"

Sorra glanced sideways and caught Gwelain's amused smile in profile. "We'll see."

The swords gleamed under the stage lights, which shone from so many angles that the combatants had no shadows to anchor them as they moved. They swung and blocked, parting and coming together, testing for weaknesses before striking again. Tullian feigned a high swing and instead came in low, and the goblin barely blocked his blade before it touched his silver breastplate.

"Reaver prefers an axe," Gwelain said, "but he's using a dulled sword like the rest of my soldiers."

"Did Tullian request that change?" Sorra asked.

"No, I ordered it. Reaver needs to learn a little humility, and I'd hate for the show to be over too quickly." Gwelain sounded bored, though, as if she might be regretting that decision even if it kept Tullian safe from accidents that might kill him and fulfil Linnea's vision of her defeat.

"Tullian!" Gwelain called, her voice resonating through the theatre as she stood, spreading her arms so the wide sleeves of her dress spread like the wings she'd had in her portrait. Every goblin on stage stood at attention, their eyes locked on their queen. "It seems my soldiers don't stand a chance against you."

Reaver's lips parted in a snarl, but he directed it at the stage floor instead of his queen or her guest.

Gwelain folded her hands before her, waiting.

Tullian nodded stiffly. "I believe they're going easy on me, Majesty. You've chosen well, and all are worthy of their positions."

A few of the goblins appeared to relax at the pronouncement, and Sorra wondered what the penalty would have been if Tullian had declared any of them hopeless.

Gwelain dismissed her soldiers with a wave of her hand. They left the stage, but a dark shape lurked in the wings.

"A fine demonstration, Tullian." Gwelain motioned for Sorra to stand beside her, and Sorra obeyed.

Tullian frowned up at them. "I'm glad it pleased you, Majesty."

"I didn't say that," Gwelain said. "It was fine, but dull. There's no danger without bloodshed, no thrill in an even match. I crave entertainment."

Tullian rested the tip of his sword on the stage and folded his hands over the pommel. "What would you prefer, Majesty?"

He didn't sound as though he really wanted an answer. Sorra wasn't sure she did, either.

"Enough goblins, I think." Gwelain clapped her hands. Seconds later a pair of soldiers dragged a human in servants' clothing onto the stage and dropped him. He collapsed onto his knees, his hair hanging over his face.

Sorra's hand was on the queen's arm before she could consider how dangerous it would be to touch her. Gwelain's upper lip twitched, exposing her teeth as she glanced down, and Sorra pulled away.

"I'll fight Tullian," she said. "I can swing a sword, but I'm still bad enough at it that it will be terribly amusing for you."

The servant looked up, and Sorra's breath caught as she recognized the man who'd posed as Beau, who had let them into the castle.

After he'd run off, Tullian had said that Sorra's actions had been those of a villain, that her recklessness could get them killed. She struggled to keep her breakfast down as she understood that it wasn't her life or Tullian's she might have put in danger.

"Give him a real weapon." Gwelain's voice carried through the theatre as it had before, but in more menacing tones. "Let's see whether this is more amusing."

One of the soldiers handed his sword to the servant. It wasn't especially large, likely not much heavier than the one Sorra now wielded with relative ease, but he held it as she had in the beginning, gripping it with both hands as he gave it a few tentative swings.

Tullian didn't raise his own weapon.

"My apologies, Majesty," he said. "I fear this servant is not trained in any way that would make it possible for me to stage an interesting battle for you."

Gwelain sat, rolling her eyes. "I don't want you to stage anything. He disobeyed my orders and requires punishment. We'll see whether a few rounds with an experienced knight can teach him a lesson."

Sorra took her seat beside the queen, perching on its edge, gripping her skirt tight in both hands.

Tullian leaned in and said something to the servant, who nodded. They raised their swords, and Tullian took a lackadaisical swing, giving the servant plenty of time to raise his weapon to block, then spun slowly and swung again, with the same result.

"I'm bored," Gwelain called. "It will not go well for anyone if I remain in this state much longer."

The fight sped up. Tullian struck again, landing a blow against the servant's arm with the flat of his blade. It would leave a bruise, but if that and a heaping dose of humiliation were all the punishment the poor fellow received, Sorra supposed he'd be getting off light.

She hadn't thought of him since he'd run from the garden, but now remembered clearly how terrified he'd been—not of her, but of Gwelain.

Another blow. The servant's sword clattered to the stage and Tullian waited for him to pick it up.

"Ridiculous," Gwelain muttered.

"It's his personal code of honour," Sorra said, not sure why she felt the need to defend Tullian when he was happy to let Gwelain despise him. "He's sworn to protect those weaker than himself, not to press his advantage over them. He'd no more hurt that man than he would a child."

"Ridiculous and foolish, then." Gwelain cast a sideways glance at Sorra. "His code is a promise to a dead queen who offers him nothing in return."

"It's more than that," Sorra said. The servant swung his sword and made contact with the armour that covered Tullian's chest, and the knight stumbled harder than seemed realistic or necessary. It *was* ridiculous, but Sorra admired it all the same. "It's not about the promise, it's about who he is. Without his code and the purpose it gives him, I'm not sure what he'd have left."

"Hmm." The queen's eyes shone with interest. Sorra wished they wouldn't. A bored Gwelain somehow seemed safer than this. "I wonder how far that goes. Enough!"

She stood again.

The servant dropped his sword and leaned forward, his back heaving with his breaths. Tullian turned, expressionless, to face Gwelain.

"I'll make you an offer, Tullian. I vow on my life and on my magic that I'll show you where the heart is. All I ask in return is that you kill this traitor first. Here. Now."

The servant didn't look up or offer what would surely have been a useless plea for his life. He only sank to his knees, head bowed, and waited.

Tullian didn't move, and he didn't answer.

They'd come for the heart. Sorra imagined it might save them days or weeks of searching if Gwelain kept her promise, but Tullian would be disgraced in his dead queen's eyes if he killed an innocent person. By gaining an advantage in his quest, he'd prove himself unworthy of completing it according to Linnea's visions.

Gwelain clearly didn't think he'd accept.

It was a test. A tease. But Sorra couldn't help wishing he'd surprise everyone, judging the act necessary even if it cost him a slice of his honour. The visions might not be the only path to victory after all, and the servant would die either way.

She hated herself for her ability to see the advantage of unexpected violence and wondered whether she'd count the costs differently if she were the one with a sword in her hand.

The servant sobbed. "Do it," he said in tones that barely reached the spectators above. "I have nothing left to live for here."

Tullian closed his eyes, whispered a few words, and sheathed his sword.

"I cannot," he said. "Not for Your Majesty's amusement, not for any reward."

Irritation and relief flooded Sorra in equal measure, leaving her drifting between her old self and the person she was trying to become.

"Interesting," Gwelain said, though she sounded not at all surprised. "Have you lost interest in the quest your deceased queen set for you?"

"No, Majesty," Tullian said. "But the path to victory will not be washed in the blood of innocents. Goodness and honour will win in the end."

"Will they?" Gwelain snapped her fingers, and Reaver stepped onto the stage, his battle axe gripped in both hands. "In my experience the winners are those who do what needs to be done. You, servant. You have betrayed me, but if you can survive against my soldier for half a minute, by any means available to you, I swear I'll let you go free."

Tullian drew his sword and turned toward Reaver as he would have stood against any goblin trying to collect taxes.

Sorra gripped the balcony rail tight to keep her hands from trembling.

Half a minute. Tullian could immobilize or kill a goblin in that time, especially when Reaver wouldn't dare risk harming him.

The servant backed away, empty hands held up, helpless. Reaver darted around Tullian, and Sorra waited for the knight to attack.

Tullian hesitated, then lowered his sword.

The axe came down, and before Sorra could scream, the servant's head had rolled across the stage, leaving a dark trail as his body collapsed and his blood drained from his neck, spreading in a dark pool across the glossy wooden boards.

Sorra closed her eyes and forced herself to breathe through the storm that raged within her—the shame at what her actions had led to, the anger at Tullian for clinging to his honour when the same outcome could have offered them an advantage.

Gwelain is clever, she reminded herself. *There was a trick to this. Giving in to her demands might have been the first step toward Tullian becoming the traitor she needs.*

But when she opened her eyes, it wasn't Tullian Gwelain was watching, but her.

"You are dismissed, Tullian," Gwelain said without looking back at him. He left, as did Reaver. "What do you think, would-be hero? You came to my castle dressed in his armour, clothed in his worthless honour. Would you have chosen differently?"

Sorra leaned on the railing, letting her hair fall to cover her face. It didn't blind her to the stage, though, or the wasted life spilled across it.

The servant had died because she'd defied Tullian's rules and chosen her own path into the castle. It had seemed right at the time, a small price to pay in terms of her own heroic merit, and this was where it had led.

Perhaps Gwelain had meant to show her the foolishness of Tullian's convictions, but all Sorra saw were the consequences of her own minor villainy.

It wouldn't do to say so, of course. Better to pretend she thought Tullian was wrong and let the queen believe she had a chance of driving a wedge between the heroes.

But she'll know if I lie.

Another test, another judgement, but Sorra couldn't imagine what the rules might be.

Honesty, then. At least I'll know where I stand.

"I'd have done the same," she said, turning to face the queen. "Though not for honour."

Gwelain had taken her seat again and motioned for Sorra to do the same. "Explain."

She sounded interested, not angry. Sorra didn't trust it but forced herself to sit. "Respectfully, Majesty, what you promised Tullian could have ruined you if he'd surprised you by lopping that poor fellow's head off."

Gwelain's eyes narrowed. "You believe a queen would go back on her word?"

"No, Majesty." Sorra resisted the urge to brush away the sweat she felt forming on her brow. "I believe you'd have kept to the word of your promise, as you did with Beau."

"But?"

But there's more to it, Sorra thought. *If only I knew what.*

Tullian had chosen at the last second not to intervene. It wasn't fear that had held him back. He'd stood up to goblins before and knew Reaver wouldn't dare risk harming him.

But that was before. Outside.

Her breath caught.

"When you welcomed us as your guests, Tullian swore he wouldn't attack you or anyone else in your castle," she said, her words picking up speed as the realization spilled out. "You knew he wouldn't kill that servant, but you also knew he's never failed to defend your citizens against taxes when he had a chance. If he'd done the same on that stage, if he'd attacked Reaver to give the servant time to escape, you'd have been free to imprison him or throw him out of the castle."

Which would leave me alone with you, she added to herself, and fought off a shiver that would have given away her fear. *I'd never find the heart or free Beau on my own.*

But it was more than that. Sorra tried to school her face into pleasant neutrality as dread pooled in her stomach.

She knows about the blessing.

She thinks I'm the traitor from Linnea's visions.

Tullian had become irrelevant the moment he'd sworn her to the quest. The only question was how long Gwelain had been manipulating their journey to draw them into her trap.

The queen stared at her for a moment, then chuckled. "Very good. I should put you on stage. You're far more amusing than anything else that happened there today."

"Thank you, Majesty," Sorra said, which only seemed to amuse Gwelain more.

"You're honest," Gwelain said. "Bold, too, and I think cleverer than that knight realizes—he wouldn't understand my thinking as quickly as you have, which shows that you and I have as much in common as I had hoped. He wants to change you, doesn't he?"

"He's trying to help me be better."

"That's his mistake," Gwelain said, standing and smoothing her skirt. "There's great potential in the things you've been taught to suppress, but he's blind to it."

Before Sorra could think of a response, a goblin appeared at the top of the stairs. He bowed low at the waist.

Gwelain turned to him. "What?"

"Majesty, there's a matter that requires your attention. Quite urgent."

"Isn't it always?" Gwelain stalked away, then paused and glanced over her shoulder. "We'll continue this discussion soon, Sorra."

Sorra stood and curtseyed awkwardly. "Of course."

Gwelain followed the servant down the stairs, leaving Sorra alone with the corpse on the stage.

Ignore him. Think.

Tullian had said to listen and observe, to find advantages. Gwelain had just exposed her true intentions, but that wasn't enough.

Information about the queen's urgent business would be far more useful.

Sorra waited, counting seconds, putting space between herself and Gwelain. As she did, she looked at the body one last time, carving it into her memory.

This is where my natural inclinations lead. Whatever potential Gwelain sees in me is better left to rot. I'll be good. Heroic. Anything but what she wants me to be.

But as she crept down the stairs, Sorra wondered again how heroes constrained by morality could ever hope to defeat a monster who was free to do whatever it took to win.

CHAPTER FORTY-TWO

By the time Sorra reached the bottom of the stairs, Gwelain had vanished.

Of course she's gone, you ninny, the voice in her mind whispered. *You fault Tullian for being overly cautious, then hesitate while opportunity slips between your fingers.*

"Would it have been better to be caught?" she whispered back to it.

The voice didn't answer, but there was something infuriatingly smug about its silence.

The castle, too, was silent. No voices or creaking doors to indicate where Gwelain had gone, and still no sign that her noble monsters had risen for the day. When Sorra looked closely, though, the sky-blue carpet was paler in patches to her left where the pile had been flattened by two sets of long, narrow toes. As she watched, the fibres eased back to their intended position.

It was a direction, and better than nothing. She followed, her own steps quick and careful, pausing when she reached the junction between two corridors.

Someone cleared their throat behind her. Sorra turned slowly, ready to explain how very lost she was without the map she'd left in the theatre.

Hannah stood with a pile of clean, white linens resting on both arms, not trying to hide her irritation.

"If you're looking for the queen," she said before Sorra could speak, "she's unavailable. I wouldn't want to be you if you're caught sneaking about without permission. I don't have time to escort you, but if you keep going straight here, you'll find stairs that will lead back toward your room."

But she nodded her head hard to the right, down a bright hallway where white roses grew up the walls.

"Thank you," Sorra said. "I was lost, that's all."

"And now you're not." Hannah turned and marched back the way she'd come.

If Corvin was listening, he'd hear that she'd ordered Sorra to her room. Whether Sorra actually went or whether she followed the nod elsewhere was apparently not her concern.

Probably safest for her not to know, Sorra thought as she turned down the rose-scented hallway. She still wasn't sure how far any human in the castle could be trusted but suspected that Hannah might be an asset as long as she wasn't risking her own hide in the process, and that was far better than nothing.

She'd passed a half-dozen locked rooms and had nearly given up before Gwelain's voice reached her, muffled by a door that stood slightly ajar.

Sorra pressed her back against the wall, her heart galloping. She didn't feel any guilt over eavesdropping when Gwelain was so willing to do the same through Corvin, but she trembled at the thought of what would happen if someone caught her.

"The timing isn't ideal," Gwelain said. "It should be done with some subtlety if it's to be approached this way at all." Sorra strained to pick out her words and commit them to memory. The queen spoke clearly and not particularly quietly, but it sounded like she might be at the far end of a large room, and Sorra didn't dare push the door open any further.

Sorra couldn't make out the response of whoever Gwelain was speaking to. Someone, she suspected, who was accustomed to taking up less space and drawing less attention than the queen.

"I know, but it will require adjustment," Gwelain said. "If his father is that ill, we might be looking at weeks or even days rather than months or years."

His father.

The words hit Sorra in the gut, stealing her breath.

There was only one person whose death would affect Gwelain's plans.

"No, I won't tell him," Gwelain said. "No one but us needs to know. He's sure about the severity?" Another pause, and Gwelain sighed. "Very well. I'll want your magic at its strongest in coming days. We'll make an evening of it, bring in more humans, whip up anticipation and bloodlust. I want everyone ready to leave on short notice, but don't reveal too much. When Ranthorn dies, we'll only have a few weeks to claim the crown before it goes to one of his other offspring."

Sorra forced herself to breathe, to nail down every important detail and conclusion.

She's speaking to Corvin—arranging human victims to feed his blood magic. Andonia's king is dying. We're out of time.

She knew she should go straight back upstairs to tell Tullian everything. To do otherwise would risk pushing her limited supply of good luck well past its limits.

But when she reached the stairs outside the throne room, she turned away from them, toward the dining room. It was stark and cold, lit only by the light from the hallways on either side, empty of voices, music, and life as she passed through on her way to the library.

I'll tell Tullian I risked the detour because we need Beau's help. He's the only one we can really trust who knows this castle, and we need to move quickly.

No point explaining everything twice.

It was true enough, but that wasn't what kept her moving through the library.

All she could think as she stepped out onto the balcony overlooking the garden was that Beau deserved to know his father was dying.

The garden was empty. Though the sun shone down pleasantly enough, what had seemed a scrap of enchanted wilderness the night before now appeared to be little more than a weed-choked courtyard. No beetles floating about like fairy lights, no ethereally floating moths, no moonlight captured in what now showed itself to be a shallow, murky pond.

And worse, no Beau.

Sorra stood at the railing and tried to remember the details of their conversation. He'd said something about visiting the kitchen if she needed to get away from goblins. Perhaps just a bit of friendly advice, but maybe more.

Sorra ran, crossing through the empty dining room again to reach the stairs down to the kitchen, mouthing a prayer to anyone who would listen.

The kitchen was awake and alive, warmed by a wall of ovens and thick with the scents of baking bread and a stew that bubbled over a fire in the corner. Six human servants bustled about, stepping around each other in a perfectly choreographed dance that kept them out of each other's paths as they washed, chopped, mixed, and kneaded.

They all ignored the finely dressed prince shelling peas into a wooden bowl at the far end of the room but paused to watch suspiciously as Sorra entered.

Beau barely glanced up.

Careful, then.

A large man in a white chef's cap resumed his work fitting piecrust into a pan large enough that a child could have slept in it, but he watched Sorra carefully. Sorra pretended not to notice and flashed an apologetic smile at another cook as she nicked a ripe plum from a basket on the counter.

"Didn't have much stomach for breakfast," she explained.

The cook grunted and returned to stirring the stew.

"I'll take this back to my room, then," Sorra said, projecting her voice.

No one answered, and Beau didn't look up. Sorra left as casually as she'd entered. It didn't feel like enough, but anything else that needed to be said would have to wait.

It would never be safe for her and Beau to meet under Gwelain's nose, but she hoped the rewards would justify the risk.

CHAPTER FORTY-THREE

Tullian stood in the space between their bedrooms, arms crossed. He'd removed his armour and sword, looking a bit undone but no less intimidating for it. He swept a withering glare over Sorra's dress and raised his eyebrows in an unspoken question.

Sorra supposed this was better than finding him weeping and tearing out his hair over his inaction in the face of human suffering, but having his emotions redirected into anger at her didn't seem like a *vast* improvement. She ignored the queasy clenching of her stomach.

"We should speak in my room," she said.

Tullian didn't move. "I told you to wear your armour."

Sorra crossed her arms. "You suggested I should and offered good reasons. I decided not to for my own reasons that I'd be pleased to discuss with you, but it's hardly the most important thing at the moment."

He didn't move, so Sorra stepped past him and into her room. After a moment, he followed.

Sorra left the door ajar.

"This is what she wants." Tullian motioned toward the dress. "You dressing to please her, socializing with her over a light lunch and a bit of gory entertainment."

"Good. Let her think she's winning me over. Let my clothing lower her guard." Sorra fought to keep her voice even. "You can afford to wear armour because Gwelain knows you're useless to her. By wearing this dress I'm letting her think I might not be." She paused. "She thinks I'm the traitor, Tullian. And her believing I'm the key to her victory might be the only thing keeping us from rotting away in her dungeon. I have to keep her interested if we want a chance to find the heart."

"And what happens when she hooks you with the bait you think you've set for her?" Tullian snapped. Then he sighed. "You're sure she's trying to win you over?"

"As sure as I am of the fact that she won't succeed. She nearly told me in as many words."

Tullian nodded but didn't look entirely convinced. "Did she say why?"

"No." There were limits to the practicality of honesty, and anything touching on Sorra's blessing or her own unheroic side felt dangerous. "Maybe it's only that she knows it won't be you."

The door opened, and Beau stepped into the room. Tullian's eyes widened, but he didn't offer a greeting.

Sorra cleared her throat, and both men turned to her. "This room is a safe space for us to talk. At least, Varek told me it was. If it's true that he can't lie…" She turned back the carpet to reveal the symbol carved into the floor. "He said this is protection. No one can listen to what's said inside this room."

Tullian crouched and traced his fingers over the lines. "It looks like the ones at our last hideout, but I've never had a feel for magic. What do you mean he can't lie?"

Beau stood beside the carving, brow furrowed as he looked it over. "His mother cursed him to suffer if he spoke a lie," he said absently. "And this is no exception. It's simple, but clear enough in its intention. If he said it would work, it will."

Sorra smiled. "You've studied magic?"

"I'm not allowed to. No one in my family is." Beau shrugged. "But most of the books in the library are written in the language of the Bright Ones. I've had a lot of time on my hands over the past decade or so. I can't write it or speak it, but my reading is passable, and I can get some sense of it even in this more complicated, condensed form."

"Most impressive." Tullian bowed. "A pleasure to meet you, Prince Beauregard. I've heard you might be an important part of our plans moving forward, but I'm afraid I wasn't informed we'd be meeting today."

You didn't give me a chance to tell you, Sorra thought, but kept her mouth shut.

"Likewise, Tullian." Beau offered his hand, and Tullian shook it without hesitation. "I'm afraid Sorra hasn't had time to tell me much about you, but the fact that she considers you a worthy companion makes me believe I should disregard the queen's less flattering opinions of you."

Tullian laughed. "Some of them, at least."

Sorra tensed. This was good—just a quick introduction and they were already getting along. But there was something about the respect Tullian offered, immediately and without question, that rubbed her against the grain.

Beau is a prince, she reminded herself. *It's not personal.*

"Please call me Beau, at least when we're in here," Beau said. "Titles have caused me nothing but problems for some time now."

"Of course. It was good of you to come." Tullian sat in one of the chairs by the fire and offered the other to Beau.

Beau looked to Sorra before he accepted, and she nodded. A small courtesy, but it eased a little of the tension that had crept into her shoulders. She leaned against the wall beside the fireplace, facing them.

"I almost didn't come," Beau said. "It's dangerous for us to meet like this, even with protections. But if there's any way I can help without risking a war, I want to do it. I understand you might not trust me with your plans right away, but—"

"We might not have a choice," Sorra said. Tullian frowned at the interruption, but it was with his usual disappointment in her manners rather than true anger. She ignored him and took a long breath, steeling herself for what had to come next. "I followed Gwelain after she left the theatre and overheard her speaking with her mage, saying she needs to change her approach because time might be short." She forced herself to look to Beau. "It sounds like your father is ill. Deathly ill, maybe. I'm sorry."

Beau paled. "He was always so healthy. I'd hoped—" He clenched his jaw, cutting off the thought. "Nothing to be done about it. Gwelain's not likely to let me go home to say goodbye."

"Or even to tell you it's happening," Sorra said. "She doesn't know I heard her, and I think we should keep it that way."

"Any small advantage is worth holding on to." Tullian rubbed his forehead. "She has too many, even if she's lost her ability to listen in on our plans. The more I think about it, the more I realize she's been ahead of us every step of the way. She wanted Sorra here and sworn to the quest."

"Even if she has the advantage now," Beau said, "that doesn't mean she has to keep it. She got what she wanted, but so did you. The only question is what we're all going to do with the time we have left."

Sorra watched closely for signs that the news of his father's illness had shaken him. He seemed steady enough, and he wasn't wrong.

"Right," Tullian said, then pulled Selim's notebook from his pocket—not the notes Tullian had read from on their journey, but the slim volume Selim had written in the old language. Sorra flinched internally as Beau took it. She'd never been allowed to touch its pages and hadn't known Tullian carried it with him. "Sorra believes you're the Mind Linnea spoke of in her visions. You're familiar with them?"

"I am. My father made sure of it before I left home. He didn't place much stock in the visions but wasn't willing to overlook any potential advantage."

"Hmm. Perhaps he'd be pleased to know the Might, Mystery, and Mind have gathered," Tullian said. "Selim was to be our Mind when we came in search of Linnea's heart, and even if he wasn't a part of the visions, his private notes may yet contain the key to our victory. Gwelain thought it worth silencing him to keep their secrets, and I myself can't read them."

Beau cradled the book's spine in one hand and frowned as he scanned each page, pausing over one near the end.

"There's a lot here. Suspicions, reasoning, second-guessing."

Tullian leaned in closer. "But he reached a conclusion."

"He did." Beau handed the book back to him. "He suspected Gwelain knew more than any of you. Something about the lost visions and her reading them before they were destroyed."

Tullian paled. "Impossible. No one but the mages and the scholars had access to them."

"And not everyone is as loyal to their oaths as you are," Sorra said, speaking as gently as she could. "Someone in Embercliffe has to have told Gwelain about the king's illness. No one is crossing the border with messages, but if magic were involved..."

Tullian's nostrils flared. "It's possible. If Selim was right—and I assume he was if Gwelain thought it worth silencing him—she's watching for signs and warnings we can't possibly know about."

Sorra swallowed hard. "And they led to her bringing us here."

Bringing me *here,* she thought. Gwelain knew about the blessing. Who could say what else she knew?

Tullian glowered into the fire. "Then this, too, must be used to our advantage. Linnea would not have seen our potential victory if Gwelain had already won." He turned to Beau. "She doesn't know we have this information, or our Mind."

"And it must stay that way," Beau said. "Not only for the sake of advantage, but for Andonia. If Gwelain finds out I've helped you, even with something as minor as a translation, she'll be free to attack Andonia. She's firm in her plans to use me to take the throne as long as she's confident of success, but if things seemed to be falling apart, I'm not sure what she'd do. It could mean another curse, or worse. I can't risk breaking the treaty when my father's plans may be close to completion."

"But you'll help us?" Sorra asked.

Beau leaned his head back and closed his eyes. "I'll do what I can, but we'll need to be careful if we meet again. Varek has given us a gift for whatever his reasons might be, but it would have been far more useful if he'd placed his protection almost anywhere else in the castle. There's no good excuse for me to be here, and the only other protected rooms I know of are the royal apartments."

Sorra easily thought of a few good reasons for Beau to come back to her room or for her to visit his, but none that would please Gwelain.

She waited for Tullian to say something helpful about heroism and the need to take risks so Beau could help more. He'd accepted Beau as the Mind far more easily than he had Sorra as the Mystery, perhaps because the prince looked and spoke like the sort of hero he'd been expecting before she showed up to shake him into action. A stirring speech, even a stern lecture on why the visions and not his father's plan would be their road to victory…

But Tullian nodded. "You are correct, of course."

Sorra glared at him. "You're saying he shouldn't help us?"

"I'm saying caution is warranted, even with time running short. As long as Gwelain remains on her current path, we might predict her next steps. If her plans change, our task will become far more difficult than it already is." Tullian kept his focus on Beau as he spoke. "But you're here now, and you must know things we don't. Is the heart in the castle?"

"It is." Beau sat up straighter. "I don't know where. She's able to draw on its power from anywhere in the castle, but her power weakens if she's away for too long."

"And she doesn't take it with her if she leaves?" Tullian asked.

"No. It's here, and she believes it's safe. There are only a few places in the castle that are strictly forbidden to me, where being caught would qualify as a violation of her orders." Beau spoke as though he'd been thinking about it for some time. His hands might have been tied when it came to acting against Gwelain, but his mind had been free to roam. "The dungeons are one. The north tower is another, as is whatever lies beyond the door off the east side of the throne room. But it's probably in the central tower above the royal apartments. It's the most secure location in the castle. You can't get into those rooms without me, Gwelain, her mage, or Varek opening the door, and the tower at their centre is guarded."

"Hmm." Tullian steepled his fingers under his chin. "If we can't get into the central tower without your help, we might at least eliminate the others and learn something useful if we could search without being caught. I don't suppose she's planning a royal tour of her lands any time soon?"

Beau smiled sadly. "That would be convenient, wouldn't it?"

"It would." Tullian nodded slowly, thinking. "She believes Sorra is the traitor from the visions. Perhaps if I searched while she's busy wooing her… but then her mage would still be an obstacle."

"And her guards," Sorra added. It was beginning to feel as though Tullian had forgotten she was in the room. "We need to get all of them away from the castle, or at least distracted within it. A theatre performance we can sneak out of, or that royal tour, or—"

"Or a hunt," Beau said. "She hasn't been on one in months, and she loves a bit of bloody sport."

"We know," Sorra said, remembering the scent of the queen's dog breathing in her face. "Please tell me you don't mean hunting humans."

"Not this time." Beau spoke softly, and Sorra understood that it wasn't an attempt at a joke. "You two are supposed to be making yourselves useful, and there's nothing more useful to Gwelain than entertainment. Tullian, if you ask her to take you on a hunt and promise a good show, I think she'll accept. And she likes to keep her mage close."

"Leaving Sorra to search?" Tullian asked.

"Of course." Sorra stood up straighter. "You can be the distraction. I'll find an excuse to stay behind and learn what I can." The thought terrified her, but it felt right. It felt like being a hero, like spitting in the face of the fate her blessing had promised. "I can do this."

She hoped the concern sketched across Tullian's features was for her safety and not for the future of their quest. "Promise me you won't take unnecessary or impulsive risks. Your goal will be to find the heart or confirm where it isn't. Nothing that will get you in trouble. Any further action we decide to take will require planning and preparation."

Sorra forced a smile. "Of course."

"Good." Tullian stood. "I'll find Gwelain and keep her occupied with my proposal while you two work out details of the search. A proper hunt requires planning, and I'll want to discuss every detail with her immediately." He went to the door, paused, and looked back as if he wanted to say more.

Warnings, Sorra suspected. *Don't take too long, stay focused on the task, don't be caught leaving.* She was accustomed to such unnecessary reminders from those who didn't trust her to remember for herself.

But he only nodded to Beau and left.

Sorra collapsed into the chair he'd vacated and kicked off her slippers, then drew her feet up under her skirt so she could rest her chin on her knees.

"How does that feel?" she asked, keeping her voice unnaturally light.

"How does what feel?"

"To be assumed competent. To be seen as a hero without having to prove yourself over and over."

"Ah." Beau thought for a moment. "It does make life easier. I overheard some of your conversation before I came in. Does he really worry you'll betray Andonia?"

"I don't know. He's scared someone will, and he knows it won't be him. That doesn't leave a lot of options." Sorra picked at the hem of her skirt. "He doesn't know about the blessing."

"I assumed not." Beau didn't sound concerned. "I suppose he'd take it as seriously as he does the visions?"

"I think so. And he really does believe in those, so don't let him catch you questioning them. He might re-think that trust he just offered you so easily."

"I'll play along." Beau smiled, but it faded quickly. "I wish I could stay to help you. Even if our plan works perfectly and we get most of the goblins out of the castle, you'll be in danger."

"I know. But this is why I'm here." Sorra tried to sound more confident than she felt. "If we can find Linnea's heart and take it from Gwelain, she won't be able to threaten Andonia again. There will be no need for a treaty, or for you to stay here. You'll be free."

"I would be."

"You don't sound happy about it."

Beau looked down at the floor, studying the symbol Varek had carved as though deciding again whether to trust it.

"I've spent a good portion of my life expecting this would all end with me losing everything," he said. "In the early days, I imagined my father coming up with a clever plan to invade these lands or to find a way around his agreement with Gwelain so he could bring me home with all the information I was gathering. He didn't. And I realized, probably later than I should have, that his only option might be to let things reach a point I thought was our last line of defense."

Sorra unfolded herself and pulled her chair closer. His voice had gone low and quiet, as though he hardly dared speak even in a protected space. "Which is what?"

"A letter of abdication."

"But you still carry the heir's mark."

He nodded. "I am still the heir to the throne. The letter that would make it otherwise is signed in my blood, magically bound to airtight legality just as the agreement with Gwelain was, and the marriage contract I signed a few weeks ago. The difference is that this one was sealed and made to become legal only when opened."

"So it lets Gwelain keep thinking she has her clear path to the throne but gives your father a way to block her even if she married you?"

"Exactly. The letter will be opened in the event of his death. It would break the agreement and free Gwelain to attack again, but I've bought my father a dozen extra years to plan his defenses. I hope he has some brilliant plan, or at least that his mages and soldiers are ready to fight."

"And that's it? You'll have lost the crown forever?"

"I would, according to the laws. I used to hope it wouldn't come to that, but after I lost that wager and had to sign the marriage contract, I resigned myself to losing everything." He smiled sadly. "But then you came tumbling into the throne room, stirring things up, making me think there might be a way to end things without putting Andonia in danger, without abdication."

"Isn't that good?" Sorra asked.

"Maybe. But letting myself hope for it feels dangerous, especially if it leads to me taking the kind of foolish risks I've managed to avoid for so long."

"I understand." She reached for his hand. "If you'd like, I can do the hoping for both of us. You stick to thinking of our next steps and helping in whatever ways won't unleash a fresh curse on our people. If there's anything to the visions and you are the Mind, it will be enough."

"I can do that." Beau twined his fingers between hers and squeezed tight. "I'd like to kiss you again."

"I'd like that, too." Sorra felt as though her next words might kill her and cursed the idea of duty and responsibility. "It's probably best not to. We're already taking risks that—"

"I know." But he turned her hand over and raised it to his lips, placing a kiss in the middle of her palm and sending a warm, tingling sensation up her arm and through her body. "Keep that one, then, for when you need it."

It was a silly, childish idea, and therefore one she'd never have expected from him. She closed her fingers and held her fist to her heart, swallowing the lump in her throat.

She wanted to ask him whether there would be more of this when the dust had settled but didn't want him to make impossible promises. If they succeeded in defeating Gwelain and returning Beau to Embercliffe before his father's death, that letter never needed to be opened. He'd still be king. It was what she'd come for, what he wanted.

There probably wouldn't be much room for kissing commoners once he'd married a foreign princess, and even if there were, she wouldn't want him that way. She'd take what she could behind the queen's back, but only because Gwelain was an evil creature bent on destroying everything they both loved.

Anyone Beau married freely deserved better.

"Right," he said, as though something had been settled. "We should go over the locations you'll try to search tomorrow. I can't tell you what you'll find, but I can at least get you there."

Sorra nodded, wishing she could slow time so they could have a little longer to talk about other things. She couldn't, though, and in the end, it would do her no good to pretend they could ever have more than this.

As Beau talked about dusty hallways and forbidden staircases, she tried to convince herself that saving the world together could be enough.

CHAPTER FORTY-FOUR

Sorra hadn't faked sick in years, having figured out early on that even real fevers, vomiting, aches, and pains were unlikely to earn her a day in bed. Still, it had worked a handful of times in her life, if only for getting out of uncomfortable social situations.

The first part of her plan went smoothly enough, once she'd bowed out early from the evening's festivities and had figured out the trick of emptying the contents of her stomach into the chamber pot.

She spent the night next to the fire, wrapped in blankets. By early morning a sheen of sweat covered her face and had soaked through her nightgown, and she didn't need a mirror to know how sickly the dark circles beneath her eyes would appear.

It hurt to sacrifice sleep, but if she'd given her blessing any wiggle room, it might have let her doze through the arrival of her breakfast, ruining everything. The night seemed as bottomless and empty as her stomach, especially with no clock to mark time's passing. She caught herself drifting several times before she caught the shuffle of movement outside her door.

She leapt into bed, leaving the blankets mussed.

"Oh, my dear!" The maid who entered with Sorra's breakfast tray was a stranger. Sorra tried not to let her disappointment show. "Are you all right?"

"I don't think I am." Sorra rolled onto her side and hugged a pillow to her stomach, looking as pathetic as possible. "I hope it's only the unfamiliar food."

She gestured to the chamber pot, which she hadn't dared open for several hours no matter how her bladder insisted, then let her hand fall back to the mattress.

"Goodness." The maid tried to lay a hand on her forehead, but Sorra turned away, unsure of whether a fever was called for. The maid stepped back. "I don't suppose you feel like breakfast, then."

It hurt Sorra to turn it away after losing her previous meal, but she shook her head. "I couldn't possibly eat now."

"Of course not."

"Thank you. And I don't suppose I'll be going on the hunt today. Would you have someone inform the queen?"

The maid nodded. "I'll just take the chamber pot out and come back for your breakfast tray." She looked over the tangled blankets. "And I'll bring fresh bedding. Always helps me feel better when I'm ill."

"Thank you," Sorra murmured, pretending to close her eyes but watching through her lashes as the maid left her.

Sorra checked the door and found it locked, as it had been since supper. She'd hoped yesterday's map-guided freedom had set a new pattern for life in the castle but had known not to expect anything to be that easy.

Hannah would have been better. She might have left the door open while the queen was away, and Sorra had spent much of the night deciding how to convince her. This new person seemed kinder and more accommodating, which made Sorra trust her less.

Another way, then. If I could catch the door and jam the latch when she's finished here—

A knock startled her out of her thoughts.

"Yes?" She got back into bed and pulled the covers up over her chest.

Gwelain entered, dressed in forest-green trousers and a flaw-lessly fitted, high-necked jacket that would give her full freedom to ride and to hunt. There was nothing especially flashy about the outfit, but Sorra envied the effortless elegance she'd never be able to imitate even if she wore identical clothing.

The goblin queen sat on the edge of the bed, her pearl-scaled toes curled against the carpet. "Troubles, little hero?"

Sorra pulled the blankets higher. "I'm terribly sorry, Majesty. I don't believe I can go on the hunt today. I have nothing left to throw up, but there are rumblings farther south. I'm afraid I'd slow you down when I needed to stop along the way to—"

"Never mind that, I understand." Gwelain's nose wrinkled. "We wouldn't want terrible smells alerting the animals to our approach, would we?"

Sorra smiled weakly. "I am sorry, Majesty."

She hated lying there, appearing weak and helpless before her enemy. Still, it occurred to her that this might be the opportunity she needed if she could play her cards right.

"Majesty, I wonder whether—"

"It's terribly inconvenient for you," Gwelain said, speaking over her. "I'm sure you'll be bored all day if you stay in bed. If you feel well enough to walk, perhaps you'd enjoy taking in the sculpture gallery? It's on the upper level, right turn past the golden pool, you can't miss it. Or there's a lovely little garden outside the library, if you'd prefer fresh air." The queen gave her a cold smile. "But you've seen that, haven't you?"

Sorra gripped the blankets tighter. "I have, Majesty. It's lovely."

"Hmm. I'll leave your door unlocked, then."

They watched each other for what felt like far too long, neither of them moving or speaking.

Another test, then. Or worse, a trap.

Sorra had expected to need her wits about her to talk the queen into letting her be free for the day—to lie, to act innocent, to be subtle enough that Gwelain wouldn't realize what she was up to. Instead, the queen was smiling, cold and calculating, offering Sorra exactly what she wanted.

I know what you're up to, her shining eyes said. *And I have nothing to fear from you.*

Either she was confident that Sorra wouldn't find the heart, or that it wouldn't matter if she did. Or worse, Sorra realized as cold dread pooled in her bowels, this was what Gwelain wanted all along. This was her game, and she had been playing a half-dozen moves ahead of them from the start.

But we have our secrets, too. She doesn't know that I know where to look, or that we know to search for the missing visions as well as the heart.

The reassurances fell flat under Gwelain's gaze, which sparkled with what might have been interest or malice.

"Thank you, Majesty," Sorra said. "The statue gallery sounds lovely. I hope you'll all be careful out there. Hunting is a dangerous business."

Gwelain rested one hand on Sorra's leg and squeezed hard enough that Sorra felt the sharpness of her golden claws through the blankets, then stood.

"Everything is dangerous, little hero," she said, speaking over her shoulder as she stepped out of the room. "Especially when your business interferes with mine."

The door closed, and Gwelain's words hung in the air.

It was several minutes before Sorra could convince her body to abandon the safety of her bed and prepare to hunt for a queen's heart.

~

The morning sky was clear, as was Sorra's view of the meadow beyond the castle's front courtyard. A few dozen goblins milled about, ignoring the human servants who held the reins of nervous horses, all of them waiting for the queen to appear.

She's going to call it off.

Sorra paced away from the window, then back to it, white nightgown billowing behind her. The servant had paid another visit, leaving Sorra with clean blankets, a fresh chamber pot, and an assurance that she'd return with lunch, but Sorra had decided not to dress for her own hunt until the goblins were gone.

Maybe it would be for the best if Gwelain did cancel her plans, she thought. *More time to plan. Less chance of me making a mess of things.*

A black-clad figure approached the crowd. Corvin. Beau had promised to keep him occupied, drawing his attention away from Sorra as often as possible. A dozen dogs joined the waiting group, leaping and snapping at each other in their excitement.

Big dogs. Sorra was glad of the distance that kept her from seeing their more monstrous features.

She's not going to call it off.

Her empty stomach clenched.

Beau had mentioned four places he thought she should search, only three of which she had any hope of accessing on her own. The map he'd drawn marked the locations of every place he'd never been allowed to visit. Sorra had committed it to memory as well as she could, then burned it.

Search for answers in the blank spaces, she reminded herself, warmed by Davina's advice whispering in her mind as confirmation of her next steps.

He had said the central tower above the royal apartments was the most secure space in the castle, which meant the heart was probably there. It would be impossible for Sorra to reach it on her own, but there were still the other forbidden spaces. Gwelain seemed confident she wouldn't find the heart even if she had the day to search, but maybe Linnea's Mystery would uncover something else in the places the goblin queen kept hidden from her prince.

She might narrow the search, assuming she managed to stay alive and keep out of trouble along the way.

At least my track record for not dying is good.

She shed her nightgown and dressed in a grey tunic and trousers, pairing them with her old boots, leaving her sword and armour in the wardrobe. Freedom of movement felt essential, and a sword would raise questions if anyone saw her.

I'm just going for a little walk with the queen's permission.

She tucked her dagger into her boot, then returned to the window.

Tullian had arrived, armour shining in the sun, and one of the servants offered him a broad-backed chestnut mount. Sorra watched as Beau helped Corvin onto a black horse, then mounted one splotched with brown and white.

Sorra bristled with nervous energy as the rest of the goblins mounted up, leaving a stunning white horse riderless. Gwelain strode toward them, dark hair floating loose behind her. The horse shied as she took the reins and mounted, and she kicked it into a gallop, leaving the others to fall in behind her as she rode for the forest.

"Gods, Linnea, whoever's there," Sorra whispered, "let Beau and Tullian be safe."

After they disappeared into the woods, she forced herself to wait through a dozen more breaths, just to be sure, then crept out of her room and down the stairs.

Two soldiers stood at the doors outside the throne room when she looked down into the palace's entryway. She didn't recognize them as Gwelain's personal guards, but they were imposing enough to make it clear she wouldn't be searching there any time soon. Instead, she headed for another staircase Beau had noted on his map that would open near the kitchen.

If anyone stopped her, it would be simple enough to explain that she'd been on her way down for a bite to eat now that her stomach had settled a little.

There was no need to lie, though. Most of the goblins had joined their queen for the hunt, and the soldiers outside the throne room were the only ones she saw as she skulked through the twisting maze of halls and descended a dusty wooden staircase.

Humans worked in the kitchen, clattering pots and barking orders, but none looked up as she passed.

Too easy, Tullian grumbled in her mind. Sorra told him to hush, but listened for trouble before she passed through the door Beau had indicated on his map.

The stairs to the dungeon were bright and lovely, but what lay beyond the door at the bottom felt entirely disconnected from the pretty, airy spaces above. The room was roughly carved from the stone beneath the castle, its dark walls and low ceilings lit by flaming torches instead of magical lamps, the air dank and thick with an unpleasant mingling of mildew, rot, and waste. Cells with rusting iron doors lined both walls of a narrow passage with a wooden door at its far end. Sorra walked slowly, watching for movement or any sign that Gwelain had punished Linnea by locking her heart in such a depressing place.

Every one of the cells was empty save for a dusting of musty old straw, and Sorra's relief grew with every one she passed.

A prisoner might ask for help, might even threaten to expose her if she refused, and she wasn't sure there would be a way to make Tullian proud without ruining everything.

She counted a dozen cells before she reached a door at the end, which stood ajar. There were no sounds coming from behind it, though light flickered at the crack.

Sorra pulled gently against the handle, then more firmly when the heavy door didn't move. The opening widened, and Sorra paused until her heartbeat calmed.

Nothing. She opened it further, slowly and cautiously, and peered inside.

She clapped a hand over her mouth to keep from screaming.

There was a man in the cramped little room, but he was no threat to her or to anyone. He'd been strapped to a vertically tilted metal frame, his head pointed toward the bloodstained floor, his emaciated torso cut open, his innards removed.

His eyes were gone, too, leaving the empty sockets staring helplessly at Sorra.

Taxes. She gagged. The poor fellow's suffering was over, but if Tullian was right, his soul wasn't at peace. It was gone, possibly burned up for the sake of magic.

And if the old knight was right about the goblins feasting on the flesh that was left over after the pain was done and the soul was taken, they weren't finished with this body.

Sorra fled, stomach lurching, only stopping to catch her breath when she'd reached the top of the stairs.

No heart, but it wasn't hard to guess why Gwelain would want to keep Beau from visiting a place that would remind him of his enemies' darkest and most horrifying habits. She imagined how

Gwelain would laugh if she could see her now. The thought brought with it a flash of anger that cleared her mind.

The north tower, then.

Sorra checked her boots to make sure she wasn't leaving a trail of dirty footprints behind her, then climbed the stairs to the second floor. She kept Beau's map in mind as she walked past bowls of polished jewels on pedestals, turned left past a wall where golden coins flowed like a never-ending waterfall into a pool crossed by a silver bridge, and followed a corridor lined with mannequins wearing stunning ballgowns. Finally, she spotted a plain oak door at the end of a narrow hallway, just as Beau had described.

"Hey!"

Sorra forced herself to turn as one of the soldiers from outside the throne room stalked toward her, his tail twitching behind him like an irritated and unusually scaly cat's.

"Where are you going?"

"I—I was looking for the sculpture gallery." Sorra's voice trembled, but there would be nothing suspicious about being scared of an angry monster even if she hadn't been doing anything wrong. "Queen Gwelain said I could enjoy it while she's gone."

He frowned, creasing the hairless skin of his pale brow. "You've gone the wrong way."

Sorra widened her eyes and blinked at him. "I turned right past the waterfall. She said to go right."

"You went left. Are you stupid?"

Sorra looked down at her hands. "I have trouble with directions."

"Then allow me to assist you."

Under other circumstances, the condescension and irritation in his voice would have set Sorra's temper aflame. As it was, she only felt relief. Better to let him think her an annoyance than a threat.

It was a short walk to the statue gallery, a long room with curved walls forming a tunnel of glass panels, allowing sunlight to stream in from every direction. Statues carved from granite and marble stood facing each other in two lines, leaving space to walk between and around them.

"Thank you," Sorra said.

The soldier grunted. "Think you can manage to find your way back on your own?"

Sorra bowed her head. "Left turn where I went wrong before, straight back to the stairs up to my room."

"And which one is left?"

Sorra swallowed back the sharp answer she wanted to give and held up her left hand.

The soldier stalked out of the room, grumbling to himself.

Sorra wandered the sculpture gallery, unsure of whether he'd double back to check on her. The statues were a strange assortment that looked as though they might have been collected from all over the world. A few with clearly human forms stood closest to the entrance. As Sorra made her way to the far end of the room, the statues she passed became larger, stranger, and more beautiful. They had pointed ears like Gwelain and her goblins but boasted an array of odd features beyond what the queen had bestowed on her creations—broad antlers, massive feathered wings, and thick fur carved in impossibly life-like detail. Their bodies frequently resembled those of humans but ranged in size from a well-developed man who stood only as tall as a child to a shockingly handsome fellow with a thick beard and laughing eyes who towered over the rest, his jagged stone crown resting at a rakish angle on his long, thick hair.

The Bright Ones. Legends to Sorra and to every human in Andonia, but to Gwelain they were family. Perhaps she hated them, if Tullian's story were true, but she also honoured them, or at least what they represented.

The far end of the room had no windows and lay in shadow. A dozen smaller statues stood facing Sorra. Goblins like the ones from the old stories, squat and muscular, with rough skin and sharp little eyes. None displayed the kind of beauty Gwelain had given the creations that had replaced them, and they were as out of place in the gallery as they'd have been roaming the halls of her castle. They'd served Gwelain and fought for her, but Sorra could see how their rough appearances would have displeased their queen after she'd grown up among the Bright Ones. These monsters had never been what she wanted. She kept their images close but had left them standing guard over a broken statue that lay behind them.

Sorra stepped past the old goblins, careful not to catch her clothes on the swords and spiked clubs they held over their heads. Nothing about the broken statue marked her as anything but human, but she wore a crown smaller and more delicate than the one that adorned the handsome king who stood in the sunlight.

"Linnea," Sorra whispered, and knelt beside her. The statue smiled kindly up at her, but the eyes had been chipped away, and a rough hole marred the centre of the old queen's marble chest. Dust and bits of stone still littered the tile floor, and the iron bar that seemed likely to have done the damage lay forgotten in a dark corner.

There was a purpose to stealing her heart, the seat of her power, Tullian had said. *But to blind her helpless body? That's spite. That's all it is.*

"I'm sorry," Sorra said, speaking to Linnea herself even as she looked down at the statue. Tullian had said her spirit couldn't rest until her heart was returned to its rightful place. Maybe she'd been hearing Sorra's useless prayers all this time. "I'm trying, I swear. If there's any way you could help us along…"

The statue smiled blandly up at her, and no other answer came.

Sorra turned and stalked out of the gallery, not glancing back at Gwelain's forgotten subjects or the Bright Ones. She paused outside the room, and when she was sure the soldier had truly left her, she followed her steps back to the door Beau had said would take her to the north tower.

He'd suspected it would be unlocked, and Sorra was only halfway surprised to find he'd been right. When a queen had the kind of power Gwelain had, holding life and death—and in Beau's case, the fate of his people—in her hands, orders and threats worked as well as locks and keys.

She passed through the door quickly and stepped into an empty room lit by lamps that cast cool moonlight instead of the sun's rays. Three passages opened off it, each visible through an open archway. Two looked much like the rest of the castle, with thick carpets and paintings on the walls.

The third was different. Where the rest of the castle was polished and brilliant, it was dusty and crumbling. Instead of shimmering white stone, the walls were grey and dull. A painting hung not far in, its colours faded, its frame broken and hanging by one corner.

"The humble path it is, then." Sorra stepped into the cold air of the hallway, which curved gently to the right until it ended in a stairway like the one that led to her tower room. The stairs were coated in a layer of undisturbed dust. If this wasn't an abandoned tower, it was at least one that wasn't frequently used.

Sorra sighed. Another dead end, perhaps, but at least no one would be along to see the footprints she couldn't help leaving behind.

She climbed, watching for signs of Gwelain's trickery. There were no lamps, but her path was lit by a flickering blue light from above.

Unnatural, she thought. *Careful, now.*

But she kept going. There was no sense in turning back after she'd come so far, not even if her breath grew shallow with fearful anticipation as she neared the top, ready to run if a trap awaited.

There was no door, no lock, no slavering hound waiting around the last bend. Nothing but that strange light to hint that this was anything but a place Gwelain had somehow forgotten within her own walls.

The staircase ended in a room that filled the width of the tower, its far wall lost in shadow. Sorra's breath caught in her chest as she entered, her fears momentarily drowned by wonder.

A disembodied heart floated on a stone pedestal in the centre of the room, casting its strange blue-green glow over the bars of the gilded cage that surrounded it. The light shifted gently with each rhythmic beat.

Sorra stepped closer, captivated and horrified. The heart itself was a deep, dark blue, traced over with veins of pure gold, and though no blood flowed through them, they pulsed with whatever magic kept the heart alive.

Linnea, Sorra thought, and raised a hand toward the cage without intending to.

Something moved in the darkness at the edge of the room, and the heart's beat quickened in time with Sorra's.

Varek stepped into its light, smiling, and moved with surprising grace to obstruct her path to the stairs.

"Well done, intrepid human," he said, his voice an icy rumble that sent a chill up Sorra's spine. "Welcome to the treasury."

CHAPTER FORTY-FIVE

"Don't worry." The air of the room had a flattening effect on Varek's voice, but Sorra caught the amusement in it. "I have no intention of harming you."

Sorra almost laughed, then remembered he couldn't lie without consequences, and she saw no evidence of painful eruptions on his face or hands.

"I suppose you'll have to tell Gwelain I was here, though," she said. "She could do me harm."

Varek shrugged. "She expected you to search the castle while she was gone and asked me to stay behind to keep an eye on things. I doubt there will be any punishment. The game wouldn't be much fun for her if you didn't try to win." He glanced around the room, and Sorra followed his gaze to take in the cobwebs and shadows. "Not much of a treasury, is it? She prefers to keep her wealth where others can admire it, and her by extension. The heart is the only thing she worries about protecting."

"Doesn't seem too carefully guarded to me."

"Try stealing it, then." It wasn't a challenge. He still sounded amused.

"It won't hurt me?"

"It won't hurt you."

The larger part of her wanted to disbelieve him, and she

reminded herself again that he couldn't speak a lie. She waited until Varek stepped back, then moved closer to the cage.

It had no door, and the bars were too closely spaced to pull the heart out between them. She held her breath and touched a finger to one of the bars, pulling it back quickly. There was no pain, so she tried again.

They didn't move no matter how hard she pushed and appeared to be anchored in the stone pillar. When she tried to slide a finger between them, she met resistance, though there was no visible barrier.

"It's impossible to steal it, then?"

"Until Gwelain dies or voluntarily gives up control of the heart, only she can open its cage." Varek yawned, clearly bored by the conversation.

"And we can't kill her, can we?"

"Even if you could, you'd destroy Linnea's heart in the process. I believe we established the other night that you don't want that, so I'd say you're out of luck unless you can talk Gwelain into severing her connection to it."

The familiar ache of disappointment bloomed in Sorra's gut. Finding the heart should have felt like victory, but they'd gained nothing.

Or at least that was what Gwelain wanted her to believe.

She narrowed her eyes at Varek. "Did she ask you to guard the heart so you could get me away from it, or so you could discourage me?"

"Both will please her, I'm sure." Varek stepped closer. "Are you discouraged?"

"I haven't decided."

"Then you can think it over in your room." He motioned toward the stairs.

Sorra didn't move. "You didn't want Gwelain to know we spoke before. Can her mage not hear what you just said?"

"No one outside of this space can hear us."

Sorra's mind sharpened. "Then I have questions for you. I know about your curse and why it would make you want to help us. If we can work something out—"

"We can't." Varek frowned, obviously wary. "When Gwelain asks me what happened here I need to be able to tell her I found you, offered honest and appropriate discouragement, and then immediately ejected you from this space and warned you not to return."

Not *I won't*, but *we can't*. A problem to be solved, not a door slammed in her face.

"Then do it." Sorra held out one arm. "Escort me out so you're not lying when you say you did. Then all you should need to do is not tell her how we turned around and came right back in so we could speak freely. Please. There must be some way we can help each other."

Varek's jaw muscles tightened. "You have a knack for manipulation and half-truths."

"Thank you."

"It does not make me more inclined to trust you. Out, now, and know that if you return, Gwelain will punish you for it." He grabbed her roughly by the arm and dragged her to the stairs, forcing her to stumble alongside him. She was still trying to figure out where she'd misstepped when he turned around on the third step and marched her back into the room.

Sorra rubbed her arm. His claws hadn't pierced her sleeve, but she thought they might have left bruises. "You'll speak to me, though?"

Varek pulled his claws through his hair as he paced the room, circling Sorra and the heart. "Not for long. And I make no promises about answering your questions. I can't lie to you, but I'll keep my silence if answering truthfully will put me in danger. You have good reason to fear Gwelain, but so do I."

"All right."

"And I won't trust you." His steps slowed. "You're human, and therefore your interests are opposed to mine. More importantly, you can lie. You can make promises you don't intend to keep."

"I know." Sorra wanted to defend herself, but he was right. He had fearsome claws and a bit of magic on his side, but she did have an advantage over him. "But I think you want things to change here, and that's what I've come to do. Am I right in thinking you'll be free of your curse if Gwelain loses the heart's power?"

Varek scowled. "You are."

"Then we should help each other. I know my word isn't worth anything, but I promise I won't tell Gwelain we've spoken, or that you're helping us."

"I'm not helping you," he said. "And our interests are not as aligned as you assume. We're only talking. You'll answer my questions, and I'll allow you to ask five of me, but if you irritate me with them or place me in danger, we're through."

He held up his left hand, five long, claw-tipped fingers extended.

"Agreed." Sorra struggled to decide to ask. It would be stupid to jump to *how can you help us defeat Gwelain* when he would so clearly refuse to answer.

Varek crossed his arms. "You first. Where did you go before you found this room?"

Sorra relaxed slightly, relieved he'd asked a question she could answer truthfully without revealing anyone else's secrets. "Before this I was in the sculpture gallery, where one of the soldiers left me after he found me close to finding this place. I saw the humans, the Bright Ones, the goblins, and Linnea. Before that, the dungeons."

Varek grimaced. "And saw some interesting sights there, I imagine."

"One, anyway."

Sorra looked at the heart. It was a beautiful thing, but wrong. Out of place, exposed in a way that seemed shameful and humiliating, ripped from the protection of Linnea's body. Such offences seemed common enough in this castle, though. She'd seen as much with her own eyes.

She considered the mutilated body and its connection to the visions. Linnea had warned them about Corvin but hadn't provided any details about the threat he posed. It wasn't the most important question to ask, but it might be one Varek wouldn't be overly cautious about.

She cleared her throat. "I saw a man's body. That's... I mean, Gwelain uses this heart's power, but Corvin draws power from others, doesn't he?"

Varek's thumb bent to touch his palm. "Not in the same way. You know about blood magic?"

"Tullian said it was about death or souls or pain. I guessed that's what happened to that prisoner."

The heart's steadily pulsing light reflected strangely in Varek's eyes. "Blood magic is an incredible source of power, and it's one that humans stole from us. Magic was never meant for creatures like you. You're weak and clumsy with it, unable to create illusions that stand up to true scrutiny, nearly helpless in the face of injuries I could easily heal. Watching a human mage work is like watching a dog riding a horse."

"But blood magic makes a human mage stronger."

"It does, though that's still nothing compared to what a truly magical being can do with it, and it would take most of them a lifetime to learn what comes naturally to us." Varek sat on the floor with his back against the wall and motioned for her to do the same.

Sorra sat close enough that they'd be able to speak quietly but out of claws' reach. There was always a chance her next question might be the wrong one.

"Blood magic used by the Bright Ones is harmless to the magic-bearer," he said. "But when a human uses blood magic, it destroys their ability to act as a vessel and hold magic within them. After they've done it once, their only option is to store their power in an object outside their bodies, then to keep it filled by torturing and killing again and again if they don't want to face the unbearable emptiness of a life without magic. It is greater power, but at a foolish price."

The disgust in his voice was unmistakable but clearly directed at the humans who dared to reach for power that wasn't theirs rather than at the act of murder or the theft of a soul.

But he'd offered something there. Corvin didn't carry magic within him, and that meant it might be stolen.

"You don't like Corvin." Sorra remembered at the last moment to drop her voice, changing a question into an observation she hoped would reveal another reason for him to stand against the queen.

Varek chuckled, low and dark. "I do not. My mother finds him endlessly useful, but I despise him."

"It must be hard for you, seeing a human in that position when Gwelain could be using you instead."

Varek's lips tightened, baring more of his teeth, making those that were already exposed more threatening. "Watch yourself."

A sore spot. Dangerous, but informative and possibly useful. If his resentment against Gwelain went deeper than the curse, that was even more reason for him to risk betraying her.

"Sorry," she said, and shifted closer. "You said you couldn't trust me, but I'm having the same problem. I want to understand you—why you came to me that first night, why you're speaking to me even if you won't tell us how to defeat her. I want to be sure you're doing this for your own reasons, not on her orders."

Varek looked into her eyes, unflinching. "Gwelain does not know I'm speaking with you now, and she doesn't know we've spoken aside from a few words at the feast and in the theatre. She isn't using me to set you up for failure, and she can't use me to feed you false information. I have my own reasons for being curious about your plans and for wanting to see this power taken away from my mother, but they're complicated."

"I'm listening." Sorra let her head rest against the wall, forcing her body to relax in a way her mind couldn't. Pointed questions would put his guard up, but if allowed to speak freely about whatever had turned him against Gwelain, he might reveal more than he realized.

They both watched the heart for several beats before he spoke again.

"You should understand what's at stake." Varek didn't look at Sorra, remaining focused on the heart. "Gwelain is my mother. She is my queen. She has accomplished much, but she isn't worthy of the power she has. She isn't the heart's true master."

"Because she stole it, I suppose."

Varek smiled. "How precious of you to think power is a matter of morality. I believe there are ways by which Gwelain could fully claim the heart as her own, but she's afraid to expose it to potential harm. She's content to leave it here, keeping it as a prisoner instead of truly owning it. Security is more important to Gwelain than maximizing her power."

"I see. You think she shouldn't have the heart because she's not power-hungry enough." Sorra tried not to sound as though she were judging him but couldn't help wondering whether goblins and humans were more different than she'd realized.

Varek's lips quirked up at one corner, tightening against his lower canines. "That's one way of looking at it, I suppose, but overly simplified. I think she shouldn't have it because she's short-sighted and foolish. Do you want to know why no one outside this room can hear us speaking?"

Sorra squinted into the shadows.

"There are no protective enchantments here," Varek said before she could guess. "They're not necessary. Because of Gwelain's weakness, the heart remains its own entity. Outside of the treasury Gwelain has full control of its magic, but Linnea is queen of this tiny territory. Perhaps she was a private woman in life, and that trait clings to her heart. Perhaps it's spite, or some natural quirk of her power, but magic worked outside this space has no effect within it. No listening, no watching. Here, the heart is in control."

Sorra frowned. It was useful information—if they did find a way to open the cage, no one would know they were doing it. But there had to be more, and Varek clearly wasn't going to offer it without prodding.

He was waiting. Holding back what she needed, but perhaps willing to offer it if she asked the right question.

He'd brought up the heart's defenses on his own, either to mislead her into wasting a question or to nudge her closer to answers.

Trust, then. At least I'll find out if he's playing fair.

She sighed. "What does that leave Gwelain with when she's here?"

Varek raised his hand and pinned his smallest finger under the claw of his thumb. His smile widened unpleasantly. "It leaves her with nothing at all." He opened his hand and a tiny flame appeared on his palm, dancing until he closed his fist and snuffed it out. "No magic from outside, but I can use my own magic here, and so can Corvin. Gwelain can't, because she has none of her own to use. Once she possessed Linnea's heart, she stopped using her own natural magic. It was impressive once, but it's either withered from disuse or Linnea's magic has actively destroyed it from within. All of Gwelain's power comes from this heart now, and she can't use it when she stands in its presence. Her established enchantments remain in place elsewhere, but in this room she is nothing more than her pathetic self. It must be horrifying for her."

He sounded as though the idea pleased him.

"That's it, then." Sorra scrambled to her feet. "All we have to do is follow her into this room and threaten her so she'll cut her ties to the heart to save her own life."

He didn't answer.

Because I didn't ask.

Sorra held back a frustrated sigh. "Is that how we defeat her?"

Varek followed her movements with his eyes, still resting the back of his head against the wall. "It seems unlikely. She rarely comes to this room. If she does, she raises a magical barrier at the bottom of the stairs that keeps out every living soul in the castle, friend or foe. She allows Corvin to accompany her as an extra layer of magical defense, but no one else. Even her guards wait below, unable to enter until she lowers the barrier—which she could do from here if you were waiting to attack her. It responds to her voice, no magic required." He looked back to the heart, then closed his eyes. "I told you security was important to her."

A third finger curled down.

Two questions left.

The missing visions, perhaps. If he knew anything about them and would spill those secrets, it could change everything.

Or Gwelain's plans for what would happen after King Ranthorn's death.

Or she might ask what other leverage would convince her to let the heart go, though the answer to that was likely nothing.

Sorra paced around the cage.

"It's destroying her," Varek said, without opening his eyes, "yet she clings to it. And what has it truly gained her?"

"A marriage," Sorra said, not to defend Gwelain but to keep him talking. "A path to the throne, if that's her true plan."

"A *legitimate* path to the throne," Varek said, sneering. "I despise her for that, too—her obsession with taking what was given to a half-human mongrel. Her own magic wasn't enough for her when she saw Linnea had more, and she hasn't been satisfied with her crown since she began to envy Linnea's. Her own subjects were never good enough, though she was happy to let them die in her foolish war against your people. I was too young to fight, so all I could do was watch them go and see fewer of them return from each battle. My older siblings and goblins I'd known all my life, all dead. My father, probably, though I never knew who he was. She lost them and she lost the war, and it made no difference to her. She was happy enough to replace her loyal subjects with pretty faces and shallow praise."

With every word, the hatred in his voice grew deeper and colder.

Sorra looked more closely at him. "I hadn't realized you had so much goblin in you."

He looked down at his hands and smiled ruefully. "Three-quarters. The blood of the Bright Ones runs far stronger, though, so fractions and portions don't mean much."

"Clearly," Sorra said, thinking back to the statues of the old goblins, all of them small and ugly and twisted. "You favour your mother's side."

"You think me beautiful?" Varek's voice dripped with mockery.

Sorra hesitated, confused by what should have been a simple answer given how monstrous and terrifying he'd seemed at first glance. But when she looked past that first impression, there was something of the Bright Ones' beauty about him, lurking even in his mossy skin and imposing teeth, and she realized she liked it far better than the pretty hues and shimmering scales Gwelain had given to her supposedly improved creations.

It wouldn't do to say that, though. He'd think it was shallow flattery or, worse, an attempt at flirting.

"I think you're... taller than the old goblins."

Varek laughed, and Sorra's cheeks warmed. "Never mind that.

My point is that I don't fault Gwelain for craving power, but it pains me to see how she wastes it in the pursuit of her petty vengeance. She uses Linnea's magic without considering the costs and consequences."

"For example?"

Another finger curled to touch Varek's palm, and Sorra winced. Her focus had slipped, and the momentary lapse would cost her a more valuable piece of information.

"My own situation." Varek drummed his claws against the floor. The soft tapping made Sorra think of a giant cockroach's feet skittering on stone, and she tried not to shudder. "Spells or enchantments that Gwelain works with her stolen magic draw from her power for as long as they remain active—another sign that she isn't the heart's true master. She cursed me impulsively, and in her blind rage neglected to leave a way to put an end to it. This curse comes at a small cost, and perhaps the control it gives her over me balances the scales, but it's a part of a pattern. She curses nations, she spends her magic keeping death out of her lands... it all adds up, even if she's more careful now, and that's why she wants a mage to take care of minor tasks."

"Like keeping track of interesting conversations."

"Exactly. Or minor curses, magical punishments, assisting her with transforming humans into goblins, various things." Varek held out one hand. Sorra took it with little hesitation and helped him to his feet. He brushed his palm against his dark jacket, then approached the heart and rested his hands on the stone pedestal, his fingers curving around its edge. "This power has changed her, and I believed for many years that her mismanagement of it would be her downfall. Now I fear it won't. Her plan for taking Andonia's throne is solid. She'll never be the heart's true master, but once she gets it to Embercliffe and cages it there permanently, there will be no way to take it from her."

"And you'll be cursed forever."

"I will. I doubt her victory will be good for anyone else, either. She might play at being a good queen for a while, but there's no telling what will happen once she grows bored of playing with Linnea's toys."

"Then help me." Sorra stood across from him, placing the heart between them. "If removing the heart from her control would break your curse, tell me how I can do that."

"I don't see how you can. Not on your own, not with the knight, not even with your prince's help." Varek stated it as a simple fact, without pleasure or regret. "I hoped when you arrived that you might change things. I know about your curse, too."

"Blessing," Sorra said, though she wasn't sure the difference mattered enough to warrant correction. "I didn't realize you knew about that."

"My mother likes to think out loud, occasionally in my presence. She also likes to gloat when she feels she's been particularly brilliant." He paused. "You can't use it against her, can you? Can't order your mayhem to rain down on your enemies?"

"No. It only seems to hurt those I don't want it to, and the odds of me and her becoming fast friends seem slim."

"True enough. So the answer remains no. I don't see how you could do it. At least, not without my help. I've been working on some things that might, under the right circumstances, give one an advantage. Not me. But someone."

"Then join us. Free yourself while you still can."

Varek's nostrils flared. "No. I'm tempted, of course. I can't steal the heart myself because she so frequently asks me whether I'm planning to do just that. Not as often as she used to, but habitually enough that I can't afford to make plans and risk having to lie about them. But if you were to do it…" He shook his head. "I want to be free of my curse and see Gwelain humbled, but I would suffer it and her for a thousand more years before I'd see the heart in the hands of humans who would use it to retaliate and destroy the remnants of my people."

"I thought the old ones were all dead."

He smiled sadly. "There are still some in the forests and mountains, though they're never invited to the castle for tea. They're happy enough to have been discarded, and for me to be the only member of my family who pays them any mind. They deserve better. Better than Gwelain, and certainly better than human kings would offer them."

"I don't suppose a promise that we'd leave you alone would suffice."

"No goblin in his right mind would trust three humans to keep their word once they no longer needed him."

"So our choices are to destroy the heart or give up."

Varek shrugged. "I can't see the future. I don't know how things will change. All I know is that much of it will depend on who wants victory the most and what they're willing to sacrifice for it."

He fell silent, and Sorra tried to think of one last, perfect question.

Then Varek's gaze sharpened, focused somewhere beyond Sorra's left shoulder. "We need to leave. They're returning earlier than I expected."

Sorra's mind raced. She'd lost track of time, focused as she'd been on the number of questions he'd allotted. Now she felt every passing second, running like sand between her fingers as Varek took her arm and led her again toward the stairs.

"Wait, I get one more question." She tried to stop, but only managed to slow his steps. "The visions—what does she know that we don't? Or what is she planning?"

Varek's grip tightened. "She doesn't speak to me of the visions, but you're right to think she knows what was lost to your people. And if you think she tells me all her plans, you haven't been paying attention."

Bad questions. Better to have asked about Ranthorn, or what lay in the other two rooms forbidden to Beau, or about what rare occasions caused Gwelain to visit the treasury. But Varek forced her onto the first stair, and she didn't dare speak where Corvin might be listening.

Her thoughts kept churning as he guided her out of the north wing and into more pleasant parts of the castle.

He said we can't do it without his help, which means he can see a way forward if he gets what he wants.

Which we can't give him, because he wants the heart destroyed.

But there has to be a path to our victory.

All attempts to reassure herself fell flat. She'd found the heart, but she'd lost the hope she'd carried with her when she'd begun the hunt.

But I didn't come here to fail. If—

Her thoughts vanished as they rounded a corner and found two of Gwelain's soldiers standing at the bridge that crossed the golden pond.

"Prince Varek," one said, and they both bowed slightly. "Your mother has returned. She's requested a private meeting in the throne room."

"Very well," he said, his voice taking on an imperious tone. "Let her know I found her guest wandering the palace and am escorting her back to her room. I'll meet with her shortly."

"Forgive me, my prince." The soldier on the left, who had caught Sorra snooping earlier, bowed deeper toward Varek but cast a sly glance at Sorra. "But it's not you the queen wishes to speak to."

CHAPTER FORTY-SIX

Sorra focused on placing one foot in front of the other as she approached the staircases outside the throne room, flanked by goblins.

She knows I broke the rules.

I'm not her chosen traitor. She set me up to fail. She's going to send me away so she can focus on Tullian.

A wave of dizziness passed over her as she considered what other punishment Gwelain might have in store.

I should hope *she only sends me away.*

She'd walked straight into it, confident in the idea that Gwelain needed her.

She'd made mistakes before, but not like this. It would be bearable if she'd been able to tell Beau or Tullian what she'd learned, but Gwelain would never allow it.

Her steps slowed, and one of the goblins gave her a hard shove. Sorra swallowed her nausea and forced herself onward.

A blade of sunlight cut across the carpet below as the tall doors across the rotunda cracked open. Voices followed, along with silhouettes that became solid forms as Sorra's eyes adjusted to the light—four humans, surrounded by armoured soldiers. A hulking goblin held a blond-haired man by the upper arm, which was lost in the monster's grip. The man tried to pull away, twisting to look at the woman and the two children behind him who were being herded along by the other soldiers.

The big goblin hauled the man forward, laughing when he stumbled.

Gwelain's voice filled Sorra's mind. *I'll want your magic at its strongest in the coming days.*

Souls to feed Corvin's magic.

We'll make an evening of it, bring in more humans, whip up anticipation and bloodlust.

The children wailed, clinging to the woman's skirt, tripping her. She reached down to touch them, but there was no comfort she could offer. Her eyes were wide, her cheeks tracked with tears, her mouth open in an expression of mingled fear and disbelief that made Sorra's heart lurch.

Sorra reached for her sword without thinking, then remembered she'd left it in her room. Still, she stepped forward, only to be jerked back when one of the goblins behind her grabbed her by both arms.

"Let me go!"

The goblin chuckled. "Why? You want to join them?"

A fresh chorus of laughter drowned out the children's cries as the woman fell. She tried to get up, but one of the soldiers shoved her with his foot, sending her back to the floor.

She looked to Sorra. "My lady, I beg you, help! Please!"

"Please, please!" the goblins echoed in a chorus of high-pitched mockery. In a moment they had her on her feet again, and before Sorra could find her voice, they'd hurried the family along toward the dungeons.

Warm tears tracked Sorra's cheeks, but she stopped fighting. There was no right way forward, no way to fight or to free those poor people, no way to ease their fear or the pain that surely awaited them.

No words or actions that would change the inevitable.

I'm helpless.

And that's exactly how Gwelain wants me to feel.

The fact that the humans' arrival had matched her approach to the throne room was no coincidence.

Sorra gritted her teeth. "Let me go. The queen is expecting me."

"By all means." The goblin released her, then stood aside and gestured toward the stairs.

Sorra tried not to think of the family. If Gwelain wanted her distracted and distraught, she would do her best to deny her the pleasure.

She reached the bottom and proceeded alone along the short passage to the throne room. The doors slammed behind her, and Sorra flinched.

Sunlight streamed in through the glass ceiling, giving the room an air of warmth and cheer that Sorra saw but couldn't feel, and she squinted against the brightness.

Gwelain stood at the centre of the room, still dressed in her hunting clothes, back straight, claws clasped gently before her.

"Come closer, my dear." The queen's voice was gentle but cold.

Sorra decided not to ask about the humans. Bait cast by a predator was best ignored.

Gwelain smiled. "You're looking better."

"I'm feeling better, Majesty, thank you." Sorra's voice held steady. "You're back earlier than I expected. I hope the hunt wasn't unpleasant."

"No, no, it was fine. A little dull, but that gave me time to think." Gwelain held one hand out, opened toward Sorra. "Come. It's time we spoke openly and honestly."

Sorra's belly cramped. "Come... where?"

Gwelain's smile widened as she turned to cross the room, headed for a door that blended almost seamlessly into the pale woodwork.

The door Beau's never been through. Sorra's heart hammered as Gwelain opened it and motioned for her to pass through.

The little room beyond contained a desk and a wooden stool—a clerk's office, perhaps, to be used for royal business. A large tapestry depicting a swarm of goblins tearing apart a unicorn covered most of the rear wall. The beast's mouth was frozen in a scream, its pearly coat streaked with blood.

Gwelain pushed the tapestry aside, revealing the entrance to a tunnel with a rough stone floor that descended steeply, curving away from the throne room.

"After you," Gwelain said.

Sorra didn't dare disobey, but with each step, she prayed this place wasn't forbidden to Beau because it was another path to the dungeons. She didn't hear any weeping ahead, but that was a small comfort.

"Did you find the statue gallery?" Gwelain's voice filled the tunnel.

"I did. It was interesting. Shame about the broken one."

Gwelain chuckled behind her, and the hairs on the back of Sorra's neck stood on end. "Yes, poor Linnea. Favourite of the king, coddled and spoiled, given these lands to rule over—one final insult to me from a king who couldn't let go of our past even when he was ready to let go of this world. But that's not what I wish to speak about."

The queen didn't say anything more as the tunnel carried them underground. The air grew thick and humid, and the gentle music of flowing water reached them from somewhere ahead.

A curtain of hanging vines blocked the tunnel. Gwelain stepped through, then held them back as she had the tapestry to allow Sorra to step into the cave beyond.

Rays of sunlight shone through an opening in the stone overhead, illuminating long stalactites that hung like jagged fangs and shorter stone formations that rose from the cave floor to mirror them. Mosses formed a lush green carpet speckled with clusters of tiny brown mushrooms, and ferns as high as Sorra's waist grew in thick clumps like miniature forests.

Sorra took a few steps toward the shallow creek that crossed the cave, awestruck, her fear momentarily forgotten. Her feet sank pleasantly into the moss.

"Like it?" Gwelain asked.

"It's wonderful."

Gwelain sighed. "As I expected." She approached a cluster of boulders near the water and sat on the tallest of them, her legs crossed at the ankles. She looked as regal there as she did on her throne, and every bit as imposing.

"Sit."

Sorra sat, clasping her hands on her lap to keep them from shaking.

"My goblins saw beauty in places like this, too," Gwelain said. "The old ones. The true ones. I tried to introduce them to real beauty and finer things, but they craved these wet, stinking, unrefined places." A glittering blue beetle landed on her knee, and she flicked it away. "I hated you, you know, when you first barged in to interfere with my business."

Sorra's chest tightened.

"I couldn't figure out what Beauregard saw in you," Gwelain continued. "So raw, so plain, so ugly in so many ways. I hated you for trying to steal what was mine. For the fact that he wanted you even when you offered so little. I wanted to kill you. Do you know why I didn't?"

"Because you knew Tullian wouldn't be the traitor you need?" Sorra asked, hoping that still held true.

"Very good." Gwelain lowered her voice like she was sharing a secret. "I hated that, too. Needing you. Any of you. The old heroes were so damned stubborn, and I'd begun to fear my plans would all be for nothing if I didn't have the traitor from Linnea's visions. But then you came along, an element of unexpected chaos."

Sorra winced. "That does seem to be my lot in life."

"But so much more than that!" Gwelain sounded pleased. Sorra didn't trust it but liked this conversational turn better than the threat of violence or banishment. "I despised you, but then I saw how I might use you. I could have forced it, you know. Tortured you into submission or done the same to Tullian until you gave in to stop his pain."

"Then why didn't you, Majesty?" Sorra wasn't sure she wanted to know, but asking felt like a foregone conclusion.

"Because you're meant for greatness, and I believe you're clever enough to choose it for yourself."

"Greatness?" Sorra's shoulders stiffened. "My birth blessing says otherwise."

"No." Gwelain pointed one claw at Sorra, her eyes flashing. "I understand that you've been manipulated into seeing it that way, but your upbringing blinded you to the truth. I wish to enlighten you, and to make you an offer. Hear me, consider it, and I promise I won't punish you for your adventures earlier today."

Sorra shifted uncomfortably. "Just listen?"

"Just listen."

Listening wasn't so bad. Gwelain hadn't ordered her to agree to anything, and there was nothing the queen could offer that would sway her from her quest or her intention to see Beau crowned without a goblin queen at his side. And the fact that Gwelain was rushing to make an offer was promising. She might make other mistakes in her desperate attempt to grab her victory before time ran out.

"All right. I'm listening."

Gwelain sat up straighter, more relaxed than she'd appeared before. "Why did you leave Andonia to come here? Were you not worried your blessing would make everything go wrong, or that you'd somehow make things worse for Beauregard if you tried to help him?"

"I did worry, Majesty. A little." There was no point lying yet. "My thinking was that I couldn't know whether the blessing or the arrow had brought me to Beau in the first place. It seemed like my blessing had a hand in everything going wrong, but I hoped there was more to it. That the blessing had won a battle in ruining Beau's plan, but the arrow might still win the war by leading me to a way free of it. I have two destinies now, the blessing or the arrow, one terrible and one great. I decided to believe in the one that gave me hope."

"How precious." Gwelain's eyes shone. "How perfectly logical a thought for you to have based on what you understood."

"I'm afraid I don't see anything precious about it, Majesty." Sorra tried not to sound irritated and failed. "My blessing has brought me nothing but misery, and nothing but harm to others. Is it amusing to you that I'd want to be free of it?"

"No." Every trace of humour vanished from Gwelain's expression and tone. "Your logic amuses me. Your conclusion angers me. Your blessing isn't what's brought such trouble to your life. Your misery was a gift from the people who fear it and you. I heard what you told Beauregard, how every part of your upbringing was designed to negate your potential and hobble you so you couldn't walk the path laid out for you."

Sorra looked away, watching the sunlight sparkling off the creek's burbling waters. "They were trying to protect me from myself, and themselves from me. My mistakes, my disasters, the chaos that follows me no matter how I try to avoid it... I never meant to hurt anyone."

"Never?"

Sorra rubbed her throat to loosen the tightness that gathered there. "Maybe once or twice, when my temper got the best of me."

"And did it feel good to cause trouble on your own terms?"

Sorra knew the right answer was 'no.' Spilling ink over a bully's artwork was petty revenge, not the righteous action of a hero against an enemy.

But Gwelain would guess it was a lie.

"Sometimes. When they deserved it."

Gwelain laid a hand over Sorra's. "Of course it did. You were allowing your true nature to shine through, and I suspect you accomplished what you intended without any of the obstacles you faced when you tried to be *good*." She wrinkled her nose. "Your blessing is a deadly sharp blade you've clutched tight in your hands to keep it from harming others, and all you've accomplished is making yourself bleed instead. If you embraced who and what you truly are, you'd have nothing to fear." She squeezed Sorra's hand tighter. "Do you see it? Your blessing is as true as your sisters', and your destiny is greater than any of theirs."

Sorra opened her mouth to argue, then stopped herself as the pieces clicked into place.

It took her a moment to find her voice. "*Great* doesn't have to mean *good*, does it? Not even for destinies."

Gwelain clapped her hands, delighted as a mother at her child's first steps. "There! I said you were clever. The blessing said you'd walk in shadow where your sisters walk in light, but why should that not lead to a glorious destiny? I myself am great and powerful, and I stand at the verge of claiming everything that was unfairly denied me, though I know your people wouldn't call me good. But,

Sorra, it is so good to be me. If your destiny were tied to mine, you would know what goodness is."

Sorra squeezed her eyes closed. It was hard to think straight when she looked into Gwelain's golden eyes.

"That's not goodness," she whispered. "Forgive me, Majesty, but I don't long for selfishness, or to harm others for the sake of my own glory."

When she looked up, Gwelain was still smiling, but there was pity in her eyes. "Do you not long for these things, or have you only been trained to deny yourself? Can you open your eyes to see how you've twisted yourself into something you were never meant to be, all for the sake of running from your gifts? I could offer you so much, Sorra, if you offered me the one thing I need. Wealth. Comfort. Freedom like you've never known. Power over those who have harmed you."

Sorra heard her, but her thoughts were trapped in the idea of a great and terrible destiny and how cleanly it solved the problem of conflicting fates. It all rang true at a deeper level, too.

It felt right when I hit back, or hit first.

Being good has always felt like trying not to breathe, but I was punished when I inhaled.

Gwelain wasn't wrong on any point. Sorra's aunt, her teachers, and most of Cottsbridge had feared and hated her from the moment they learned of her blessing, and they'd taught her to fear and hate herself. The thought kindled the anger that always seemed to burn low, deep inside her, and for a moment she imagined what it would be like to mend what her upbringing had tried to break, to have the kind of power everyone said was too dangerous for her to hold.

To repay those who had punished her for the crime of being born.

Gwelain smiled as though she could read Sorra's thoughts—or more likely, the shifting expressions she was doing a poor job of hiding. "They already fear and hate you, Sorra, and that won't change no matter how you try to warp yourself to please them. I'm simply offering you some benefit to sweeten things otherwise."

Sorra tried to ignore her.

If she's right, the arrow did show me a path to the great destiny I was born for. The story is already told, and all I have to do is embrace a gift I didn't ask for and play my part.

It felt true.

But not good.

Even if it was destiny, Tullian was right. She had a choice—the fact that Linnea had foreseen two potential outcomes only proved it.

Maybe that's the Mystery's role. I'm the rogue wind blowing through fate, one that even Linnea couldn't predict.

Tears burned her eyes.

So I can choose to fight my nature forever for the good of all, knowing there's no escape from my pain down that path. Or I can harm everyone I love for the sake of embracing my own greatest destiny.

She been wrong to think there could be no harm in listening. Knowledge could hurt more than the bite of a whip, especially when it placed freedom and ease just out of reach.

She wouldn't accept, no matter what else Gwelain offered to tempt her to her side. But she felt the blessing as she never had before, carving deep into her heart so it wouldn't harm anyone else.

Sorra steeled herself. "You say you'd offer me freedom, Majesty. You wouldn't wish to control me?"

Gwelain's laugh was like the creek, gentle and musical. "Of course I would! But I'd use you for your true purpose. You'd be a war horse charging across the field of battle instead of hobbled in a draughty barn or hitched to a grinding wheel for the rest of your life."

Sorra didn't answer but nodded for her to go on. Hearing her out was the only way to escape so she could try to forget this conversation had happened.

"I hated my old goblins at first," Gwelain said. "I made something of them, though, and later I used my knowledge of them to make something even better. When I create my beautiful monsters, I place a seed of darkness in their hearts, cold and sharp. As it grows, it frees them of their humanity." She brushed a claw against Sorra's cheek, and Sorra fought the urge to pull away from the gentle touch. "You already have so much of that in you—your stubbornness, your beautiful rage, your flashes of cold logic, your spite. You try to blunt all of it, but it shines through. Even your attempts at heroism only show off keen ambition. You fail only because your potential has always been misdirected. I see what you could be if you, too, were freed from your humanity."

Sorra sucked in a hard breath. "You want to make me one of your monsters?"

"Of course." Gwelain's fingers twitched with excitement. "Linnea's vision said the traitor would be my creature, and I intend to make it so in every possible way. It's an offer I only make to favoured humans. The best of them become my nobility. Others serve me as soldiers. None of them wish to return to what they were before."

An image rose in Sorra's memory—three bodies hanging over a blood-soaked yard, probably killed by humans but certainly left to rot by their own kind, one bearing a scar where its tail had been removed long before its death. Creatures who, perhaps, had regretted what they'd become and had tried to escape.

"That may be, Majesty," she said, as diplomatically as she could, "but I think you know what my answer has to be. No single destiny outweighs that of a nation, or those of the people I love. And—not wishing to offend—I have no desire to become a goblin."

"I thought you'd say that. You'd see things differently if you were free of your humanity and your unfortunate upbringing, but I can't change that yet. There is one more thing you might wish to consider, though." Gwelain flexed her claws, letting them gleam in the sunlight. "There is the matter of Beauregard."

Sorra's heart lurched. "What about him?"

"Well, you becoming a goblin would solve some issues there." Gwelain sighed and shrugged one shoulder. "Your humanity is part of what draws him to you. If you became something greater, something he finds repulsive, that would be one less reason for me to hate you. And one more reason for me to let him live."

The whisper of regret in her voice chilled Sorra. "Respectfully, Majesty, you can't kill him. You need him alive for his coronation. He's not king of Andonia yet."

"And you've seen how convincingly I can replace him."

"But he hasn't named you next in line if he dies. These things are signed in blood, aren't they?"

Gwelain turned her face to the sun. "You won't find an obstacle I haven't already planned to overcome. The truth is if I keep him alive, it won't be because I need him, but because he amuses me. His resistance is endearing, and every defeat he suffers is terribly satisfying. But I'm growing bored. And, more to the point, even if his father dies, I won't set foot in Andonia until the final piece is in place." She looked back at Sorra, her smile frozen. "You, little hero. Little traitor. If you refuse me, my plans will fail, and then what reason do I have to keep him alive? But if you were no longer a temptation to him, if he remains obedient for the sake of his people, and if my path to victory is assured, what reason would I have to kill him?"

Sorra's thoughts scattered like a flock of sparrows, and she tried to chase them down before they could fly away.

She would kill him. She doesn't know about the letter of abdication, and that might keep her off the throne... but what does it matter if Beau isn't there to take it instead?

I can't let him die.

But I also can't give her what she wants.

The space between *yes* and *no* was a tightrope, and Sorra doubted she'd be able to keep her balance for long. But Gwelain hadn't demanded an immediate decision, only a conversation.

Sorra swallowed the acid that rose in her throat.

"This is a difficult decision, Majesty. You've given me so much to think about. I feel duty bound to refuse you, but..." She paused. "Does the transformation hurt?"

"Terribly!" Gwelain grinned. "Or rather, it would if I didn't put them to sleep before magic broke their bodies to re-form them."

"I see. And would I be myself afterward?" Sorra held her breath, hoping Gwelain would read her questions as final objections and not a way of stalling.

"Unfortunately, yes. You'll sign a contract in blood, magically binding, which will include assurances that you won't harm me. I think you'll quickly lose that desire once you understand the gift I've given you, though."

"And would I have to eat human flesh?"

"Have to? No. But you'll be denying yourself a delicacy if you don't."

"Oh."

Gwelain's lips twitched, hinting at a smile. Sorra hoped that meant she saw hesitation, and therefore possibility.

"I know it's hard to see things in a new light so quickly." Gwelain stood, and Sorra walked beside her toward the cave's entrance, eager to end the conversation and leave the queen's presence. "You'd see it all instantly if I could change you now—the world would be wonderfully and beautifully different, and in time you'd learn to let go of old ideas. But choice must come before change if we wish to do this the civilized way. You'll have time to think this evening. Supper will be waiting in your room. We're having a party tonight that our human guests will not be invited to attend."

Sorra had managed not to think of the prisoners, but their cries came back now, and the desperate helplessness she'd felt as she'd watched the soldiers dragging them away.

An entire family to feed Corvin's terrible magic.

She tried not to wonder whether children made better victims.

"Thank you, Majesty," she murmured, afraid her voice would break if she spoke louder.

The walk back seemed shorter than the trek down the tunnel, and they reached the door to the throne room sooner than Sorra expected. The sky above the glass ceiling was a dazzling display of sunset orange.

"Think carefully," Gwelain said. "And don't take too long. I will have my victory. You can stand at my side when that moment comes, or you can waste yourself trying to stop me."

"Thank you, Majesty," Sorra said again, unable to think of anything else. She tried to keep her steps unhurried as she walked across the throne room.

"Oh, Sorra?"

Gwelain's voice hooked into her, drawing her back when all she wanted was to flee. "Majesty?"

"I almost forgot. We returned early from the hunt because your friend Tullian had a mishap. He's alive, but a little worse for wear. He'll be resting in his room for a while, the poor creature."

Icy claws gripped Sorra's heart as she pictured Tullian on his deathbed, brought down not by Gwelain's orders, but by his own proposed hunt.

Sorra didn't try to think of an answer, and for the first time since her arrival at the castle, she allowed herself to run from the goblin queen.

CHAPTER FORTY-SEVEN

The tower stairwell echoed with the slap of Sorra's boots and her ragged breathing. Tullian's door stood open at the top, and she burst in, prepared for the worst.

The bed was empty, its blankets pulled tight and tucked in sharply at the corners.

Someone cleared their throat behind her, and Sorra spun, reaching again for a sword that wasn't there. Beau held her door open, silently motioning her closer.

His presence would have offered comfort if not for the bloodstains on the arm of his shirt. He caught her looking as he eased the door almost closed behind her.

"Not mine," he whispered, and nodded toward her bed.

Tullian lay against her pillows, dark circles haunting the skin beneath his half-closed eyes, looking older than he ever had before. His right sleeve had been cut away, and a bloodstained bandage circled his arm from wrist to shoulder.

He raised his left hand, beckoning, and Sorra hurried closer, her breath trapped in her throat. She took his left hand in both of hers as she sat. His skin was cold, but he appeared thankfully whole aside from the injuries to his arm.

"What happened?"

"Damned wolves," Tullian muttered.

"Tullian took down the golden stag," Beau said. "He'd just ended its suffering when the wolves attacked. We fought them off, but he was injured."

"Obviously." Tullian shifted, settling deeper into the pillows.

Sorra looked to Beau. "Do you think Gwelain planned this?"

"She can't risk killing me by her hand or her influence," Tullian said, slurring his words a little. "Not her plan, but she certainly took advantage. Bandaged me up and insisted I take something to dull the pain." He scowled. "Made me dizzy. I wouldn't have made it up the tower stairs without the prince's help. Do stop petting me, Sorra. I'm quite all right."

Sorra released his hand, which she'd been stroking like a wounded sparrow without realizing she was doing it.

Beau pulled one of the armchairs closer and sat. "Did you find anything while we were gone?"

"Too much. I'm not sure where to begin."

"At the beginning, perhaps." Tullian sounded like he had when he was drunk, though a little gentler. "But quickly."

"Right." Sorra tried to gather her thoughts, but it felt like a lifetime had passed since they'd last spoken. "I found Linnea's heart in the north tower."

Tullian's bleary gaze sharpened. "And?"

"And it's in a golden cage only Gwelain can open. Varek was there. He warned me off, but I convinced him to answer a few questions." Sorra caught the disgust in the twist of Tullian's lip and continued before he could interrupt. "He was… not openly helpful, but I think as honest as he could be. He has plenty of reasons to want Gwelain to lose the heart, and he's taking huge risks to try to balance the odds. He doesn't see how we can defeat her without his help, but he doesn't want to see the heart in human hands. He wants it destroyed."

"Then he's no use to us." Tullian spoke firmly. "There is no room to negotiate on that."

"But he was helpful today, and if Gwelain's curse holds, he was truthful."

"What did he say?" Beau asked.

"That the heart isn't usually guarded, but that there's an enchanted barrier Gwelain can raise and lower to close the tower off when she's in there, and she usually takes Corvin with her as extra protection. The reason she needs to take precautions is that she's powerless when she's in the heart's presence. It won't let her draw from its magic when she's in that room, and her own has atrophied or been destroyed by Linnea's."

"An easy place to threaten her with harm, then," Tullian said.

"If she ever went in there." Sorra's fingers plucked at the hem of her tunic. "She would if she needed to move the heart to Ember-cliffe—she'd have to if she's the only one who can open that cage. But she'll only do that when it's time for Beau's coronation, and only if she has her traitor. But if we could get her in there without Corvin or her guards…"

"Not by physical force," Beau said. "She's too strong when she has Linnea's magic."

"No. But maybe that's how Varek thinks he could help us. I wonder whether we could work something out with him, whether maybe he's the Magic. We can't destroy the heart, but if Andonia's future king promised it would never be used against him…" She trailed off as the thought met its unfortunate end. "But he says he can't trust human promises. There has to be a way, though."

Beau tapped his fingers against the arm of his chair, obviously considering something. "We might not need him."

"He said we needed him," Sorra said. "And he was telling the truth. Not one painful boil."

Beau seemed unfazed. "You said he doesn't see how we can do it without him. Were those his exact words?"

Sorra struggled to remember. "Yes."

"Then he was telling the truth about his belief, but that doesn't make his belief true. There could be something he's not seeing."

"Like the missing visions!" Sorra sat up straighter as a bolt of excitement shot through her. "I asked about that, too—Gwelain hasn't told him about them, or her plans. Maybe the only reason he can't see our way forward is that he doesn't know about some missing piece."

She still liked the idea of Varek being the Magic, of having another misfit on the team to balance out the proper heroes she was currently speaking with. But maybe he'd played his role already in protecting this room and offering information, or his role would become clear once they'd found their own path forward.

Tullian listed to one side and pushed himself upright, waving Beau off when he reached out to help. "Gwelain isn't likely to reveal anything to us about those missing pieces, but there's another thing we need to consider. Remember, Linnea said Corvin was the key to Gwelain's rise and her fall. It could be that we're meant to win him over somehow, making *him* the Magic."

Beau grimaced. "You might not think so if you'd spent more time with him."

"Very well. But perhaps he holds her secrets and is the key to us learning about the rest of the visions, or some other information that would show us our way forward. Or we're meant to destroy him, leaving her without her mage when she's powerless in the heart's presence."

Sorra shivered. If the visions and their quest were a puzzle, it would feel like the picture was beginning to take shape. But too much was still missing.

"He'd be easier to kill than Gwelain would," she said. "Varek talked about that, too—I don't think he'd shed a tear if it happened. Corvin uses blood magic, which means he can't keep it in his body. It's all in an external vessel of some kind."

"His amulet," Beau said. "No question. He once had a servant killed for spilling wine on it—it's fragile, it's valuable, and I'd guess the only time he takes it off is when he has his pre-sunrise bath every night."

Tullian nodded. His chin rested on his chest for a moment, and it seemed to take immense effort for him to lift it again. "Every night?"

"Better than clockwork. Or, if you think he's the key because of information we need," Beau continued, "we might find it in the central tower. I thought the heart would be there because it's the most secure location in the castle, but maybe there's something more valuable there—something that could ruin Gwelain's plans if we found it."

"The missing visions," Sorra whispered.

Beau nodded. "My point is, Corvin goes in there a lot, I've never been allowed to, it's very well protected… What we're dancing around here, ultimately, is that you need to get into the royal apartments. If it's to kill Corvin, there are servants' passages in the walls that open into each room, including the one where he bathes and his bedroom—everything is laid out in a circle around the tower. If you want to find out what's in the central tower…" He frowned. "That's a bit trickier, but not impossible. But you can't get into either without me. And if I'm caught…"

"You won't be," Sorra said. "Not if we do it now. They've brought in a family of humans to feed Corvin's blood magic. It's going to be a big event—we're to be shut in our rooms so they can enjoy their evening. Corvin will be distracted and won't know what we're up to. We could get into the tower, see what Gwelain is hiding, and then decide whether to leave you lurking behind the walls, Tullian, if you decide killing him is the best— Tullian?"

His chin rested on his chest again, and his next breath came as a deep snore. Sorra gave his left arm a hard shake. "Tullian!"

He snorted and raised his head. "I'm listening. This would, indeed, be a perfect opportunity. If we can know things, or break the mage's… thing…" He pushed himself out of the bed and, in the same motion, collapsed into Beau's arms. Tullian grumbled as he allowed himself to be placed back on the bed. "I'm beginning to believe we're cursed beyond Gwelain's intentions," he said, somewhat indistinctly. "She couldn't have set the wolves on me, yet it happened, and just in time for her to muddle my mind and weaken my body when we need them most. Everything that goes right is really going wrong."

Sorra exchanged a glance with Beau. He gave nothing away, but she guessed he, too, was thinking of her blessing.

Your blessing is a deadly sharp blade you've clutched tight in your hands to keep it from harming others, and all you've accomplished is making yourself bleed instead.

Maybe Gwelain was right, but guilt was useless now. If giving in wasn't an option, the only thing to do was to keep moving forward. No obstacle could be worse than the prospect of embracing her greatest and darkest destiny.

"We'll get through this," she said, for her own sake as much as for Beau's or Tullian's.

"We will," Tullian muttered. "Linnea promised us the prospect of victory, and we shall seek it as soon as I'm on my feet. Perhaps that's for the best. This *appears* to be a perfect opportunity, but it may only be another chance for Gwelain to gain an advantage if we act rashly—a trap to tempt Beauregard into breaking his father's treaty, perhaps, freeing her to resume her violence when she doesn't get her traitor."

Beau nodded, then looked away.

Sorra gaped at Tullian. "Gwelain won't respect the treaty for any longer than it serves her. Surely Beau acting against her now is a worthwhile risk."

"Risks must be calculated," Tullian said, and yawned. "Even if we do nothing, we hold the power to deny Gwelain her victory. If we act, it must be with the certainty that we're not shifting the odds further in her favour. The path to victory will be made clear. Until then, we must remain humble, obedient to the... the visions will show when..." He yawned again. "In time, that is."

"We don't *have* time." Sorra took Tullian's hand again, this time to hold his attention. "I saw Gwelain after you returned from the hunt, and she made me an offer. She wants her traitor, and she wants me. Now. If she's rushing, we can't afford not to. Beau and I can go without you and figure things out."

Tullian gripped her hand tight. "And what did she offer you in return?"

"Power. Position. I refused her, of course, but—"

"Then Andonia is safe." Tullian made himself more comfortable. "As long as she doesn't get her traitor, her plans are worthless."

"But Beau will die if she doesn't get what she wants."

Tullian closed his eyes. "As we all must be willing to do for the sake of Linnea and Andonia. Beau knows this as well as I always have. Let me rest my eyes for a few minutes before we... hmm."

His snores filled the room.

Sorra resisted the urge to shake him awake again. He was right. He was no good to them in this state, and rest would do him good.

But waiting was out of the question.

She looked to Beau, who seemed unshaken by the threat against his life. "What does he mean, you're willing to die? What were you talking about before I came in?"

Beau's hands curled into fists on his lap, but he spoke without emotion. "Many things. The treaty, my duty, the sealed letter I left behind in Embercliffe, and how he can see it all tying into Linnea's vision of victory. He holds some strange views but has some plausible—"

"And your death?" Sorra prompted. Tullian's ability to twist any new information to fit within the scope of Linnea's visions was the last thing she wished to discuss.

"The odds of me surviving have never been good. For now, Gwelain believes she needs me alive to take the crown and to sign the order naming her as my successor in my blood. She won't kill me until that's done."

"She didn't seem concerned about any of that," Sorra said.

"It doesn't matter anyway." Beau took a long, slow breath. "Once my letter of abdication is opened, her plans will fall apart. I'll no longer be king, and she'll no longer be queen, and she'll kill me. My hope is that it will happen only after we've returned to Andonia, and that the magic-enforced consequences of her breaking the treaty by harming me will leave her vulnerable."

"And what? Your father's assassins kill her and destroy Linnea's heart in the process?"

Beau paled. "Tullian expects otherwise, according to the visions. But I can't know my father's plans."

"No, you can't." Sorra's voice dropped to a rasping whisper. "Because he sent you here as a sacrifice, with no way of knowing whether it's going to matter, with nothing but orders to *do nothing* for the sake of a treaty Gwelain only respects for as long as she can use it to take the throne. He threw you away to buy himself time, and now he's going to die and leave you to face the consequences of his inaction."

Beau flinched, and his gaze hardened. Sorra felt no urge to apologize for insulting his father.

"You matter." Tears burned her eyes, and she wiped them away. "You might be willing to die to keep Gwelain off the throne, but that's not good enough for me. I intend to claim the victory Linnea said was possible, or to take it anyway even if none of this was what she saw in her visions. You said your destiny was tied to mine, and I'm choosing a destiny where you live. Where you fight for yourself even if your father said not to, even if Tullian says not to. Where you forget about duty and decide what you want and take it."

His expression had softened as she spoke, and now his lips twitched in a smile. Sorra's cheeks warmed. "Did I say something amusing?"

"No." Beau stood. "You're absolutely right."

Before she realized it was happening, his arms were around her, his lips on hers. Sorra gasped and closed her eyes, letting herself fall into him. Her tongue brushed his lips, and her hands found their way to his arms, then his shoulders.

He pulled away, slowly and reluctantly, but let his lips hover a breath away from Sorra's.

"That's not what I meant," she whispered.

"I know." He rested his forehead against hers. "But if we're taking risks, that seemed like a good place to start."

She reached up to touch his face. "Does that mean you'll help me? Tonight?"

"I will. I believe your destiny is to save Andonia. If helping you means risking my father's plans..." He tensed. "Tullian believes I need to preserve the treaty so Gwelain's plans as we understand them don't change, but I've been idle for long enough. If my choice is between the promise I made to my father or following the course of action I believe is right, I will act. I only hope I'm not risking Andonia's safety out of my selfish desire for survival."

"It's not selfish. You won't get caught. And once Gwelain is defeated, there will be no need for a treaty, letters of abdication, or any plans your father has made."

Beau dipped his head and kissed her throat, then her earlobe. Warm, aching pleasure flowed through Sorra's body.

"We'll go now," he whispered. "I think I can get you into the central tower. When Tullian wakes we'll be ready to plan our next steps."

His breath made her shiver. "I swear we'll be careful. Get me in and I'll take care of the rest. You can open the doors and wait for me in your room, where you're supposed to be."

He stepped back, a faint smile on his lips. "Quiet, now. Corvin may be distracted, but we can't risk him hearing us."

Sorra found her sword and put it in its place at her side, then eased the door almost closed behind her, not wanting to be locked out. Beau led the way down the tower stairs.

It wasn't how she might have imagined him sneaking her into his room, but this was better than nothing.

CHAPTER FORTY-EIGHT

Silence filled the castle like a living, breathing entity. The sun had long since set and the goblins should have been roaming the halls, feasting and dancing and doing whatever else their hearts desired, but it seemed they'd all chosen to attend whatever gruesome festivities Gwelain had planned for the evening.

No humans roamed the castle, either, perhaps having been locked away as Sorra should have been or knowing better than to be about on a night when blood would scent the air. The lamps on the walls were turned low, offering the light of an overcast evening, making the entire building feel as dull and abandoned as the north wing.

Voices pierced the silence as Sorra and Beau approached the theatre. Its doors were all closed, but shouting and shrieking and laughter penetrated the thick wooden panels, and beneath them drifted music so cheerful and bouncy it would have been at home on a fairground. It made Sorra's stomach turn, knowing as she did what sorts of games the goblins might be enjoying with their human guests.

The voices fell silent, leaving an auditory vacancy that was quickly filled by a chorus of screams, which were in turn drowned out by more shrieks and jeers.

Sorra's feet grew heavy, and she stopped walking just past the door to Gwelain's box. Would the queen be there now, smiling as she watched her monsters delighting in suffering that would feed Corvin's magic? Or would she prefer to stand on the stage, basking in the blood spatter, intoxicated on suffering?

Beau brushed a hand against her arm, drawing her attention. He looked as distressed as Sorra felt, as though the screams were tearing him apart as they were her. But he shook his head and continued down the corridor, leaving Sorra to drag her feet onward.

He was right, of course. There was nothing the two of them could do against dozens of goblins. Even if they could sneak into Gwelain's box, she'd have her magic to protect her, and Corvin's if hers should fail. She'd be surrounded by guards, too, with swords that could harm as easily as any spell. A prince and an apprentice hero could use Gwelain's and Corvin's distraction to make the humans' deaths mean something, but not by throwing their own lots in with them.

It hurt to tear herself away, though. She wasn't sure Tullian would have chosen differently, but it felt cowardly and painfully unheroic to turn her back on such suffering.

To end more, she reminded herself. If this was what life under Gwelain's rule looked like here, it wouldn't be better for the people of Andonia when their time came. And if Varek was right, Gwelain would be unstoppable, her power protected forever once she'd permanently caged the heart in Embercliffe, her cruelty only limited by her imagination as she found new ways to amuse herself and her dark-hearted nobles.

A worn-out knight, a common girl with shadows in her soul, and a prince whose hands were bound against doing harm to their enemy seemed unlikely to fix anything, but they were all that was left.

So she walked away, leaving four people to face their deaths and the destruction of their souls, and added them to the list of crimes she'd make Gwelain pay for.

Beau led Sorra up a wide, sweeping staircase she hadn't discovered on her previous explorations. It ended at a smaller version of the castle's main doors, though the gemstones here were pale green and the silver scrollwork was dotted with needle-like protrusions.

Beau pressed his finger to one, hard enough to break his skin and leave a bright drop of blood behind.

He pulled Sorra close as the doors swung open, holding her tight against him as they stepped through and the doors closed behind them.

Walls of smooth, pale wood curved away in both directions, unadorned with tapestries or paintings, forming the hallway encircling the base of the tower. The floors were warm oak, glowing in the clear twilight illumination.

Beau paused, listening, then followed the hallway to the left. Several doors were set into the outer wall, but between them there was still no decoration, no obvious displays of wealth.

Of course not, Sorra thought. *There's no one here she needs to impress.*

Beau opened one of the doors and held it for Sorra to enter the dark room beyond. He moved confidently into the shadows, and as the door closed, a match flared to life, followed by a lamp that sat on a table next to a large bed. Not a sunlight lamp, but plain oil, no different from the ones Sorra used at home.

Beau caught her watching its flame. "I don't like magic in here," he said. "It's the only room in this damned castle that feels like it's my own."

"You said once that these rooms were protected," she said. "Can we speak?"

"Quietly." Beau stepped past her and touched the symbol carved into the door—not identical to the one on the floor of her room, but nearly. "Gwelain rebuilt this castle from the ruins of an old one her grandfather used as one of his retreats. For when he tired of the overwhelming beauty of his other homes, I suppose. His magic was strong enough that it still has some effect even now. Every room in this part of the castle has its own protections. They're old and imperfect, but it takes some effort for Corvin to hear anything from outside."

"How do you know?"

Beau flashed her a mischievous smile, and for a moment he seemed like someone else entirely—perhaps the man he'd be if he didn't have the fate of a nation resting on his shoulders. "Years of experimentation. As I've said, life here hasn't always been terribly exciting. One finds ways to fill the hours." His smile faded to a wistful shadow. "It makes me miss my brothers and regret not knowing them better. The youngest was only a child when I left but already an expert at causing trouble. He'd have pushed every boundary and probably figured out how to pick every non-magical lock in this place. It took me far longer to figure out how to use trouble to my advantage, learning what I could and couldn't do without being noticed."

Sorra pressed a hand to her chest and gasped dramatically. "Prince Beauregard, did you just admit that someone so irresponsible and troublesome could have managed things better than you?"

He laughed under his breath. "Maybe that's why I thought there was hope for you."

"Once you got over your initial disappointment in me, of course."

His smile broadened. "Naturally."

In another life, in another place, it would have been a perfect moment. Not sappy declarations of love, but the kind of easy openness she'd wished for at the cabin, a hint of the depths of a personality he'd buried under a lifetime of responsibility and a decade of denying his true self. A glimpse of someone she might have let herself trust and love fully if they'd been ordinary people living unremarkable lives.

"Well." She looked around, taking in the mahogany furniture, the papers scattered over the round table at the centre of the room, the cold fireplace in the corner, the narrow door in the far wall—anything to keep from looking at him and seeing the warmth in his gaze. "What's next, then?"

He pulled a dagger from beneath his mattress and hid it in his boot. "Now I try to get us into that tower. With any luck, we'll find a detailed outline of Gwelain's master plan and a diagram picturing a terrible weakness we've overlooked."

"And you said you didn't dare hope."

Beau flashed a quick, nervous smile. "I really don't know what's in there. We might not find out at all. The door isn't just locked—it's guarded. Let's hope we're not the only ones willing to take a risk tonight. Quiet, now. We don't want to alert the servants."

Before Sorra could ask more, he crossed the room and stepped into the hall.

"The entrance to the central room is just ahead," he whispered as they passed another door in the outer wall. His steps slowed, then stopped. "You can wait here if you like. The door isn't dangerous, but it's guarded by... well, it can be disturbing."

Sorra watched as he disappeared around the curve. His voice came back, barely audible, his words indistinct.

Her curiosity quickly got the better of her. As she rounded the curve and approached Beau's low, gentle voice, she spotted a shelf jutting from the outer wall. Something made of gold sat on it, a single display of wealth in the otherwise barren space. Sorra squinted.

Not wealth at all, but a glass jar of honey with a long-handled wooden spoon resting in it.

Questions about the honey faded as she turned to Beau, who had fallen silent.

An arch of darker wood outlining a closed door broke the expanse of pale wood opposite the shelf. The door leading into the tower had been carved with the life-sized image of a naked woman, her limbs horribly twisted and broken, her mouth gaping unnaturally.

It was a horrible thing, yet beautiful in a way that amplified Sorra's discomfort and disgust. The carving was a perfect portrait of hopelessness and suffering that could only have been created by an artist who found beauty in pain.

Beau's warning had been a kindness, and Sorra wished she'd denied her curiosity, just this once.

The carving moved, turning to cast its blank gaze on Sorra.

Sorra gasped and stepped back, her body jerking involuntarily, her heart hammering. The surface of the wood moved as smoothly as water but creaked gently as the image shifted again, tilting its grotesque head to one side.

Beau glanced at Sorra, then turned back to the door. "This is Sorra. She's with me, for the same purpose."

The wood moved again as the carved chest rose and fell in a quick, silent sob and the face turned away.

"I know," Beau said. "I understand. I wouldn't ask if it weren't the only way."

The carving didn't move again.

"Beau?" Sorra's voice had gone, and the question came out as an airy whisper.

He held out a hand, letting it hover close to the surface of the wood. "She's afraid," he said, speaking to Sorra but watching the carving. "She has good reason to be. She already suffers, but there's always some way they can make it worse."

Sorra studied the carving. This image was more clearly human, its movements more obvious, but the essential similarity to the tree that had once been Tullian's friend Selim was undeniable.

"Who is she?"

"I don't know." Beau's hand dropped to his side. "She's been here longer than I have. Someone who displeased Gwelain enough that death was too merciful a punishment, I suppose. She's trapped here, able to crave sweetness she'll never taste again." He nodded to the honey on the shelf across the hall, visible but out of reach. A tiny cruelty, but it spoke of everything the poor creature lacked. "She suffers pain and humiliation, aware of the passage of time, fearing whatever they've threatened will happen if she opens to allow anyone but Gwelain's trusted few into this room."

Sorra cleared her throat and found a scrap of her voice. "Gwelain told you this?"

"She did, when she ordered me never to acknowledge this poor soul who's not meant to hear a kind word."

The face turned slowly back toward them.

"Do you speak to her often?" Sorra asked, though she suspected she already knew the answer.

"Only at times like this, when the people who would punish me for it are occupied with important matters outside these walls. At first, I used it as a way to test the old king's protections—a disobedience Gwelain would correct if she knew about it, but not an act against her that would break our agreement. It's become more than that over the years, though. A secret bit of defiance. And, I hope, a small comfort for this poor soul, even if there's nothing else I can do."

The carving's eyes closed tight, the wood beneath them darkening as droplets of water formed on its surface.

Something screamed in Sorra. Beau had called the door disturbing, but it was more than that. Anger and despair battled within her at this vision of suffering no one could possibly have deserved, and at the unbearable weight of the creature's helplessness against the power of the queen's cruelty.

A fine way to guard the tower, though. No matter how terrible this soul's suffering, it might always be made worse. A direct threat might persuade her to open, or willingness to take an axe and destroy what had already been so grievously harmed. But no hero would do any such thing.

So what does a hero do?

Sorra stepped closer to the door, trying to erase the dread she felt, even knowing this was no monster.

"Is there anything in that room that would help us take back Linnea's heart?" she asked. "Information, plans, anything at all we might use to break her magic?"

The carving—*the person*, Sorra reminded herself—opened her blank eyes and nodded. Her mouth moved, but there was no sound and no way to interpret what words her slack lips might be trying to form.

"Is anyone up there now? Are there traps or protections beyond yours?"

The woman shook her head slowly, then froze in place, looking at Beau.

Sorra held her breath, waiting for the Mind to play the cards he'd been storing up his sleeve over years of building trust. If he promised the spirit would be set free once they'd seen whatever was hidden in the tower, if he guaranteed no harm would come to her, she would believe him. It was a lie, but one that might save them all.

"We hope your assistance will lead to Gwelain's downfall and your freedom, but I can't promise you anything," he said, and Sorra's stomach sank. "If you let us in, we'll try to make sure no one finds out, and we'll do everything we can to see those responsible for this punished. But I know the consequences could be terrible if we fail, and I leave it to you to decide whether you want to risk it."

The trapped soul tried to speak again, then hung her head. The wood smoothed, drawing her into it, and the door swung inward. Sorra stepped through, onto the spiral staircase beyond, but Beau hung back.

"Thank you," he whispered, and pressed a hand against the door.

Shame twisted Sorra's stomach into knots.

He's the kind of hero Tullian was looking for, she thought. Goodness and playing by the rules had their drawbacks, as Tullian had proved. But there was merit there, too.

Beau passed Sorra, heading up the stairs as the door closed behind them.

"Wait." Sorra grabbed the hem of his shirt and tugged until he turned to face her. "Go back to your room."

She kept her voice quiet, though the door had said there was no one above who might be listening.

There was little light in the stairwell save for a dim glow from above, but Sorra caught Beau's frown. "Absolutely not."

She pushed past him and stood on a higher step. "You've done your part. There's no sense risking you getting caught here or getting hurt if there's trouble. You're too important."

The furrows on his brow deepened. "So are you."

"No." Sorra took a deep breath. "Do you know how stupid your father is?"

"What?"

She gestured past him, toward the door. "You gave her an honest choice. You didn't threaten to find an axe and force your way through, you didn't exaggerate our odds of victory to convince her to help us, you didn't demand this as owed to you for past kindness. You made it acceptable for her to refuse."

"And she probably should have, but she deserved the choice." He spoke without hesitation. "Gwelain has taken everything from that poor soul but her ability to judge and choose. Manipulating her in those ways would have robbed her of the only power she has and made me no better than anyone else who uses her."

"So you were kind to her when it didn't benefit you, and you didn't use that kindness to manipulate her when you needed it returned," Sorra said. "And not because of some code of honour or set of rules, but because you judged it to be right."

Beau sighed. "And that makes me a fool, I suppose?"

"No. It makes you the king Andonia deserves, and your father's a stupid horse's ass for not fighting harder to see it happen. You need to make it home alive before your father dies, which means not getting caught here." She rested a hand on her sword's hilt. "I'll be fine."

"Of course you will. I'm going to see to it myself. Andonia needs good kings, but it also needs true heroes." His tone didn't invite argument.

Sorra's heart fluttered. She tried to ignore it but felt her resolve softening.

"Fine," she sighed. "But I'm going first."

"And I'll be right behind you."

Sorra tried not to smile as she turned away. She meant what she'd said, but it eased her mind to have him at her back as she climbed the stairs, telling herself she was ready to face whatever they might find above.

CHAPTER FORTY-NINE

A stair creaked beneath Sorra's boot halfway up the long climb. She paused, listened, then continued upward.

The stairs opened directly into a windowless room lit by the flickering glow of a hundred candles someone had left burning without concern over setting the room's contents ablaze. As Sorra stood at the top of the stairs taking it all in, she wished it had burned before she'd had a chance to set eyes on any of it.

The room didn't seem to have a single defined purpose. It was a study, perhaps, given the big wooden desk covered in books and papers. And it was a mage's workroom, its shelves packed with jars, bowls, knives, bottles, and books.

And it was a museum of horrors.

The armchair to the left of the stairs was upholstered in a patchwork of mismatched leathers in varying shades of brown and cream. Acid rose in Sorra's throat as she recognized how they reflected the palette of human complexions, and she turned away.

The jars on the shelves held dried herbs, but also stranger items —frog's eggs with tiny tadpoles squirming within, live beetles attempting to climb the glass to escape, strange purple berries that pulsed with something like a heartbeat.

A tongue preserved in clear liquid, twisting and squirming.

Eyes, brown and blue and green, staring blankly in every direction from within their glass housing.

A desiccated human hand, barely more than bone wrapped in leathery skin.

Everywhere she turned, Sorra found a new source of discomfort, a new urge to run and pretend she'd never come, but she forced herself to take a step into the room.

This was Corvin's place, but also Gwelain's. Anything might be important.

The scents of smoke and melting tallow hung heavy in the air, thick enough that Sorra thought she might choke as she turned.

Her chest tightened, stealing her breath as she found the wall behind the stairs covered by a gallery of human faces—or rather, the skin that had once covered them, cut free and stretched flat, attached by black thread to golden frames. The spaces where their eyes should have been stared blankly back at her.

She looked away, but the image was burned into her mind.

Beau took a sharp breath behind her as he reached the top of the stairs.

"Come on," he whispered, and walked toward the desk. "We already know what Corvin is."

Sorra couldn't keep herself from examining the workbench on her way across the room, though. She didn't dare touch anything, but the sight of bloodstained wooden bowls and rusted knives was enough.

She'd known, but she hadn't truly understood what it meant for someone to use blood magic. A person who could cause pain and suffering, who could kill for the sake of power, wasn't just selfish or evil. It had to be more than that. He couldn't possibly think of himself as human and still revel in their misery.

Gwelain hadn't made Corvin into one of her little pets, but he had become a monster all the same.

Beau picked up a sheaf of papers from the desk and shuffled through them, then set them aside and opened one of the books. Sorra tried to read as he turned the pages, but everything was written in the old language.

"Anything useful?"

"Not to us. Spells, notes…" He gestured to the loose papers. "Lists of ingredients to locate."

Sorra decided not to ask for details.

"There has to be something." She stepped back and spotted a trunk under the desk, black with dark iron fittings. "What about in there?"

Beau crouched and dragged the trunk out. Its surface was covered in short hair like horse's hide. There was no lock. Sorra supposed one wasn't necessary when the object in question was already in a room guarded by a tortured soul set within the most secure part of a nearly inaccessible castle.

The chest contained hundreds of sheets of paper written in that strange language, each of them signed in brown ink in a variety of hands.

As he read one over, Beau paled. He read the next, frowning, then picked up several more and skimmed over them, holding them closer to the candles that burned on the desk as he examined the signatures.

"Contracts," he said, his voice tight. "Agreements signed by those Gwelain has turned into her goblins, mostly, though there are others. Signed in blood, magically bound."

"And?"

"And they're not the sort of thing anyone would sign. Ever." He held one out, though the words meant nothing to her. "They agree to the change, but also to terrible consequences if they ever betray her, death being the most merciful. Even after death they agree that their souls will be Gwelain's to control. If they die within the bounds of her grace—her phrasing—they'll remain to serve her, whatever that means. If not, their spirits will be consumed to feed the magic of whoever she consigns them to." He looked through the papers again, shaking his head. "They've signed over the families they've left behind for immediate consumption, and in some cases, they've agreed to have their human memories stolen to make them entirely new creatures. It doesn't make sense."

"Gwelain said her goblins were people who had pleased her and proven their loyalty. If—"

The sound of footsteps thundering up the stairs silenced her. There was no time to close the chest or hide before Varek reached the top, breathing hard, his teeth bared.

Beau drew his dagger, but Sorra stopped short of freeing her sword from its sheath.

"What are you doing here?" Varek demanded.

Sorra stood as tall as she could. "What we can on our own, since you won't help us. We need information if we want to make plans. Isn't that what you want us to do?"

Varek stared at her, eyes wide with disbelief. "You're more foolish than I realized. If you're caught here, you'll ruin everything for all of us. What did you hope to find? A diary outlining her secret weaknesses? A magical sword that will cut through the bars of the heart's cage? And you." He turned the same look on Beau. "I thought you were dull, but not entirely stupid."

Beau held the contracts out to Varek, untroubled by his anger. "Explain these."

Varek snatched them from Beau's hand, his claws wrinkling the pages. "Contracts. They have no bearing on the quest you've gotten yourself wrapped up in. Leave them. You need to go before the others get back."

"Are the festivities over?" There was an edge to Beau's voice Sorra wasn't accustomed to.

"They will be soon." Varek dropped the contracts into the trunk and slammed it shut, then shoved it back under the desk with one foot. The trunk scraped over the floor, setting Sorra's teeth on edge. "If you're caught here, I can't lie for you. Leave. Now."

Sorra didn't move. Neither did Beau.

"Is there anything in this room that would be useful to us?" Beau asked. "The missing visions, her plans for Andonia. Anything?"

"No." Varek spoke through clenched teeth. "Not much of interest unless you're curious about the intricacies of blood magic or old paperwork."

Beau glanced toward the black trunk, now hidden under the desk. "I am curious about those, actually. How did she make anyone sign them?"

"Is the answer worth wasting your lives or freedom over?"

"I think it might be. Especially if you don't want to tell me."

Varek's claws balled into fists at his sides, then relaxed. "It's nothing to me, unless you waste so much time that we're caught here."

Sorra touched Beau's arm. "He's trying to help us."

"Then he can answer quickly."

Sorra frowned, but Beau didn't seem to notice. The change in him was strange. He'd been so kind to the soul trapped in the doorway but was unable or unwilling to offer basic courtesy to another of Gwelain's victims who was trying to help them.

"They didn't know what they were signing," Varek said. He glanced over his shoulder, listening for something.

"They couldn't read?" Sorra asked.

"That would have made it easier, wouldn't it? Magic proved more useful."

"The contracts aren't binding if they've been altered," Beau said. "By magic or otherwise."

"They haven't been altered." Varek smiled grimly. "The words on those pages were there when the documents were signed, but they were covered by an illusion to make them look like they said something far more agreeable. It's simple enough that even an accomplished human mage can do it if he matches illusion to expectation, and it's quite effective. From a logical perspective one might argue the legality, but magic doesn't deal in shades of grey. They signed those contracts willingly."

Beau looked as though he might vomit.

"Does that satisfy you?" Varek asked.

Beau didn't answer. Sorra touched his arm, and he seemed to come back to himself, but his gaze remained distant.

"Out." Varek stepped behind the humans, not touching them but standing close enough that Sorra stepped away, toward the stairs. She wanted to run but forced herself to stop and turn back.

"The soul in the door—she won't suffer for this?"

"I don't plan to tell anyone you were here. If you're not caught, no one but me will know she disobeyed," Varek said.

"Thank you." Sorra walked toward the stairs, but Beau didn't follow.

"That's not good enough," he said. "If you truly mean what you seem to be implying, swear she won't be punished for this in any way. Not by your hand, and not by anyone else's."

Varek's upper lip curled. "You sound like your wife. No trust, only careful questions to turn her curse against me. Fine. I will not punish the guardian spirit for this, or make her suffer otherwise. I will not instruct anyone else to do so on my behalf. As to what will happen if anyone else finds out what she's done, I can't make promises. At that point I'll be too worried about the state of my own hide to worry about hers or anyone else's. Does that satisfy you?"

"It'll do."

Varek glared at Beau with cold hatred. He wasn't as powerful as Gwelain, but he was a goblin prince with blood of the Bright Ones flowing through him. To be questioned, to be manipulated by a mere human, to be mistrusted by those he was trying to help despite his lack of faith in them, had to sting his pride.

Sorra understood Beau's caution and their history, but her heart ached for Varek.

"Come on, then." Varek brushed past Sorra and led the way down the stairs. The humans followed, Sorra's steps quick, Beau's plodding. Varek snarled something under his breath, and the door opened for him. He paused, listening, then led them to the left.

Voices reached them from the far end of the circle. Varek looked back, eyes wide, and opened a door in the outer wall.

"In," he ordered. "Go."

Sorra and Beau stepped into a room covered from floor to ceiling in white and gold tiles. Sorra stumbled, missing her step at the edge of the big, square tub sunk into the floor. Varek grabbed on to the back of her shirt with one hand to keep her from falling as he closed the door with the other.

Sorra looked around as she caught her breath. Deep tub, a panel of wood cut through with a lace-like pattern set into the back wall, gold hooks on the wall for hanging clothing or towels—or a delicate magical vessel a mage didn't want splashed with water. She looked to Beau, and he nodded, then touched a finger to his lips.

"*Vorlrathnul*," Varek murmured, and steam thickened the air as the tub filled with water. His voice had a more musical quality as he spoke the old language than it ever did as it contorted itself to the harder edges of modern Andonian speech. *"Broulgrenthsi."* The scent of cedarwood and some exotic flower rose from the water.

A knock from outside cut through the air, and Sorra flinched. Varek motioned for the humans to stand against the wall, out of sight of the door. They obeyed, and Sorra reached for Beau's hand, steadying herself against the waves of panic that threatened to sweep her away.

Varek opened the door enough to speak around it without being seen by whoever stood outside.

"What?"

"You left before the fun was over." Gwelain's voice. Demanding. Perhaps suspicious, but Sorra let herself hope she didn't sound accusing. "Is everything all right?"

Varek glared at Sorra and Beau. "As well as it ever is. But I've had enough. I grow tired of the company you keep and wished to be alone."

A single, oozing sore erupted on his forehead. Then another next to his nose, and a third on his chin. Blood and clear liquid flowed in thin streams. More appeared, smaller, larger, erupting over his face and throat. His lips parted in a silent, pained snarl as he rested his forehead against the back of the door.

Gwelain clucked her tongue. "I swear you grow duller by the day, Varek."

Varek's shoulders rose and fell with a long, slow breath of the sort Sorra knew well after years of calming her own temper. "Why are you here?"

"I've just had news from my contact in Embercliffe, with more to follow at any moment. We're going to be quite busy, and very soon. I've ordered Corvin to finish up quickly."

Varek nodded, though Gwelain couldn't see. "We'll speak when I'm finished here."

"Don't take too long."

Varek pushed the door closed, then knelt and splashed water over his face.

"Varek," Sorra whispered, releasing Beau's hand.

Varek stared down at his reflection in the wavering waters of the tub. "Don't tell me you're sorry," he said. "Just hope that whatever the news is, it's enough to distract her from anything else I might need to lie about. If you go now, I might have time to fix this mess before I see her."

He stood, shook the water from his hands, and opened the narrow door in the back wall—the one Tullian might use to sneak in to kill Corvin. That conversation seemed like it had taken place a lifetime ago.

"I'll take you through the servants' corridors," Varek said. "It will be a few minutes before Gwelain rouses any of them to tend to her."

He didn't wait for an answer before he stepped into a dim hallway so narrow his shoulders nearly brushed the rough stone walls.

Sorra followed, and a few seconds later the light from the bathing room dimmed as Beau stepped through the door.

"I thought the royal apartments were sealed off," Sorra said.

"They are." Varek spoke quietly over his shoulder. "There's another door, but it's locked by enchantment. Now hush."

A staircase led them downward until Sorra guessed they must be at ground level or lower, then ended at a door with an old-fashioned iron latch. Next to the door, barely visible, a mark carved into the stone—the last line of the old king's protection against magical eavesdropping before they stepped back into the outer castle.

Varek brushed a layer of cobwebs aside and leaned close to whisper a string of words at the lock. The bolt clicked, and he pushed the door open. When he turned back, his face was still festering with sores.

The urge to apologize welled up, and Sorra squashed it down. Varek was right. Words wouldn't fix anything.

"Go," he whispered. "Close it tight and it will lock itself behind you. Cover your tracks." Without another word, he hurried back up the stairs, leaving Sorra to catch the heavy door before it could close with them trapped inside.

Beau stepped through the doorway and into a musty cellar full of wooden crates packed with potatoes that had been forgotten for long enough that they'd collapsed into wrinkled sacs covered in long, wilted roots. The faint smell of rot turned Sorra's stomach, as did the sight of glass jars full of food old enough that whatever had been inside had turned to mud.

She paused before she closed the door.

Varek had handed them a path back into the royal chambers that they might need later. Even Tullian would call her a fool if she gave that up.

The lock was a simple, heavy bolt. Once slipped into place, the door would once again be a dead end. Propping it open wasn't an option, though. Varek might come back to check, or a servant might notice it standing ajar.

The lock needed to be jammed to keep it from sliding home and the door held closed firmly enough that a push from the other side wouldn't give away its secret.

Sorra looked to Beau to see whether he was thinking the same, but he was staring at nothing, lost in his own mind.

Sorra snapped her fingers, drawing his attention, and motioned to the door. He held it open as she searched the room.

Nothing seemed promising. The crates would do for putting weight behind the door once it was closed, but worthless until the lock was either broken or stuck. The potatoes wouldn't help. Neither would the ancient glass jars of questionable liquids.

A memory tickled the back of her mind—hours she'd spent canning with Mrs. Blotchkin, listening to her drone on about how things used to be done. The memory seemed irrelevant, as so many distracting thoughts tended to be. But the memory broadened, and Sorra recalled wrinkling her nose at the smell of the thick black paste the old woman insisted on using to seal the jars even when there were more modern methods available.

The stuff was vile, but undeniably effective.

Sorra held her breath and forced one of the jars open, trying not to slosh any of the liquid on her clothes. The underside of the lid was ringed with the hard black tar she remembered well, and when she worked it between her fingers, it became pliable. She had to open three jars before she'd collected what she thought might be enough, and though she carefully closed them again, the stink of rot made her eyes water.

The warmth of her hand softened the tar as she crossed the room and applied it to the open lock, pressing it into the space around the bolt, then smoothing it so the door would close. Beau tore a strip of cloth from one of the potato sacks, and Sorra pressed it into the sticky surface until the tar oozed through the gaps, then smoothed it again.

She waited five seconds. Ten. When she tapped her finger against its surface, the tar had hardened. Beau released the door, and she closed it, holding her breath. When she pulled again, it opened easily.

Sorra's body hummed with excitement and apprehension—pleasure at her success and fear of it somehow being turned against her.

When the door was closed again, she pushed a stack of potato crates against it. Beau, moving slowly, added a few more on top, then another layer in front. They were heavy. With any luck, the door would feel locked to anyone pushing it from the other side.

Beau rubbed his arm absently, lost again in thought.

Sorra waved her hands to get his attention and mouthed *what is it?*

He shook his head and took her by the hand. They made their way out of the cellar and into a larger storage room that smelled more of dried herbs and fresh onion than of rot and mildew. From there they passed through the kitchen, which was as dark and quiet as anywhere else in the castle.

Sorra hardly dared to breathe as they crept back to her room, their movements silent until they'd slipped inside.

Tullian still slept, filling the room with gentle snores.

"Should we wake him?" Sorra asked.

"Soon." Beau sat on one of the chairs and rested his head in his hands. "Varek was wrong. We did learn something important tonight."

Sorra knelt on the floor in front of him and took his hands in hers, then waited until he met her gaze. "What? The contracts?"

He took a shaking breath. "You wondered why Gwelain seemed so confident about not needing me, and there's the answer."

"What answer?" Sorra felt stupid for having to ask.

"You said earlier that she might have one of my father's mages in her pocket. Maybe more than one. Varek said even a human could work a convincing enough illusion to trick someone into signing a contract. I can't know for sure who she's got, but if you're right, and if it's the mage who wrote my letter of abdication—"

Sorra's throat tightened. "Then you can't know what you actually signed."

"I think we do know, though." Beau's voice was flat. "I've been assuming that she still needed me to officially name her next in line for the throne, that I could still hold that over her after we were married. But she's had it all this time. I didn't sign a letter of abdication. I signed a note of succession that will become legally binding the moment it's opened, whether I'm there to confirm it or not."

"It's all right," Sorra said, willing it to be true. "She can't do anything while your father lives. We still have time."

"No. We don't." Beau rolled up his sleeve. "I know what the news from home is." He turned his arm over, revealing not the heir's mark, but fresh black lines in the shape of a crown. "I should leave. She'll be looking for me. Looking for this."

Sorra wanted to say something, to do anything that might somehow negate the defeat in his voice, but she couldn't move. Couldn't breathe.

Then he stood to go, and she found her body again. She still couldn't speak, but she put her arms around him. He responded slowly, as if he wasn't quite sure how. Then his arms tightened around her, holding on to her like a drowning man might grasp a rope thrown to him from a passing ship. She clasped her hands behind his neck and kissed the corner of his mouth.

Neither of them heard the door open, but every hair on Sorra's body stood on end as she registered the soft click of talons on the wooden floor.

"Well," Gwelain purred. "Isn't this cozy?"

CHAPTER FIFTY

Sorra pulled away from Beau, clasping her trembling hands behind her back.

"Beau has received troubling news," she said, taking in every hint of the queen's mood—the narrowed glint of her eyes, the shadow of a dangerous smile. "Human loss requires comfort, Majesty."

"Does it?" Gwelain touched a claw to her chin. "I suspect you've been offering him quite a lot of human comfort since your arrival."

Beau watched Gwelain, not answering in word or action, and Sorra decided to follow suit as well as she could.

If they claimed it wasn't what it looked like, Gwelain's natural question would be what it was. Admitting they'd been conspiring against her would leave them in an even worse position.

But the silence stretched out, broken only by the occasional snore from the knight sleeping on the bed, the tension drawing so tight Sorra felt it would suffocate her.

"This was my fault," Beau said.

Sorra stepped in front of him.

"Don't lie for my sake," she said, as firmly as she could manage. She understood his urge to protect her, and under other circumstances it would have been admirable. But they had more to lose if he appeared to have stepped out of line. "He brought Tullian to my room after your return, Majesty. I shouldn't have kept him. I'm sorry. I didn't—"

"Didn't what? Didn't mean to kiss him? Didn't remember he's married to someone who could easily destroy you both?" The queen's voice carried a false lightness that set Sorra's nerves prickling. There was a sharp edge to it, one that would cut deep if she wasn't careful.

"I meant to," she said. "I remembered. And I'm still sorry."

"Sorry you were caught." Gwelain stalked the room, pacing between the tub and fireplace, hands clasped behind her back. "Apologies aren't enough. I need to be certain it won't happen again."

"It won't," Beau said. "A momentary lapse, my queen."

Gwelain turned to face them, sizing up the humans with keen interest. "Leave us, Beauregard. Return to your room. I'll see about using some of my dear mage's freshly harvested power to arrange a new enchantment, just to be sure. If you ever touch her again without my permission, you'll turn back into a bear. Seems fitting, doesn't it?"

Sorra clenched her jaw, afraid of what would come out if she risked speaking. A taunt, perhaps, about why Gwelain couldn't afford to waste her own magic on such a thing. Gwelain had her backed against a cliff's edge, and the urge to lash out was strong.

Beau, too, seemed to understand that pleading or arguing would only make things worse, but his posture radiated controlled anger. "If you think it necessary, my queen. But perhaps there are more important matters to address, by magic or otherwise."

Gwelain smiled. "Indeed. Go. We'll speak when I'm finished here."

Beau didn't move. Gwelain sighed.

"Don't be stupid." She dropped her voice to a threatening murmur. "Disobedience will only make it worse for both of you."

Beau didn't glance at Sorra again before he strode from the room.

"Forgive me, Majesty," Sorra said, "but it might make your ascension to the throne difficult if you show up in Embercliffe with a bear on your arm."

"True. Better to replace him, then." Gwelain closed the door and went to Tullian, laying a hand against his brow before stepping back, arms crossed.

The old knight stirred, then opened his eyes, blinking against the light. He caught sight of the queen and pushed himself up to sit on the edge of the bed, wobbling slightly.

"Stay where you are," Gwelain said. "I want you listening, not fainting at my feet."

Tullian scrubbed a hand over the side of his face and sat up straighter, though he still listed slightly to his left. Sorra could only imagine how it pained him to appear before his enemy in such a dishevelled, weakened state.

"Apologies, Majesty," he said, tugging his fingers through the wild halo of steely hair that framed his head. "I didn't know you'd be visiting."

"Nor did I realize you'd both be here. I suppose you haven't heard the news of Ranthorn's death?"

Tullian glanced at Sorra. "I had not. So Beauregard is king of Andonia."

"And I am its queen." Gwelain tilted her head, bird-like. "You may rise now, if you wish to bow."

Tullian looked away, as did Sorra when the queen turned to her.

Gwelain didn't seem surprised. "I see. One of you will, though. Everything is in place for my ascension save for one tiny detail, and I won't have you standing in my way any longer. You have until morning to decide which of you will abandon your quest, become one of my little monsters, and swear yourself to me. Whoever comes to me first will lay the path for my victory and will be rewarded appropriately."

"And when neither of us comes?" Tullian asked.

"Then I'll enjoy finding the best way to break your will. Pain seems like a fine place to start. Not enough to kill you, but enough to make you willing to do anything to end it." Gwelain shrugged. "I hope it won't come to that. Your suffering would be lovely, but I'd prefer to see this taken care of quickly. Beau will only hold his claim to the throne for so long before my plans are ruined."

Sorra and Tullian exchanged a glance, and Gwelain laughed.

"Don't think you can defeat me by running out the calendar," she added. "I've devoted more than a dozen years and countless magical resources to this plan, but in the grander scheme of things, it's nothing to me. Should you fail me, I'll find another way. Another traitor, certainly, should this prove to be the wrong time for the visions to be fulfilled. I can wait another century if that's what it takes. Can you say the same?" She chuckled, low and dark. "I know a certain prince who has no visions to protect him, who would become tragically disposable very quickly."

Sorra's body went cold.

When neither of the heroes spoke, Gwelain turned to Sorra. "I'll give you until sunrise. Remember my offer, and consider what's best for everyone. The great, dark destiny spoken of by your birth blessing still lies within your grasp. I'd hate to see you waste it."

Before Sorra could form an answer, Gwelain swept from the room, leaving the door open behind her.

Tullian cleared his throat, but Sorra didn't turn. The queen's departure should have been a relief, but Sorra couldn't help wishing she'd stayed, or that she'd had the decency to finish tearing everything down instead of leaving Sorra with the choice of how to do it herself.

"Sorra." Tullian spoke her name as an order, and Sorra forced herself to face him. He stood, steadier than he'd seemed before but holding on to the bed's footboard for support. "What destiny is she speaking of? What blessing?"

Sorra's mouth turned dry, her throat thick enough that she hoped for a moment she might choke to death on her own dread and put the matter to rest without having to speak a word. But her lungs kept drawing air, and the clouds of white midges that swarmed at the edges of her vision passed.

Tullian's cheeks reddened. "Speak, girl."

"I'm trying." Sorra focused on her thundering pulse, willing it to slow. It didn't. "She speaks of an irrelevant issue, but one she thought she could tempt me with. A sort of curse spoken before my birth that said I'd walk in shadow and bring destruction on all those whose lives I touched. It's proved itself true in the past, most clearly when I caused Beau to lose the wager that led to him marrying Gwelain. I've been trying to escape it by becoming a hero." Her voice came out a dead monotone. "I wanted to tell you."

"And why didn't you?"

Tullian whispered the question. Sorra wished he'd yell. The heat of his anger would be better than this—cold, distant, like the tolling of a death bell.

She blinked back tears. "Because it didn't matter! Look how far we've come. Neither of us could have made it here if we hadn't worked together, and you never would have joined me if I'd told you about the blessing."

"Of course I wouldn't have!" Tullian's fingers tightened around the wooden footboard, and he stood straighter. "No wonder things keep going wrong. No wonder every step that seems to bring us closer to victory only pulls us deeper into Gwelain's plans. You knew you were delivering her traitor." He paused. "And she knew?"

"It doesn't matter who knew. She's wrong. Or she will be." Sorra pulled her sleeve back, exposing the black songbird etched onto her skin. "I haven't abandoned our quest, and I have no intention of doing so. We still have time. While you were sleeping, Beau and I went to the royal apartments."

"You what?"

"We learned that Gwelain's spy may have tricked Beau into signing over the throne to her—"

"You what?" Tullian repeated. A vein pulsed in his forehead.

"And that's bad," Sorra said, holding her hands out in a peace-making gesture. "But we also found a way for you to get in—a door through a storage room off the kitchen, normally locked by magic, but it's open now. If you want to, we can..."

She trailed off, unsure of what would come next. Killing Corvin would only mean anything if they could get Gwelain into the tower where she'd be weakened.

And without her traitor and her assurance of victory, she'd abandon her plans rather than expose herself to harm.

Sorra's hands dropped to her sides. "It's something."

"It's nothing," Tullian spat. "All we've gained is greater certainty that she's been ahead of us all along, with no way of knowing what other traps she's set, or how else she might tempt you. The best thing we can do now is try to run, though she'll never stop hunting us. Or we could kill each other, if we can't escape." He stepped away from the bed, testing his balance. "It would have been better for me to stay where I was. To let her kill every human in these lands if that was what it took to prevent her victory."

"But the visions say she'll have her traitor or she'll be defeated. One or the other." Sorra tried to speak calmly, but her voice broke. "We don't win by doing nothing, remember?"

"Then perhaps we don't win." Tullian squeezed his eyes closed. When he opened them again, they shone with tears. "You are not the Mystery, and I was a fool to think I could turn you into a hero. You say you won't give in for the sake of saving your prince, but he's the reason you came, the reason you chose not to tell me about this destiny of yours. And now here we are—one of us to die for our victory, or one to meet her destiny by betraying Andonia."

"Tullian, listen to me! I won't. Even if she tortures me. Even if she threatens Beau, or you. Even if I have to die for our victory."

He only seemed to be half-listening, calm and resigned even as a tear trickled down his cheek. "It was a mistake to swear you to the quest. My mistake. My responsibility. I cannot let you be tempted to betrayal, no matter what sacrifice is required."

His left hand searched at his side for his sword, but it was gone. Sorra caught sight of it leaning against the fireplace, and before she could look away, he followed her gaze to it.

Sorra moved closer to the open door.

This was Tullian, the man who had knocked her into the dirt dozens of times but had always helped her back up, even before they'd been anything like friends. Who had told her the old stories, who had thought her capable of discipline and even heroism, who had placed his faith in her when he'd thought all hope was lost.

But he was also a knight who had made sacrifices before, making sure his companions died before they could betray Linnea. A man who believed in the visions, who had nothing if he didn't have his honour. Even if it broke his heart, he would do whatever he thought necessary to serve his quest and his queen.

Tullian bared his teeth in a pained grimace, then turned to

collect his sword. "It shouldn't have been this way," he whispered, barely loud enough for Sorra to hear. "It's all wrong."

Before he could turn back, Sorra slipped out the door and darted for the stairs.

"Sorra!" Tullian yelled after her. "Sorra!"

She didn't stop, and she didn't turn back.

CHAPTER FIFTY-ONE

The castle swarmed with goblins scurrying from room to room like ants fleeing a kicked nest. Sorra shied away from them at first, hugging corners and holding her breath, but quickly realized they had no interest in her panicked eyes and tear-tracked cheeks. Their gazes slid past her as they hurried by, some followed by human servants carrying armloads of clothes, some appearing lost within the familiar walls of a castle that might have been their home for a hundred years or more.

It made them strangely human, and though Sorra didn't pity them one bit, she understood what it must mean to them to be shaken from their complacent, spoiled positions and faced with the proposition of a move, a change, even a war.

Change brought unknown dangers, and even for monsters, adventure wasn't always as grand as one might imagine it to be.

Sorra resisted the urge to break into a run, knowing it would give panic a foothold she couldn't afford to offer. Down the stairs first, past the theatre, following the route they'd taken to the royal apartments, but Beau's face wasn't among those she met along the way. The door to the apartments was locked, and though she knocked at its uneven surface until she was sure her knuckles would be bruised, no one answered.

But he might not have obeyed.

She backtracked, ignoring the narrowed eyes of a pair of

armoured goblins who stalked past the dining room as she made her way toward the kitchen. It, too, was a hive of activity as human servants collected food and supplies, all talking over and bumping into each other. A pot clattered to the floor, and someone let out a string of curses.

A dozen humans, but Beau wasn't one of them.

Please, Sorra prayed as she hurried up the stairs. *Let him be waiting for me in the garden.*

The dining room and the corridors beyond stood empty. Whatever lay behind the doors in this part of the castle was of little interest to the goblins as they collected the scraps of their lives. But when Sorra reached the library, a line of bright lamplight shone from beneath the door, and Sorra's heart jumped.

Please.

But it wasn't Beau who turned to face her as she entered. Varek stood at the far wall of shelves, a heavy book held open in one hand. His green skin was clear and smooth, showing no trace of the marks his lie had left.

He closed the book and placed it back in its spot before he crossed the room, reaching past Sorra to close the door.

"What are you doing here?" he whispered, leaning in close.

She was about to say *looking for Beau* but stopped herself. This was another kind of opportunity, if they could talk.

"Is this safe?" she whispered back.

"Of course not. Corvin is likely occupied, directing the packing of his things or enjoying one last bath before we leave, but that doesn't mean anyone, anywhere is safe."

Sorra took a deep breath. Up close, Varek's clothes smelled a little like the cave below the castle, moss and damp stone. She stood on her toes to place her mouth closer to his pointed ear. "Quickly, then. Do you still think there's a way to defeat Gwelain?"

He didn't answer for a moment. Thinking, Sorra supposed, examining the angles. "Did she deliver her ultimatum?"

"Yes. We only have until sunrise before we're hauled off to be tortured. Beau's life is in danger—he'd negotiate for your future safety, or almost anything you want."

"Except the heart's destruction, I assume."

"Except that."

Another silence that felt longer than it probably was. Sorra fixed her gaze on the tall glass doors and the darkness beyond them, untouched by dawn.

"There may be a way." Varek spoke quickly, his whisper tickling her ear. "Your foolish human queen's visions may have been correct. You will need my magic, and the knight's sword, and some contribution from Beauregard before the story she foretold reaches its end. Do you think you could talk them into accepting my help?"

Sorra thought of going back to face Tullian, and a wave of dread passed through her. Bad enough that he knew about her blessing—now she'd have to propose bringing a goblin prince in on their plans.

But surely he'll see, once he's calmed a little. If I can offer a way forward...

"I'll try," she said. "And then what?"

"I don't know." He sighed. "I *could* help you. But even if your new king would offer terms, how could I trust him when he has no reason to care what becomes of me or my people?"

"He's good," Sorra said. "He's not like Gwelain, keeping promises only as long as—"

His hand closed around her arm, and Sorra jumped. "Someone's coming," Varek said, barely audible. "Listen carefully. We have not made plans. I won't be lying if Gwelain asks whether we have, and it will remain so for now. Speak to your knight, ensure—"

He fell silent, shoved Sorra behind the door, and with a wave of his hand doused the lamps, leaving the room lit by starlight as it had been the first time Sorra had passed through it, then by a rectangle of lamplight from the hallway when Varek opened the door.

"There you are." Gwelain's voice. A rippling shiver flowed down Sorra's spine. "I need to speak to you."

"Not here," Varek said.

Gwelain sniffled. "There's no one here to listen."

"But I have things to do elsewhere. You wanted us ready by dawn, did you not?" Varek's voice faded, and Sorra imagined him leading the queen away.

Go, she thought. If the queen knew she and Varek had been talking, Sorra might not get a chance to bring him into any plans even if Tullian gave his blessing.

The queen's skirts rustled outside the door. "We're all busy, Varek, but I want…"

Her voice faded, and Sorra released her breath. The door hadn't quite latched, but she didn't dare touch it until she was sure the queen was really gone. She did risk a look out at the garden, though. Varek would have mentioned if Beau had been there, but it still disappointed her to find the little yard lit by glowbugs and the moonlight that glinted off the pond, but no prince.

She listened at the library door, telling herself it was to make sure no one would see her leaving so soon after Varek, knowing it was an excuse to delay going back to speak to Tullian.

A potential ally is a peace offering, she reminded herself, and pushed the door open. *And even if he wants to argue against it, at least we'll be talking about something other than my blessing.*

The reasoning felt painfully hollow, but she made herself walk back toward the tower stairs, barely glancing at the crowd of goblins outside the throne room. Her mind was full of words and phrases that she tried on and discarded as insufficient for the task ahead.

Her boots scuffed against the stairs as she climbed, her feet heavier with each step.

"Tullian, there's hope," she said under her breath, practicing a tone that would command respect. "We have an ally. I still believe we're the heroes Linnea saw, even if we're not what the scholars expected."

Her door stood open. Sorra took a deep breath and held it as she stepped into her room, bracing herself for an attack.

Tullian was gone.

She crossed to his door and knocked, but he didn't answer.

Sorra's stomach sank, heavy with uneasiness that only worsened when she returned to her room and spotted the white paper on her bed.

She picked it up, her movements slow, then read the note written in Tullian's familiar, careful script.

Sorra—

*Though it pains me to say it, you are correct: it is wrong for us to
remain unmoving, to use caution as an excuse for cowardice.
Whether we are truly the Might and the Mystery is of no consequence now, and I shall take the next steps alone to ensure
Linnea's victory. I pray my actions will clear the way for you and
Beauregard (may his reign be long, provided it does not involve a
goblin queen) so that you may carry on unhindered by Gwelain's
spy and the protections he offers her in vulnerable moments.
If I am successful, I will bring about the sign assuring our victory
and therefore close the door on the possibility of Gwelain's. Use my
sacrifice to whatever advantage presents itself.
I fear the uncertainty that lies ahead of me, but not as much as I
fear what will happen if my lack of action leads you to temptation.
I will be watching. Do not let your destiny be Andonia's downfall.*

—Tullian

Sorra read the letter twice, hoping she'd misunderstood the first
time, but its meaning was clear.

She'd told him how to get into the royal apartments, and Beau
had mentioned where he'd find Corvin at this hour.

Tullian clearly didn't expect to survive the encounter. He might
destroy Corvin's vessel and deprive him of magic, and he might kill
him. But Gwelain's guards would be nearby.

*He thinks he can fulfil Linnea's vision by making Gwelain's monsters
kill him.*

Sorra crumpled the note and threw it into the fire.

"You idiot," she spat. "You can't force destiny."

His faith had always been strong enough that he'd believe a
foolish plan like that would work. And maybe killing Corvin would
offer an advantage. There would be no mage to eavesdrop or to
guard Gwelain if she entered the tower to collect the heart for
transport to Embercliffe.

*But it's not enough. We don't have a plan. We still need Linnea's
Might.*

For a moment she understood Tullian's frustration with her own recklessness, his need to plan and weigh every option, and she wished he hadn't chosen this moment to surprise her.

Tullian's faith was unshakable. Sorra's was not. The only thing she was sure of was how unprepared she was to see the quest through without him.

She only hoped he'd taken long enough to make his decision and write his note that she'd still have time to catch him before he made a terrible mistake.

CHAPTER FIFTY-TWO

The stack of potato crates had been toppled, and the door to the servants' passage opened easily when Sorra pulled on its handle. She didn't dare call out as she climbed the dark stairs, taking them two at a time, ignoring the protestations from her exhausted body.

Her hope of catching Tullian vanished as sounds of shouting and swords clashing met her at the top of the stairs. She hurried on, knowing there was nothing she could do but unable to stay away.

Fighting to quiet her breath, Sorra reached the door to the bathing chamber. She peered through the tiny openings in the door's latticework panel.

Though everyone else's schedule had been upset by preparations for leaving the castle, it seemed Corvin's had remained undisturbed. Tullian had found him in the bath.

The mage was dead. His naked body floated in the tub, throat slit, blood tinting the water. His robes lay in a crumpled heap in the corner next to the shards of emerald and gold that had once been the vessel for his magic.

But Gwelain hadn't left her mage unprotected while she was busy elsewhere. Two guards faced Tullian with their swords drawn. There wasn't much room to fight, but Tullian was attacking with incredible energy and speed. His right hand was still unusable, but he fought respectably with his left.

The soldiers might have been content to keep him contained, but Tullian harried them, forcing them to defend themselves even as they tried to avoid harming him. He'd left his armour behind, and their queen would not be pleased if they killed the hero.

"Useless!" he bellowed. "Is this how you plan to defend your queen in a land where everyone hates her? Pathetic."

He darted forward, and the tip of his sword sliced into one of the soldiers' throats. The goblin stumbled from the room, one hand pressed to the wound, and two more stepped in.

"I'll kill every one of you!" Tullian attacked again and defended himself when one of the soldiers struck, aiming for his arm.

Sorra's heartbeat rang through every part of her. She barely breathed until she grew dizzy and forced herself to take in air.

Run.

Tullian fought on, defending himself from stronger and more confident attacks, convincing the soldiers that he had no intention of doing anything but cutting his way through them and escaping.

Finally, one of the goblins roared and thrust his sword forward in a strike aimed to upset Tullian's balance when he spun to block it. Instead Tullian held his sword arm out to his side and let the blade sink into his chest. Sorra held back a cry as he fell to his knees, turning away from his enemies and offering Sorra a clear view of his face and the sword protruding from his body.

The soldiers backed away. The one who had struck fled, leaving his sword buried in the hero whose death would spell Gwelain's defeat.

Sorra pressed both hands to her mouth, muffling a sob.

Tullian laughed, then coughed. Blood spilled over his lips, and he raised his eyes to the ceiling as he tore his thin cotton shirt from the neck down, opening it to reveal the wound that would kill him.

"There," he said, and wrapped both hands around the sword's hilt to pull it free and release his blood to join Corvin's.

Tears spilled over Sorra's cheeks.

Maybe this is what Linnea saw after all, she thought, grasping at hope.

Tullian adjusted his grip.

Gwelain stepped into the room, her golden eyes flashing as she took in her mage's ruined body and the sword that pierced her enemy.

"I don't think so."

She waved one hand and whispered a long string of unfamiliar words, thick sounds that flowed musically off her tongue.

Tullian's eyes widened. His lips moved, but his hands seemed frozen in place as the skin around his wound darkened and puckered. The greyish hue spread over his chest and up his throat, turning his skin to bark. A strangled choking noise rose from his throat as his arms flew out to his sides, twisting into branches covered in tiny silver leaves. His thickening body split the seams on his clothing, and roots spread across the floor.

His face was the last thing to change. It wasn't like his friend Selim, where Sorra had needed to search for a face in the gnarls and rough bark. Tullian's was clear, its agony obvious in every perfect line as he twisted away from the queen.

Sorra forced herself to take shallow, silent breaths through her nose, to stay standing even as her legs threatened to collapse beneath her.

She knew she should run. She couldn't.

Gwelain smiled and ran her claws over Tullian's face.

"That could have been disastrous," she said, smiling. "Don't worry, brave knight. I know it's unpleasant, but you're still alive." She looked down at Corvin and frowned. "If only we could say the same for him. What a mess."

She snapped her fingers, and her personal guards stepped into the room as the other soldiers hurried out.

"Take him to the throne room," she said. "Find the girl and make sure she comes to me alive."

She left, and her guards followed, one holding Tullian's branches, another lifting him at the roots.

Shouts and barked orders erupted outside the room, then faded.

Sorra wanted to curl into a ball on the floor of the servants' passage. For the moment it was safe. But they'd come soon. They'd look for Tullian's entrance, and they'd find her.

The ache in her chest was unbearable. She hurt for Tullian, and she hated him for his useless bravery and pointless sacrifice. Even if he'd been right and his death would somehow have forced their victory, he hadn't died.

Both potential outcomes still lay open, a fork in the mist-shrouded path ahead.

She pinched her inner arm hard, and once she had her own attention, she ordered herself to move.

There was nowhere to run now that she was Gwelain's only chance at claiming her traitor.

But maybe there was still time to find a place to rest while the world crumbled around her.

CHAPTER FIFTY-THREE

Sorra sought shelter, as desperate as a rabbit chased from its
burrow by baying hounds.

Nowhere was safe, but there were quiet places.

When she reached the corridors outside the library, voices
reached her—rough, excited, barking words she couldn't quite
understand. She threw her weight against a closed door that
opened easily, slamming into the wall behind and offering an
opening into an unfamiliar hallway, dark and narrow, that spiralled
upward as she followed it, one hand grazing its outer wall to steady
her steps.

At the top, another door. She opened it cautiously, watching and
listening. Voices, but distant, and to her right, the waterfall made of
gold she'd passed on her search for Linnea's heart.

She considered hiding in the treasury—a place Gwelain
wouldn't visit if she could avoid it, and one forbidden to nearly
anyone else.

*Or maybe she'll have her guards waiting there in case I decide to
destroy the heart, and her with it.*

Sorra turned instead toward the sculpture gallery. The path was
clear and the room silent when she stepped in, with no lamps lit to
expose her to anyone who might be looking through its windows
from some other part of the castle. There was only moonlight, cold
and thin, to illuminate the gallery's pale inhabitants.

She told herself it was only a trick of her mind that the sky in the east seemed paler than in the west, and that she only imagined the room was cold enough that she saw the ghost of her breath.

The statues' blank stone eyes stared down at her as she passed between them, a jury of the dead whose favour she feared she hadn't earned. But they were soon behind her. So were the stone goblins, once she'd passed by the half-circle of their grotesque forms and crawled into the darkness at the end of the room, letting it swallow her whole.

Linnea's statue lay where she'd last seen it, sketched in what little light reached its sheltered resting place. Sorra crawled over it and pressed her back to the wall, knees pulled to her chest, drawing heaving breaths.

Don't cry. There's no time. Just think.

But no thought could ease the pressure. There was only Tullian's blood, Tullian's face frozen in the bark of a tree, and the knowledge that everything had gone wrong, as it had been destined to the second she'd become involved.

Sorra sobbed into her arms, releasing the flood of overwhelm and regret that would otherwise have torn her apart. When it was over, she was calm, a sea after a storm, but nothing else had changed. All that was left in her was cold, darkness, and dread.

She wiped her eyes on her sleeves and pulled tighter into herself, shivering, as she began to sort through the broken pieces of ideas she'd collected, unsure they added up to anything but certain that if there was an answer, it had to be there.

There was the possibility that Tullian was entirely correct, that her well-meaning lie of omission had led them to disaster. It hurt to consider, but she resisted the urge to turn her attention elsewhere.

Maybe if she'd told him about the blessing, he'd have refused to help her. Tullian would have carried on as he had been for so long, denying Gwelain her traitor.

And Gwelain would have given up, and some other group of heroes would have come along some day to fulfil the visions. Beau would have died for her failure but as the willing sacrifice he'd always suspected he would become.

Or maybe Beau's father's plans were now in motion, and all

she'd done was to put Andonia's new king in danger by tempting him to disobedience.

"But this was my destiny," she whispered. "I was supposed to be here."

As she looked back on the impossibly short span of time since she'd left Cottsbridge, it seemed inevitable. The arrow leading her to Beau, her wayward cleverness ruining his plans but revealing the opportunity for her to become a hero and escape her blessing. Tullian had said that every step forward had only brought them closer to defeat, but...

But what?

Sorra forced herself to keep breathing.

But I don't want that to be how the story ends, with me ruining everything by trying to be good.

Very well, Davina's voice whispered in her mind. *If that outcome isn't acceptable, set it aside and see what else you can make with all those sharp and scattered pieces.*

A fresh tear slid down Sorra's cheek. She hadn't thought of her sisters often since she'd left Andonia, but now more than ever she wished for their grace, their wisdom, and above all their ability to do things right. Or if not them, Tullian, even with the blinders of his faith and his sharp rebukes.

Anyone who might manage things better than she herself could. Someone capable, someone clear-headed, someone who would know the right thing to do without having to make a dozen wrong choices first.

But there was no one. Only Sorra and the stone queen lying on the floor, her face and her chest chipped and scarred.

Blinded. Heartless.

Sorra could see her better now. The sky was lightening outside the gallery windows.

She ignored the threatening sunrise and turned back to the task at hand. Davina—or rather, herself posing as Davina—was right. If one version of the truth was bad, there had to be a better one. Gwelain hadn't won yet, and Tullian had failed to die, which meant both outcomes might still be possible.

Options, then.

Tullian had mentioned running away. He'd also mentioned killing each other, but Sorra set that aside as both too horrifying and too tempting as a means of releasing herself from responsibility. Running was different, though. Beau was probably under guard by now, but if she could find Varek and convince him to help her escape, and if she could make it back to Andonia...

The trail ended there. She didn't know what Gwelain's plan might be if she didn't get her traitor, so she wouldn't know what to warn anyone about. She could tell them what she'd seen, warn them that their king-for-now was married to the goblin queen and they'd best make sure Gwelain didn't cross the border. For that she might be hailed as a hero, but it would leave Beau to whatever fate Gwelain thought appropriate once he became entirely useless to her.

But I came here to save him, and I mean to do it.

That left staying, and trying for victory in the hopes that this would all somehow lead to the better fulfilment of the visions.

"I don't have much to work with," she whispered, hoping that words and sentences would corral her ideas, or at least herd them in a definite direction. "A vague promise from Varek—no, not even that. The idea that he could help. Not that he will, because he still can't trust humans. Corvin is dead, so he can't listen in, but there's no more time to speak, anyway. But him being dead does mean he can't protect Gwelain when she goes to the treasury to collect the heart to take it to Embercliffe with her—if she goes alone, she'll be helpless, and if she takes Varek to protect her, he might turn against her..." She sighed. "Which would be perfect except that she won't go into that room until she needs to move the heart to Embercliffe. She won't do that until she has her traitor and assurance of her victory according to the visions, which I can't give her for exactly that reason."

Sorra screamed into her arms, muffling the noise.

"I wish I'd never heard of the visions," she said, speaking directly to Linnea's placidly smiling statue. "How have they helped us? Beau's hint of 'east of the sun and west of the moon' was more help in finding the castle than us following the humble path, which might have been about any number of things along the way."

She kicked the wall, which hurt her foot but released some frustration.

"It's too many pieces," she decided, still whispering to the statue. "What if I set the visions aside and made something of the rest of it?" The answer came quickly, surprising her. "It'd be obvious then, wouldn't it? I'd say we needed to give Gwelain a false sense of victory, manipulating her into putting herself in danger because she thinks she's safe. The only way to do that would be to give in, become her traitor and her monster—" Sorra paused, then pushed past thoughts of exactly what that would mean for her. "And then she'd go to collect the heart, expecting a smooth road to claiming Linnea's throne, crown, and country. She'd let me negotiate for Beau's safety if it meant her getting what she wants. He and Varek would join me, and Varek might know how to get into the tower and sever her connection to the heart so Beau could take it home. Varek would have to trust us enough to agree to that, but..."

Her imagination only caught on that detail for a second before the pieces fell neatly into place.

"But Varek would trust me if I were a goblin and had as much to lose as he did if Beau broke his promises. Our fates would be tied together. I'd still trust Beau. It might be enough."

It was perfect, in theory. Devious in its way, but Sorra saw nothing wrong with manipulating Gwelain after all her tricks.

But it was only perfect when she set aside the visions. They'd proved themselves consistently true in hindsight, if not always helpful as a roadmap, and they clearly stated that Gwelain would rise to power if she had a traitor by her side who had turned away from Linnea's quest.

Not will. May. Andonia's greatest enemy may *rise to power.*

Sorra's breath went out of her in a quick rush.

The scholars believed the two outcomes were mutually exclusive. Gwelain clearly did as well, and was confident that her victory would come naturally once she'd won over her traitor.

But none of Linnea's other visions were *if this then that.* They were *this is what will be.*

So what if both outcomes are true? What if they're not mutually exclusive, but sequential?

What if the traitor opens the door to Gwelain's possible victory, but then to her defeat?

And at Gwelain's defeat, her magic would crumble. Tullian's enchantment would fail, and he would become human again.

And bleed.

And die.

A terrible outcome, but the one he'd wished for, and the hero's death would come on the day of Gwelain's defeat, just as Linnea's vision said. He would be free, and so would Selim and all the people trapped in Gwelain's timeless lands.

There were too many unknowns, too many possibilities. Tullian would have called her misguided and foolish for considering it, but the idea wouldn't leave her.

Gwelain said the blessing and the arrow's guidance could both be true if I aided her victory, but what if they could also work together for her downfall? I could fulfil my blessing by becoming a monster and a traitor, then escape it by making an unexpected move in this game Gwelain thinks she controls.

It felt right and terrible. Right and terrifying. And, worst of all, right and risky.

"It's not, though," Sorra said, climbing to her feet and brushing the dust off herself just for the sake of moving. "It can't be right. The scholars would have seen it."

But they'd made mistakes. They'd only chosen men as their heroes in the past, though nothing in the visions said they had to be. Sorra knew she wasn't smarter than them, but she had never been taught to wear blinders as they had, formed from assumptions and outdated thinking.

Not smarter. Just more able to see.

"Which only leaves a larger problem," Sorra said, her voice thick and dull. "I don't want it to be right."

If the plan worked perfectly, she'd be turned into a goblin. There was a chance that this, too, was magic that would end when Gwelain lost her power, but she doubted she'd be so lucky. Gwelain had spoken of breaking bodies to reform them, which sounded rather permanent.

"Funny, isn't it?" She crouched beside the statue and looked into the jagged grooves where its eyes had been. "All this time I've known I was meant to be a villain but was trying to dress myself as a hero so everyone would finally love me. Now I have a chance to be a true hero, but it could forever mark me as a monster, just like the blessing promised."

She brushed a tear from her cheek, then traced the same damp path down the statue's face. "Are you listening, Linnea? Have you been listening all along?"

The trail dried and faded, leaving the statue as impassive as ever.

"I don't want this!" Sorra's voice rose to a desperate, pleading rasp. "Show me another way. Show me this is wrong. Shift time, go back and choose someone else to feature in your damned visions. Or, if I'm not supposed to be here at all, let me go back and die in Cottsbridge before I had any notions of heroism or happy endings. Please."

The dead queen didn't answer. There was no sense of peace or reassurance, and no other solution came to mind that might save both Beau's life and Linnea's heart, or that would allow her to keep her humanity and save Andonia.

If I'm wrong, I'll be handing Andonia over to its greatest enemy.

If I'm right, Beau keeps his throne. The heart returns to Andonia with him. Tullian dies and spends eternity with his queen, the humans here get to live and die as they should, and I'll make sure Varek gets a world that's as safe for goblins as it is for humans—my life will depend on it.

There were so many places it could all go wrong. The idea of a happy ending for anyone still felt like a dangerous fantasy.

But if the choice was an orderly march to defeat or a wild dash toward a sliver of hope, Sorra knew what her choice had to be.

If my dark blessing is our only hope, then chaos is our path to victory.

Her eyes burned. Her chest ached. She wished she could turn to stone like the similarly wounded statue before her, forgotten in shadows and left to crumble while someone else took care of destiny.

But her heart kept beating. The sky outside the gallery lightened to violet, then deep, burning orange.

Sorra took a shuddering breath. "If you're still here, Linnea, help me. If I still have a chance to negotiate, I'll need to be clever to avoid Gwelain's tricks. I could still fail. I probably will. I'm not ready for this. But I have no other cards up my sleeve, and I can't do anything except play the hand I've been dealt. Help me see how to play it well."

She walked slowly through the gallery, her heart and her feet heavy as she passed between the Bright Ones. She looked up at them, hoping for reassurance, but nothing had changed except the light.

They had abandoned this world.

Linnea had tried to make it better.

Now Sorra would find out whether her greatest destiny was to save it or destroy it.

CHAPTER FIFTY-FOUR

Sorra moved as though encased in glass, seeing the goblins, the treasures, the beauty, and the bustle, but noting it all distantly, as though none of it had any relation to herself. Voices touched her ears as insignificant murmurs, and scents of sweat and perfume barely entered her consciousness. The goblins she'd shied away from on her flight to the statue gallery parted before her, residents of another world as she walked forward, her gaze locked on the next turn, the next staircase.

Her fear remained, but it now nestled deep within her, cozy as a cat drunk on fresh cream. After a lifetime of denying and fighting the chaos that surrounded her, accepting its inevitability felt right, if not at all good.

Whether the choice was right or wrong, it was made, and all that was left was to see where it led. Her fear of the goblins was nothing compared to the blinding terror she felt for herself and her destiny, and even when Reaver and a soldier companion fell in behind her, escorting her with grinning teeth bared and axes drawn, her steps didn't falter.

Kill me now, she thought without passion. *Let me do what Tullian couldn't. Spare me knowing where this would have led.*

It was her own voice in her mind. Not the dark, taunting one. Not her sisters. She listened, but none of them spoke up.

So Sorra descended the stairs as alone as she'd ever been, even surrounded by enemies.

The doors to the throne room stood open, flanked by a handful of goblin courtiers who had paused to watch. She saw herself through their eyes—dishevelled, her face marked by dried tears and exhaustion. Pathetic, bedraggled. The impression rolled off her, along with the shallowly amusing idea that she had once cared what anyone saw when they looked at her.

Early morning sunlight, clear and gentle, lit the throne room from above. The thrones still stood in their place, but where there had once been an open expanse of black and white tiles at the centre of the room, a garden blossomed. Tullian stood at its centre, his roots sunk deep into dark earth, his twisted branches reaching for the sun.

Gwelain stood facing the tree, dressed in an open-backed white dress, speaking to him as though certain he could hear.

The glass walls Sorra had imagined surrounding her shattered, leaving her cold and exposed, a part of the world again as Gwelain motioned her closer. Every detail stood out, far too clear—the gilded claws, the faint tremble of Tullian's leaves in the still air of the throne room, the hilt of the sword that still protruded from what had once been his chest. She wondered whether he felt it, or whether he could feel anything at all.

"I was beginning to think you'd taken the coward's way out," Gwelain said, turning to face her. "I hope your presence here means you've had a change of heart, or at least seen reason now that this fool isn't standing in your way."

Sorra didn't answer. She met the queen's gaze, though. It was easier than looking at Tullian.

"I think he'll do well here even after we're gone," Gwelain continued, as though Sorra had asked. "Plenty of light, good soil, and a source of water that should serve him long enough to live out his natural lifespan."

"You are most merciful, Majesty," Sorra said, her voice flat.

Gwelain smiled, cold and lovely. "Is that why you're here? For mercy?"

Movement near the thrones caught Sorra's attention. Varek

approached, frowning. He wore black but had managed to make himself unnoticeable in the bright and shining room.

"I suppose I have," Sorra said, turning her gaze back to the queen. "And to come to an agreement I hope will serve both of us."

Gwelain plucked one of Tullian's silver leaves and twirled it by its stem between her fingers. "Negotiations? I hardly think you're in a position to bargain at this point."

"I think I am, though." Sorra wished the conversation were happening anywhere but in front of Tullian, but Gwelain wanted him to witness this, to make him suffer his defeat as fully as possible, to make it as painful for Sorra as she could. And a defeat it would have to be—the queen couldn't be allowed to guess that Sorra was abandoning her quest for any reason other than to save Beau.

She would believe it. She already thought of Sorra as a low creature, devious and selfish.

So Tullian would have to think the same. Sorra hoped she'd live to prove them wrong but felt less certain of her plan than she had when she'd been alone with the imagined ghost of Queen Linnea.

There was no turning back now, though.

She cleared her throat. "According to Linnea's visions, you can only rise to power after one of her servants bows to you and becomes your creature. I am the last of her heroes."

Gwelain shrugged. "There will be more. The visions must be fulfilled eventually."

"Maybe. But not now. Not soon. Without me, your carefully laid plans around Beau and your claim to the throne will be for nothing. I can't hold out forever, but I can last long enough to take this from you."

Gwelain's smile remained, but her eyes turned cold. "You really think you can be that brave?"

"I know I can be that stubborn. Or you can have me now. I'll accept your offer under certain conditions, and you'll be free to leave for Embercliffe today, with plenty of time for Beau to claim the throne before it passes to someone else."

Gwelain laughed as she stalked toward the thrones. "Varek,

didn't I tell you she was amusing?" She sat and rested her chin on one hand. "Very well. Let us hear your demands."

Sorra glanced at Varek, but he was as unreadable as ever, offering no sign that he thought she was doing the right thing, no discouragement, nothing that revealed they'd ever spoken more than a few words to each other.

But his presence made her feel a little less alone, and that was better than nothing.

"I will renounce my quest and my allegiance to Linnea," she said. "I will swear myself to you and allow you to turn me into a goblin, but only if you agree to certain conditions."

Gwelain rolled her eyes.

Sorra stepped closer, turning her back to Tullian. It wouldn't change anything. He would still hear. But she couldn't say more with his leaves dancing at the corner of her vision.

"In exchange, you will agree to spare Beau's life." A terrible thought occurred to her, and her stomach sank. She looked to Varek. "He is still alive, isn't he? The real one."

"He is," Varek said.

Gwelain looked from Sorra to Varek and back. "You know about my son's little problem, do you?"

"Yes, Majesty. I trust that you're coming to these negotiations honestly, and his confirmation of facts won't be a problem for you."

Gwelain let out a long breath, nostrils flaring. "Go on."

Sorra pressed on, afraid she'd lose her nerve. "The real Beauregard of Andonia will stay alive, healthy, mentally capable in every way, with his memories intact and all his senses working, with no alterations in form or function or lifespan no matter what actions he takes in the future." Her thoughts danced, jumping from obstacle to obstacle as she imagined how Gwelain would worm her way around technicalities. She thought of the contracts the queen had made her goblins sign and her devious deal with Beau, letting the ideas flow instead of trying to herd them into rational paths, following each shining point as it appeared to her. "He, as his true and identifiable human self, will return to Embercliffe as king of Andonia, and his ongoing safety will be the price you pay for my sacrifice."

"Is that all?" Gwelain asked, far too pleasantly. "Consider it done."

"Not quite." Sorra stood up straighter. "I want irrevocable, magically enforced consequences to apply if you go back on this promise, even after my transformation or whatever else might happen to me. If any harm ever comes to Beau through your actions or negligence, you will lose your connection to Linnea's power and her heart will be free. Forever."

Gwelain gripped the arms of her throne. "I'm afraid such a thing would be impossible," she said, her voice smooth as silk even as her posture betrayed her irritation. "No mere contract could ever be stronger than my power."

Sorra looked to Varek. "Is that true?"

Gwelain shot him a warning glare, but he appeared not to see it.

"It is, partly," he said. "If you signed in your own blood in the traditional way, Majesty, the contract would not be stronger than your magic. It would, however, be stronger than your bond with the heart. The consequence proposed here would come into effect the moment you broke the agreement, and your control would be severed."

Tension drained from Sorra's body, leaving her aware of her exhaustion. Whatever happened to her, Beau would be saved. Even if Gwelain made it to Embercliffe—and Sorra prayed she wouldn't —he would still be free to finish what Tullian had started so long ago.

Gwelain's golden claws tapped out a quick, uneven rhythm on the arm of her throne. "Is it your aim to save him, or to trap me into severing my connection to the heart?"

"I hope you intend to keep your promise, Majesty. But the consequence seems fitting, and it shouldn't be a problem as long as you aren't planning to go back on your word."

The tapping continued. Gwelain stared down at Sorra, and Sorra held her gaze.

"Very well. There's a standard contract already drafted that permits me to turn you into one of my little monsters." Gwelain snapped her fingers at Varek, and Sorra caught the irritated twitch of his lips. "Varek, go find it in the anteroom and make the necessary alterations regarding Beauregard and her renunciation of... well, everything. Your magic will be sufficient for this, I think."

Varek nodded, but the glance he shot at Sorra as he passed offered a clear warning.

And an unnecessary one. If a lifetime of errors and miscalculations had taught Sorra anything, it was to learn from her mistakes —and better yet, those made by others.

"An established contract won't do," she said. "I'd like a new one, written in my own language where I can see each word as it's inked."

Varek looked to Gwelain.

"You're trying my patience," Gwelain said, nearly snarling.

"I have a habit of doing that, Majesty, and of not trusting folks to have my best interests in mind. You can blame my upbringing for that, if you'd like."

Gwelain nodded to Varek, and he entered the little office Sorra and Gwelain had passed through the previous day. When he returned, he carried a delicately carved wooden lap-desk in both hands. He sat on the empty throne, barely perched on its edge, and opened the desk to remove a clean sheet of white paper, an inkwell, and a quill pen fashioned from a black feather.

"There's no trick to that paper?" Sorra asked.

"None," Varek said. "Nothing's ever been written on it before. The ink is only ink, the quill is a regular quill. Magic will only come into it at the signing."

Gwelain scowled but motioned for Varek to go ahead. Sorra read over his shoulder as he laid out exactly the terms she'd proposed regarding Beau's safety and the consequences should Gwelain break her promise, word for word. Gwelain didn't speak again until Varek looked to her for further instruction.

"In exchange," Gwelain said, "Sorra must agree to renounce her loyalty to Linnea, to Andonia, and to the foolish quest that brought her here. And to her humanity, of course. Permanently."

"My physical humanity," Sorra said. "But I keep my memories, my mind, my will."

Gwelain tapped her claws together. "As though I'd rob you of any potential pain and regret by taking any of them."

Too easy, Sorra thought, but Gwelain went on.

"Clever little Sorra will agree to become a goblin in the fashion of my soldiers and nobles—a pretty little monster in whatever form the magic chooses for her, with the usual seed of darkness planted in her heart. But she will retain her ugly little personality and her memories, and she will swear loyalty to me. She will be mine to use as I see fit, and she will forever be magically bound against doing me harm. The consequence of any attempt at such will be the destruction of her body and her soul."

Sorra flinched. She'd hoped Gwelain wouldn't specifically keep her from continuing her work but wasn't surprised. She'd never convince the queen she'd had a true change of heart or deserved any level of trust. It would be up to Beau and Varek to use the opportunity she and Tullian had given them.

Corvin dead. Gwelain vulnerable the moment she went to collect the heart.

The Mind and the Magic would have to be enough.

Varek paused, quill raised above the paper. "Forgive me, my queen, but I want to be sure I have the exact wording you want. You did say *forever*?"

Sorra drew a sharp breath. It wasn't quite a warning, but his hesitation reminded her how the clauses in the goblins' contracts had horrified her. "Not forever."

Gwelain's claws dug channels into the wooden arms of her throne. "What difference does it make?"

Sorra didn't dare look to Varek for guidance.

"I..." Sorra glanced around the room, hoping for an answer. All she found was Tullian, who had been denied his death and his chance to serve Linnea in the lands beyond. "I don't know what happens after death, Majesty, but I wish to be free to experience it. You may change my body and control my future while I live, but I insist that my soul remains my own. It will not be yours to enslave or destroy. Our agreement ends when my body dies."

Gwelain's lips tightened.

Sorra didn't dare speak again.

"Your counsel, Varek?" Gwelain said at last.

Varek read over the contract, then looked to Gwelain. "If your desired outcome is to have her sign the contract and become the traitor, freeing you to collect the heart and—"

"Yes, yes," Gwelain muttered. "According to the visions and such."

"Then I would suggest, if I may, that you allow this concession. Unless, of course, you believe she'll somehow harm you after her death."

Gwelain bared her teeth at him. "Are you implying I might be afraid of ghosts?"

"Not at all. I am, however, attempting to establish whether this is something you wish to waste time on when you have other preparations to make before our departure." His voice, though still rough, had taken on an obsequious, placating tone Sorra hadn't suspected him capable of. "Perhaps in an honest contract eternity is too much to demand if a lifetime will get the job done."

"Until her death, then." Gwelain rubbed the pads of her fingers against her temple. Sorra hoped that a headache would soon be the least of the queen's problems. "Are we finished?"

Sorra studied Gwelain. The queen smiled, clearly satisfied even after her concession and in spite of whatever pain she was in. But no matter how Sorra looked at it, she couldn't see where the agreement left a door open for Gwelain to harm Beau, or to keep him from standing against her now that his safety would be guaranteed even if he broke the treaty.

Perhaps she was only pleased about removing Sorra from the quest, binding her actions even if in her heart she still wished to fight. And, of course, anticipating the victory she now believed was within her grasp.

Sorra lowered her chin and looked to Varek from beneath her lashes. He stretched his neck to one side, then the other, finishing his movements in a barely noticeable nod.

White lights crowded the edges of Sorra's vision.

Varek wanted her to sign. Whether or not this was the path to victory he'd imagined, he thought she'd done the best she could with it. The question was whether she trusted him.

She knew what Tullian would say if he could speak—that this

was the worst thing she could do, that she was the greatest mistake he'd ever made, that she'd be better off dead.

She knew what Beau would say, too. He'd never let her sacrifice her humanity and risk handing Andonia to Gwelain for the sake of saving him.

But this wasn't their decision.

"We're finished," she said. "As long as the queen will sign first."

Varek took another quill from the little desk, this one adorned with a white feather. Gwelain held out her right hand, and he pricked her finger with the quill, holding it in place until the base of the feather turned red. The colour flowed upward, spreading to its tip. As Gwelain signed her name, the colour bled into the paper.

Sorra sat on the floor cross-legged, and Varek settled the desk on her lap. She held out her right hand. There was little pain when the quill pierced her skin, but a bead of blood remained on her finger when Varek pulled it away.

Gwelain leaned in to watch as Sorra took the quill in her hand, which trembled so violently she had to pause to steady it before she could sign.

Let me be right, she prayed silently. *Let every mishap have been a step closer to victory. Let me be the Mystery, blessing and all.*

She tried not to think of what she stood to lose, or the risk she was taking as she signed her name below the queen's. Her blood glowed faintly as it sank into the paper, sealing her fate.

Gwelain snatched the contract away from her and held it up, examining the signature. Then she handed it to Varek and grabbed Sorra's arm, roughly pushing her sleeve back.

The black songbird that had marked her as Linnea's servant was gone.

Gwelain crouched, placing her face close to Sorra's. "Say it out loud."

Sorra swallowed hard. "I renounce my loyalty to Linnea and the quest to retrieve her heart," she whispered.

"Louder."

"I pledge myself to your service, Queen Gwelain." Her voice came out in broken, grating shards.

Gwelain stood. "On your knees, then."

Sorra clenched her jaw to keep her chin from trembling as she knelt before the goblin queen.

"Rise."

Sorra obeyed but kept her eyes downcast.

"Look at me." Gwelain waited until Sorra met her cold, hard gaze. "What do you think, Varek? Should I kill her the second the transformation is complete, or let her live a few moments longer to regret it?"

Sorra felt as though she'd been punched in the stomach. "Majesty, you can't. That is, surely there's a purpose for me. The visions…"

She trailed off as her words were lost under Gwelain's delighted laughter.

"Yes, the visions." Gwelain calmed herself but grinned madly. "My favourite is one your scholars never read, I think. There were two deaths foretold, one on each potential path to victory. On the way to Linnea's heart being restored to its so-called rightful place, a hero's death." She looked to Tullian and clucked her tongue. "Not to be, was it? On the path to my victory, another vision. The traitor's lifeblood spilled instead, and the shifting sands made solid before the goblin queen's feet as she steps boldly toward her hard-earned fate." She paused. "At least, that's the best I can translate it into your ugly tongue. Do you see? You have a role in my victory, and it's as easy as can be. I don't have to trust you to act on my behalf. I only need you to die."

Sorra couldn't speak.

Gwelain flexed her claws. "Varek, aid me in making her one of my goblins. Once that part of the visions is complete, I think I'll spill her blood in the garden to fertilize the soil for her dear mentor."

Sorra's lips moved, trying to beg for her life. She stilled them before her breath could fill her voice. Begging would only delight Gwelain and would do no good.

"My queen," Varek said. "Mother. Would you allow me to offer counsel?"

Gwelain sighed, irritated. "In my best interest?"

"In the interest of your personal satisfaction, Majesty," he said with a little bow and a hint of a dark smirk that seemed to please Gwelain. "It would be a shame to kill her without your husband first seeing his beloved little human as a traitor and a monster."

Gwelain frowned. "He'll know of it either way."

"And he'll believe it, no doubt." Varek clasped his claws before him. "Forgive me. You know my feelings toward him, and perhaps you'd be right to think me selfish for saying this, but mightn't it be more satisfying—for both of us—to wait? Telling him what she did would be fine, but showing her to him, alive and monstrous and re-made into something like your image, would make him hate her in a way he could never hate a corpse. I'd like to see that. I think you would regret it if you lost your chance to see it, too."

His cruel words sucked Sorra's breath from her chest.

Varek couldn't lie. If he said he desired Beau's suffering, he meant it.

But it's not all he wants, she reminded herself. *He wants to see the heart taken from Gwelain. Even if he's only delaying my death to further those plans, so be it. He doesn't have to be good. He just has to get me what I want, too.*

If a bit of cruelty was what it took to delay things long enough to bring Beau on board... well, she'd chosen to trust Varek this far.

But a part of her wished he hadn't stepped in. To die as a goblin would be terrible, but living long enough to face Beau when he saw what she'd done might be worse.

Gwelain smiled as she turned back to Sorra. Varek did not.

"You may be right, Varek," Gwelain said. "I congratulate you on your clear thinking. It would be a shame to deny Beauregard the bitter conclusion to this misguided little romance. A king needs to be stronger than he is now. Harder, if I'm to be saddled with him for the rest of his natural life. This will be good for him."

Sorra wondered if Varek saw through Gwelain as clearly as she did, and whether Gwelain understood how pointless her justifica-tions were. This decision wasn't about shaping Beau into the king she wanted him to be.

It was the same as her treatment of Andonia. She wanted to rule it legitimately, but if she couldn't, she'd gladly burn it to the ground. And if she couldn't have Beau's admiration and affection, she'd burn them out of him by destroying everything he might have loved in Sorra.

Possession or destruction. Maybe it was all the same to her in the end, as long as no one else had something she couldn't.

"Let's finish this, then," Gwelain said. "I'll want her back on her feet before we show her off to him." She stepped closer to Sorra, her lips parting in a vile grin. "I'm afraid we won't have time to put you to sleep. Try not to scream loud enough to draw attention and ruin the surprise. Varek, your assistance, please."

Sorra only heard a few syllables of Gwelain's magic before pain gripped her body, setting her skin on fire. Her muscles convulsed, arching her back past its natural range of motion. She fell to the floor, writhing, praying to Linnea for unconsciousness or death.

Neither came. She screamed, and Gwelain's laughter echoed through the throne room.

CHAPTER FIFTY-FIVE

Diffuse sunlight burned Sorra's eyes when she opened them. She squeezed them closed and tried again.

The underground cave came into dazzling focus around her. It was the same place she'd visited with Gwelain, but everything had changed, as if this were the true cave and the version she'd seen before merely a shadow of it.

The moss she lay on was more comfortable by far than any bed she'd ever slept in, and though the wool blanket that covered her had a rough texture, the scratch of it against her skin pleased her. The burbling of the creek was the most fascinating music she'd ever heard, and the veins of quartz in the walls were more lovely than diamonds. Everything was clearer and sharper, from the beams of sunlight to shadows so thick they seemed to have weight of their own. She could pick out every leaf on a little vining plant on the far side of the cave and saw more shades of colour than she'd imagined existed.

She breathed in deep to convince herself she was alive. The faint scents of moss and lichen and mushrooms were still present, but she picked out notes she hadn't before. The sweetness of rot, the sharp bite of damp stone, the complex richness she'd previously noted only as "soil."

She'd thought the place lovely on her first visit, but now it put

Gwelain's shining castle and all its treasures to shame, and she wondered how she hadn't realized it before.

She closed her eyes again.

It's because I was human then.

Her awareness shifted from the cave to her own body. She didn't remember losing consciousness, and most of what she'd suffered was blessedly buried somewhere deep in her memory, but she remembered the agreement and the beginning of the transformation.

She raised her hands and stifled a gasp. Her skin was its old, familiar colour, though it had lost the warm tan it had picked up over the summer.

That was the only thing she recognized.

Her arms were longer than they had been. So were her fingers, which were tipped with dark claws—not as dangerously impressive as Gwelain's, but completely inhuman nonetheless. She touched one to the back of the opposite arm and found the claw sharp, but her skin was tougher than it had been before. She pressed harder. Her claw didn't break through, but there was pain.

Different pain, though, which brought little desire to escape from it. Present, but not *bad.* She pressed harder and shivered at the sensation.

Sorra had never been particularly aware of the shape of her teeth, but what she felt when she moved her tongue was horribly wrong. Larger teeth. Sharper. Not exposed like Varek's or Gwelain's, but hidden behind her lips. Still, they were the teeth of a predator, deadly tools made for tearing flesh.

She touched her face but couldn't tell whether it had changed until she moved her fingers to her hairline, where two short horns curved back from her forehead, crowning hair that felt thicker and softer than she remembered. She tucked the dark strands behind her ears, which now came to long points.

Down then, exploring with dreamlike detachment. Her arms ached as she moved them, but there was strength in her body she'd never felt before. She sat up, observing the pain in her stomach muscles, and pushed the blanket down to her waist.

Her breasts were unchanged, but behind them her heart beat

more eagerly than it had before. She slipped her hands under the blanket and found herself naked. Softer hair than she remembered. Harder thigh muscles.

She steeled herself and threw off the blanket.

Her legs had been replaced with a monster's. Shorter thighs and shinbones, elongated feet with long, thick toes and curving claws. From her toes to her knees the skin was covered in coppery scales.

Like a bird. Or a dragon.

Like Gwelain's, but not pearlescent or pretty.

She flexed her toes, and the horrible things came alive.

The sight of those feet moving at her command broke something in her. She cried out and leapt up, knowing she couldn't escape but desperate to try. She stumbled and pitched backward as she tried to place her feet flat on the ground and only found her footing when she stood on her toes.

It felt horribly natural.

She took a few steps, cautious at first, then bolder, finding balance easy. Her new feet changed her gait to one that felt as much like dancing as it did like walking.

She reached behind her.

No tail. No wings, though a line of scaly skin traced down the length of her spine.

She was still standing with her hands behind her when Varek pushed through the vines at the cave's entrance and stepped in carrying a covered tray. He looked away quickly, and Sorra bent to snatch up the wool blanket and hide her body.

A wave of dizziness hit her, and she sat down hard in the moss, holding her breath so she wouldn't cry.

Varek set the tray down next to her and sat without waiting to be invited.

"This was an interesting choice," he said, nodding toward her new form. "Some would call it stupid."

Sorra tried to pull her knees to her chest, but her legs were wrong, and she gave up. "I think it was objectively stupid." Her tongue moved strangely against her new teeth, giving her a slight lisp, but her voice was the same. "All I want to know is whether it was useful."

Varek removed the lid from the tray, revealing a silver goblet filled with dark liquid, a bowl holding three raw eggs with bright, golden yolks, and a plate of sliced meat, red with blood.

Sorra wrinkled her nose. "I can't eat that."

"You can, and you should. Your ordeal drained you, and this is what your body needs if it's to recover."

Sorra leaned closer. The smell of raw flesh repulsed her mind, but her mouth watered.

"Tell me the meat isn't human."

"This isn't human. It's cow, actually."

She picked up the bowl, held her breath, and slurped the eggs down whole. The slimy whites didn't turn her stomach as she'd expected, and the flavour was mild and pleasant. She pinched a thin slice of meat between her claws and lifted it to her mouth, trying not to think about what she was doing.

She tasted, chewed, and swallowed. Her appetite roared to life, and though she tried to go slowly so she could savour the new texture and delightful flavour, the meal was quickly gone.

"Drink," Varek said. "That's not human, either."

With less hesitation than she'd felt toward the rest of the meal Sorra lifted the goblet to her lips and drank, letting blood wash over her tongue, rich and warm and good, trying not to think of how hard it would have been for her human body to swallow a single drop.

She wiped her lips on the blanket. "Does this mean there's a reason for me to recover beyond Gwelain wanting me back on my feet before I die?"

"That's up to you." Varek looked into her eyes.

She didn't know what hers were like now, but his had changed like the cave had, becoming deeper and more varied in the shades of bronze and dark gold that radiated through the irises. She hadn't noticed before how thick his eyelashes were, or how the green of his skin wasn't so strange after all.

She suddenly felt shy but resisted the urge to look away.

"Why did you do this?" he asked, more gentle and curious than he usually seemed. "Why did you give her what she wanted? You might have escaped and made a life somewhere far from Andonia."

"Not one where I could have lived with that choice." Sorra looked down at her hands. "I didn't want this. But you said—" She stopped. "Is it safe to speak now that Corvin is dead?"

"He's gone. No one is listening."

At least that's something, she thought, though the price Tullian had paid for it was far too high.

"Gwelain can't use magic to defend herself when she's in the heart's presence," she said.

"True."

"She has to go to the treasury to collect the heart if she wants to transport it to Embercliffe. But for that to happen, she needed her traitor." She shivered, though the humid air was warm and pleasant. "Even if I'm dead soon, I hope you or Beau might take advantage of that somehow. Or if not here, on the road to Andonia." She sighed. "I didn't know enough to plan beyond getting her into a weakened position. But I thought that if the visions were sequential instead of alternate paths, she could have her traitor and still be defeated."

"Impressive thinking for a human mind."

Sorra ignored the twisted compliment. "Tell me you can use this somehow."

"There might be a way. She's resting now. The heart is still in its tower, but she'll want to collect it and leave as soon as she's finished with you." Varek looked toward the pale stalactites that hung from the ceiling. "What do you think of this place?"

The change of subject caught Sorra off guard, but she answered without hesitation. "It's wonderful. I thought so before, but now it's... it's perfect."

Varek smiled sadly. "I'm glad you think so. Gwelain's creations generally prefer the kind of beauty she offers them in her castle, clean and structured and deliberate. What surrounds us now is the kind of beauty favoured by goblins—real ones. I much prefer it, myself." He looked to her, apparently unguarded and open. "What will you do now that you're one of us?"

Sorra frowned. "I think the plan is for me to die quite soon."

"Say you survived this in spite of your best attempts to destroy yourself and the world you know. If you had a future, how would you use it?"

Sorra's stomach clenched.

The answer was both obvious and painful.

"There's no future for me in Andonia."

"True enough." Varek thought for a moment. "If we fail and Gwelain makes it to Andonia, she'll see to it that our kind are most welcome, but she will not forgive either of us for any attempted betrayal. If we succeed, humans will remain in power, which has never been good for our kind. But you seem to trust your human king. He might pardon you."

"I know. But I can't go home. I can't face my sisters or hope for a normal life there, or anywhere among humans."

"No." His claws dug deep into the moss. "Does this knowledge free you of your desire to see the heart returned to human hands? Do you wish to destroy it to ensure it won't be used to harm you?"

Sorra noted hesitation, as though he knew what her answer would be.

"No. I know it sounds foolish, but I think the world needs Linnea's magic. But humans don't have to be your enemies. If we help him save it, Beau will see that we're protected. You, me, whatever's left of the old kind. He'd release these lands to you and agree not to use the heart against us as long as we don't cause trouble."

Varek laughed bitterly. "Like children sent to our room to think about what we did?"

"Like reasonable creatures who did a service to Andonia and deserve to live in peace. Would you want that? To rule, I mean. Even if Gwelain survives this, Beau would never agree to her holding power."

"Nor would I want her to. I'd like that, though. Power of my own, not the scraps she's allowed me." He didn't sound happy about it, though. "You believe he'd keep promises like those?"

"Yes." She couldn't imagine it for herself but felt sure such a life was possible for Varek even if she didn't survive to see it. "If you have a plan that will get the heart away from Gwelain without destroying it, if you'll help Beau take the heart back to where it belongs, he'll agree. I don't suppose relations will ever be warm, but with Gwelain out of the way, he'd have no reason to see you as an enemy, provided you didn't act like one."

"I suppose I'll have to trust you on that, now that your fate depends on it as much as mine does." Varek climbed to his feet. "I do have a plan. It's dangerous and by no means guaranteed to work, but it will give us a chance to end this today."

"What is it?"

Varek smiled. "I'll tell you as soon as that king you're so fond of agrees to your terms." He pulled a watch from his pocket and glanced at it. "If he's capable of following instructions, he should be here any moment."

Sorra pulled the blanket tighter to her chest and glanced around the cave as though Beau might already have materialized. He hadn't, and neither had any sort of clothing. She combed her hair forward in an attempt to cover her horns, then changed her grip on the blanket, hiding her claws.

"Does he know about what's happened?"

"To you? No," Varek said, unconcerned. "He knows about the knight's actions and that you're here, but not—"

He stopped as Beau stepped into the cave, his eyes wide as he absorbed the lovely underground space that Gwelain had never revealed to him.

He spotted Sorra and ran toward her.

Then his steps slowed as his face twisted into an unguarded expression of horror. He fell to his knees beside her, his eyes widening as he looked into hers.

"What did she do to you?" He glared at Varek. "Did you have a part in this?"

Sorra reached for his hand. The way he flinched away from her claws threatened to rip her heart from her chest. He could have touched her without consequence now that Corvin and his fresh curse were gone. He simply couldn't stand to.

It hurt, but she supposed this pain would be nothing compared to what was to come.

Sorra clutched the blanket tight again, hard enough that her claws tore the fabric. "I agreed to this," she said. "It was the only way to make sure you stay alive long enough to end the fight. The contract Gwelain signed is clear. If she harms you, she loses the heart. You're free to fight her."

Beau's gaze roamed over her face and her arms, lingering on her horns.

"You're a goblin."

"Yes."

"You turned your back on your quest and gave her the last piece she needed to secure her victory. You risked everything. To save me." It wasn't a question, but he said it as though begging her to correct him.

"Yes. Not only you, but to give us a chance to save Linnea's heart and Andonia's magic, and for you to take the throne. Even if I'm wrong, you'll still be alive to fix things."

He stood, backing away before she could reach for him again.

"My life isn't worth this!" He gestured to her body, and Sorra curled in on herself as if she could make the monstrous truth disappear. She told herself it didn't matter, that his anger didn't hurt.

Varek had been right. If Gwelain had killed her already, Beau would have mourned Sorra's death and turned his anger on Gwelain. Now, though, he looked at Sorra as though she were the monster who had killed the woman he'd cared for.

Varek stepped between them, facing Beau.

"It was a calculated sacrifice," he said. "Her idea, her decision, and one that offers us a chance to end this before Gwelain can take the crown and lock the heart away forever. Much as it pains me to say it, we'll all need to work together if we want to make Sorra's sacrifice and the knight's mean anything."

Beau sat on one of the stones near the creek, his head in his hands.

Sorra wished her heart had changed as her senses had, making her just monstrous enough that she could stop caring what a human thought of her.

Varek crossed his arms and nodded toward Beau. "Go ahead," he whispered. "Time is short."

Sorra stood, cautiously finding her footing again as she wrapped the blanket around her torso, and sat on the stone Gwelain had occupied the last time she'd visited the cave, preparing herself to negotiate for Varek's participation and his future.

For my future, if I have one, she reminded herself. Varek was allowing this because she wasn't negotiating as a human, and she owed it to him to remember that.

"We'd like an agreement in place before we move forward," she said.

Beau raised his head. "We?"

"Those of us without a future in Andonia," she said, and swallowed the tightness in her throat. "Which will be in your hands, if all goes well. Varek is willing to agree to seeing the heart returned to Andonia instead of its destruction provided you agree that these lands will belong to goblins as a country separate from Andonia. And, more importantly, provided you agree that the heart's magic will never be used against Varek or his people."

"Under any circumstances?" Beau spoke to Varek. He hadn't looked at Sorra since he'd lifted his head. "That's convenient."

"Any goblins who act as enemies will be treated as such, of course," Sorra said, answering before Varek could step in. "You'd be free to keep the border closed if you wished, and the accompanying death penalty. But if the goblins—that is, if we keep the peace and keep to our own lands, we must have nothing to fear from Andonia or its magic."

Beau looked ill. "Will we even remember these lands exist?"

"You will," Varek said. "If Gwelain had created that enchantment from her own power it might have lasted after her death, but she used magic that isn't truly hers. Once she relinquishes her authority over the heart, whatever she's created using its magic will crumble. The world will remember these lands. Age and illness and death will return."

"And you'll be able to lie again," Beau said. "I'm sure that'll be a relief."

"It certainly will." Varek flashed him a grim smile. "I find beauty in many bleak and painful things, but unadorned truth is too ugly for me to bear much longer."

Sorra barely heard anything after *whatever she's created using its magic will crumble.* She looked down at her hands, then to Varek.

He shook his head. "Her defeat will not free you from this."

"I see." Sorra straightened her shoulders. "Does that suit everyone, then? The heart goes back to Andonia, the goblins are left in peace here in their own lands. Everyone gets what they want."

"Not everyone." Beau took several breaths before he spoke again. "Very well. If you and Varek help me return the heart to human hands in Andonia, these so-called Forgotten Lands will belong to the goblins." He looked into Sorra's eyes without fear. "You'll be safe from me and all who follow after me as long as you remain a friend to Andonia. That's the best I can offer you. I can't promise all will be well or that your kind and mine will ever resolve our differences, but I can give you a chance to live in peace. You will be safe. And I hope you'll be happy."

The anger was gone, leaving his voice heavy with sadness that echoed the weight in Sorra's chest.

He doesn't hate me.

The thought should have pleased her, but it only made the pain worse. He wasn't angry because of what she'd become. He was grieving what he—what they both—had lost.

Sorra looked away and reminded herself that there had never been a place for her in his life as king.

Beau cleared his throat. "Varek, did Tullian killing Corvin shift the odds any further in our favour?"

"It hasn't been as advantageous as he likely hoped," Varek said. "The enchantment that closes off the treasury is still in place and will protect Gwelain when she goes in to move the heart from its current cage to the one it will travel in. A word from her and the door will open to whomever she summons, but I suspect I won't be invited except to carry the cage out once she's safely away. She won't want to maintain contact with the heart once the transfer is complete, and once she leaves the tower, her magic will return."

"Is that cage as secure as its current housing?" Beau asked. "Could it be stolen?"

"It's more portable, but stealing the cage wouldn't remove the heart's magic from her control," Varek said. "She'd realize what was happening and take action before you could get far."

"Tell us your plan, then," Beau said.

Varek hesitated and glanced at Sorra. "The magical barrier that protects Gwelain when she's in the treasury has been in place so long she may have forgotten its exact details, but I haven't. It keeps out every living being, friend or foe."

"But not the dead," Sorra whispered.

"Correct."

Sorra thought of the body in the dungeons, of what might remain of the humans sacrificed to Corvin's power, then realized how much fresher a body Varek might soon have access to.

"Does this have something to do with how you influenced the wording of the agreement?"

Varek nodded. "Gwelain doesn't care for the practice as I do, but I've done some experiments in reanimation, hoping it would be useful for exactly this reason. I believe my skills are up to the task."

Beau looked to Sorra, confused. "What does that have to do with your agreement?"

She ran her tongue along the insides of her teeth as she thought it over. "Gwelain wants to see your reaction when she shows you what I've become. Once she's had that bit of fun, she's going to kill me, at which point my contract with her will end."

"Exactly," Varek said. "After that, you'll be free to betray her and harm her and do whatever you please without risking body or soul."

Beau glared at him. "She's not going to be able to do much if she's dead."

Sorra motioned for him to wait, trusting there was more to the plan but afraid to hear what it might be.

Varek's grim smile did nothing to ease Sorra's nerves. "You will die, Sorra, and I will trap your spirit inside your body. No heartbeat, no breath. Dead as dead can be, even after I heal whatever wound killed you, but your soul will remain a passenger as I pass your body through a barrier no living being can breach. Then I'll release your soul back into your body, which will return to true life, armed and ready to steal another heart Gwelain could never quite manage to claim as her own."

He spoke as though everything he'd said were simple, obvious, and above all, possible. Beau stared at him, his brow furrowed.

"Just like that?" he asked. "Dead, then alive because you said so?"

"It's quite complicated," Varek admitted. "Impossible, I suspect, in a place where Lord Death could claim a soul after its body died. Here, the rules are different, at least as long as Gwelain's enchantments hold. It's also the only option that takes advantage of Sorra's little gamble and gives her a chance to survive." He turned to her. "How are your fighting skills?"

"Passable," she said, struggling to move on to new questions when her mind was stuck on his last idea. "If I have full use of my body, and if Gwelain doesn't have magic on her side, I might at least back her into a corner. She can't call on Corvin to help her now."

"And she certainly won't get help from me." Varek obviously took pleasure in the idea.

"You'll stand against her, then?" Beau asked.

"I will. I'd wait another hundred years for this victory if I had to, but I'd prefer to take it now, even if it means compromising and trusting an agreement with a human. Good enough?"

Beau nodded but didn't seem satisfied.

"It's not enough for you to catch her with the heart free of its cages," Varek said. "She has to voluntarily sever her bond with it, and she'll only do that if she believes the alternative is worth the sacrifice. She won't believe you'll risk destroying the heart, but if you can force her to open the door to let her guards in, I might be able to enter and use my magic to persuade her. Make sure you don't touch the heart. It will burn you, and anyone who isn't its true master. Even Gwelain isn't able to hold it for long."

Beau didn't seem to be listening. "About Sorra's return from death," he said.

Varek sighed. "What?"

"Your plan isn't good enough." Beau stood and faced Varek. "You'll need to be there to bring her back once she's through the barrier?"

"Unless you think you can do it."

"And what happens if you don't?"

"If I waited too long, there would be damage even I couldn't repair." Varek didn't seem pleased to acknowledge his weakness. "If

I didn't bring her back at all, her soul would be trapped in her rotting flesh."

Sorra's breakfast rose in her throat.

Varek narrowed his eyes at Beau. "You don't trust me to do it? I lose as much as you do if she doesn't come back."

"I trust that you need her." Beau spoke calmly but firmly. "I am concerned, however, that Gwelain will have her guards ready to keep us away, and that you'll be killed in that fight, leaving Sorra helpless. That's not a risk I'm willing to take."

"Let me think." Varek paced beside the water. "I could place a time limit on her soul's containment. That would bring its own risks, though. If it brings her back before she's through the barrier, we'll have lost our chance."

"But she'd still be alive to fight, and free from her contract."

Sorra told herself to stand up and tell them it wasn't necessary, to be brave enough to take a greater risk in return for a greater chance of success. She couldn't make herself move. The idea of slowly going mad as her new body decomposed around her was too horrifying to entertain.

"I trust you to bring me back," she said. "But Beau is right. At least this way if something happened to you, he might still get me through the barrier in time."

Varek looked away. "Consider it done, then."

"So that only leaves the question of why you need me," Beau said. "I suspect it's too much to hope that I'll simply be swinging a sword at anyone who attacks you."

"Far too much," Varek said. Sorra hadn't imagined him capable of the pity she caught in his voice, and it frightened her. "There are still problems with the plan. Sorra needs to die of an injury I can heal fairly easily. I'll be quite drained after setting things up and will still have difficult magic to work on her after her death. Ideally, she'll die from a single wound. I can account for lost blood, but we'll run into trouble if she has injuries that keep her from fighting when she's brought back. We can't afford broken bones, a crushed skull, horribly mangled innards. A single stab to the heart, perhaps."

Beau's jaw tightened. "Which means one of us needs to do it."

"You, yes. When Gwelain reveals Sorra to you, you'll convince her that you're angry enough to kill. She might order you to do it, or you might need to ask her permission. It shouldn't be hard. This is exactly what she wants for both of you."

Sorra looked to Beau, but he turned away.

"I can't do it."

"Don't, then," Varek said, any trace of sympathy gone. "The alternative, of course, is to let Gwelain break every bone in Sorra's body and leave her to bleed out while the rest of us deliver the new queen to her throne in Andonia."

Beau ran his hands down his face. When he let them drop, his features had taken on the calm, authoritative expression Sorra assumed he'd wear frequently when he became king.

"Promise me word by word that you'll work the magic exactly as you've said."

"I swear it," Varek said, biting off each word of truth he had to speak to prove himself. "I'll contain Sorra's soul within her body after her death, heal her wounds in preparation for her return, and ensure that her soul will be released before her body suffers from its loss, prioritizing her survival above our success. Will that do, Your Highness?"

Beau held his gaze. "I suppose it will have to."

Sorra pushed herself awkwardly to her new feet and stepped between them. Though she understood Beau's caution, there was no need to be so cold, so suspicious. Varek had protected them from Gwelain in the royal apartments, had saved Sorra's life once already, and was offering Beau a chance to keep his crown and take the heart home with him despite his mistrust of humans. To humiliate Varek by using his mother's curse against him seemed unnecessary.

"Go, then," Varek said. "If Gwelain has finished her beauty sleep, try to keep her occupied a little longer."

Beau looked as though he had something else to say, but he kept it to himself. He turned away, and soon Varek and Sorra were alone again.

"I'm sorry he was so rude to you," Sorra said. "You deserve better."

"No need to apologize." Varek pulled a folded sheet of paper from his pocket, then a nub of charcoal. "He cares for you and wants to live the rest of his life knowing you have a chance at happiness, even if he's not a part of it. It's pathetic, but I understand that my pride means nothing in the face of such emotion."

He sat on a rock, and Sorra stood beside him as he scratched out a few notes on the paper.

"Do goblins never feel things like that?"

"I don't know." He looked up at her. "Gwelain has twisted things so it's hard to tell what's possible. There's more loyalty among goblins than you've seen, or at least there always was among the old kind. More peace. Who's to say there isn't love? Not in Gwelain's ballroom, but perhaps elsewhere."

"Places like this, maybe?"

"Maybe." Varek watched her for a moment, without the suspicion he'd so obviously carried when she was human. "She's right, you know. You'll make a good goblin. You still have your human flaws, but it might be beneficial for me to keep you close once Gwelain is dealt with. There are so few I trust among her creations, and so few among the old kind with your intelligence." He scratched out a few more notes, then tucked them away and stood again.

Sorra tried not to be flattered, but the knowledge that he wasn't lying made it difficult.

"This will really work?" she asked.

Varek held out his hands, and she took them. His claws scratched against her skin, but she found she didn't mind.

"There are no guarantees," he said. "But I think it will. Are you ready?"

Sorra pulled her hands from his. "Will it hurt?"

"Not this part," he said. "That will come soon enough."

CHAPTER FIFTY-SIX

Time took on a strange quality as Sorra waited for her next orders. Varek had left her after he'd performed his painless magic, saying only that there was work for him to do and promising that someone would return for her. She couldn't tell how long she was alone. It could have been minutes or hours, every moment the same in its sense of calm presence as she let herself sink into her new body and its unfamiliar way of experiencing the world. There was apprehension, there was worry, but they were nothing more than ideas. The future and its concerns weren't welcome within the cave.

When Varek returned carrying an armload of clothing, it took her a few breaths to return from the dreamlike state she'd slipped into.

"I hope these still fit," he said. "I suppose Gwelain would have preferred rags, but I brought the things you wore under your armour instead. Everything but your boots, of course."

"It's perfect, thank you." Sorra ran her fingers over the fabric. Its buttery softness felt different from when she'd had human skin, deeper and richer, but no more appealing than the wool blanket or the moss she'd been resting on. She looked up at him and frowned. "Are you ill?"

The difference was subtle, but his skin, formerly the rich green of a shadowy forest, had paled to a sicklier hue. Greyish circles had gathered under his eyes, and his movements were slower than they'd been. He'd changed his clothes and now wore a black doublet that buttoned up to his throat over dark breeches—fancy, even dashing in a ridiculously old-fashioned way, but doing nothing to improve his appearance.

"It will pass," he said. "I've used a lot of magic today, and I don't have my mother's resources to draw from." His lips twisted into a bitter smile. "Kind of you to notice. She didn't. Or didn't care to ask."

He turned away, and Sorra dressed. The trousers felt tight in the wrong places, and the fit of the shirt had changed. Her shoulders were broader than they had been, and her arms longer. Clothes that had once fit perfectly now felt like they belonged to someone else.

"Done," she said, and Varek turned. He brushed her hair back from her face, pulling his claws through, tugging out the tangles. The sensation rippled pleasantly from Sorra's scalp to her toes, and she shivered.

Varek didn't seem to notice. He pulled a silver clip shaped like a moth from his pocket and fastened her hair back from her face, leaving her horns and her pointed ears exposed.

"There," he said. "That should please her. She'd hoped for more from your transformation. Skin like mine, perhaps, or some more monstrous change that would have made you truly ugly."

Sorra pulled her hair forward over one shoulder and brushed her claws through it. "She said my spirit didn't need much transformation. I suppose my body agreed."

"Perhaps. But here. Look." He took a small mirror from his pocket and handed it to her. Sorra braced herself, then lifted it. She couldn't see more than a little of herself in it at a time, but as she turned her head and adjusted the mirror's angle, a picture formed.

Same eye shape, but they seemed larger, their dark brown irises now encircled with gold that bled toward her pupils. The same face shape, save for her widened jaw and her lips, which appeared more prominent thanks to the larger teeth hiding behind them.

She touched the side of her face, where the rose mark still spread over her skin. That more than anything assured her that she was still Sorra. She wasn't beautiful like Gwelain, but she saw nothing in the mirror that struck her as ugly. She was only herself, the monster she'd always been destined to become.

Now that it had happened, she wondered what she'd been so afraid of.

Varek's fingers brushed hers as he took the mirror. His skin was cold enough to raise bumps on Sorra's. "Time is up," he said. "Gwelain is waiting in the throne room."

"Of course she is." Sorra hadn't thought of Tullian's circumstances since she'd wakened, but her feelings hadn't changed. She'd have given anything to spare him the pain of seeing what was about to happen.

Almost anything, she thought. *I won't turn away from this. Our victory will be his freedom, one way or another.*

Varek took hold of her arm, and she allowed him to march her like a prisoner through the passage that led back to the throne room.

Sorra squinted as they stepped through the doorway. The castle's clean, pale beauty seemed garish to her now, utterly contrived and lacking in charm. The white walls hurt her eyes as they hadn't before, and the pattern of the floor nauseated her. The only relief was in the natural forms of the new garden, and she didn't dare let her gaze linger on that.

Gwelain looked radiant, lively and excited as a child waiting to open a gift. "You're looking well," she said. "How are you finding your new body?"

"It's extraordinary, Majesty, just as you said." Even now a strange sense of calm filled Sorra, and she wondered whether it was her altered mind or some aspect of Varek's magic. "I feel stronger than I ever knew was possible. The world is different to me."

Gwelain lifted Sorra's chin and turned her head from side to side, then stepped back, satisfied. "I wasn't lying when I said it was a gift. Do you wish to beg for your life now that you understand what I've given you?"

Sorra looked away. "I might, Majesty, if I didn't know how pointless it would be."

Gwelain chuckled. "You almost make me wish it were otherwise. Go, now. Hide in the shadows. Varek, you'll stand with me."

Sorra walked to the corner behind the thrones, her movements quick and strong, letting herself imagine for a moment that she might disappear and be forgotten.

She wanted to focus on the idea that this might all work out, that Beau would soon return home with the heart and she'd find a life for herself somewhere in these lands, but all she could see was the next few minutes—pain, death, being helplessly trapped in her body as she waited to see whether Varek was as good with magic as he claimed, trusting him and Beau to take care of her as she endured helplessness like she'd never experienced before.

And that was if everything went perfectly.

"Beauregard!" Gwelain clapped her hands together. "There you are."

Beau entered, slowly and cautiously. He was dressed for travel in brown breeches, knee-high leather boots, and a long jacket cut to allow easy movement. He looked like the dashing heroes Sorra had once imagined when her sisters read her stories at bedtime.

"You requested my presence?"

"I have a belated wedding present for you." Gwelain slipped her hand under his arm, gripping it possessively as she guided him to the centre of the room.

Without meaning to, Sorra bared her teeth.

"It's a practical thing, really," she said. "I know how hard it must be for you, never being able to touch that girl again after your little adventure together, so she and I came up with a solution that will make things easier for everyone."

Beau stopped and Gwelain turned to him, grinning.

"What did you do?" Beau asked, his voice filled with fear and anger that he likely didn't need to fake, and which clearly delighted Gwelain.

She set her hands on her hips and pouted theatrically. "Now, there's no need to sound like you're accusing me of something horrid. I've only helped Sorra reach her full potential and stop running from her little destiny. Come out, dear."

Sorra stepped into the light and walked closer to Beau, forcing every step.

She told herself Beau was performing brilliantly as she observed the perfect expression of horror and rage that crossed his face, far more than he'd shown in the cave. It was all perfect, though—the tension in his body, the clenching of his fists, the redness in his cheeks.

Almost as though he'd been holding back for her sake before, and this was the truth even if it wasn't the surprise Gwelain believed it to be.

Sorra reminded herself that it meant he cared, but that didn't cushion her from the bolt of pain that shot through her heart as he stalked closer, looking at her like she was truly a monster.

"What did you do?" he asked again. Not a yell, but a whisper. Less dramatic, more real. And directed at Sorra this time, not Gwelain.

She wished the floor would open so she could let the earth consume her instead of facing another moment of his disappointment, real or not.

"She saw what you must," Gwelain said. "That she couldn't win, and that the only path that benefitted her was to join me in my victory instead."

Beau didn't look away from Sorra. "You've betrayed Linnea. Andonia. Your family."

He didn't say *and me*, but Sorra heard it anyway. She told herself not to cry. "Yes."

Gwelain stood next to Beau, but Sorra barely saw her.

"What should we do with her?" Gwelain asked.

Beau held Sorra's gaze. They both knew the answer, but he didn't speak until she dropped her chin in what Gwelain might read as defeat, but Sorra meant as a nod.

Do it.

"Traitors deserve death," he said. His voice broke, and his eyes shone with what could have been anger, sorrow, or even fear.

"If you insist," Gwelain said. "You may stay to watch if you wish or leave to finish your preparations for the journey." She flexed her claws and smiled.

Sorra's heart skipped, and Beau's eyes widened.

Gwelain might not take her time with the kill, but she'd make it worth the wait. Magic, pain, and as much damage as she wished to inflict—too much for Varek to fix in his weakened state.

Varek was listening, but he couldn't step in without risking a lie.

Beau placed a hand over Gwelain's deadly claws, gentle but firm. "I am the king of Andonia. I'll deal with her the old way. Personally."

She frowned at him. "It's best that I do it. I fear your tendency, even now, may be toward a quick and merciful death."

Beau watched Sorra, his gaze cold and hard, as he spoke to Gwelain. "And how would you see it done?"

"I'd prefer that you do it my way, if you insist on doing it yourself." Gwelain tilted her head to one side, eyes narrowed. "Will you promise me that?"

"I will."

"Good." Gwelain perched on her throne, ready for the show. "Make it entertaining. Hit her, break her bones, unleash your anger. I want to watch her suffer before I offer you a weapon to finish the job."

Sorra tried not to let her chin tremble or her legs quake.

Beau shot Gwelain a look so sharp it seemed to Sorra that the queen should bleed all over her lovely white dress. Then, in one smooth movement he might have practiced a hundred times he pulled a dagger from his boot and reached his other hand behind Sorra to pull her close. As Gwelain leapt to her feet, he drove the blade into Sorra's heart from beneath her breastbone.

Sorra gasped. The pain was incredible, but not as sharp as she'd expected, at least until he pulled the blade free. Blood washed over the front of her shirt and pattered to the floor. Her legs weakened, and she grabbed on to his arm, still looking into his eyes as he gently lowered her to the floor, his back to Gwelain and Varek.

Everything at the edges of Sorra's vision darkened.

Beau moved his lips. There was no sound save for his shaking breath, but she read his words perfectly.

I'm sorry.

She tried to lift her hand to touch his face and brush away the tears that threatened to fall and give him away, but she couldn't find her arm. It seemed to have disappeared, along with the rest of her body. She drew in a shallow, gasping breath, and then even that was gone. Her awareness pulled back into her body, leaving her small and lost. She still saw through her eyes but couldn't move or focus them. It was like watching the world through a dark tunnel as Beau released her and walked away. She heard, but the sounds were muffled.

And she felt nothing as Gwelain crouched beside her to check for signs of life.

Her heart lay still. She couldn't breathe, and though panic overwhelmed her as it would have if she were drowning, she couldn't move to save herself.

She screamed, but there was no breath, no movement, no sound.

"You disobeyed me," Gwelain snarled. All Sorra could see were her scaled feet and Beau's blood-spattered boots, visible through a thin curtain of hair that had fallen over her eyes.

"I have no choice but to have you as my queen," Beau said, his voice heavy with quiet rage that Sorra clung to as an anchor against her terror. "But I will not allow you to turn me into a monster. You will not make me cruel, now or ever. Go. Retrieve your damned heart so we can leave this place."

He stalked away, a blurry form against the blinding white of the room.

Gwelain's feet shifted as she took a half step after him. "He'd better watch his tone if he knows what's good for him."

"You can't harm him," Varek said, his voice distant and disembodied.

"What's good for his people, then. There are still ways to punish him." She paused. "Is everyone ready?"

"Ready and waiting outside," Varek said.

"Good. I'll summon you when the heart is ready to be carried out."

She left, but nothing else happened for what felt like far too long when time was so short. Then Varek crouched in front of Sorra and turned her head so she was looking up at him.

"You did well," he said, speaking quietly, "and your king did better than I expected." His brow furrowed, and he brushed back the hair that had obstructed her vision. "It must feel wretched to be trapped in there. Remember that you're all spirit now. You can't suffocate when you're already dead, even if it feels like you will, and any pain you feel is imagined. Stay strong. This will be over soon."

He moved out of sight. "I'll heal you now and restore what I can of your blood."

She felt nothing. Then the room shifted as her body moved.

"I'm putting your belt and weapons on you," Varek said. "Sword at your left hip, dagger at your right. Fighting will feel different in this body, but I trust you'll adapt."

The room rocked again, pitching horribly to one side before the floor retreated and everything turned upside-down. Another movement and she found herself looking up at the glass ceiling with its heavy wooden beams before the sun turned everything white.

"I can carry her."

Beau's voice, but she couldn't see him. Then the light vanished as he hovered a hand over her eyes, shading them.

"No." Varek walked out of the sunlight and away from him. "You need your arms free to keep us safe until I get her to the barrier. Gwelain will be in the treasury by now, and we don't have much time before Sorra returns."

They left the throne room. The world passed in a dizzying blur, and Sorra wished she could close her eyes. She didn't feel sick, only disoriented and helpless. She trusted Beau and Varek, even if they didn't trust each other, but having no choice but to rely on them was more torturous than she'd expected.

Just a few more minutes.

She had no breath she could control to calm herself, so she focused instead on the rhythm of Varek's steps.

Shouts shattered her brief peace. Varek's movements became quicker, and somewhere close by the clash of swords joined the angry voices.

"Go!" Beau yelled.

Sorra wanted to tell Varek to stop, but he ran on, up a flight of stairs and past the waterfall of gold coins.

"He'll handle it," Varek said. "Three soldiers, and not her best. I expect he'll be free to follow us soon."

Sorra knew Varek hated not being able to lie but was more glad of his curse in that moment than she'd ever been before. He hated Beau. If he said he was a capable enough swordsman to handle this, it was an honest and hard-won opinion.

He hadn't needed to say it, but he had for her sake. She wished she could thank him.

They passed into the north wing and the dusty corridor that led to the tower.

Varek stopped short.

"What're you doing here?" Reaver's voice.

"What're you doing with her?" The other one. Of course Gwelain had stationed her favourite guards outside the barrier. She trusted her magic, but nothing and no one else.

"That's none of your business," Varek said.

"I think it is," Reaver growled.

Varek backed away. Sorra's head rolled on his arm, and she saw Reaver advancing, axe drawn. The other followed a few paces behind, unsheathing his sword.

Varek set Sorra down against the wall, lying on her back.

Don't leave me, she thought.

The guards passed—Varek was still retreating.

Please.

Weapons clashed. Varek shouted a spell that Sorra hoped would knock the guards flat. Instead, the world canted sideways, then rolled and blurred as her body moved, righting itself as she stood facing the end of the hallway, where a purple wall of light barred entry to the stairway leading to the treasury.

The floor rushed toward her as she fell, then disappeared again as her body righted itself like a puppet on strings.

Sorra tried to look back at Varek but had no control. She was still trapped, still small, but now her body was moving forward, jolting with each step it took closer to the stairs.

The sounds of fighting continued behind her, a little louder and closer than they'd been before.

Not closer. Clearer.

Her vision, too, was slowly changing, the tunnel becoming shorter and wider. A distant sensation tickled her brain—faint awareness that her fingertips existed.

The spell that bound her soul within her body was weakening, whether she wanted it to or not, and the stairs were still much too far away.

Varek shouted something that ended in a snarl of pain. Sorra's body broke into a run, stumbling like a newborn foal finding its legs for the first time. With the stairs just a few paces away, she felt herself expanding to fill her body.

She pitched forward, passing through the barrier. Her toes caught on the bottom step, and though she tried to raise her arms to break her fall, her cheek and arm took the brunt of the impact as she landed.

Her lungs filled with air and her heart thundered back to life, racing like a flooded springtime river. She gasped and bit back a cry as a sensation like a limb waking up from numbness but a hundred times more painful gripped her entire body.

She lay on the stairs, her face pressed to the cool stone, until her limbs stopped trembling and the pain passed. Her arms shook as she pushed herself to her knees, then pressed one hand against her heart. It fluttered with her fear, but it felt strong, and though the front of her shirt was stained with her blood, there was no fresh flow.

Her body was still weak, but it was so much better than being dead that she wanted to scream with joy.

Instead, she let herself relish a few strengthening breaths, then drew her sword and climbed the stairs without looking back.

Whatever Varek was suffering, it was his to deal with.

She had her own monster to face.

CHAPTER FIFTY-SEVEN

The heart's blue light flickered at a frantic pace as Sorra's shaking legs brought her closer to the top of the spiral staircase. She steadied herself, drawing long breaths even when it hurt to pull air into the depths of her lungs. They still felt halfway dead, and her heart refused to beat in anything but a sluggish, uneven rhythm.

Another breath, and the pain lessened. A few more minutes and the enlivening process might complete itself.

But she didn't have a few minutes. Sorra pictured Gwelain in her white dress smiling down at the heart as she set a pretty new cage on the floor to await transport, ready to reclaim its power the moment she stepped out of its presence.

Sorra forced herself onward, testing the strength of her legs and the unfamiliar balance of her weight as she walked on her widely spread toes, trying not to let her talons click against the stairs.

She raised her sword. It felt wrong. Or rather, her fingers did— too long as they wrapped around the hilt, her talons bulky and inconvenient when she laid them beneath the heel of her palm. She tried curling them around the outside and nearly lost her grip, and set them back where they'd been, telling herself it would be fine if she stopped thinking about it.

She braced herself as she reached the top of the stairs, ready to face the beautiful monster who had harmed so many for so long.

Instead, she found a stranger.

Gwelain stood with her back to the door, facing Linnea's heart. Her black hair hung in greasy, lifeless clumps over bony shoulders. She still stood straight and proud, but the sculpted muscles her backless gown had previously displayed were gone, and her spine stuck out in hard knobs that cast shadows in the pulsing light that filled the room.

Sorra drew in a trembling gasp, and Gwelain's narrow shoulders hunched defensively as she slowly turned.

The queen's lips curled, exposing her teeth. One of her lower canines was broken, leaving her looking lopsided and feral. The rage written on her features faltered as she recognized Sorra, exposing what might have been doubt or fear before she caught herself and raised her chin, defiant.

"You're alive," she said, sharp and accusing, and sniffed the air as though to confirm it. "I saw you die. Explain yourself."

Her haughty royal tone remained intact, but her once honey-soaked voice had roughened and sounded more like Varek's than her own. Chipped grey claws twitched by her side, then grasped her skirt, pulling its panels forward to cover the dulled, dusty scales on her legs.

Sorra's sword dropped to her side. She raised it again, blinking to shake herself out of her shock, willing her arm to quit trembling. *The heart*, she reminded herself. *The quest.*

The heart still floated above its pedestal, but the bars of its cage had vanished. A golden birdcage sat open on the floor, waiting to receive it.

But Sorra couldn't look away from the greenish veins pulsing at Gwelain's temples, or the unchanged brightness of her eyes set against the bruise-like purple of the skin beneath them.

Varek had said the queen's magic had become weak as she'd relied on Linnea's instead. Now, in the only place where Gwelain couldn't use the heart's power, it was clear that her magic wasn't the only thing that had suffered. Her stolen power had allowed her to clothe herself in illusions so perfect there had been no need to properly care for the reality that lay beneath them.

Sorra cleared her throat and adjusted her posture, perfecting it as Tullian had taught her.

"Did you really think you'd win so easily?" She injected some of Gwelain's royal disdain into her own voice. "Did you think you were the only one with secrets? The visions warned you we'd have magic on our side. We'd hardly have been foolish enough to come to your castle without it."

The lie rolled off her tongue, and she allowed herself a moment of gratitude for it. Gwelain had robbed Varek of so much when she stole his ability to bluff and flatter and deceive.

"I know you're powerless here," Sorra said. "You are unarmed and lack the protection of Corvin's magic. And you're right. I was dead. Our agreement is therefore over, and I am free." She took a step closer. "Abandon all claims to Andonia's throne. Break your bond with Linnea's heart and your marriage contract with Beau, and I will allow you to leave unharmed."

Gwelain laughed, a wild shriek that stung Sorra's ears. "You think you can threaten me into giving up everything?"

"Not everything. You'd have your life, which is more than you left me with."

Gwelain spat on the floor and flexed her claws. "Your death was better than you deserved. And whatever your plan is, it will fail. Your blood sealed my victory. All that remains is for me to claim it, and you will not stand in my way."

She glanced at the heart, exposed above its pedestal, and rushed at Sorra, teeth bared and claws reaching.

Sorra braced herself, finding her balance in her unfamiliar body, sword held defensively.

But Tullian had never taught her how to fight an unarmed opponent. The closest she'd faced was a dog, and then she'd been fighting to kill.

And I can't kill her.

But she can kill me.

She moved into Gwelain's attack, aiming to slice into the queen's arm before her claws could meet flesh, struggling to maintain her grip as she swung. But Gwelain darted to her left and leapt, shifting her gaze from Sorra to the top of the staircase.

Sorra dropped her sword and threw herself at Gwelain, knocking her off course and meeting a flurry of claws and slashing talons as they hit the floor. Sorra pushed away, rolled to her feet, and backed toward the stairs, hesitating over her fallen sword.

Pick it up, Tullian bellowed in her mind. *Where's your training?*

She ignored him. The weapon had served her well as a human hero, but it didn't fit her now any better than her armour would have. If her new body wouldn't play by the old one's rules, the game would have to change.

Gwelain climbed to her feet and stalked across the tower's dusty stone floor, tensed like a cat about to pounce.

"I will leave this tower and reclaim my magic. Stand in my way and I will kill you again, by my own hand. Stand aside and you may survive long enough to run and hide."

Sorra gritted her teeth. "You are weak. You have no more magic than I have. Release the heart and you may survive long enough to—"

Gwelain moved faster than Sorra expected, landing a blow against Sorra's right cheek and coming in with a slash of her claws to the left. The cuts landed below her eye, and Sorra snarled at their sting.

Pain, but bearable. Enraging, but not incapacitating.

Another blow came, aimed at her stomach, and Sorra stepped back, her gait flowing now. Natural. She hit back, swiping with her claws, tearing through Gwelain's dress, reddening it with blood at her waist.

Blow after blow followed until the fight became a blur, Gwelain attacking and Sorra defending, desperate to keep the queen from escaping, denying herself a deadly attack when Gwelain left her throat exposed. Death's weakness had left her, and her new body offered every advantage Gwelain had promised—strength, agility, keen senses. But even without her magic, as run-down and broken as she appeared, Gwelain fought tirelessly.

Sorra thought of Tullian wasting away in a drunken stupor, tortured by his failure but afraid to act, backed into a corner where the best he could do was to deny Gwelain her traitor. Sorra's attempts at defense now were no better, preventing Gwelain's escape without pushing for a victory that might risk the heart's destruction.

But a stalemate was no longer an option. Gwelain had no reason to hold back. She would win, if only by exhausting Sorra.

Varek would help, if he'd survived his own fight, but only if Gwelain opened the door.

Victory or defeat. There is no other ending.

Sorra stepped back to dodge another attack aimed at her eyes and found only air behind her. Her heart skipped as she grabbed for the wall next to the stairs, her claws scrabbling against unyielding stone.

Gwelain rushed at her as she fell.

Sorra forgot Tullian, Beau, Varek, and the heart. No training, no quest, and no vision would help her now. She let out an animal growl as she twisted and grabbed on to Gwelain's arm, pulling her into her fall. The edges of the stairs scraped against Sorra's arm, but she landed on top of Gwelain as a loud snap echoed through the stairwell. Gwelain screamed, and Sorra's blood sang with strange joy.

She hauled back, slowing their descent as Gwelain fought to continue it, and tangled her claws in the knotted locks of Gwelain's hair.

"Enough!" Gwelain screamed.

Sorra didn't answer. She found her footing and dragged the squirming queen back into the heart's chamber. Her muscles burned.

Monstrous strength and agility were fine gifts, but it seemed they had their limits.

She pushed Gwelain face-first to the floor next to the heart and dropped, pinning Gwelain's back under one knee, catching one flailing arm to pin it behind her. The other lay at the queen's side, bent in too many places.

Gwelain twisted her head to look up at Sorra, teeth bared. "You can't kill me," she snarled. Mucus flowed from her nose, mingling with the tears that stained her skin. "I may die, though, and Linnea's heart will be destroyed all the same. My arm is broken. I believe something else may be as well, deep inside. The pain is—"

She screamed as Sorra grabbed her broken arm and squeezed.

Underhanded, Sorra thought in a voice that sounded a little like Tullian's and a little like her own. *Cruel. Unheroic.*

So be it, she answered.

She believed Beau would be a good king because he would respect his subjects and do what was best for them, because he would follow the high road and refuse to stoop to the level of those who would do otherwise.

That was good. Necessary. In a perfect world, it would be enough.

But the world wasn't perfect. Not yet. And this was Gwelain, not one of her victims.

Maybe it's still wrong. But a monster can do what heroes wouldn't dare.

Gwelain bucked beneath her, and Sorra squeezed until she stopped.

"I don't think you're going to die any time soon," she said. "You're tougher than you look, even now, and I think there might be enough of your old magic left in there to keep you alive for a while. But you're right. I can't kill you."

She released the broken arm and drew the dagger from her belt.

"I can keep hurting you, though. Maybe break your legs or cut a few tendons so you can't run. What was it you said you'd do to me and Tullian if we didn't bow to your wishes? Keep us alive but torture us until we'd do anything to end the pain? Seems fair that I make you the same offer."

She pressed the tip of the dagger to the stringy muscle above Gwelain's shoulder blade, ignoring the pleasant tingle that ran over her skin as a bead of dark blood welled up around it.

Gwelain gritted her teeth and squeezed her eyes closed.

Harder, then. The blade slipped deeper. Gwelain's eyes flew open.

"*Issisthruail!*" The command came sharp and loud. "Reaver! Aristhos!"

Sorra drew the blade free.

Gwelain had given the command.

Somewhere below, the magical barrier had vanished.

Sorra held her breath.

CHAPTER FIFTY-EIGHT

S ilence.

Gwelain twisted to look at the stairs, and Sorra gave her a warning cut with her dagger.

Varek's fight had been as critical as her own. If he'd fled or been defeated, Gwelain's guards would come and end things, and Andonia's greatest enemy would rise to power, just as the visions had said.

If he'd won, and if Beau had survived his own fight to join him…

Footsteps approached. One set, talons clicking against stone.

Sorra's claws dug into Gwelain's arm, still twisted behind her back.

Please.

Varek stepped into the room, still looking pale and weak, but alive and otherwise whole.

Sorra waited, but Beau didn't follow. Her throat tightened as she stood, leaving the goblin queen to sit with her broken arm cradled to her chest as she glared up at her son.

"Varek," Gwelain growled, and used the plinth beneath Linnea's heart to pull herself to her feet. "Where are my guards? My other soldiers?"

"They're either dead or still fighting with your husband." Varek sounded unconcerned. "Their king, actually, which I suspect could get them into trouble."

Gwelain pulled herself to her full height. "I don't suppose you've come to help me."

Varek spread his hands out in front of him. "I can't lie, mother. No, I'm not here to help you."

"And you're responsible for this bit of treachery?" Gwelain gestured at Sorra.

"I am." Varek spoke without hesitation.

"I should have known. But this changes nothing." She grabbed the heart. The scent of burning flesh filled the room, and Gwelain snarled.

The travel cage still sat in its place on the floor, its door open and waiting.

Sorra kicked it away, feeling no pity.

Gwelain hissed, then ran for the doorway.

Varek spoke through bared teeth, uttering the language of magic in rolling, growling syllables. A flash of light blinded Sorra, and she squeezed her eyes closed to clear them.

When she opened them, Gwelain stood with her legs frozen to the ground, immobile, while her upper body pitched forward like a ragdoll. She gripped the heart tighter, and its frantic beating sent waves of light fluttering over the room.

The skin visible around it blistered and oozed.

Sorra glanced at Varek. He looked worse than he had moments before, having now used far more magic than he could possibly afford. But the spell held, even as Gwelain struggled.

"Do you know why it burns you?" Varek asked. "Why it fights you, why you can't use its power when you stand before it?" He picked up the cage and set it just out of reach, then walked a slow circle around Gwelain. She watched him, her eyes wide, her teeth bared in clear agony. "It didn't burn Linnea when it was hers, and it wouldn't harm anyone who possessed it as fully as she did. You couldn't, could you? You were too cowardly to take such a risk. You never cared to understand magic beyond seeing how it could serve your petty desires, and now you have nothing."

"And yet it remains mine," Gwelain whispered. "I can bear this pain. Unless you wish to destroy the heart to free yourself from my power over you?"

Varek smiled sadly. "I do wish to be free from your curse and your control. I wish I could lie to you now and threaten to destroy you and it in one stroke, but I've made an agreement with the humans and have promised it will be returned to Andonia."

Gwelain glared at him for a moment longer, then released a pained laugh.

"He won't destroy it," Sorra said. "But he could keep you here like this, suffering until you release the heart to us." She didn't know how much longer his magic would last but guessed Gwelain might suddenly be questioning what she believed about her son's abilities. "And when your flesh has burned away, we could take the heart. We might not break the bond, but we can take it far away."

"You wouldn't be able to use it," Gwelain whispered.

"And neither would you," Varek said. "You would remain like this, without power or beauty or the pathetic illusions and aspirations you've fed yourself on for centuries. All you'd have would be yourself. I can't think of a worse fate."

Gwelain's nostrils flared.

"Break your bond with the heart." Sorra moved closer, unafraid. "Release it so we can return it to Andonia as Linnea intended, and we'll let you live. If you do it now, your burns might heal."

Gwelain looked from Sorra to Varek and back again.

Tullian had called her spiteful. She'd tried to break Beau because she couldn't have him and seemed now to be considering whether the loss of her hand would be an acceptable price to pay for making sure her enemies couldn't use what they wished to take from her.

She gripped the heart tighter in her blackening fingers. "All these years I thought I was overestimating my son when I should have been more cautious."

Varek smiled grimly. "I've never lied to you without suffering for it."

"No. But you're slippery. I asked if you intended to steal the heart, but I never asked whether you were helping someone else to do it, knowing that you despise humans as I do. I thought being a prince and enjoying power over them would be enough for you."

"It might have been harder to misdirect you if you'd thought of anything beyond your own shallow ambition," he said.

"Ambition." Gwelain snarled, then sighed. "Better your hands than theirs."

She lifted Linnea's heart to her lips and whispered something, then screamed and threw the heart to Varek, revealing the ruined, blackened skin of her palm and fingers.

Varek snatched the heart out of the air and snarled in pain as he turned away.

A low rumbling echoed through the treasury as several stones disappeared from the wall and sunlight poured in through a new hole in the ceiling, accompanied by chaotic rumblings from elsewhere in the castle.

And then, faint and far below, screams.

Whatever magic Gwelain had used to rebuild her castle from the ruins of her grandfather's was vanishing.

Sorra picked up the travel cage, holding it with its open door facing Varek. "Quickly! We have to get the heart out of here."

He glanced over his shoulder at the cage, then down at the heart he now held in one hand. His claws tightened around it, threatening to pierce the glowing muscle beating frantically against his searing flesh.

"You gave your word you wouldn't destroy it." Sorra spoke in tones more suited to ordering a dog to drop a bone than to addressing a prince. "You promised it would go back to Andonia."

He laughed. "I did promise, didn't I? And it will."

He raised his empty hand and sent a flash of green lightning at Gwelain. She collapsed, the life fading from her eyes.

Sorra dropped the cage and ran to her, though there was nothing to be done.

"What are you doing?" she shouted. "I promised she'd live!"

The tower trembled again, and several of the wood panels that formed the treasury's roof fell to the floor as a section of the stone wall collapsed outward. The room steadied, and a gust of wind howled through the openings in the wall, wild and eerie to

Sorra's ears after weeks in a land where the weather never changed.

She stood and turned to Varek. His back was still turned, the light of the heart flickering unsteadily against the walls as he held it out, admiring it.

"Varek, look at me! Say something!"

He ignored her, instead speaking over the heart in sharp, commanding syllables. It settled into a steadier rhythm as blue light washed over his hand, sinking into his skin.

Panic filled Sorra, familiar and dreadful.

"Varek!"

He turned to Sorra, and her own heart seized in her chest before stumbling back into a panicked rhythm.

One of his eyes was gone, the skin around it marked by old scars.

He smiled and touched his face with one claw. "The carefully chosen price of great magic," he said. "Gwelain couldn't stand to look at anything so imperfect, no matter how it benefitted her as I spied on you. Do you find me beautiful now that her illusions are gone?"

Sorra thought she might vomit as the words of her blessing echoed through her memory.

The path she walks will lead her to darkness, bringing dishonour to her family and destruction to everyone around her.

A scream gathered in her throat, and she swallowed it back. It would do no good.

Even when I win, I lose.

"You're the mage the visions warned us about," she whispered. "Not Corvin."

Varek nodded. "I was the true power, much as it shamed me to serve someone who couldn't cage the heart as its true master. I could do nothing but wait and obey until someone came along to fulfil the visions." He opened his doublet, revealing a gaping hole in his chest, the flesh around it still torn and raw, his ribs jagged where they'd been broken to remove his breastbone and the heart beneath. "Thank you, Sorra. I truly couldn't have done this without you."

Violent tremors gripped Sorra as he pressed Linnea's heart into the space where his own should have been, roaring with pain.

Let it kill him, Sorra thought. *Let him be wrong.*

Her hope died as Varek's snarls turned to laughter. Bone grew over the heart, then muscle and skin.

His colour returned as the heart vanished, caged not in gold but in its new master's flesh.

CHAPTER FIFTY-NINE

Sorra's knees weakened. She sank to the floor but held her head up, not wanting Varek to mistake physical weakness for supplication.

His chest glowed faintly until he buttoned his doublet over it. His skin had returned to its rich, mossy tone, and with each passing second, he appeared stronger. The creature who had looked little better than a walking corpse moments before now might have stood among the Bright Ones represented in the statue gallery, inhuman but brutally lovely even with his scars.

"It's impossible," Sorra said, knowing how childish it was to believe she could argue away the truth standing in front of her. "You were cursed to tell the truth. We made a plan. You said Corvin was her mage, that your magic kept him from listening."

Varek crouched in front of her, his hands dangling between his knees. "I never made a false statement when I spoke to you. I withheld information and chose not to correct assumptions that benefitted me, but I didn't lie." He reached out to brush her hair back as he had before, but Sorra flinched and pushed herself away, scrambling across the floor until her back touched the wall.

Another stone fell, barely missing her head.

Varek shrugged and stood. "I told you the truth about why Gwelain didn't deserve the heart. I never said I didn't want her dead, only stated the fact that the heart would be destroyed if you killed her before she let it go. I meant every word when I said the world would be better off if it were destroyed than if it remained in her hands or was returned to humans—I simply neglected to present my true intention as a more desirable option. As for Corvin, Gwelain decided as soon as she learned of the visions that a decoy was in order. Linnea had put a target on her mage's back, and Gwelain relied on my magic far too much to risk losing me. Corvin served her as a lesser mage. He listened to her subjects just as I said, and my magic kept him from doing so when you were in your room."

Sorra's tongue and lips felt numb, but she forced herself to speak. "But the protections were only against anyone listening." She glanced at his scars. "You were… watching?"

He smiled. "The whole country could have been protected against eavesdroppers and I'd still have been free to read lips. Not all magic requires sacrifice, but mine was well worth it." The amusement faded from his voice. "You did surprise me once, the night you found my workroom in the central tower. I glanced away from our rituals and saw your tender moment with the future king but couldn't see you making your plans. I believed you'd keep each other busy while I was focused on strengthening my power, and by the time my work was finished and my attention free, I was too late to stop you."

Sorra remembered the horrible artefacts in the workroom, the screams from behind the theatre's doors. "All those human deaths were for the benefit of your power, then? Not Corvin's?"

"Both, actually. The humanity of Linnea's heart might keep me from using blood magic in the future, but I'll have no need of it once I fully control her power." He smiled again, and Sorra's skin crawled. Even with his scars, he was monstrously beautiful, which only made his ugly words more terrible.

"You said you'd return the heart to Andonia."

"And it will arrive there safely." He pressed a hand to his chest. "Gwelain had the right idea with her curse, but she lacked the power and conviction to do anything truly significant with it. She could have made the Andonians pay for her defeat and taught them their true place in the world's natural order, but she settled for a human king and a dead woman's crown."

Something crashed below them, and the room tilted with a hard jolt. Sorra tried to dig her claws into the floor, knowing it would do no good if the tower fell but too frightened to try to run, too numbed by the realization of what she'd done.

"I was right, then," she said, her voice flat. "The visions were sequential. *Should the queen's pledged champion die by the enemy's order or intention, on that day shall Gwelain meet her end.* I pledged myself to a queen, and she ordered my death. It led to her defeat, just as Linnea said. But the rest is also true."

Varek nodded, pleased. "*When the hero pledged to Linnea bows to the goblin queen and becomes her creature, then will the door be opened so that our greatest enemy may come to power, raining misery and destruction upon Andonia.* I've always liked that part."

Sorra spoke around the hard lump in her throat. "She wasn't Andonia's greatest enemy. You are."

She tried to say more but couldn't get the words out.

He couldn't come to power without me giving Gwelain what she wanted.

I opened the door.

She'd been clever enough to see a path to Gwelain's downfall, but not to imagine a greater threat when every interpretation of the visions had been sure they referred to her.

"You came closer to seeing the truth than any human who came before you." Varek seemed genuinely pleased. "I was beginning to think you wouldn't get there, or that the foolish knight would talk you out of seeing what he'd blinded himself to. It was a delicate balance, setting you up to see enough without letting you understand everything."

A fresh chorus of screams rang out from somewhere outside the castle. Varek offered a hand to Sorra. She refused it, instead climbing unsteadily to her feet and finding her balance on the tilted floor.

"You've fulfilled the visions and your destiny," he said. Not mockingly as Gwelain would have, taunting her with her failure, but with warmth that hinted at admiration and gratitude. "You are your people's greatest enemy. They will hate you for what you are and what you've done. The only question now is where you'll stand when I unleash Linnea's power against those she once loved."

Sorra clenched her jaw hard enough to send pain radiating through her head, trying to think, trying to keep her world from crumbling with the castle.

"Sorra."

He stood before her, radiating magic she felt in a way she hadn't when she was a human or when the heart was Gwelain's to command. His old power, too, no longer hidden, mingling with Linnea's.

He wouldn't make the same foolish mistakes Gwelain had. He would be stronger, more clever, more dangerous, less predictable.

"I also wasn't lying when I said I couldn't have done this without you," he said. "And I meant what I said about your potential and your future. Gwelain was a fool to waste you. Come with me. Be my weapon if you wish. Or, if you'd prefer it, be the voice of reason I need so badly. Teach me what mercy is, help me see why I shouldn't make humanity scream loud enough for the Bright Ones to hear them from another world." He took her hand. "Your role in my reign has only just begun. Let it be as my ally and not my enemy."

Sorra pulled her hand away and looked down at it, claws and all.

"My magic made you as much as Gwelain's did," he said. "I won't take back this gift I've given you. Come with me. You can still become something far greater than you ever were as a human."

"A lovely offer," Sorra said, her voice weaker and more frightened than she liked. "Does it feel good to be able to lie?"

He chuckled. "Freedom is a wonderful thing. But perhaps I'm being sincere. Perhaps you can save me and Andonia. Or you could learn to embrace what we are once the seed of darkness in your heart takes root. Either way, your greatest destiny is still tied to me."

Sorra took a backward step, searching for her new body's strength, hoping it would be enough. "Maybe it is. But I'll never become what you are."

His lips twitched with amusement. "We'll see."

The sun shining through the hole in the roof glinted off Sorra's sword. She dove for it, still gripping her dagger tight in one hand, knowing her claws alone would do no good if he attacked her. Varek whispered a spell and the sword spun away from her, knocking against the stone plinth at the centre of the room and skittering to its edge.

Varek gasped and pressed one hand to his chest, his lips parted in a silent snarl.

"Is something wrong?" Sorra asked as she climbed to her feet again. Her legs were still weak, but she thought she could run if he wasn't ready to grab her as she passed or strike out with his magic.

His snarl shifted to a maniacal grin that exposed far too many of his teeth. "Nothing unexpected. Gwelain had reason to fear true possession of Linnea's heart, but you needn't worry about me. It will learn to serve me, and I will shape its magic in ways Linnea herself never dreamed. And then Andonia will—"

Another rumble rose from beneath them, and the clattering of stone against earth.

"Andonia will be safe if you're buried in rubble," Sorra said, and took a step toward the downward slant of the room.

"Don't." He spoke with authority, but Sorra caught the fear in his eyes. "If I die, so does Linnea's magic. And so do you."

Something wild burst within Sorra, bittersweet sorrow and rage and a hopeless sort of joy. Her blessing had led her to the worst version of her greatest destiny after all, but there was still a chance of slowing him down.

He won't let himself die. Not now. But I can hurt him. I can buy time.

She threw herself against the wall, knowing her weight couldn't possibly mean much to a tower that had stood as long as this, certain that her blessing would somehow shore it up and thwart her good intentions once again. But something moved. A stone fell from the wall next to her foot, and then a floorboard clattered to the stairs below.

Another rumble. Another shift.

Varek shouted and threw his hands up. The sound itself should have been enough to tear down stone walls, and for a moment it drowned out Sorra's thoughts. She covered her ears, closed her eyes, and crouched. His voice faded to whispers, long, complicated phrases that rolled and seemed to build on each other in complex patterns she couldn't begin to comprehend. When she looked up, Varek's arms were still outstretched, his brow shining with sweat from the effort of his spells.

"Impressive." She gave him plenty of space as she moved toward the stairs. He glared at her, but his only answer was the continued string of magic that she imagined was keeping the tower standing. "Will it fall as soon as you stop? Or if I pick up my sword and drive it through you?"

He snarled, breaking the pattern of his spell, and her dagger flew from her hand, joining her sword as both were swept out through the hole in the wall. Another section fell from the ceiling.

Varek resumed his mumbling but turned to face her. He was clearly in pain, and the effort of his magic had brought a sheen of sweat to his brow, but there was an amused glint to his eyes.

He has caged the heart, but he doesn't fully control it yet.

Linnea is still fighting.

He fell silent and lowered his hands slowly, cautiously.

Sorra gathered all the strength that remained in her and raced down the stairs, her heart slamming harder as she leapt over a broad space where they'd collapsed, stumbling down the last few steps and finding her footing again as she ran through the room at the bottom.

A rumble behind her, then a crash like the end of the world as the tower collapsed, opening the castle to the bright sky above.

She kept running, barely able to hear her own terrified screams.

CHAPTER SIXTY

"**B**eau!"

Dust coated Sorra's throat. She coughed, still running.

The carefully lit, serenely elegant passageways of Gwelain's castle had vanished, replaced by the broken reality that had lain beneath her magic all along. The only illumination came from thick shafts of sunlight cast where sections of the roof had disappeared, leaving other areas lost in darkness.

Sorra paused at the junction of two hallways she knew she should recognize. Nothing was as it had been. Moss dotted the dark stone walls, the gleaming suits of armour were revealed as rusting and incomplete, and rags hung where there had once been beautiful tapestries.

She turned by instinct more than decision and ran again. Even the correct path might lead to a dead end if parts of the castle had collapsed. Speed was the thing.

"Beau, where are you?" Her voice was rough as a crow's call, sharp with panic.

The waterfall of coins had vanished, and the bridge over its golden pond had become a rickety wooden plank spanning a shallow, algae-choked puddle. Sorra covered her nose as she passed, confident now in her direction.

The castle's great front doors stood open, one hanging drunkenly from its bottom hinge. Though tarnished and missing a few gems, these, at least, were recognizable as their former selves. Sorra took the stairs toward them two at a time. Three steps from the bottom they crumbled beneath her. She leapt, braced herself, and rolled to a stop next to the doors.

Screams rang through them from the courtyard outside. The goblins. Maybe the servants, too, if they'd made it out.

She brushed the dirt from her clothes. "Beau, are you—"

"Sorra."

She barely heard the voice, weak as it was, calling from the throne room.

Human, but not Beau.

"Tullian?" She hurried closer. The throne room was still lit by the sun shining in through its glass ceiling, but everything else had changed. The black and white diamonds of the floor tiles were now cold grey flagstone, and the air was hazy with the dust from its crumbling walls.

The tree was gone. Tullian lay where it had stood, fully human and completely naked, the sword still protruding from his chest.

Sorra tore a musty tapestry from the wall and hurried to cover him with it, stepping over a wide crack that ran across the floor.

He raised one hand, and she grabbed on to it as she fell to her knees beside him, sobbing, no longer able to hold back her overwhelming shame and terror.

"Sorra," he whispered. "What's happened?"

"I've ruined everything. I'm so sorry." She bit her lip hard to focus herself. Tullian deserved the truth, and he didn't have time to waste listening to her tears. "You were right. So was I, but it doesn't matter. I figured out that the visions were all true, that Gwelain could only be defeated if she got her traitor first."

"And her certainty of victory then led to her opening herself to defeat." Tullian's skin, pale and covered in dust, matched the colour of his hair. Only his eyes, still sharp and bright, kept him from resembling Gwelain's statues.

"And it worked. She released the heart. She's dead now. But the scholars were wrong. She's not the greatest enemy Linnea saw in her visions. Varek was her mage all along. He tricked us, and he has Linnea's heart caged in his own body now. I escaped before the tower collapsed, and I've made everything worse. If he died, Linnea's heart has been destroyed with him and her magic is gone. If he didn't, that's probably worse. I think his plans for Andonia are going to make Gwelain's look like a garden party."

Tullian coughed, then groaned. "Stop crying, girl. You're not finished yet."

Sorra squeezed her eyes closed. "I'm so sorry, Tullian. If I'd listened, or if I'd done nothing, if I hadn't come and made a mess of everything…"

Tullian pulled his hand free from hers, but only to brush her tears away. "No. You were sent here to change things, and the story Linnea foresaw is not finished. Without you, Gwelain might have held the heart forever, securely caged here, or if she'd found a way, permanently in Embercliffe. It is now controlled by a dangerous enemy, but one who dares risk bearing it within himself, exposing it for the sake of claiming its power." He seemed to be listening to something, but Sorra heard nothing but his breath and her own. "Did it harm him?"

"It burned him until he said some words to it and put it in himself. Then no." She paused. "Unless—no, something was wrong when he used magic to hold the tower up. He did it, though."

Tullian nodded. "Gwelain struggled at first, too, and she hadn't claimed it as he has. There might be time."

"For what? I've tried my best and it's done no good. What if I try to do more and only make things worse?"

"You may. But you have set events in motion that Linnea believed would lead to her heart's restoration. Her death, the theft of her heart, Gwelain's defeat and Varek's rise have all come to pass, but more remains." He coughed again, spraying the front of Sorra's tunic with bright blood. "You may not see the path forward clearly, but this is not the end. It is only another step, and a necessary one."

"You really believe that?"

"I have to." He smiled, then gasped as his back arched with pain. "I've had time to think, and no choice but to listen to voices I was unable to hear before." He grabbed for her hand again and gripped it tight. "You must continue the fight. Varek is alive. It's true that you'll never be the hero I wanted you to be, but that's for the best.

You are not a failure or a villain. You are not a mistake, Sorra. You are the Mystery, the first piece of the puzzle."

Sorra brushed his hair back from his face, unsure of how else to comfort him. He was rambling. Dying. "You were the first. The Might."

"No! Listen!" His eyes widened, and his gaze shifted to look past her shoulder. Sorra turned. There was nothing there. "I was necessary, but I am not the one foreseen. That vision, the one where all is made right—the Mind, the Might, the Mystery, the Magic—is only beginning. The traitor's blood has opened the enemy's path to power, and he may claim it. Or he may not. Seek Linnea's victory. Find the Might, Magic, and Mind where only you would choose to look."

His eyes lost their focus as his grip on her hand weakened.

Sorra rested her clawed fingers gently against his cheek, turning his face so he'd meet her gaze. "Don't go, Tullian. I still need you."

"And I'm needed elsewhere." He looked past her again, smiling. "I expect I'll remain close by, watching until Linnea is at peace."

An icy shiver flowed up Sorra's spine. "Is she here?"

A tear traced its way over Tullian's temple, cutting a wavering line through the dust. "She is, and she always has been. She's as beautiful as ever, and she watches us with love. And Selim, my dearest friend. You're free. I'm coming."

There was no final gasp, and no fight to hold on.

Sorra held back the sob that fought to break from her aching chest. He didn't want her grief. Only for her to fight.

He knew Varek lives because Linnea is still here. Her heart remains.
The fight isn't over.

She leaned in and placed a kiss on his forehead.

"I'll do my best. I can't promise more than that, but I swear I'll try."

The wall behind the thrones cracked, and stones rained down on the floor. Above her, glass shattered, showering Sorra with broken shards. The wooden beams that had held it in place groaned.

"Sorra!" Beau stood in the doorway, his clothes drenched in blood. Her heart leapt.

At least one part of the plan hadn't gone as wrong as it possibly could. Andonia's king was alive and free.

He looked up. Sorra followed his gaze to the beams, which shifted and cracked. The one directly above her canted dangerously to one side, barely supported by its neighbour.

She stood and took a step toward him, but the broken glass bit into her bare toes, making quick movement difficult even on her thick, scaly soles.

Beau ran toward her, his boots crunching and slipping over the debris.

Gwelain laughed in her mind, teasing as Sorra recalled her threat.

I'll see about using some of my dear mage's freshly harvested power to arrange a new enchantment, just to be sure.

Not Corvin, but Varek.

"Don't!" she yelled, her voice high with panic. "Get out! Go back to Andonia and tell them Gwelain is dead, but—"

Another tremor gripped the castle, and the room's exterior wall fell, stealing what little support had been left for anything above.

Beau collided with her and pushed her to the floor, covering her body with his own as the remains of the ceiling fell.

CHAPTER SIXTY-ONE

Sorra tried to breathe, but even her new body wasn't strong enough to pull in air when she was crushed beneath so much weight. She squirmed and twisted, trying to make space, pushing against the warm, soft blanket of fur that covered her.

It moved, groaned, and lifted enough for her to take a breath of dust-choked air that she immediately coughed back out.

Beau stood over her, four sturdy legs braced against the ground, and shrugged off the weight of a wooden beam that would have broken a human back.

"Beau," Sorra whispered when she found her voice.

"Are you all right?" he asked. He took a step back, a frown wrinkling the ursine face Sorra had learned to read so well back in Andonia. Her heart ached to see it again, dear and comforting and so completely wrong that she wanted to scream.

He lifted a forepaw and stared at it, blinking slowly, then examined the remains of his torn clothing that had fallen to the floor.

"You touched me," Sorra said. "Gods, I'm so sorry."

He sat down hard. "I touched you after Corvin died, and I didn't change. His enchantments are broken. It was safe."

"But you had Gwelain's permission to touch me that time. She ordered you to kill me." Sorra buried her face in her hands. Wherever Gwelain was now, she was surely delighted. "Corvin wasn't her mage. Varek was, which means he did this to you. Gwelain is dead, and he has Linnea's heart. It sounded like he might need some time to figure out how to use it, but it's his just as it was Linnea's, caged in his body." She tried not to think of the hole in his chest where he'd ripped out his own.

No wonder he'd seemed pale and weak. He hadn't lied—he had used too much magic, but it had been as much to sustain himself as to save her.

"And he's alive."

"Which means his curse still stands." Sorra reached out and brushed a claw through the fur on his cheek.

"I see." Beau pawed away some of the debris that covered Tullian's body. "I heard a little of what he said to you, though clearly not enough. He told you to carry on with the quest despite..." He swung his head toward her. "Everything?"

"It seemed that way. I'm supposed to go find the other three heroes who are meant to save Andonia. He thought Linnea was here, and it was like he could hear her speaking, but he was dying. He might have just been seeing what he expected to."

"We can't know, I suppose." Beau snorted and pawed at his nose, clearing the dust that had settled on it. "But we can see what has happened. The visions have come true. Not all of them yet, and not in the ways anyone predicted, but I think it would be foolish to quit if there's still hope, even if your faith remains shaken."

Sorra smiled, though her heart felt like it might tear in half. "Even without considering the visions or my blessing or destiny or anything else, I think I have to keep going. I made this mess. If there's any chance it's a step along the path to making things right, it's my responsibility to get there. Tullian would call me horrible names if I didn't. He thinks I'm meant to, even if I'm not exactly the *adonthai* Linnea said would do it."

Beau's furry brow creased. "*Adonthai?*"

"Heroes in Linnea's language. The kind of bold, right-minded, selfless fellows the scholars kept sending on these quests. The kind of person Tullian was trying to shape me into so I'd be worthy to join him. He didn't speak the language, but he carried that word with him."

"I know the word," Beau said. "But *adonthai* is... it could mean hero, if you wanted it to. But it literally means something more like 'one who performs a good work'. Action, not character or title or anything else. Why wouldn't that be you?"

"I can think of a few reasons." She reached down to close Tullian's eyes. "That does give me some comfort, though. If the human scholars had that wrong, maybe he's right and I am one of the four Linnea saw. That means I still have a chance, and that the others might be somewhere out there, waiting for me to find them."

Beau nudged at her hand until it rested on his head. "For *us* to find them. I never believed I was the Mind or had any part in a mystical vision, but I can help you."

"I can't ask you to do that." She took a step away and winced at the sharp pain in her foot. It still felt different from human pain, but it remained a warning not to cause further damage. She made her way out of the field of glass and sat to pluck the shard from the thin skin between her toes.

Beau followed.

"You've suffered too much already because of my involvement in your affairs," she said. "You're free now. You're not sworn to this quest."

"Neither are you, now," he said, speaking in a gentle rumble that warmed her through. "Yet you're carrying on."

"You have other duties." She flicked the bloodied glass over her shoulder. "If you're not a part of the visions, your destiny doesn't have to stay tied to mine."

"I know. It's my choice."

Sorra groaned, exasperated. "I'm giving you a way out of my mess, Beau! I've already ruined so much. I don't want you to get hurt again."

He sat beside her. "You've saved me, Sorra. Not only from Gwelain, but from myself. From my inaction, my acceptance of duty when it asked me to become nothing... None of this has turned out as I expected, or as anyone might have wished. But I have hope now." He touched her cheek with his nose and sighed. "I confess I much prefer order and rules and clarity, but if your chaos is the way forward, I'll let the storm carry me where it will. Provided, of course, it keeps me next to you."

Don't cry, Sorra ordered herself, but her eyes burned.

"You've already forgiven me for betraying Andonia? You were so angry."

"Angry, but not at you." He smiled. "Well, perhaps at first. A little. But any anger in me at the moment of your death was at the cruelty of destiny, demanding your sacrifice for our victory. At Gwelain. At whatever gods or energies or stars asked so much of you. I have no need to forgive you."

"And you don't hate what I've become?"

"I could never hate you, Sorra. I've hated many goblins, but I hated the monsters they were on the inside. Your appearance has changed, but my loyalty..." He cleared his throat and looked away. "That is to say, my feelings have certainly not changed."

She threw her arms around his neck and buried her face in his fur.

"Come on," he said. "Ride until your foot is healed."

Sorra climbed onto his back, and he carried her out of the throne room, through the castle's front doors, and down the ramp beyond.

The courtyard was empty. The goblins had scattered, or Varek had collected them while she'd been busy with Tullian.

Or perhaps he'd killed them, preferring his own army of monsters. She wished she'd asked him how many of the old goblins still lived, back when he couldn't lie to her.

"Where do you think the humans went?" She glanced over her shoulder as they left the castle ruins behind them. No voices rose from the rubble. The only sound was the river as they approached, and the wind as it rustled through the forest beyond the meadow, carrying the fresh scent of earth and trees.

Overhead, dark clouds gathered.

Gooseflesh broke out on Sorra's arms. She hadn't felt the kiss of a breeze since she'd stepped into Gwelain's lands, and it awakened something wild within her.

"Perhaps the servants fled to a nearby town," Beau said. "I would have."

He splashed across the shallow river, stopping in the middle to drink and to let Sorra wash her wounded foot. Then they sat on the far side, looking back at the ruins of what had once seemed a perfect storybook castle.

Varek had called Gwelain's magic illusions, but they'd nearly been real. He'd despised her for wasting her power and claiming so little of it, but it had been unimaginably strong.

And he'll have more.

Gwelain had possessed the heart for more than a century before she'd been able to use it to curse Andonia. Sorra doubted Varek would take so long, but she hoped he'd struggle for long enough to give them time to gather their heroes, break Beau's curse, and prepare for an attack.

Just this once, let that much luck be on our side. Let Varek keep hurting. Let the magic fight him.

"Will we go to Embercliffe?" she asked. "If there's still a king's mark under that fur, there's still time for you to take the throne."

"And if not, we can at least warn my family about what's coming. They'll help with your next steps."

Sorra looked down at her claws. "I won't be welcome in Andonia."

"Hmm." Beau looked her over. "It might not be terribly difficult to disguise you, though. Long skirts. Hats. Gloves."

"Drape myself in a bedsheet and pretend to be a ghost instead of a goblin?"

"If it comes to that." He raised his nose to sniff at the breeze. "We should make our way to the border as quickly as we can. See if we can outpace the rain."

And Varek, Sorra added to herself, not daring to speak his name aloud. Let him be distracted by his new magic or his old goblins. She had no intention of calling his attention back to her if she could avoid it.

Sorra mounted again, glad to be off her feet, hoping she'd inherited a bit of quick healing with her new body even if Gwelain's pretty monsters didn't have magic of their own.

"Which way to the Gate?" Sorra asked.

Beau turned. "South. Shall we?"

Sorra sat straight and tall, imagining herself an unlikely knight on history's strangest steed. "Let's go."

~

The rain seemed like a miracle at first. After a few hours, though, when Sorra's clothes were wet through and Beau's fur slick with it, her attitude changed. Even the sound of a bird chirping somewhere in the forest didn't lift her spirits.

Beau had fallen back into his habitual silence from their first days together. Sorra hoped he was working out a plan for how they'd get into Andonia and to the castle in Embercliffe without trouble. She herself had no ideas, and no real concept of what the capital city or its people would be like.

But I'm the one who's supposed to find the heroes. If the visions are still true, the path will become clear once we're there.

The thought sounded nice. Tullian would have embraced it, but it didn't make her feel any more confident.

Sorra gripped Beau's fur tighter and leaned forward as a familiar pub came into view.

"I know this place," she said. "This is where I found Tullian."

"Friendly town?"

"Not particularly. Or generally, for that matter." She slicked her wet hair back from her face, wincing as the side of her hand found the unfamiliar bumps of her horns. "But things might be different now if they realize how everything has changed."

But the streets were quiet. Even in the rain Sorra had hoped people might be out celebrating—it had been so long since they'd felt it on their skin.

"I should knock at a door and ask for some warmer clothes," Sorra said. "Or not. I suppose they'll be more afraid of me now than they were before."

"Perhaps not," Beau rumbled.

Sorra slipped off his back but kept one hand on his neck as they walked down the street. "They went through centuries of creatures who look like me collecting taxes. I'm the enemy."

Beau didn't answer but stopped outside a house where three empty rocking chairs creaked gently in the breeze.

Nap time for old men, Sorra thought, but the skin at the back of her neck tingled as she passed the empty rockers. She wished the ancient trio were there, unhelpful though they'd been before.

She wished anyone was there.

She knocked at the door and waited. When no one answered, she pushed it open.

"Hello?" she called as she stepped inside, leaving Beau in the shelter of the covered porch. "Is anyone home? Don't be frightened, I've come with good news. Gwelain is dead, and—"

She fell silent, the breath sucked out of her. Two corpses sat at the kitchen table just inside the door, one collapsed forward into its breakfast, one leaning back with its mouth hanging open. Both were dry as dust, their skin stretched tight over bone like they'd been there for decades or longer, white teeth grinning below empty eye sockets.

One wore a white dress covered in a pattern of faded forget-me-nots, threadbare and patched at the elbows.

The other wore trousers and stockings, and its flowing white beard covered most of its yellowed shirt.

Sorra turned away, nauseated, as Beau squeezed through the door. He brushed past her on his way to the bodies, sniffing the air.

When his nose touched the old man's arm, its head rolled forward, snapping off its neck and thumping to the floor.

Sorra fought back the gag that choked her and hurried out onto the porch, taking in gasps of cool, fresh air.

Beau joined her a moment later.

"You knew," she whispered.

"I suspected." He sat, and the boards creaked under his weight. "I hoped they'd live on once her curse was broken, but why would she arrange for such mercy? Time has returned, and they've been swept away with it."

Sorra didn't answer.

"It's not your fault," Beau said, speaking gently.

"I know." Sorra wiped her eyes on the back of her hand. "I just wish they'd had a chance to live out their lives. To be happy again. I wish…" She stamped a foot against the porch, at a loss for who to be angry with now that Gwelain was gone.

Varek might have worse things planned for Andonia, but this was all his mother's work.

Beau nosed her hand, his breath warm against her skin. "You didn't give them freedom in life, but they've found it in death. Wherever souls go when their bodies perish, they've gone."

Sorra took one more deep breath and nodded. "I hope it's peaceful."

"So do I."

Sorra was about to return to the house to look for a sweater when screams rang out from the direction of the stable. She exchanged a glance with Beau, then ran toward the noise, Beau keeping pace beside her, then pulling ahead.

He stopped at the edge of town and crouched behind a bush at the side of the road. Sorra caught up and joined him.

He didn't have to warn her to stay hidden, or to stay quiet.

A grey-haired man dressed in the same uniform as the soldiers at the Gate had driven his sword through a goblin's chest, leaving it bleeding out on the dusty road. Another goblin, a bluish-skinned creature Sorra recognized from the feast on her first night at Gwelain's castle, collapsed to his knees. His arms were bound behind his back, his fine pink jacket smeared with dust and blood.

A dozen human soldiers looked on, some amused, some appearing bored or restless. None seemed to have anything to say in opposition to the proceedings.

"Please," the goblin said. "We haven't set foot in your lands. Gwelain is dead. We only wish for peace."

The soldier standing behind the goblin opened his throat, silencing him.

Sorra bared her teeth but didn't let her impulsive desire to attack carry her forward. The goblins were monsters, Gwelain's creatures through and through, but this one had been powerless and begging for his life. Perhaps the soldiers looked at them and saw only the beasts who had carried out the slaughter at the Gate, but it was wrong.

Andonians are supposed to be the good ones.

"What do we do?" she murmured.

Beau's ear twitched. "I'm not sure. They're Andonians. They're my soldiers, if I'm still king. If my father sent them before he died, if they've been waiting for the enchantments to break so they could enter these lands..."

Sorra's throat tightened. "You think he had a plan after all?"

"Perhaps. Or maybe they're just soldiers who noticed there was a way north, taking out their frustrations on the first goblins they saw. Either way, they're our first taste of what we'll find in Andonia."

He stepped out from the bushes. The soldiers turned, and most drew their swords.

"Peace," Beau called. "I have news of Gwelain's defeat, and of a greater threat against Andonia."

An arrow whistled through the air, barely missing Beau's shoulder as he stepped to one side.

"Stop!" he roared. "I am Beauregard Alphinex Regus Tolineau, heir to the throne of Andonia. Gwelain has held me prisoner in exchange for peace, and—"

Another arrow drove itself into the dirt at his feet.

"That's a warning, beast," someone called from the left of the group. A middle-aged soldier with a thick, iron-streaked beard stepped forward, another arrow nocked to the bow at his side. "We know of the enchantments protecting these lands, and that they have altered to allow our presence, or to allow the so-called goblin queen to enter Andonia. We are here to prevent it, on orders to kill every monster we find. I don't remember instructions about talking animals, but I'm thinking you qualify."

Beau growled. "You will listen. I am cursed by an enchantment, but my companion and I must reach Embercliffe to speak to the mages and to whomever my father left in charge. Escort us and you will be rewarded. Threaten us again and I'll see you all hanged."

The archer raised his bow and took aim. "Surround the bear. Don't let it escape."

The soldiers spread out, more apprehensive than they'd appeared earlier. But then, the goblins had been captives and might not have chosen to fight back. A massive bear was unexpected, unpredictable.

Beau backed up until he reached Sorra.

"Get on."

She climbed onto his back and gripped his fur tight.

"Another goblin! Kill them!"

Sorra couldn't tell whether it was the same soldier who spoke. Beau had already wheeled around and was pelting down the road as a rain of arrows fell.

She kept her head down and let him run.

CHAPTER SIXTY-TWO

They didn't slow until long after the shouts had faded behind them. Beau gasped for breath, and Sorra slid to the ground to walk beside him.

Thick forest surrounded them. The rain had stopped, and songbirds sang among the branches as sunlight cut through the leaves, lighting Beau's fur in patches as it dried.

"We just have to get past the mountains," Sorra said. "Someone in Embercliffe will recognize you somehow. Your mother, maybe. Wouldn't she know you no matter what you look like? Or your brothers?"

Beau grunted. "Maybe, if we can get to them. Clearly we won't have assistance from soldiers along the way."

"Common people might help us get there, though. We could try to get to my sister Davina. She's clever. She'll think of something." She paused. "But we can't go through the Gate."

"No." Beau nodded ahead. "We're walking west now. If Gwelain's enchantments are all broken and the old maps in her library were correct, we should be approaching a pass through the mountains that's been lost for quite some time. We'll enter Andonia farther from Cottsbridge or Embercliffe than we'd planned, but the odds of it being guarded seem slim."

Sorra fell into the rhythm of walking, losing herself in the gentle whisper of dead leaves rustling beneath her feet as they approached the mountains. As Beau had promised, a wide pass cut between two worn peaks, a new path to the south.

There was no road through the pass, but the tree cover was thin enough at the top to offer a dazzling view of the forest that spread out beyond it, rocks and trees ablaze with sunset light.

"Are we in Andonia?" Sorra asked.

"I think so." Beau sniffed the air. "I thought it would feel different the moment we passed the border."

Sorra laid a hand on his shoulder. "The border was only what Gwelain created. It's gone now. The Forgotten Lands are open to Andonia."

"And it to whatever threats were hidden in the north for so long." Beau started forward again. "We should make camp for the night. Move forward in the morning."

He didn't sound excited, or even hopeful. Sorra tried to think of something to say and came up empty, so she busied herself making a nest of leaves next to a tall boulder. They had no blankets, no matches, no axe to cut firewood or knife to slice kindling.

Beau lay on his side, and Sorra cuddled into the warm fur of his belly, resting her head against him as the stars came out.

"Embercliffe," Sorra whispered. "Is it lovely?"

"It is, if it hasn't changed since I last saw it." Beau's voice rumbled pleasantly through his body, and Sorra sank deeper into it. "It will also be teeming with soldiers. But if we can get past them, that's also where we'll find the mages. They'll be our best chance of restoring our human forms so we can move on with your plans."

"Plans. Right." Sorra stared up into the sky. "If Tullian is right and I'm meant to find the Mind, Might, and Magic, the visions around them are the ones we need to pay attention to now. *Marked by birth and by life. Born not under the light of the moon.* They could be in Embercliffe, right?"

"Could be." He lifted his head and turned to her. "Linnea said the quest began in Embercliffe, so it's as good a place to look for them as any. Perhaps the Magic is the mage who makes us human again. And not all soldiers will remain against us."

He laid his head back down, and his breathing slowed.

But Sorra couldn't settle, exhausted though she was.

The scholars knew how to find mages and soldiers, she thought. *They tried it, and they failed. If this is my destiny, I'm meant to do things differently.*

Tullian said I should seek the other heroes where only I would think to look.

She tried to remember the exact wording of the visions. She'd been watching for a few so closely that others had grown rusty in her memory, and it took work to pry them loose.

"She didn't say Embercliffe," she said, not sure whether Beau had fallen asleep but needing to think out loud. "She said their journey would begin where hers ended."

The words jostled several memories loose. They seemed unrelated, but there was something there—something brighter and clearer than the vague idea of Embercliffe.

Sorra closed her eyes and tried to see the connection between the memories.

A queen.

A coronation.

A business card with an unfamiliar address written on it.

She gasped.

Beau shifted. When Sorra looked to him, he was watching her with sharp interest. "What is it?"

"The heroes' journey begins where their broken queen's ended. Her life's journey ended in Embercliffe," Sorra said, climbing to her feet. Energy coursed through her body, and the thought of sleep abandoned her. "But there were other journeys, weren't there? When she fled her coronation, her journey ended somewhere else."

"Queen's Run." Beau stood, too, and shook the leaves from his fur. "Do you know any likely heroes there?"

"No one I truly know, and certainly no one Tullian would have called heroes. But I wonder."

She paced, tugging both hands through her hair, willing her thoughts to fall in line.

"It's ridiculous. Worse than my idea about sequential visions, maybe."

"Which turned out to be correct, if not complete," Beau said. "Tell me."

Sorra stopped and turned to him. "*Adonthai* could be anyone? Truly? Even a goblin?"

"A goblin, a princess, a farmer… depends what good they've done."

"Or what good they're going to do, even if they might not be doing it now?"

"Perhaps."

Sorra pressed both hands to her face, blocking out the world so she could picture the pieces of the puzzle.

The Mind, the Mystery, the Magic, the Might.

Marked by birth and marked by life.

There had been four of them under the bridge the night she'd sold the arrow, one more than they needed if Tullian was right about Sorra being the Mystery.

The scholars had expected heroes, knights, wise men, and royally sanctioned mages and had assumed they'd all be men of good character. If they were wrong about them being men, she suspected they could be wrong about the rest.

"The arrow introduced me to three women from Queen's Run who might fit the bill. They didn't give me the impression that they were exactly on the right side of the law. One was clearly their leader. She seemed clever, even devious, and uninterested in risking having the sheriff's eye on her even to help clear my name. She had strange eyes, two different colours."

Marked by birth, she thought, and her stomach fluttered.

"Another was a witch. She recognized the magic in the arrow, and she was missing a finger—her sacrifice, I suppose. Like Corvin's ear."

Marked by life. Not a random scar, but one that specifically marked her for her role in the quest.

Beau snorted. "Certainly on the wrong side of the law, then. And the third?"

"She carried knives and had scars like she'd survived more fights than anyone has any right to. Mind, Magic, Might. There was a man with them, too. Sneaky, with quick fingers. I don't know where he fits into all this."

"Well, I expect it will take more than four people to save the world, no matter how clever or strong any of you might be. They don't sound like heroes, but they're a place to start, and certainly one only you would consider. And they're waiting where Linnea's journey ended, if not the one the scholars assumed." Beau nudged her hand with his nose. "If you believe it was more than coincidence that set them in your path, we should find them and see what comes of it."

Beau's eyes were shining, and Sorra wondered whether his heart was beating as hard as hers.

"You don't mind a detour to Queen's Run? You could still go to Embercliffe without me. It would be the more reasonable choice."

"Did I not say I'm with you?" He grinned more naturally than she'd ever seen when he was in bear form. "If I'm your destiny, you are mine, and if the arrow is leading you down one path, I won't leave you to follow another. I have never believed in the visions as Tullian did, but I believe in you."

Sorra hugged him tight, breathing in the scent of his fur as he wrapped a foreleg around her and squeezed awkwardly.

It was all wrong. A goblin and a bear seeking a pack of potential criminals in a strange city. Not heroes, but scoundrels.

But maybe wrong is what it takes to make things right, Sorra thought as she released Beau.

She breathed in, smelling the forest air as she never had with human senses, admiring the stars and the night-darkened trees with new eyes.

"Shall we leave now?" Beau asked. "I suddenly don't feel much like sleeping."

"I think we should." Sorra's heart fluttered with what seemed an impossible mix of fear and hope. "I'm a monster and a traitor, but it seems Linnea can still use me. The queen's knights have had their chance. Perhaps it's time to find out what her knaves can do."

THE END

AUTHOR'S NOTE

Thank you again, dear reader, for joining me on another adventure. I hope you'll join me again as we see where these knaves are headed. There will be adventure, there will be danger, and I strongly suspect there will be magic.

If you've enjoyed Princes and Pawns and have a few minutes to do so, please consider leaving a review or posting about the book to help other readers find it. Your recommendations are more powerful than anything I can say about it, and I appreciate everyone who's supported the series thus far.

See you soon!

-Kate

ACKNOWLEDGMENTS

As always, there are too many people to thank, but there are a special few "I couldn't have done this without you" people who deserve to have their names here.

To Krista Walsh, Laura Dalton, Mike Lowden, Kathy Dunlavey, Margie Scheiner, and Trisha Poole, thank you for your critiques, your notes, and your encouragement.

To Joshua Essoe, thanks again for being exactly the editor this book needed and for all your support.

To Stefanie Saw, thank you for the absolutely gorgeous cover art!

To Krista Walsh again, thank you for wrangling my wayward commas and awkward phrases. And special thanks to Tammy Butler for reading the finished version to hunt for sneaky little typos.

And to my family, thank you for reminding me that the real world needs me even when I'd rather keep my head in the clouds (and that there's more to life than my books when things get difficult).